Critical Incidents

Critical Incidents

Lucie Whitehouse

4th ESTATE • *London*

4th Estate
An imprint of HarperCollins*Publishers*
1 London Bridge Street
London SE1 9GF

www.4thEstate.co.uk

First published in Great Britain in 2019 by 4th Estate

1

A catalogue record for this book is available from the British Library

ISBN 978-0-00-826899-2 (hardback)
ISBN 978-0-00-826900-5 (trade paperback)

Typeset in Minion Pro by
Palimpsest Book Production Ltd, Falkirk, Stirlingshire

Printed and bound in Great Britain by
CPI Group (UK) Ltd, Croydon CR0 4YY

For Bridget

I leant far out, and squinnied for a sign
That this was still the town that had been 'mine'
So long, but found I wasn't even clear
Which side was which.

Philip Larkin

Chapter One

Robin surveyed the table with its heap of crumpled napkins and burger boxes, stray fries and onion rings, the pile of bleeding ketchup packets. Aftermath of the cholesterol bomb. They'd had breakfast back in London, too, but as the road signs had started to portend BIRMINGHAM, her stomach started churning, and by the time they'd reached Warwick Services, it had felt completely empty or at least gnawing in some other way that made eating fifteen quid's worth of Burger King seem like a good idea. Whoppers, milkshakes, the works – no section of the menu overlooked. Now she had stomach ache *and* she felt sick.

Across the table, Lennie's stomach was a toddler-style pot under her Blondie T-shirt. She put her hands on it and grimaced. 'Ugh. I feel like I've swallowed a sofa cushion. Full of grease.'

'It was a two-seater. I got the fluff and loose change from down the back, too.'

Lennie laughed and for a moment, everything seemed brighter. There was still a chance this would all be irrelevant in the grand scheme, wasn't there? A blip. Once, on one of the long nights when Lennie was a baby, she'd whispered in her ear that together, they could do anything. She would do anything for her, of course; but also, *because* of her, she, Robin, could do anything. *Right*, said a snide voice.

She stood quickly and began piling their rubbish onto the trays, crushing her burger box with a savagery that startled Lennie from her texting. 'Once more unto the breach?'

A thump, hard but fleshy, as if a large bird – a pheasant, even a swan – had dropped from the sky and landed deadweight on the roof. They both jumped but a second later a smirking face loomed at the passenger-side window. For the love of god. Robin took a long breath then pressed the button to lower the glass.

'Luke.'

Her own eyes looked back from a face that was her own, too, but pale and more defined, the jaw made square by pads of muscle. 'Shocked you, did I? What are you doing sitting back here? There's a parking spot outside.'

'Someone must have just gone.'

Her brother made the *yeah, right* expression he'd been giving her since he was six. 'How are you, Lennie? Can't be many people who've staked out their own grandparents. Old habits dying hard, Rob?'

She flung the door open and moved to get out, remembering at the last second that she'd undone her jeans. 'What are you doing here?'

'Same as you – come to spend time with the rentals. Though just the afternoon in our case.' He smirked again.

Robin came round to the pavement and stooped to look at the roof. She couldn't see a dent, but still. 'Why would you hit my car, you . . . fuckwit?' she hissed.

'Afraid it'll affect the resale value? What?' The injured innocence he did so well. 'You're going to have to sell it, aren't you, if you're as broke as Mum says? Can't drive an Audi if you're begging. Even if it *was* second-hand.'

'We're *not* begging.' She glanced at Lennie, just getting out, then glared at him: *Watch it.*

'Would you be back here if you weren't?'

'Hiya, Lennie. Robin.' Natalie, Luke's wife, lunged at them. She was like a newly hatched bird, Robin thought, all beak, eyes and pushy hunger, thrusting herself into the middle of every situation to ensure she wasn't overlooked or slighted in some other unguessable way. Her fringe absorbed make-up from her forehead and hung in damp-looking, fresh-from-the-egg strands.

'Right.' Robin opened the boot. 'Since you're here, Luke, make yourself useful.' She handed him a box. 'It's only light.' She wasn't going to give him an excuse to put his back out and malinger with his PlayStation for weeks. 'Natalie, have you got a spare hand? It's just a bag of—'

'Sorry.' She held up a set of lilac claws. 'I've just had my nails done.'

On balance, Robin thought as she locked the car, Luke had done her a favour accosting her out here. Better to have the opening skirmish under her belt than walk into an ambush. And being pissed off was useful, armour of a sort. She'd thought she was over the worst but as she'd turned into Dunnington Road, she'd felt a moment of suffocating panic. Here it all was again, as if the sixteen years in between had just fallen away – collapsed: the pairs of Fifties semis facing off across the wide street, their bay windows netted prissily against anyone who could be bothered to peer over the rosebushes or the brace of mid-range saloons in the tiny front gardens. It was all so low-rise, so stunted: nothing reached higher than two storeys.

The sky yawned overhead for bleak white acres, uninterrupted. She was seized by a sense of personal jeopardy, actual threat: if she was under it too long, exposed, it would suck out her soul.

As they rounded Terry Willett's white Ford Transit – the bane of her mother's existence, herself aside, for twenty-five years – she saw number 17 for the first time and waiting in the ground-floor bay, trapped like a bug between glass and net curtain, her dad. She watched him light up like he'd heard it was Christmas. In a whisk of nylon lace he was gone. 'Chrissie,' she imagined him bellowing, 'they're here!'

Seconds later, the outer porch door opened. Lennie ran to him, the bag bumping against her back. 'Hello, sweetheart.' He held her away to look at her. 'You've grown again, haven't you? Who said you could do that?' He lowered his voice. 'I've got some Creme Eggs in for you – we'll have one after lunch.'

Lunch.

Lennie turned, eyes wide. Robin shook her head: *Say nothing*.

They could smell it now, the scent wafting through the open door: roast beef, roast potatoes, Yorkshire puddings, gravy, carrots, sprouts, peas and god knows what else. *Shit*. Why hadn't her mother said something? No – why hadn't she *known*? Of course she was going to cook the fatted calf. And that was why Luke and Natalie were here, wasn't it? Luke wouldn't drive five minutes to see her but he'd never miss a free lunch.

Over Natalie's head, her dad winked. When the others had moved inside, he took her bags then pulled her into a hug, crushing her face into his sweater. His smell, it never changed: Ariel detergent, Camay soap and, faint but unmistakeable, the stealthy cigarettes that he disappeared off to smoke twice a day and still believed her mother knew nothing about. Her ribcage buckled as he gave her a final squeeze. 'Good to have you back, love.'

'I knew you'd be later than you said so I aimed for three o'clock and it's a good job I did, isn't it? Was there traffic?' Christine slid the potatoes back into the oven, straightened up and retied the apron over her cream blouse and floral skirt. The pattern was yellow roses, not unlike the one on the oven gloves, the blinds and the covered stools. Robin felt like a biker crashing the Women's Institute garden party.

'Hi, Mum.'

'Hello.' Christine touched her cheek briefly to hers. 'I'll get the greens going now you're here. So was there?'

'What?'

'Traffic.'

Robin glanced at Lennie. A couple of minutes ago, when she was bringing in her suitcase, Lennie had come racing out of the house to tell her there were starters – *'Cheese soufflé!'* – and pudding, too. 'What are we going to *do*?'

'Nothing. And not a word.'

'But . . .'

'We eat. Just do your best.'

The tea towels, Robin noticed, had the roses, too. 'It was pretty busy,' she said. 'Especially round the Oxford turn.' Before the epic Burger King, they'd had several goes at catching a stuffed pink alligator with a mechanical claw, and they'd lingered round the books in Smith's so long they'd attracted the security guard.

'It's normally worse going *into* London, isn't it?' Christine said, sorting broccoli florets into portions. 'How nice, to have Elena here.' She turned and gave her a side-hug. 'Now, the boys are having a beer, Robin, and there's lemonade.' She lowered her voice. 'Natalie's not drinking at the moment but don't make a song and dance about it.'

'Really? The thinnest woman in the West Midlands? Is she on another diet?'

'Sssh. They're trying again. Don't say anything.'

'Trying what?' Lennie whispered.

'To have a baby.'

'Oh.'

'Have you got a drink, Mum?' Robin asked.

'I'm going to have a spritzer once everything's on the table. Would you like one?'

'No, thanks, I'll have one of these.' She picked up a beer from the cluster on the end of the counter. 'Purity? I haven't seen this before.'

'It's local – the brewery's out near Studley, I think. Your father likes it.'

Robin flipped off the cap and took a sip. 'Yeah, I can see why. What?'

'At least use a glass. And take that jacket off before we sit down, please. And those boots. You look like . . .'

She couldn't help herself. 'A dyke?'

Christine suppressed a shudder. 'Like you're going yomping across the Falklands.'

They managed the soufflés without major incident. As he'd pulled out her chair, her dad had murmured, 'Don't have a fight, will you? For your mother's sake,' and he'd done his best, steering the conversation towards such anodyne topics as the decking that Natalie and Luke were laying in their garden – or rather Natalie's brother was relaying, Luke having botched it – and the restaurant in Moseley where they'd been for their anniversary, which now had a Michelin star, apparently.

'A Michelin star in Birmingham – who'da thunk it?' Robin said.

'Actually,' said Natalie, tight-lipped, 'there's five.'

The main course proved a bridge too far. The temperature in the room seemed to be rising, the oxygen level decreasing in inverse proportion. Robin had had the same piece of beef in her mouth for a minute but her stomach was drum-taut, painful when it met the table-edge. Glancing to her right, she saw Lennie – genius! – disappear a roast potato into a piece of kitchen roll on her lap. She pushed back her chair to go and get a piece for herself but Luke, obviously afraid of losing his sitting target, cut Dennis off mid-sentence.

'So, Robin,' he said, 'Mum and Dad told me, obviously, but I'm still having problems getting my head around your . . . situation.'

'Which part is troubling you?'

'Well, for a start, how did you actually *get* fired? We thought, me and Nat, that you were some sort of golden girl down there, the great white hope of Scotland Yard.' They looked at each other, struggling not to snicker.

'Luke,' warned Dennis.

'What? I'm trying to understand.'

In another situation – any situation with no Lennie – she'd grab him by the collar and bounce his head off the wall. He'd done it to her enough times when his two-year advantage still counted. But then she'd turned eleven and knocked one of his front teeth out and that had been the end of it. The beatings, anyway.

'Well,' she said, 'in layman's terms, to help you *get your head around it*, my boss wanted to charge a bad man with a murder he didn't commit just because he was bad and the public would be better off if he was inside, but I didn't think it was right, so I said so and he – my boss – didn't like it.'

7

'And you got fired for that?'

'Yes. They're quite hot on insubordination in the police. I'm guessing it's not such a big deal at Carphone Warehouse. Or is it T-Mobile these days?'

'Robin.' Dennis put a hand on her arm, calming or admonitory, she wasn't sure.

'But from what Mum told me,' Luke said, 'it wasn't just that your boss didn't like it. The guy – the *bad man*,' he made a face that Robin yearned to plunge her fist into, 'has gone AWOL, hasn't he? So he's out there somewhere, a known killer, because of you.'

'He didn't do it.'

'But you don't *know* that.'

'I didn't have evidence to prove it – I needed more time – but I'm pretty sure.'

'And that's enough, is it? The great Robin Lyons says so? "Oh, I'm pretty sure he didn't do it, let him go – oh look, he's killed someone else, that's a shame."'

'*Beyond reasonable doubt* – heard of that? You can't just lock people up because you think they're bad apples.'

'I don't know why not,' said Christine. 'That always seems like a good idea to me. Put them away before they can do the damage.'

Robin gave herself credit for not rising. Even a couple of years ago, she wouldn't have been able to let that pass.

'But, sorry,' Natalie took a prim sip of her water, 'if you really *were* highly thought of' – Princess Di eyes over the rim of the glass – 'would one thing like that be enough to get you fired?'

'Ah, that's the bit she's not telling us, isn't it?' Luke grinned. 'It *wasn't* just one thing – she was on a written warning before. She's been busting that poor guy's balls from the moment he started there. This was just the final straw.'

'Language.'

'Sorry, Mum, but I'm right, aren't I? She couldn't keep her mouth shut and this is what happened. With Adrian, too, I bet – no wonder he dumped her. That poor bas—'

'Luke!'

A moment of seething silence in which Robin could sense Lennie gathering herself. She put her hand out – *Don't* – but it was too late. 'Ade loves Mum,' Lennie said, voice tight. 'He asked her to marry him.'

'Len, it's okay. You don't—'

'But it's *true*. You were the one who said no so even if you had a fight, it doesn't change that, does it?'

'He asked you to marry him?' Christine was staring. 'And you said *no*? For god's sake, *why*?'

'Because I couldn't . . . I just didn't . . .'

'Oh, you,' her mother cried, 'you, you, you. What about anyone else? What about poor Elena? Do you ever give her a second's thought in all this, when you're going around acting like you're—'

'What? How could you even—'

'Robin – be quiet. Christine.' Dennis had his hands out to the sides, boxing-ref style.

Her mother closed her eyes against the cruelty of the world, and the burden it had put upon her.

'I'm fine, Gran,' Lennie said. 'Honestly.'

A hiatus, this time ended by Natalie. 'So how long will you be here then? Your dad said you're going to work for Maggie Hammond. That doesn't mean you're going to *stay*, does it?'

'No.' *Please fucking god.* 'Maggie's got a lot on so I'm going to help her until I straighten things out at the Met.'

'Doesn't she work for the council?'

'She's self-employed, they're just one of her clients. It's not just benefit fraud; there's suspect insurance claims and—'

'From Homicide Command in London to catching scroungers on the sick in Sparkhill,' crowed Luke. 'How the mighty have fallen.'

'Luke, for the last time,' said Dennis.

Cheeks flaming, Robin stood up. Blood pulsed in the backs of her hands. 'Better to have fallen than to never even have *tried* to stand on your own two feet. You . . .' The swirl of words and arguments and fury bottlenecked in her throat – she couldn't choke them out. 'You're pathetic,' she managed. 'Just . . .' She remembered Lennie. 'Bugger off.'

She swung out of the room and took the stairs two at a time, her mother jabbering away behind her, a diatribe unchanged in twenty years: '*I won't have that language in this house; this is my home; I won't have her behaving like this, Dennis; I just won't.*'

Robin slammed the bedroom door as she'd done a thousand times before, the wall shuddering as it always had. Sudden silence – after a few seconds she could hear herself breathing. She looked around and felt time judder to a stop.

Apart from the boxes behind the door, which Josh had sent the factory's van to collect from London last week, the room was unchanged since the day she'd packed her bags for university sixteen years earlier. The same blue gingham curtains, chosen by Christine as gender-neutral and successfully, to be fair, given that she and Luke had both hated them; the same pale blue carpet with – yes – the old stain where she'd dropped a leaky ballpoint and deliberately left it. Free-standing wardrobe in white vinyl veneer, the side that abutted the tiny desk still covered with her brother's Villa stickers circa 1994 and her own picture of Robert Smith in his heyday, all leather jacket and Scissorhands hair.

A vibration in her back pocket. Gid? She'd texted him from Warwick Services, not because she expected anything new today

– he wouldn't be at work; he'd be home with Efie and the boys watching football, cooking, regrouting the bathroom – but for morale, the feeling that on this shittiest of days she still had a line back. Hope.

Not Gid but Corinna: *How's it going over there? What's the body count?*

She thumbed a reply: *Nil – for now. Waiting til Amazon deliver acid for bath.*

Seconds later, *Good thinking. Booze/takeaway/debrief at ours Tues eve? Tell Len Peter has new Xbox game he's dying to show her.*

Wilco and YES. Feed me gin. By the pint.

She slid the phone back into her pocket feeling fractionally better. Corinna the human night-light. When she'd come down to London last month, Robin'd gone to meet her at Marylebone. She'd looked like a beacon as she'd stalked down the platform in her tangerine canvas coat with its fern-print pattern. Black polo neck, indigo skinny jeans tucked into shiny black knee boots – even Rin's hair had been kinetic that day, cut into a new bob that seemed in perpetual motion.

Len had had a sleepover at her friend Olivia's house, and so they'd got hammered, absolutely wasted, Robin swinging between rage, incredulity and grief, Rin listening, matching her drink for drink. The next day, they'd staggered up the road like Mick and Keith and eaten their way through spring rolls and meatballs and Vietnamese curry in an effort to staunch the nausea. Afterwards Corinna had done her thing, advising and problem-solving in a way that, coming from anyone else, would have driven Robin round the effing twist. 'You've started looking for your own place?' she'd said.

'Online, yeah.'

'Want me to help? I can while away a dull hour at work on Rightmove.'

'It'll have to wait for a couple of months.'

'Why?'

'No deposit.'

Corinna had frowned. 'What do they ask for, a month's rent? Or a month and a half? Can you take it out of savings? It's worth it, isn't it, even if there's a penalty for early withdrawal?'

'If it was just a question of taking it out of savings, do you think I'd be moving back? I'm flattered you think I even *have* a savings account – how long have you known me?' She'd watched it dawn on Rin that she wasn't joking, then the volley of silent questions: hadn't she had a steady job for years? A salary, not massive but solid? 'My rent here's a ton,' she said, 'and Lennie's school, even with the scholarship. Then there'll be a lot of other stuff – you know, moving. A storage locker, maybe.'

'How much will that cost?'

'Also, I had some parking tickets.' She'd hesitated. 'Which I hadn't paid, so they'd doubled. Twice. And then there's the credit cards . . .'

'Robin!'

'I know, I know, I'm an idiot – tell me something I don't know. The lottery numbers, preferably.'

'Can I lend it to you? No, don't get funny, I'd like to. I'll even charge you interest if it would make you feel better.'

'No. Thanks but no. I got myself into this mess, I'll get myself out of it. What I really need you to do is rewind the clock. Make me nineteen again, will you, so I haven't screwed up my life yet.'

'You haven't.'

'It's different this time.' As she said the words, she'd felt them settle on her shoulders like a lead poncho. 'I haven't lost my job before, have I? We know I'm relationship poison but I've always been able to count on the rest. Work.'

'You managed before.' Subtly, Corinna had tipped her head

at the next table where a man of about forty moved an expensive-looking pram back and forth with his foot. Going by his
wife's hollow eyes and limp hair, Robin had guessed their
baby was weeks old, even days, this one of their first tentative
forays back out into the world. Corinna had done that for
her, too, back then, broken her circuit between the crib, the
changing table and her thesis, and taken her out, to places
like this, to the park, a pub by the river. On the surface, the
world had looked exactly the same but for her, it had been
reconfigured, fundamentally changed. A bomb had gone off
in her life, she'd thought, and no one except Corinna had
heard a thing.

'You made a success out of a tough situation,' she'd said.

'Yeah, well, this time I've done the opposite, haven't I?'

Back in her childhood bedroom, Robin felt a bead of sweat
run between her breasts. Christine had finally got the full set
of replacement windows she'd been craving and the room was
nursing-home hot. Going over, she shoved one open. Like
punching the lid off a Tupperware box. She sucked in as much
air as her swollen stomach allowed. Below, dull little portions
of garden stretched away on either side, rectangles of winter
grass and anonymous shrubs, Homebase panel fencing. The
Richardses, their immediate neighbours, had a Little Tikes
slide and sandbox in chunky red-and-yellow plastic that
confused her until she remembered her mother saying that
Karen had 'given John and Brenda grandchildren'. *The right
way*, Robin had heard: house bought; wedding reception at a
hotel in Solihull; tiny feet only thereafter. Rather than too
young, out of wedlock, father never disclosed. Not so much
given as foisted.

She turned and faced the bunk beds – the fact of the bunk beds.
Back then, Luke used to lean over the side and flick snot-balls

13

between the rungs of the ladder as she was falling asleep; now, at the age of thirty-five, she was going to share the beds with her daughter. Everything she'd struggled for in her adult life lay in pieces around her – how had it happened? How the fuck was she going to sort it out?

Chapter Two

If you were really on the edge – and who was to say she wasn't? – a wet February morning on an industrial estate in Stirchley might be enough to tip you over. Beyond the windscreen, a leaking grey sky bulged over a huddle of building-supply mega-stores and a near-empty car park, stacks of lumber, sodden nylon holdalls of shingle and sharp sand. In the twenty minutes they'd been here, they'd seen two people, and one of those had been a member of staff pulling a trolley out of the scrubby hedge in front of Toolstation. She glanced at the clock on the dashboard. At this hour on a Monday morning her Murder Investigation team would be at full hum, the insect chatter of keyboards and phones stopping only when Freshwater, in all his ferrety majesty, swept in for the briefing, clutching the Starbucks cup he thought made him look *au courant* and dynamically caffeinated. She felt a swell of deep-tissue yearning that she quickly suppressed. She'd check in with Gid again later, see if anything new had come up.

The wipers made a grudging sweep of the windscreen and Maggie shifted, sending over another waft of her spicy perfume. Shalimar, was it, or Opium? Robin couldn't remember. At this stage, it was basically her essence, anyway – getting into the car this morning, she'd breathed it in and felt a wave of comfort. Maggie was solid, unchanged in the thirty-five years she'd known her, from the eyeliner and jet-black hair, once natural, now courtesy of L'Oréal, to the revolving collection of chunky silver jewellery set with tiger's eye and turquoise that she bought on her regular tanning trips to the Greek Islands. She looked less like a private detective, Robin always thought, than a pier-end palm reader, but likely that worked in her favour – who would suspect?

An hour ago, she'd swung her silver Ford Focus away from the kerb at St Saviour's like they were Thelma and Louise. They'd started late so Robin could walk Lennie to school on her first day but normal kick-off could be six o'clock, or earlier. 'Cul-de-sacs at dawn, basically,' Maggie'd said. 'Shots of people up bright and early, suited and booted and slinging their briefcase/toolbox in the back of the car/van, delete as applicable, are of the essence.' She'd indicated right at a Tudorbethan pub strung with banners boasting Sky Sports and Gut Buster Burgers. 'How did Lennie go off?'

'Okay. I think. Nervous but putting a brave face on. You know what she's like.'

After she'd turned the light off last night, she'd listened to her daughter flipping around overhead, the slats of the bunk creaking under her weight like a flight of arthritic stairs. 'Are you all right up there?'

'Yeah.'

'Comfortable?'

A pause. 'It's kind of weird being this close to the ceiling.'

Two or three minutes had passed, another couple of all-body adjustments. 'Mum?' Not much more than a whisper this time. 'I'm sorry I said that about Ade earlier. Sorry I got Gran on your case, I mean, not that I *said* it. I didn't like it when Uncle Luke said that about him.'

Uncle Luke's a cretin, Len – oh, the temptation. 'I know,' she said.

A minute or so; another revolution. 'Mum?'

'Hm?'

'You know when you spoke to Ms Brampton? She said I could go back to RPG, didn't she, when we move back to London?'

'As long as they have a free place, she said, it's yours.'

Another pause. She could almost hear Lennie's mind whirring in the dark.

'Do you think it's going to be really different at St Saviour's?'

*No, no, no, my love, it'll be just the same, just as cosy and shel-
tered and academically rigorous, and everyone will want to be
friends with you straight away.* 'A bit,' she said. 'It's a compre-
hensive and the area's not very well off. There'll be kids there
from some tough backgrounds – and boys, obviously. But you'll
be fine wherever you go.'

'You think so?'

The neediness, so rare coming from Lennie, had been a dart
in her chest. 'Yes. I do. And like we discussed, it's not forever.'
Please god, let it not be forever.

Next to her now, Maggie snapped to attention. 'Look lively,'
she murmured as a trolley loaded with sacks of cement nosed
through the shop's automatic doors, pushed by a man currently
suing his employers for a work-related back injury. When he
wasn't doing hard physical labour, Robin thought, he must be
spending most of his sick leave on the bench press: encased in
sportswear, his upper arms looked like Christmas hams. Amazing
how bloody stupid people could be.

Maggie waited until she had a straight shot of his face and then,
under the guise of texting, took a volley of photographs. 'We'll

get some of him loading the van,' she muttered, 'and Bob's your uncle. Like shooting fish in a barrel, this one. Here, take this.' She passed Robin the phone then sat forward to turn on the engine. 'I'll go round behind him on the way out so you get a clear view. Then we'll wait a few minutes and drive over to the site.'

'Iced buns,' Maggie said as she dropped her outside Greggs. 'Get a whole pack. And here,' she pulled a twenty from her purse, 'get some sausage rolls as well, or whatever you fancy for lunch. We might not have a chance later.'

Robin waved her away. 'I'll get it.'

'Oh, shut up.' Maggie reached over and stuffed the note into her pocket. Robin tried not to look relieved.

Inside, she joined the queue. It was mid-morning, lunchtime a way off yet, but the place was already busy, two tills going, a steady stream of customers, nasal-musical Brummie accents dipping and rising around her like carousel ponies. She had the accent herself though she'd never given it much thought until Isobel-from-Berkshire laughed at it in her first week at UCL. It was lighter these days, anyway, after a decade and a half away.

Isobel – god, when was the last time she'd thought about her? But the whole morning had been like that, an extended hobble down Memory Lane. Every time they turned a corner there was something else: the community centre where she'd been forced to do ballet; the bus stop for school; the wooden arch to John Morris Jones Walkway down which she and Corinna had disappeared to do their underage smoking. The same but different. The little precinct at the roundabout but the shops had changed. Gardens had been overhauled, extensions added. Instantly recognized, deeply known, but foreign. Even the general look of the place, the style – years in London had altered her aesthetic.

The déjà vu had started the moment she'd opened her eyes and seen Lennie's new school uniform looming on its hanger like the Ghost of Christmas Past. She'd been at Camp Hill, the grammar school herself, but for a couple of months when she was sixteen, after they were introduced by a mutual friend, she'd gone out with the baddest of St Saviour's bad boys, Sean Harvey. When he asked her, she'd said yes because she knew it would piss Christine off and because, let's face it, he was fit and she was shallow, but she'd grown quite fond of his rebel heart and precocious sexual talent. He'd dumped her after she got her GCSE results – apparently her A-stars had been an embarrassment to him. Given her current luck, she thought, she'd probably find herself sitting in a cul-de-sac outside *his* house before too long.

Catching scroungers on the sick in Sparkhill. How the mighty have fallen.

'The site' just now had been a semi-detached in Bournville where the Christmas Ham, real name Barry Perkins, was working cash-in-hand on a kitchen extension and where they'd filmed him tossing the sacks of cement out of his van like confetti. The client was Hargreaves & Partners, a local law firm acting for Perkins' legitimate boss. She had quite a bit with them at the moment, Maggie said, and another bigger firm, too, on top of her long-standing contract with the city for suspect disability and unemployment claims. With Luke's comments ringing in her ears, Robin had listened to the list and felt her soul wither.

'Foive pound seventy-foive, bab,' said the woman behind the counter.

Back in the car, Maggie ate a sausage roll in four bites then pulled off again.

Robin buckled her seatbelt. 'Where to now?'

Sparkhill, just north of her parents' in Hall Green, was almost entirely Asian, which was why Luke, the bigot, had reflexively

19

chosen it for his scroungers. The shops and restaurants on Stratford Road were a mix of Balti houses and halal butchers, travel agencies and bakeries, the windows of the clothing stores full of salwar kameez and Pakistani suits in jewel-box colours. Maggie turned off by a Sikh temple Robin didn't remember having seen before. Three storeys high with reflective windows trimmed with blue, it looked more like a call centre than a place of worship. Its red brick was the only thing it had in common with the rest of the street, a shabby collection of Victorian terraced workers' cottages.

Stratford Road had been buzzing but just a few hundred yards off the main drag, the pavement was deserted bar a single elderly woman wearing an anorak over her sari. The houses had a dormant air, the only indication that anyone in them was awake – or even alive – the flicker of television through a ground-floor window.

Maggie brushed pastry flakes off her trousers. 'Right. Time to come clean.'

'About what?'

She laughed. 'Your face! Relax, will you, I mean me, not you. There's something I haven't told you about the job.'

'What?'

'Obviously I trust you, it wasn't that, but I've always worked strictly need-to-know on this side of things and because this is probably short-term, you and me, I didn't know if it'd come up. Also, the fraud's eighty-five, ninety per cent of my work, so you had to be all right with that. I mean, obviously you're not going to be thrilled, are you, going from Homicide Command to hanging round Wickes' car park waiting for scumbags. They're hardly criminal masterminds, Barry Perkins and his ilk.'

'Maggie. You know I'd be buggered without this. Without you having offered me a job.' It wasn't just the money, she thought;

if she'd had to spend another day without *doing* something, belonging to the world of people who had somewhere to be, work to do, she might actually have gone insane.

'Oh, stop, I don't need gratitude.' Maggie pointed at the bag at Robin's feet. 'Pass me those, will you?' She took the pack of iced buns and pulled one out. The floor heaters had loosened the slab of icing, which slipped sideways across the top like an ill-fitting toupee. Her mouth encompassed the thing without it even touching her lipstick.

'Anyway, I've got a bit of a bone to throw you. It's hardly Interpol but I do some work for women in tight spots,' she said. 'Sometimes just helping them sort a problem, sometimes it's more serious. You can start off expecting one thing and it's actually something totally different.' She took another bite. 'Like, last year, I had a bigamist. His second wife came to me, she had no idea, just knew something wasn't right. I poked around a bit and that was it. I found him in the Peak District eventually with a whole other family: three kids, cocker spaniel, the lot.'

'So it's personal fraud work?'

Maggie shook her head. 'Not really. Sometimes. It's all sorts. I've had girls about to be sent overseas for marriages arranged by "uncles" who'd basically sold them as British passports – those both came word-of-mouth. One of them lived just round the corner from here, other side of Stratford Road. Her mother was the client – wanted more for her. I got her away, helped set her up elsewhere. Nice girl. She's in Leeds now, doing a degree – we're still in touch. I had a girl who was trying to get out of a cult. I've also had parents who just wanted to know about their daughter's dodgy boyfriend. Research.'

'How long have you been doing it?'

'As long as I've had the business. Since I left the job.'

'They know?'

21

'Of course. And that's how I get most of the cases. I've got a contact – Alan Nuttall, my old DS, DI now – and he rings me if something comes up, a situation where there's no actual crime, nothing the police can do, or it's like the bigamist: something's off and I help find out what. He was prosecuted afterwards, obviously, once it was clear there *was* a charge to be brought.'

'You're a dark horse, Maggie Hammond. I had no idea.'

'Need-to-know, like I said. And now you do.'

A lot of the Victorian houses Robin knew were Tardis-like, with inner proportions that seemed impossible from the outside, but this one was every bit as small as it had looked from the pavement. Dark, too; there was no fanlight above the front door, and the internal door to the front room was shut, blocking any light that way. As they followed the woman to the kitchen at the back, the phrase 'down the rabbit hole' came into her head.

It wasn't just the lack of light or space, though given her choice of small mammals, Robin thought, she'd say Valerie Woodson was more of a harvest mouse than a White Rabbit. Her shoulders hunched as she scurried ahead of them, and though her colouring was sandy – once-auburn hair fading to an odd peach-grey – her eyes were so dark, they looked like buttons, currants in a bun. Maybe they'd adapted to the conditions.

It was brighter in the kitchen, where she stood dazzled in front of them.

Maggie smiled gently. 'How about a cuppa?'

The woman spooned Nescafé into mugs Robin recognized as garage giveaways from twenty years ago while Maggie kept up a soft patter about the rain, the lead story in the *Post* on the table, a pot of snowdrops outside the back door. The kitchen was old but looked-after, the white Formica almost stain-free even as the red plastic handles dated it at warp speed. The fridge was covered with magnets shaped like pizza slices and strawberries, a London bus.

An 'I heart Devon' magnet anchored a photograph of Valerie and a girl of fifteen or sixteen. They squinted into the sun, arms around each other, their lop-sided smiles so similar they could only be mother and daughter despite the girl's extra two or three inches and dark brown hair. She wore denim cut-offs and a turquoise vest top and, unlike her mother – the small visible area of whose shins was the colour of cream cheese – she was tanned. Behind them was a beach, unmistakeably British: wind-breakers, buckets and spades, and one egregiously burned fat white back.

'Torbay,' said the woman as she carried the mugs to a small table. 'Five years ago. Six this summer.' She fetched a third chair from the front room. When they were all sitting down, they were elbow to elbow. Robin moved back a little, let in some air.

At close range, the woman looked ill. Her skin was paper-dry and blotchy, raw around the nostrils from nose-blowing. Her eyes were marbled with pink. When she saw Robin notice how her hands trembled, she moved them quickly under the table as though ashamed of the weakness.

'She left a message just before eight this morning,' Maggie had said in the car, 'Alan gave her my number. I was in the shower, and when I called her back I got voicemail. Phone tag. Anyway, she got hold of me while you were getting the food. Her daughter's missing, she says, has been for four days. We were in the vicinity so I said we'd come round, talk face to face.'

She sat forward now, silver bangles chiming against the table. 'So tell us what's going on, Valerie. As much detail as you can.'

The woman brought her hands back up and wrapped them round her mug as if it were a crystal ball. Plain gold wedding band, no engagement ring. Her nails were unpolished, cut short.

23

In fact, all evidence suggested a complete lack of vanity. Her hair was cut in an unflattering pageboy, and she wore a pilled blue round-neck sweater and the sort of elasticated trousers sold from the back of Sunday supplements. If you saw her on the street, Robin thought, she'd barely register.

'My daughter's called Rebecca,' she said. 'Becca for short, never Becky – she *hates* Becky.' A glimmer of a smile. 'That's her on the fridge, obviously. She was sixteen then – we went to Devon after her GCSEs.'

'So now she's twenty- . . . ?' said Robin.

'Two. Her birthday's in October.'

'When did you last see her?' asked Maggie.

'Thursday. In the morning, before she went to work. Just before eight, like it always is.'

'She lives here then? With you?'

Valerie nodded.

'And have you heard from her at all since? Any calls, emails?'

'No. Normally she texts me during the day – practical stuff, what's for dinner – but that day, nothing. Then I found her phone upstairs.'

Robin sensed Maggie shift infinitesimally. 'Where was it?'

'On the floor, like she'd put it on the bed and it had fallen off. It was almost hidden by the valance – I called her from the landline down here and heard it ringing but I had to ring again to find it.'

'How about her purse? Her handbag?'

'She took those. She'd have needed her Swift card to get on the bus.'

'And where's the phone now?'

Valerie stood up and fetched it from the counter, a Samsung Galaxy in a sparkly mint-green case. They looked at it without picking it up.

'Is it locked?' said Robin.

Valerie Woodson nodded. 'I don't know the code. I've tried everything – her birthday, mine, her dad's.'

'Her dad is . . . ?'

'He's dead. Graeme. He died when she was eight. Cancer.'

'I'm sorry,' said Maggie.

'Tell us about Thursday morning.'

'It was . . . normal. I've been over and over it for anything unusual. She did go to work that day, I know that, because on Friday morning when her bed hadn't been slept in and I found her phone, I rang the office to check she was okay. I got Roger, her boss, and he said she'd been there all day on Thursday and left as usual.'

'But she wasn't there then?'

'No. He was about to call here, he said.'

'Where does she work?'

'In the Jewellery Quarter.'

The Jewellery Quarter. Robin felt a cold hand on the back of her neck.

'A family silversmith,' Valerie was saying, 'Hanley's. She's been there since she finished her A-levels; they've encouraged her to go on, do book-keeping at college at night so she can take more on.'

'And has she?'

'Not yet. She says she will but now there's the other place so I don't know when she'd have the time.'

'The other place?'

Valerie frowned. 'She's got a bar job in the city centre, place called The Spot. She's been there since September. Three nights a week – Wednesday, Friday and Saturday.'

'You don't approve?'

'It would be better to do the evening course, wouldn't it? But she says she's saving up for a summer holiday.'

'Have you looked for her passport?' asked Robin.

'Yes. It's here, still in the drawer with mine.'

'And have you spoken to anyone at the bar?' said Maggie.

'Of course.' A terse note. The woman heard it and caught herself. 'I'm sorry.'

'It's okay. Just take it steady.'

Valerie exhaled heavily, as if she could breathe out the tension. 'She wasn't there that night – she wasn't supposed to be, she doesn't do Thursdays. On Friday I called to see if she was in and spoke to the manager. He was annoyed with her for missing her shift, leaving him in the lurch.'

'Right. And you've talked to her friends?'

'As many as I can. And Jane who she works with at the office. She's got new friends, though, at The Spot. I don't know them.'

'Boyfriend?'

'Not at the moment. She broke up with Nick in October and there hasn't been anyone since, as far as I know.'

'How about him?' said Maggie. 'Nick. How did he take the break-up? His idea or hers?'

'Hers. Well, he wasn't pleased, he liked her, but as far as I know, he didn't push it. There were a few phone calls then he got the message.'

'How long had they been together?'

'Four or five months. But I've been through all this with the police.'

'Valerie, do you understand why DI Nuttall says she's not a high-priority case?'

'Because of her age – she's an adult. And because there's no evidence of anything . . . untoward.' She looked down, chin quivering. 'Violent.' Robin watched her bring herself under control. 'She doesn't have any of the risk factors – she's not suicidal, she doesn't self-harm; she's not an addict; she's not in an abusive relationship. I understand what he was trying to say – people leave, they don't want to be found, that's their prerogative – but this *isn't* that. This is different. Something's wrong, I *know* it. I know my daughter. If she hasn't come home and she hasn't rung . . .'

'What's she like as a person?' Robin asked. 'What does she like doing?'

Valerie took a wad of tissue from her cuff and pressed it under her eyes. 'She likes reading. We used to go to the library a lot when she was younger and it stuck.'

'What kind of stuff?'

'Novels – all sorts. Historical, thrillers. She likes *Jane Eyre* – reads it over and over again. Lately she's been reading a lot of YA, she calls it – young adult. Well, I suppose she *is* one but it means younger, really, doesn't it? All teenagers and girls with crossbows. Fantasy. And she likes cooking. Those are hers.' She pointed to a stack of books on the counter: Ottolenghi and Polpo, two River Cafés. 'She loves the *Bake Off*, all those cookery shows on Saturday morning. She watches them then goes shopping down Stratford Road, comes back and cooks. It's not all my taste, what she makes. Too . . . herby. Lentils, little beans. What's that funny stuff – tabbouleh? But she's good at it.'

'Wish I was,' said Maggie.

'So she's a homebody, would you say?'

'No, I wouldn't. She's . . . a mixture. She likes her cooking and her books but if I said she was always sensible . . . She drinks. She goes out. She's not a wallflower.'

'You said she's not an addict; have you ever suspected she might be taking drugs at all?' Robin asked.

'No.' She seemed to hesitate. 'I don't know.'

'Remember, we're not police,' Maggie said. 'The objective here would be to find Becca, not get her into trouble. Knowing about

27

drugs is for us, to make sure we have the whole picture. We're not going to go to the police about personal drug use, okay?'

'Right. Well, maybe. I don't know. Nothing . . . serious.'

In the bag at her feet, Maggie's phone started ringing. 'I'm sorry, Valerie.' She took it out, looked at the screen then stood. 'Will you excuse me a moment?' She pointed to the hallway. 'Hello?' The tinny sound of a male voice on the other end that faded as she moved away.

Valerie Woodson looked at Robin, expectant, and for a moment she was thrown. What now? Her instinct – her training, so ingrained it was second nature at this point – was to get details of Rebecca's associates, her employers, friends, exes, but how did Maggie work? Did she have to agree formally to take on the case? Did she want to? Writing down names would look like a commitment. And what about Valerie's side of it – was there some kind of contract? A fee? What were Maggie's terms?

She played for time. 'How long have you lived here?'

'Since I was born,' Valerie said. 'I'm the only original Brit on the street now. My parents bought the house in the Fifties, I've never lived anywhere else. My dad retired about the time I met Graeme and we bought it from them. They moved out to Worcestershire, bought a bungalow near Inkberrow.'

'Nice.' Jesus, the idea of living in one house your whole life. 'Did you ever see any evidence of Rebecca using drugs?'

The non sequitur took Valerie aback, unsurprisingly. 'What do you mean?'

'Sorry – I mean, have you ever seen her with them? Found them in the house?'

'Of course not.' Now she looked indignant. 'I wouldn't stand for that.'

Robin glanced back up the hall and saw Maggie open the front door, step out and pull it closed behind her.

Valerie saw, too. 'Is it something to do with Rebecca?'

'I don't think so. No. The police wouldn't know to call us about her. We've only just made contact with you, so . . .'

'That's true. Yes, that's true. God.' She put her face in her hands. 'Sorry. It's just . . . Do you have children?'

'One. A daughter, too.'

'So you understand.'

'A little bit, yes. You must be . . . extremely worried.' Quick, she thought, deflect the conversation. The last thing she wanted to get into was her life or how she came to be working with Maggie. Her homicide experience wouldn't be a comfort, either. 'Where do they go when they're out, Becca and her friends?'

'With her old friends, Lucy and Harry, they go – they used to go, before she started at The Spot – to this thing, what's it called, The Digbeth Dining Club? Street food, she called it, lots of different stands that . . .'

The front door – Valerie's head whipped round. Following her gaze, Robin saw Maggie step inside and close it. For a moment, turned away, she seemed to pause. Then, deliberately, she walked back to the kitchen. Her face was oddly composed, un-Maggie-like. Robin tried to meet her eye but found she couldn't.

'Valerie,' Maggie said, 'I'm sorry but we're going to have to go. Something's come up. I'll ring you as soon as I can. In the next hour or so.'

The woman's chair shrieked against the floor. 'What's happened? It's Becca, isn't it?'

'Becca?' Maggie seemed confused. 'Becca – no. No. Robin, can we . . . ?'

Robin stood, her heart starting to beat faster. What the hell? It was there, she wasn't imagining it, the care with which Maggie said her name. Disorientated, she followed her down the narrow hallway and back outside. The door banged shut behind them.

It had started drizzling again while they were inside, she'd seen it through the kitchen window, but now it was properly raining. 'What's going on?'

'In the car.'

The automatic fob flashed the lights. Robin opened the door then hesitated. As she dropped into her seat, she realized she was begging: *Please, not Lennie.*

Maggie's door slammed shut. She bowed her head then took a breath. 'That was Alan Nuttall on the phone.'

Relief, followed immediately by guilt. 'So it *is* Rebecca?'

'No, it's nothing to do with this. He was calling to see if I knew about something that came in last night.'

Last night – not Lennie. Sheer, exhilarating relief – *thank god*. 'So what was it?'

'There was a house fire in Edgbaston. They're still looking for the husband – he's missing. The boy's injured, badly injured, but alive. The wife . . . she didn't make it.' Maggie reached across the gearstick and took her hand.

Robin stared at Maggie's giant turquoise ring. 'I don't understand.'

'What I'm trying to say . . . Rob, it's Corinna.'

Chapter Three

In the raw, disorientated, underground early months of Lennie's life, Robin had used to wait for Corinna's key in the door as if they were married. She'd start watching the clock at six, when the shop closed, and she'd imagine where she was now and now and now, picturing her tracking back towards them – the walk up to Notting Hill Gate, the number 94 bus – and then, at last, the rattle of the key, the thud as the carrier bag hit the hall floor. 'Hello? Lennie? Where's my favourite girl?' Normality suddenly, as if it had blown in with Corinna when the door opened. The crushing panic, the waves of *What have I done? How the hell am I going to do this?* retreated, driven back by a cold bottle of Singha beer from the corner shop and the oven on for jacket potatoes.

To do that for someone. And then – at that age. Even now, years later, Robin thought about it and was amazed. An hour after she'd jumped off the bus hurtling her and the bean that was the start of Lennie towards the appointment at the Marie Stopes clinic, she'd phoned Corinna in Birmingham and by eight o'clock that evening – the first time Robin had ever ordered herself an orange juice at a pub – Rin had been in London, sitting opposite her at the sticky table, stunned but not shocked, not trying to 'make her see sense' as Christine had screamed later but talking about how they – *they* – could make it work.

Over the next few months, Corinna had uprooted her life for them. She'd been on the WHSmith management trainee scheme then and she'd arranged a transfer from the New Street branch to the one on High Street Kensington and, two weeks before Robin's due date, she'd packed her bags and driven her Ford Fiesta down the M40 to London. She'd lived with them until Lennie was eighteen months old and she'd never once made Robin feel as if she were even doing her a favour. 'Oh, shurrup,' she'd said in the Yorkshire accent she put on when dodging anything serious. 'Helping you? What makes you think I'm not *using* you? I'd never do this without you – I'm probably going to be in Birmingham forever after this, aren't I, with Josh and the factory? This is my adventure.'

And sometimes, when she was there and Robin had had a four-hour stretch of uninterrupted sleep, it had felt if not like an adventure, at least not terrifying. Doable. Amid the anxiety – was Lennie getting enough milk? If she rolled in the night, would she suffocate? How was she, Robin, going to afford a child? – there were times when they'd start laughing at the sheer ridiculousness of their being in charge of a baby and not be able to stop. So many things: the way they'd had to take off their jeans to give Lennie a bath because the tub was cracked and leaked onto the floor; Psycho Mike-o from number 14 who'd asked Rin out three times a week; even the snails that came in under the back door overnight and left silvery trails over the grim nylon kitchen carpet. For a year and a half, that flat off Uxbridge Road had been their world, their tatty, semi-subterranean bunker of a world, and now no one else knew about it.

Except Josh, because he'd been there, too, more weekends than not. Though his dad was training him up to run their family business back in the Midlands, most Friday nights he'd arrived on the doorstep in Shepherd's Bush with a curry – 'Not the Balti Triangle but it'll do' – and stayed 'til Sunday. He'd watched Euro 2004 on their scratchy green sofa, giving Lennie a bottle, and when they'd all gone out together, he'd taken her in the baby carrier, her cheek pressed sideways against his chest, little feet bumping the tops of his thighs. He'd only been twenty-four but if anyone ever thought Lennie was his, he'd never jumped to deny her like some of her other mates had, the ones who'd treated Robin as if she was suddenly a different, mildly contagious person, The Girl Who Got Knocked Up.

The slam of a car door. Lifting her head from her hands, she saw a tall black woman in a three-quarter-length coat on the pavement outside. A second later, as the woman checked her phone, a shiny blue-black head emerged from the driver's door on the far side. Robin froze.

Riveted, she watched as the man rounded the back of the car. The hair was right, he was Indian or Pakistani, but then he looked up and – *oh, thank fuck* – she saw that the face underneath it was wrong: too young, too fine-boned, too light. And as he stepped onto the pavement, she saw that he was too short – two or three inches too short, under six feet. She leaned backwards into the cover of the dining-room curtains, heart thudding.

Energetic footsteps on the path, then the four Big Ben notes of the doorbell. Her mother appeared in the archway, eyelids swollen. 'They're here, love. Shall I let them in?'

'I'll do it.' The room tilted as she stood, the floor underfoot uncertain. Her body moved as if she were operating it by remote control – *left leg, good, now right leg* – normal communication between brain and muscles suspended. When Maggie had dropped her back a couple of hours ago, direct from Sparkhill, she'd walked up the front path like the Tin Man, stood with her

33

arms by her sides, thousand-yard staring as Maggie told Christine what had happened.

Through the pebbled glass panel beside the front door now, the shimmering outlines of the police made them apparitions, visitors from another dimension.

'Robin Lyons?'

DCI, to you.

'DS Thomas,' said the woman, showing her ID. 'We spoke on the phone. This is DC Patel.' Up close, he looked even younger than he had outside, twenty-five or -six, baby-faced. Thomas wasn't that much older, early thirties, perhaps her own age, but her vibe was completely different. Meerkat-straight, shoulders back, posture accentuated by the crisp angles of the coat and a pair of black trousers with a sharp centre crease. Her hair was cut short at the sides, the longer top shaped into a wedgy quiff that reminded Robin of Emeli Sandé. Masculine-feminine. *Got my shit together*, was the message.

'Come in.'

They followed her to the sitting room where Robin watched the woman look around, taking in the three-piece suite, a patterned aqua monstrosity whose curved backs and fluted arms recalled Botticelli and his giant scallop. It was too big for the space and so the sofa could only go against the wall, making the room look even more corridor-like than it was. Opposite was the tiled fireplace, a vase of dried grasses in the hearth, the Spode figurine of an Edwardian lady with a stupidly large hat on the mantelpiece. The least offensive thing was the gilt-framed watercolour of the Lickey Hills that had been Granny Lyons'.

'My parents' house,' she said, and saw the flicker in the woman's eyes: at her age? Robin gestured at the furniture. 'Please, have a seat.'

They took the sofa, leaving her the armchair. If you were curled up in it, feet tucked under, it was okay, shell-like in a good way, even, but sitting properly, Robin was dwarfed by it, shrunk down like Alice in Wonderland, her feet barely skimming the floor. It added to the disorientation, the sense that everything was off-kilter. Unreal.

'Thanks for talking to us,' the woman said, pulling out her notebook. 'As I said on the phone, DI Nuttall gave us your name. Maggie Hammond told him you and Corinna were close.'

'She was my best friend. Since senior school. She saved my life, I think.'

The woman's eyebrows went up.

'Not literally. Maybe literally. I'm a single mother – I got pregnant by accident in my last year at university and she moved down to London, moved in with me. She cooked dinner so I could work, changed nappies, did one of the night feeds if I was about to go insane from lack of sleep. Made it all seem like less of an unholy fuck-up. I don't know how I would have done it otherwise – I might have lost my mind. I definitely wouldn't have finished my degree.'

'Losing her must be tough for you.'

It was a statement but also a question. Unlike her mother, who'd burst into tears the moment she'd heard, she hadn't cried. There was a fierce pressure in her chest but she couldn't get to it mentally, couldn't translate it. 'I haven't begun to process it,' she said. 'I know but I don't *know*. I saw her three weeks ago – I was texting with her yesterday. Lennie – that's my daughter – we were supposed to go over there tomorrow night for dinner.' As she said it, she realized that even that, that small bright spot on the immediate horizon, had been extinguished. And there would be no more.

'What time were you texting?'

35

'Afternoon.' Robin checked her phone. 'Just after four – eight minutes past. My last reply to her at four ten.' *Last.*

'What were the texts about? How did she sound?'

'Fine, normal. Herself. I mean, she didn't mention herself. She was checking in on *me* – I only moved back here yesterday, she knew I . . . had reservations.'

'You moved yesterday?' Patel looked up from his notebook.

'Yes. From London.'

DS Thomas nodded, glanced at him: *Make a note.* 'How much do you know about what happened?'

'Almost nothing. That there was a fire at their house. Corinna's dead.' She heard herself say the words as if from across the room. 'Maggie said Peter's badly injured. And Josh's missing – what does that mean? Are you waiting for a formal ID?' She felt a wave of nausea at the thought of dental records, a body so badly burned that they couldn't be sure it was him – or even a man. She'd seen those: blackened, pink-shiny lumps of flesh, the features, genitals burned away.

DC Patel – Baby Cop – shot a sideways look at Thomas, who leaned forward, resting her forearms on her knees. 'It's very early, obviously, but as things stand, our priority is locating Mr Legge.'

'Locating?'

'We've only found Mrs Legge's body. And Mr Legge's car is missing,' said Patel.

It took her a moment but then relief flooded through her: Josh hadn't been there. He hadn't been at the house. If Peter recovered – *when* he did – he'd have at least one parent. Thank god – thank god. 'He wasn't there?'

Another sideways glance from Baby Cop, missed or at any rate unacknowledged by the woman, whose eyes were trained instead on Robin's face. 'Again, to be clear, it's early,' she said. 'Lines of enquiry are wide open and we're still waiting on the

Fire Investigator, SOCO, but even without their reports . . .
There's evidence of an accelerant at the scene. The fire was almost
certainly started deliberately.'

'What?' An electrical fault, the iron left on – she'd imagined
a malevolent spark spitting from the fire, nestling deep among
the fibres of Corinna's sheepskin rug, glowing, taking hold as
they slept unwitting upstairs. But – arson?

'Mr Legge may have killed his wife then set the fire to destroy
evidence.'

A sort of bark escaped her. She almost laughed. 'Josh? You
think Josh killed Corinna? That's . . . No. There's no way. No
way.'

'His car is missing,' said Patel again, as if that settled it.

'So? He's a businessman – he travels. He'll have been away for
the night.' Oh god – it dawned on her that if that was the case,
Josh didn't know. If he was out of contact, no one had reached
him, he still had to find out. Rin dead, Peter in hospital – she
closed her eyes.

You moved yesterday.

Suddenly Robin stiffened. The floor seemed to shift beneath
her chair.

'We've spoken to Mr Legge's secretary.' Patel's voice reached
her from a distance. 'There were no plans for him to be away.
But more importantly, the neighbours on both sides reported
seeing his car on the drive yesterday evening. Monday is bin day
over there – he took their rubbish out after ten last night, spoke
to one of them.'

Could it . . . ? Could someone . . . ?

She pressed her hands against her knees to try and stop them
shaking. *Focus*, she told herself, *focus*. 'In the extremely unlikely
event that Josh, who loved Corinna beyond all reason . . .' She
faltered, seeing Patel scribble in his pad. 'I don't mean literally

beyond reason. Just – he loved her. He really loved her. In the event that he had some sort of mental breakdown or psychotic episode – again, extremely unlikely – and killed her in a moment of madness, there's no way he would have hurt Peter.'

'Do you know how Peter sustained his injuries?' Thomas this time.

'No. But fire – smoke inhalation, burns?'

'Inhalation, yes, but actually the worst of his injuries came from the fall.'

'He fell?'

'He jumped. Into the back garden from a skylight on the second floor. Broken legs, pelvis and three ribs, one of which punctured his left lung.'

Robin covered her mouth.

'We haven't been able to talk to him, he's unconscious, but he was wearing pyjamas so our guess is he was asleep and woke to discover the fire, jumped to escape.'

She thought of him at Christmas the year before last. They'd spent it in Edgbaston with Corinna and Josh. It had worked really well; they'd all had proper time together, and Len had made trips over here to see her grandparents. In the evenings, after Josh had got him into his PJs, Peter had come to the dining table to say goodnight. Those legs – in tight jersey bottoms printed with aliens and flying saucers, they'd been long and spindly as breadsticks. She'd looked at Corinna, who'd folded her lips together to contain the laugh, the *I know, it's too much* of maternal love.

'It's an hypothesis – a theory,' said Patel.

She gave him a look: *I know what a fucking hypothesis is.*

'That having killed his wife in the heat of the moment, Mr Legge came to himself, realized what he'd done and knew he couldn't bear his son to know. But knowing also that he couldn't

38

actively kill his son – the moment had passed, whatever had led him to kill Mrs Legge – he set the fire not only to destroy evidence but in the hope that his son, who he knew to be asleep upstairs, would die from smoke inhalation without ever waking up.' He laid it in front of her, formal as a barrister.

'No,' she said. 'Not possible.'

'As Mrs Legge's closest friend, were you a person she confided in? Shared her secrets with?' Thomas.

'Yes, when there were any.'

'What sort of things would they be?'

Robin took a silent breath, tried to calm the storm in her head. *Arson*. 'Rin's dad was an alcoholic,' she said. 'He wasn't physically violent, nothing like that, but he was useless, Trevor. Worse than. Her mum was basically a single parent when Rin and Will – her brother – were growing up. Oh god – does Di know?'

Thomas nodded.

'It was the full Monty with him: sleeping rough round the coach station, going AWOL for weeks at a time, getting beaten up. Lost his teeth. Mrs Pascoe brought up Rin and Will on her own and she's a nurse so they never had much money. It's why Rin didn't go to uni – she was more than capable, she was with me at the grammar school, she got two As and a B at A-level. She wanted to start earning straight away, though, help her mother.' She remembered Corinna walking out of the British Heart Foundation in town, that Yorkshire accent: 'You know what, pet? I've 'ad it up to me neck with cast-offs. Time to get a job.'

'How about more recently than that? Was there anything on her mind? Anything worrying her?'

Robin tried to think. 'No. Nothing that would even remotely . . . They would have liked another baby.'

'But they didn't?'

39

'She had a difficult time with Peter – *placenta praevia*. He was early, she lost a lot of blood. It was Josh who was most afraid of going through that again – losing her.'

Another little note in Patel's book.

'Did she talk to you about their relationship?'

'Never negatively. Unless you count joking about how they never had enough sex – too bloody tired after work, being parents, the house, what's for dinner, you know.' Maybe they didn't; Baby Cop was too young and Thomas didn't look like she'd settle for less than perfection in any area of her life. 'But it was nothing, just idle talk over a bottle of wine, nothing to do with how much she loved him, which was a lot. They'd been together since she was sixteen.'

'You never had reason to believe she felt frightened of him?'

'No.'

'Did he try to control her at all – dominate her? Did you ever see him behave in a way you'd describe as intimidating?'

The image appeared in her head without warning; she shoved it away.

'No,' she said. 'Generous, protective, kind, yes; controlling, dominating, no.'

'DI Nuttall contacted Maggie Hammond because he knows she sometimes works with local women experiencing domestic violence.'

'Maggie knew Corinna but only through me. She wouldn't have anything different to tell you about Josh. She'd have told me – today if not before.'

'And what about Corinna herself – the other side? You never had reason to think she might have been bored of the marriage? That there was someone else? They'd been married for . . .' Patel flicked back a couple of pages in his notebook, 'twelve years.'

'No, she never even hinted at that.'

'And she would?'

'Yes.'

'If she'd met someone else or was thinking of leaving him – for whatever reason – might that be enough to make him lose control? If he loved her as much as you say.'

'Didn't happen.'

'Infidelity can make people react in extreme ways,' pronounced Patel as if he was whipping back the cloth on a remarkable truth. 'Not just men, either. Totally normal people can go completely off the deep end and behave in a way no one could predict. It could also explain why Josh would set the fire knowing his son was upstairs – these kinds of killings can be a misguided attempt to keep a family together, in death if not in life.'

'I'm aware.'

DS Thomas sat back and crossed her legs as if to signal that she was satisfied, the heat was now off. Robin braced herself.

'You were in the job yourself, weren't you?' Thomas said. 'The Met.'

Here it came.

'DCI with HMCC.'

'That's . . . ?' Patel, pen poised.

'Homicide and Major Crime Command. I led a murder investigation team.' Fifty people.

'Until quite recently.' An eyebrow rose towards the Emeli Sandé quiff.

'Just after Christmas.'

'You left because . . . ?'

'I didn't leave, I was fired.' Robin looked Thomas in the eye. 'Misconduct. It was in the papers – Jamie Hinton.'

Thomas nodded and Robin saw that of course she'd known all about it; she'd just wanted to hear her say it. How she'd say it.

'Tell us about that.'

Robin looked at her. She'd probably read the whole thing on her phone while Patel drove them over here. 'We – my team – were investigating the murder of a guy called Jay Farrell. Officially, he was a property developer – thirty-three, good-looking, big house in Hammersmith a couple of streets back from the river – but as we discovered, he also had a couple of sidelines, significantly, running illegal parties. Raves. It started with a house he was converting to flats, before the building work, but it was such a success, he started hiring places – barns, a big empty house out in Hertfordshire. Word went out on Facebook and hundreds of people turned up, the Nineties all over again. He charged them entry and sold them drugs – which he'd bought from Jamie Hinton.'

'Okay.'

'Hinton's a career crim – previous for GBH and acquiring criminal property, known gangland ties. A friend of a friend introduced them but they'd become mates themselves. They were very similar – both all about the lifestyle, the clothes, the cars, the girls. When we got Farrell's phone, there were selfies of them out together at clubs.

'But then – word is, at least – Hinton was robbed. A big stash of coke and E taken from a house in Richmond – a house Farrell knew about because he'd been there. His body was found in a park on the Thames towpath, tortured in various ways – cigarette burns, lacerations.'

Thomas raised her eyebrows, waiting for the crowd-pleaser.

'Hands cut off.'

'He was being punished for stealing?' Patel.

Top marks. 'Or so whoever it was wants us to believe. My guv'nor, Detective Superintendent Freshwater,' she couldn't quite mask her scorn, 'wanted me to charge Hinton, but I wouldn't because I didn't think he'd done it.'

'Why not?'

'Several reasons. They were mates, like I said. They had a good thing going – they were both doing very nicely out of the parties so why kill the golden goose? Also, Hinton's intelligent. If he *had* been stolen from, he's far too clever to advertise either that – *Excuse me, officer, someone's nicked my drugs!* – or the fact that he'd murdered the perpetrator. It was a set-up.'

'But you didn't have any evidence of that?' said Thomas.

'Not as things stood. So I let him go and he promptly went AWOL.'

It occurred to her suddenly that her record might make her less credible, even suspicious. Could they think she was some kind of serial aider and abetter? No, paranoid – get a grip. But even if they thought she was unreliable because of Hinton . . . 'Anyway, the dismissal was unfair and I'm going to appeal.'

'Right,' said Thomas, neutral. Impossible to judge how she meant it. 'You were with the Met for thirteen years, yeah, so you know time's critical? If this is a spousal murder, and that's the most likely explanation at the moment, whether we like it or not, it's crucial we find Josh quickly. For his own protection.'

Murder–suicide. In cases where one partner killed the other, he or she frequently killed him or herself afterwards, either straight away, at the scene, or days, even months later.

'And if something drove him to it,' said Patel, 'if she was having an affair or planning to leave him, he could plead loss of control. That's allowable as a defence. It would be manslaughter, not murder – you would be help—'

'Jon-Jaques Clinton, 2012,' Robin said. 'The Court of Appeal quashed his murder conviction for killing his wife because of the qualifying trigger – she left him for another man, wrote about it on Facebook. They ruled sexual infidelity allowable for a defence of Loss of Control, going against the legislation that had been passed in 2009.' Teaching her to suck eggs, bloody cheek. Evidently, her right as a woman to be patronized was the one thing that hadn't expired now she was off the job.

'Where would he go?' Thomas now. 'Anything you can think of. Did he have ties somewhere else? Family? Friends?'

She thought, trying to clear space in her head, but there was nothing. 'Most of his friends and family are here. There'll be university mates who moved away after – Josh was at Aston – but a lot stayed local. The Legges are Brummie to the bone, they've been here since time immemorial – even the factory's third or fourth generation.'

'Is there a place he knows well where he might try to lie low? How about holidays? Did they have somewhere they went back to repeatedly? Somewhere they all loved?'

Did, loved. Past tense. 'No, not really. They went to Italy and Greece a lot but different places every time. Different islands.' A wave of frustration. 'Look, it looks bad, I know, especially the car, but this wasn't Josh. What other lines are you following?'

'What other lines *should* we follow?'

'Burglary gone wrong.' Her turn to teach the egg-sucking.

'Though, of course, most killers are known to their victims.' *Touché.*

'Then some kind of misguided kidnapping attempt. They lived in a biggish house, Josh owned a factory – someone who didn't know better might have come to the conclusion they're loaded.'

'But they're not?'

'No. Comfortable, definitely, but not megabucks at all. The factory's not that big, a lot of the workers are part time. Or maybe they got into some kind of fight – something stupid that just grew until . . .'

'Such as?'

'The sort of thing that could happen to anyone unlucky. Road rage that escalated and the nutter followed them home. Some sort of border dispute about the garden fence that turned nasty.'

'But there's nothing like that you know of? Or any other possible motive?'

'If there were, I'd tell you.'

DS Thomas eyeballed her: would you? Robin felt her cheeks flame but refused to break eye contact. *Hold on; hold steady.*

Thomas bailed first. 'Right.' She glanced at Patel: let's go. As they stood, Robin realized that neither had taken their coats off.

'We'll be in touch,' Thomas said at the door, 'but if you do think of anything, call us straight away.' She handed Robin her card then turned to go. The temperature had plummeted since the morning and the air that came in was freezing. Robin thought of Corinna, her bag of Singha beers and potatoes, the warmth she'd used to carry with her into the flat every night. She stood and watched them as they walked away.

When they reached the car, she shouted, 'Wait!'

They spun around, expectation written across their faces: she'd remembered something; seen sense; she was going to tell the truth after all.

'If you haven't already,' Robin said, 'you should speak to Samir Jafferi.'

'*Our* guv'nor?' said Patel.

'He's a friend of theirs, too.'

Chapter Four

Rustling overhead then graunching springs. The ladder creaked as feet and calves appeared, just visible in the light round the curtains. Thighs, then the hem of her T-shirt.

Without saying a word, Robin lifted the edge of the duvet and Lennie slipped in next to her. Robin pulled her close, pressed her nose into her hair. Coconut Milk Herbal Essences these days, flavour of the month, but underneath, unchanging, the Lennieness, the smell of her daughter. She breathed it in, animal comfort.

'I keep thinking about Peter,' Len whispered. 'When he wakes up and hears about his mum.'

Robin squeezed tighter, felt her ribcage expand and contract. A cold foot – how, in the Tupperware sweat lodge? – found her shin and pressed against it. The physicality of having a child, and not just in the early days. Of course, at thirteen, Len didn't cuddle like she used to – for years, when she was two, three, four, if they'd been in the same room, Lennie had been literally *on* her – but when it mattered, here they were. There'd never been anyone else whose limbs – platonically – she'd been able to tangle hers up in without thinking, unselfconscious. Even Dennis. When he'd come home this afternoon, he'd held her as tightly as she held Lennie now, but she couldn't let herself go. She'd watched herself standing rigid in his arms, out-of-body.

Maggie had collected Lennie from school while Robin spoke to the police, so Len had already known something was wrong, but her face when she'd told her. She'd stared for a moment, aghast, and then – Robin had grabbed her – it hit home. It was the first time she'd ever lost anyone, the first time Robin had ever had to tell her someone was dead. And here, in a house that wasn't theirs, in a school uniform that she was wearing for the very first time – that she should never have been wearing at all. 'I'm so sorry, Len. I'm so sorry.'

She'd sobbed, shoulders shaking. Then, standing away, swiping at her eyes with her sleeve, she'd said, 'What can we do?'

'I don't know, love. I'm thinking. I'm trying to think.'

But her head had crackled with white noise all day. From the moment their car disappeared from view, she'd been waiting for the police to call: they'd made a mistake; Josh had reappeared; been found; there was an explanation for why he'd been doing the bins at ten o'clock but was gone by one thirty when the neighbours called 999. Not a simple explanation, perhaps – as the afternoon ticked past, she'd queasily conceded that – but a reason. Instead, there was radio silence.

Could he have had an accident? But if it'd been serious, the police would almost certainly know. They'd have checked RTIs, hospital admissions. What else? Some kind of health crisis – a heart attack, a stroke? It ran in the family, his father had had one. What if Josh had had a spat with Corinna and driven off in a huff, blood pressure through the roof? If he'd felt ill, he might have pulled over before it happened. If he was parked on the street somewhere or in a car park, no one would think anything of it. He was young – thirty-eight. They'd glance at him and see a guy having a nap.

47

But someone had set the house on fire.

Not him. Her rejection of Patel's *hypothesis* was visceral, straight from the gut: Josh hadn't killed Corinna, simple as. There were no triggers – Rin hadn't been cheating or going to leave him, and yes, she would know. But beyond that, even if she *had* been planning to leave and she'd written a double-page spread about it in the *Mail on Sunday*, Josh wouldn't have killed her. He just wouldn't.

'*Your instincts tell you?*' Freshwater's voice suddenly, lambent with scorn. 'Do they?' He'd been standing behind his desk, fists planted, knuckles white. His shirt strained in lines, neck to armpit, stuffed with mid-life-crisis muscle. Anger shimmered off him but his eyes had been gleaming, too: *Gotcha*. Here it was at last, the excuse he'd been waiting for. 'So we're ignoring the *facts* – the facts gathered by *your team*, DCI Lyons – and going with your *instincts*, instead. What the *fuck* . . . ?' His prissy fountain pen jumped in his prissy glass tray. He'd spun around, turning his back as if disgusted. Her instincts said he was hiding his face, trying not to whimper at the pain in his knuckles.

Instinct wasn't 'woo-woo woman shit' – she couldn't wait to talk about *that* at her appeal – as any cop worth his salt knew. 'Read Malcolm Gladwell, you . . .' *Fuckwit* – she'd stopped herself but barely. He'd got the message, though. The next day, she'd ordered him a copy of *Blink* on Amazon. She knew it had arrived; Gid said he'd seen it on his desk. Instinct was years of lived experience, years of watching people, their words, behaviour, body language, processed in a moment and delivered to your gut as guidance on what you were dealing with, so you could protect yourself. And her instinct told her that Corinna had never had to protect herself from Josh.

An hour ago, she'd lain with her eyes trained on the red digital numbers of the desk clock: 1.30 a.m. A full day since the emergency call, already half – half! – of the first forty-eight hours, the most valuable in a murder enquiry, when everything was freshest: scene, witnesses, investigators. With every hour that passed, the case became cooler, the odds of solving it longer.

Arson.

The lack of information was doing her head in. 'Evidence of an accelerant' – what did that mean? A jerry can dropped on the drive, or areas of petrol that had somehow failed to ignite? Was it petrol for the lawnmower, grabbed from the garage on the spur of the moment or had it been brought there, premeditated? Where was Corinna found – which room? Had she been dead before the fire started? If she was badly burned and any existing injuries had been soft-tissue . . . Veteran of hundreds of crime scenes, gangland executions, shootings, drownings, Robin had run to the bathroom and puked.

She took a deep breath now, made herself exhale slowly. Hidden by the dark, she acknowledged it, the other thing that had bound them together, she, Josh and Corinna, never spoken about but always there, the fuse on everything they'd accomplished since. Had someone found out? Was that possible after all these years? *Eighteen* years – before Lennie, before Peter, any of it. If so, why now? What had changed?

You moved yesterday.

And she'd been in the papers – someone could have seen the photo, recognized her . . . *No* – she ordered herself to stop. That way madness lay; a spiralling nightmare.

There was so much she didn't know, all of it essential for building a picture of what had happened. The effort it had taken not to ring the number on DS Thomas's card, try and glean new crumbs. By now, the initial house-to-house would be long done, and the search of the immediate area. They'd be looking at CCTV, checking speed cameras. Anyone driving away from the house had to use either the A38 or Pershore Road and there'd be cameras there – they were both routes in and out of the city centre. The time-window was three and a half hours, ten o'clock to half past one; it wouldn't take very long to find out what time Josh's car had left, and in which direction.

Who else would they have spoken to? Di and Will, of course, and they'd have family liaison there. Gerry, Josh's dad, and his sister, Kath. Poor Gerry – he was fragile anyway since the stroke, and a widower. What would it do to him, knowing that Josh was a suspect – *the* suspect? Josh, Kath and the grandchildren were everything to him. And to Rin; he'd been the dad she never had.

Robin pulled Lennie closer, breathed her in. Corinna would never cuddle Peter again – never put her arms round him and pretend to crush him while he pretended he wanted to get away. He was ten, just turned – his birthday was at the beginning of January. He'd asked for a *Star Wars* Lego kit and a trip to WaterWorld in Stoke. 'Thank *Christ* it isn't Alton Towers,' Corinna had said on the phone. 'I'd have to be tranquillized to get on one of those rides. Oblivion, Nemesis – I feel sick on the bloody spinning teacups.' She would have done it, though, even if it had taken a general anaesthetic; she'd have done anything for Peter. Not overindulgence – he wasn't spoiled or allowed to run wild on a diet of TV and processed sugar – but attention, fun, structure, family. Proper care. Corinna had been a great mother – way better than she was. *It's not fair*, Robin wanted to shout; *you fucking bastard, whoever you are, it's not fair.* Why did it have to be her?

Dennis had tried to stop her but at six thirty, she'd turned on *Midlands Today*. It had been the top story, trailed over the pulsing theme music. 'Police launch a murder enquiry after an Edgbaston house fire leaves a woman dead and her son with life-threatening injuries.' A preview of other stories to come – three teenagers jailed for a knife attack; a planning controversy; a woman looking for a bone-marrow donor – and then straight to it. Nick Owen – silver-haired, kind-eyed. He'd been the presenter since they were at school, it had to be twenty years, and now he was saying Corinna's name.

He cut to a reporter at the scene. Russell Road, where Rin and Josh lived, was busy, the woman talking over a hum of rush-hour traffic, but the houses themselves were set back behind a verge lined with trees and a small service road now cordoned off. The reporter was a few feet outside the tape, backed by a fire investigation van and a square white forensics tent. They had a uniform at the foot of Corinna's driveway.

Floodlights blazed over the area, and the bare February branches gave the scene a weird gothic beauty. But then the reporter had turned aside, the camera panned out and they saw the house itself. Across the room, Christine had gasped.

When she was little, Lennie had called Corinna and Josh's the 'snowman house'. Built in the Thirties with some Deco influence, its white stucco façade looked out from under the hat of a steep dark-tiled roof like a cheeky face, or – with the small round porthole just under the roofline – a winking emoticon. A long stained-glass window – the carrot – lit the central stairs, and the bigger, horizontal windows of the bedrooms made the eyes.

The glass was gone, shattered by the heat, and the eyes were black and gaping, lascivious soot tongues licking over the stucco above each one. The size of them – the flames must have been eight or nine feet high. The creepers either side of the front door were burned to a network of fine charcoal, intricate etchings across a face now rendered macabre, a painted Mexican skull for the Day of the Dead.

Just visible against the evening sky, beyond the reach of the

51

floodlights, was a hole at the apex of the roof, the supporting timber burned away, tiles collapsing inward like fish-scales. Peter. The skylights were at the back of the house, Robin knew, one over the back stairs, the other – the one he must surely have jumped from – in his room, over his bed, surrounded by his glow-stars. She imagined his terror at waking to find the house on fire around him. Had his door been open? Had it come into his room? The smell; the sheer noise: roaring flame, groaning timbers, the shattering glass.

Dennis had taken her hand, squeezed it so hard her knuckles ground together, and she'd heard the reporter say, '. . . DI Webster. To confirm, this *is* a murder investigation?'

The camera moved to a man of about forty-five wearing a wax jacket over a suit. Broad face, short brown hair greying at the temples. Large brown eyes.

'That is how we're treating it, yes,' he said. 'Obviously, the fire damage is significant so it'll take time to establish exactly what happened here but we do have evidence that the fire was started deliberately.'

'And you're appealing for help from the public?'

He looked directly at the camera. 'Yes. We're keen to talk to anyone who was in the Edgbaston area last night and saw or heard anything that struck them as unusual. We're also appealing to anyone who may have seen Josh Legge or believe they know his whereabouts. Mr Legge was last seen late yesterday evening, shortly before the fire started, but not since then, and we're particularly anxious to talk to him.'

A photograph appeared onscreen. Robin recognized it: Boxing Day two years ago, she'd been there when Kath took it. Josh was standing by the sitting-room fireplace, a glass of wine in his hand, wearing the chunky grey jumper Rin had given him for Christmas and the saggy old dad jeans she mocked him for. Kath had caught him at the end of a laugh, eyes narrowed, the corners of his mouth turned up, emphasizing a dimple in his right cheek. Robin had seen the expression a thousand times – Josh laughed easily, he was such a soft target – and yet it seemed transfigured now, the half-closed eyes not twinkling, fanned by smile lines, but narrowed to calculate, look askance, the smile not open but wry. Sly. As if in front of the Christmas fire, his family around him, he was envisaging the future, raising a toast.

'We're advising anyone who sees Mr Legge not to approach him but to dial 999 or contact the incident room directly on this number.'

Robin had felt a flare of frustration: were West Midlands Police up to this? They were presenting him as their suspect but what evidence did they have? They *couldn't* have any: he hadn't done it. All that talk of other lines of enquiry – as far as she could see, it was nothing but lip service. There was nothing new in the report, not a single bit of information she hadn't heard from Thomas and Patel hours ago.

Was he SIO, this Webster? If they had a DI leading, they were treating it like a simple domestic murder, a self-solver, and it was hardly that, was it, hardly the husband turning himself in at the nick, clutching the carving knife. Was he competent? He'd done all right on camera, but that was no gauge. With his broad face and wide-spaced brown eyes, the impression he gave was bovine: Aberdeen Angus in a green wax jacket.

DS Thomas had been the opposite. In the dark of the bottom bunk now, Robin felt her face go hot. *You were in the job yourself, weren't you?* She hadn't been ready for the shame. I'm not this person, she'd wanted to say as she'd sat in that godawful armchair, D-list celeb on a wedding throne; I'm a good detective – really good. This is short-term, a cock-up; I'd never buy an aqua three-piece suite!

And Samir. Their guv'nor. What would he tell them?

Lennie shifted, turning her face towards the pillow, and Robin peeled her arm from round her stomach, feeling the sweat between their bodies. The window was open and the garden glittered with frost but the cold air reached a foot into the room then stopped, repelled by the central heating. Even the wall behind her was warm.

Corinna was dead, Josh missing. Her best friends, and there was nothing she could do. She was a DCI in the Met, not even borough CID but an operational command unit, and there was nothing she could do. Whatever her skills, however well she knew the victims, she was powerless: she had to leave it to West Midlands Police. And even then, said another voice, sly, how thorough did she really want them to be?

Chapter Five

She'd done her best but Christine was too quick. In the time it had taken Robin to get down the path and into the car, her mother had somehow lost the apron, gained a pair of shoes, a jacket and – could it be? – some lipstick and materialized at Maggie's window.

Maggie lowered the glass. 'Hiya, love.' She reached her hand out and took Christine's, perma-tan, rings and forest-green nails meeting pale, moisturized, French-manicured. Robin knew Maggie took pride in subverting expectation but still, after a lifetime, she was completely bamboozled by the friendship between the two of them. It was real friendship, decades long: Maggie was woven all through Robin's childhood memories, not only there at Christmas drinks and summer barbecues but the person who stayed to do the washing-up and ended up sitting in the garden until the houses across the fence went dark and the only light in the sky was pollution. They went out together too, dinner and drinks, any film Dennis baulked at. Not that there were many, he was a sucker for a rom-com – his favourite film was *The Wedding Singer* – but Maggie was Christine's partner for the dramas, anything emotionally gruelling. About monthly, when she'd been at school, Robin remembered, her mother would get back from their outings after eleven, relaxed – for her – and pink with Chardonnay. What the hell did they find to talk about?

'How are you all doing this morning?'

Christine's breath made clouds. It was eight o'clock but the lawn behind her showed no sign of thawing. 'I don't think anyone slept.'

'You've got to take it steady, all of you. This, it's . . . beyond.'

'That's what I wanted to say to you, Mags. I don't think Robin should be working today – I told her what you said yesterday about taking the day off. She needs to—'

'I'm right here,' said Robin. 'Aged thirty-five.'

'Everyone handles things differently, Chris.'

'I know but you know what she's like. If she gets it into her head—'

'For Christ's *sake.*'

Maggie gave Robin a look then turned back to the window. 'I'll look after her, darl, and I'll drop her back later on. You take care.' She fired up the car, raising the window as they pulled off. For the full circuit of Dunnington Road, Robin said nothing. As they waited for a break in the traffic on Stratford Road, the indicator ticked like a stopwatch.

'She's worried about you, that's all.'

The lights changed and they inched towards the junction, past the little branch library, nearer the deep bland lawn of South and City College on the corner. The inexorable miles of white sky overhead. Robin felt a surge of panic. 'She's trying to take control, like she always does. Do I have to ask her now if I'm allowed to go to *work*?' A flashback to one of their old stand-up fights, her mother yelling after her as she ran up the stairs, *My house, my rules.*

'If you get some sleep tonight, we can take your car tomorrow. Would that make you feel better?'

'Make me feel less like I'm eight years old.' Robin huffed. 'Sorry. I don't want to drag you into this. But I *need* to work, that's what she doesn't understand. What am I going to do otherwise, sit around there trying to cry?' Wondering if the past had caught up with them.

Maggie took a breath, as if she were about to say something, then stopped. A moment later, 'Anything new since yesterday?'

'No.'

'It was on the radio on the way over. Heart, just local. Same thing, looking for Josh, nothing we don't already know.' She reached for the radio. 'Want to see if we can catch it again?'

As Robin shook her head, her phone buzzed in her pocket, a text. Gid? Eight o'clock, a few minutes after – he could just have come on shift. A small leap of hope: perhaps there'd been movement on Hinton. But no, when she took out the phone, the screen said 'Adrian'. It was mildly startling, the name already an anachronism.

Len just told me about Corinna. Devastated for you. Here if you need me. A

For god's sake. She couldn't stop them being in touch – she didn't want to, they loved each other, and it was good for Len to have a male figure in her life – but of course it meant Adrian would hear about everything that happened to them. Was he going to use this to reopen communication, even try to make her reconsider? She'd thought at least *that* was over and done with. She locked the phone and put it back in her pocket – she'd deal with it later.

'Where are we going?' she said.

'Val Woodson's, via coffee. I can't be messing with that Nescafé this morning.'

'You've taken her on?'

'I've told her we'll see what we can do, yeah. She's desperate and I want to help her.' Another pause. 'I also thought it would be good for you.'

'Me?'

'It's what you need now, isn't it? Something to get your teeth into – something where you can actually use your skills.' She glanced over. 'It's going to be very hard for you, being on the outside while this is going on. I thought this would give you another focus, something else to think about.'

'Thank you,' Robin said.

She watched Stratford Road slide past outside the window, One-Hour Photo and the Kerala Ayurvedic spa, a place offering cash for gold. Outside UK Furniture Clearance, a ragtag assortment of wooden cots, bedframes and awkward-looking cabinets metastasized on the pavement. She concentrated, focusing on details, looking for something she could throw a line around. If anything, the unreality was stronger this morning, the lack of sleep compounding the sense that what had been concrete was now wily, unreliable. Malign. The world had spun away – she was out on her own, free-falling.

A couple of minutes later, Maggie pulled into a spot outside a bakery three times the size of the travel agent and sari shop either side. *Weddings, Parties, Functions* read the awning, while photographs propped at the bottom of the plate-glass window showed enormous, multi-tiered cakes in colours and degrees of ornamentation from subtle to Bollywood. At eye level, a poster offered Morning Breakfast Deals at astonishing prices. *Fried egg, two toasts and beans, £2.75* – you'd be lucky to get a single slice of toast for that in London.

'Come with me,' said Maggie, undoing her seatbelt. 'Meet Gamil.'

Inside, the air was heady, the smell of coffee and eggs on the griddle cut with condensed milk, coconut and cinnamon. On the right, a long glass cabinet displayed ranks of Indian sweets in pinks and greens and caramel tones. Kaju barfi, mysore pak – an image suddenly of Aisha's wedding, the boxes and boxes of sweets they'd pressed on her because they all knew – it was a family joke – how much she loved them. Robin shook her head, flicked the memory away.

'Maggie.' A man in his mid-fifties stepped out from behind the counter, pulling off a pair of blue gloves. He dropped them in a bin and came to greet her, taking her hands in his. 'We haven't seen you for ages.' Indian sing-song met Brummie sing-song, his voice all music. Heavy-lidded eyes with extravagant bags looked out from a face that was otherwise remarkably line-free. His hair-line had receded parallel with his ears, and the deep exposed forehead and long nose with its arched nostrils gave him an avian look. At the same time, he had something French going on, the thick white cotton shirt with cuffs rolled to the elbow, perhaps, or the tan loafers. An Indian Serge Gainsbourg, minus the sleaze.

'I haven't had much over here lately,' Maggie said, 'but we might do for a bit and I wanted to introduce you to my friend Robin. Friend and colleague – we're going to be working together.'

'Robin? My pleasure.' A firm, dry handshake. 'Coffee for two? I've got a fresh pot this side, just done.'

'How are things with you?' Maggie looked at the line of people queuing to order breakfast sandwiches. 'You're mobbed.'

'Yes, morning rush, always busy, busy.' He went back behind the sweets cabinet and pulled paper cups from a long stack. 'Just as well – three kids at university. Have I seen you since? Wasim got a place at Nottingham. Computer Science.'

'Younger son,' Maggie said. 'He helps out in the shop sometimes, you might meet him if we're over here. That's smashing, Gamil, congratulations.'

'Last one. Just the A-levels now and then, pouf, all my little birds flown. Now, what are you having? Doughnut, flapjack? New muffins are just out of the oven.'

'You're all right, thanks, love. Still playing chicken with the diabetes express here, so I resist on the very few occasions I can do it without chewing my arm off. Rob?'

'No. Thank you.'

He brought the coffees over and put them on top of the display counter. 'Very hot – careful. Omelette's good if you don't want sugar. I can make it for you myself.'

'Thanks, this'll do me.' Maggie inhaled a vaporous sip from the top. 'Now, ulterior motive, I wanted to ask you if you know someone.' She reached inside her long suede coat and brought out a folded sheet of A4 printed with a grainy photo. 'He's basically the mayor of Sparkhill,' she said to Robin. 'Knows everyone round here.'

Gamil rolled his eyes. 'Show me.'

Maggie handed it over and he unhooked a pair of glasses from the V of his shirt and put them on. 'Yes,' he said, 'I don't *know* her but she gets the bus just outside, comes in two or three days a week to get something to take with her. Friendly girl, says hello, good morning. She lives somewhere up that way.' He gestured towards the shop door, left, in the direction of Valerie Woodson's house.

'You don't know her name?'

'Wasim might. Though she looks a bit older, more Faiza's age?'

60

'Yes, she left school three or four years back. Can you remember when you last saw her?'

'Not today. Not yesterday but I was in the kitchen a lot so . . . Last week, yes, that big rainstorm – Tuesday, Wednesday – the bus shelter was full so I said to the people come and stand under cover. She was there.'

'Have you ever heard anything about her?'

Gamil smiled at Robin. 'She thinks I'm a gossip.'

'You are a gossip,' said Maggie.

He shook his head. 'So mean to me. No, no rumours.' He passed them plastic lids from a box on the counter behind him. 'I see her walk past sometimes at the weekend, too, maybe shopping, but otherwise . . .'

'How do you know she lives up that way?' Robin asked.

'Ah.' A small frown, eyebrows drawing together. 'You've reminded me. There was one time, I remember it – just before Divali, the end of October – I was coming in early to deal with the festival orders, walking, and I saw her.'

'Early?'

'Four, four thirty – still dark. Bakery hours, you know.'

'What was she doing?'

'Getting out of a taxi. Coming home from a party, I think – she was a bit . . . wobbly. Big shoes, heels – she took them off, walked barefoot up the street in that direction.' He mock-shivered. 'Too cold. She was in one of those unlicensed taxis. Like a normal car. Maybe Uber, no way to be sure.'

'How did you know it was a cab?' asked Robin.

'She got out of the back, but when it went by, the front passenger seat was empty.' He shook his head. 'Too dangerous – how do you know who you're getting? When she left home, I made Faiza promise, promise me she would never do that. Black cabs only, I said, send me the receipts, I'll pay. I meant to say something to her the next time I saw her,' he tapped the paper with his fingertip, 'this girl. But I forgot. May I ask what's happening with her?'

Maggie nodded. 'She's gone missing.'

Becca's room was at the rear of the house, its narrow sash window overlooking the side return, a tiny yard and the red-brick backs of the houses behind. The bed was a single, tucked tight into the corner, but it ate up almost a third of the floor space anyway, leaving an L-shaped peninsula of carpet barely wide enough to walk around. The redundant chimney breast took a big chunk, too, and created two deep alcoves, one that housed a wardrobe, the other a chest of drawers topped with a pine-framed mirror.

Despite its size, the room was quite appealing. Robin had expected clutter, slippery stacks of magazines, heaps of clothes, a sticky basket of make-up slowly gathering dust, but instead it was minimalist. The two magazines on the shelf of the tiny bedside table – she stooped: *Elle* and *Heat* – were both lined up squarely under a library copy of *Veg Every Day* and a well-worn paperback *Jane Eyre*. The bedcover was white seersucker, the anglepoise-style lamp brushed steel. A shot glass held a tiny cactus.

'You haven't cleaned up in here?' Maggie asked.

'No.' Valerie hovered at the threshold, anxiety rising off her like a heat haze. Another person who didn't sleep last night, Robin had thought when she opened the front door. She knew about Corinna, Maggie had told her yesterday on the phone, and as she'd come in, Valerie had touched her arm. 'I'm so sorry about your friend.'

'The police asked me that, too, when they looked,' she said now. 'She always keeps it like this – she says it feels bigger when it's tidy.'

'Is anything missing, that you know of?' said Maggie.

'No, I've checked. Her jewellery's all there.' She pointed to a lacquered box on the chest. 'Not that she's got much that's worth anything, just the two rings Graeme's mother left her and a charm bracelet. I looked for her overnight bag, just in case, but it's still in the bottom of the wardrobe. She only had her handbag.'

A shallow bamboo tray next to the box held a liquid eyeliner, mascara, and an eyeshadow palette in matte greys. Without touching it, Robin read the bottom of a Maybelline lipstick: Very Cherry. 'Is this the make-up she uses?'

Valerie nodded. 'She's got another lipstick in her bag but, normally, if she's going on somewhere after work, she takes all this with her.' Her voice became a croak.

Maggie went back to the doorway and put her hands on her shoulders. 'Valerie, love, I know it's bloody impossible but try to give yourself a break, will you? You're going to wear yourself out. Why don't you have a cup of tea and we'll come down when we're finished? We'll be very careful.'

Valerie hesitated then nodded, her eyes shining with tears.

They waited until they heard shoes on the kitchen tiles and a rush of water in the pipes. 'Here,' Maggie passed Robin a pair of exam gloves from her bag and put on a pair herself. She squeezed round behind her, opened the wardrobe and looked inside. 'I'll do this, you take the chest.'

Robin tugged the shallow top drawer open, feeling the twinge in her shoulder. After Lennie had gone to sleep, she hadn't risked moving, and she'd come round from the semi-conscious state she'd eventually fallen into to find one arm completely dead. Crouching toad-like, trying not to wake her, she'd extricated herself via the end of the bed, smacking her head on the top bunk as she'd stepped down.

Becca's underwear was a mix of comfortable black cotton and skimpier, lacier things in fuchsia pink, blue and jade green designed to be seen or at least worn for a bit of a private confidence boost. Like the rest of the room, the drawer was tidy – not Christine-standard by any stretch, but neater than her own by a factor of about five; the socks in pairs, for example, rather than a static knot tossed in straight from the dryer.

T-shirts, then sweaters, all redolent of fabric softener. Robin worked her way steadily through them, shaking things out then refolding and laying them carefully on the bed. She ran her fingertips into the corners of each drawer and took out the striped lining paper. No photos taped underneath or love letters cajoling her to run away, leave it all behind; no little bag of resin or pills or even a cheeky packet of Marlboro Golds.

The clothes were cheap – H&M, Primark, Zara; tops in rayon and flimsy cotton, the knitwear more manmade fibre than wool – but they'd been taken care of, ironed and neatly folded. They'd been chosen carefully, too. The going-out things had net panels and lacy bits – racy enough – but almost everything had some design, a detail that gave it a bit of flair: a ballet wrap, a boat neck, ties at the wrists.

For all the times she'd done it, Robin hated going through people's intimate stuff. Even in a situation like this, where the aim wasn't to incriminate but to learn, maybe find a lead, it made her feel grubby. The thought of some sweaty-fingered DC raking through Corinna's underwear made her want to puke all over again. But maybe it wouldn't happen – couldn't. Given the extent of the fire damage, Corinna's clothes had likely been reduced to a heap of ash and melted hangers. Even if they hadn't been destroyed, none of them would be worth keeping; those that weren't burned would be drenched, and if they'd escaped even that, they'd reek so strongly of smoke that no one who'd loved Rin could ever bear to go near them. At least Di would be spared the task of sorting through her daughter's things. But by the same token, there would be nothing for Peter to bury his face in, nothing left that smelled of his mother. Robin pressed the idea, running her finger along it as if it were a blade. She wanted it to hurt, to cut through to the ball of potential pain she still hadn't been able to access. Why couldn't she cry? What was wrong with her?

With a screech on the rail, Maggie pushed things to one side and took out a black body-con dress. She held it up to the light.

'She bought that in the sales last month.' Valerie appeared in the mirror behind her. Robin jumped, and turned around.

'Sorry, I didn't mean to . . . She and Lucy – her best friend – they got up at four o'clock to go. The trousers she was wearing when she . . . She got them sixty per cent off – she was so chuffed. She bought me a cardigan, too. That's Lucy.' In a second, Valerie was at Robin's side, pointing to a photograph tucked into the mirror-frame of a pretty girl with light brown hair twisted into a top-knot. She wore a strappy, gym-type T-shirt and her face was flushed and shiny with sweat. 'They did a 10K run last April, the three of them.'

'He being the third?' Robin pointed at the man with his arm around the girl's shoulders, same age, mixed race. Eyes closed against the sun but grinning, a near-empty water bottle hanging between the fingers of his other hand.

'Harry, yes.'

'They look close – are they together?'

'Lucy and Harry? No. Lucy's going out with Cal – Calvin. They're just friends, the three of them. I always worried about that – three's a crowd – but it works. They've been friends for years, since they all started at Grafton House.'

'Grafton House?' said Maggie. 'The private school?'

'Graeme had a life-insurance policy. That's what I spent it on. We talked about it before he died. She went to state school until she was eleven, then Grafton.'

'Do you have Lucy and Harry's numbers?'

'I've got hers – she'll be able to give you his.'

'Thanks.'

'Becca and Harry were never involved?' said Robin.

She shook her head. 'As I say, it's always just been platonic.'

Missed opportunity, Robin thought; he was fit. She heard Corinna's voice suddenly, dust-dry, *'For god's sake, Rob. I'm dead, you're trying to find someone who's probably dead as well – a little focus, perhaps?'*

The pain – longing, loss, a desperate urge to laugh; it was sheer luck that she didn't yelp. She caught her own eye in the mirror – *steady, steady* – then Valerie's. She looked away, took a deep breath. *A little focus.* 'Yesterday,' she said, 'when you told us you checked in with her work because her bed hadn't been slept in – was that unusual? If she doesn't have a boyfriend. Does she stay over with friends? How often *doesn't* she sleep here?'

There was a pause, small but marked. 'It was when I found the phone as well that I started worrying, not just the bed. Rebecca's twenty-two. She can stay out, can't she?'

'Of course.' Maggie, soothing.

'But just to be clear, you mean with men?' Robin pressed.

'She's an attractive girl, she's never gone short of attention. She has flings, yes. One-night stands.' Valerie locked eyes with her, as if daring her to be shocked.

You'll have to try harder than that, Robin thought. 'Has she been doing it lately? Staying out, I mean?'

'Yes.'

'Would she go home with someone she'd never met before? A stranger?'

Valerie turned to the window, biting a piece of dry skin on her lip between her eye teeth. 'I don't know. No, of course I do. She would. Yes.'

Chapter Six

When Robin was in her final year of junior school, a local woman was kidnapped. Stephanie Slater was twenty-five, an estate agent, taken from a house she'd been showing in Great Barr, only a few miles away in the north of the city. It became a major national news story, one of the biggest manhunts in British history. Christine and Dennis whispered about it in the other room, waited 'til she'd gone to bed to watch the news, but the details had been in the air, all anyone could talk about: the ransom money snatched from a railway bridge, the coffin-sized box inside a green wheelie bin in which Slater had been locked in darkness for eight days, told that if she moved she'd be electrocuted. After she was released, she described how she'd talked to Michael Sams, and kept talking, so he'd be forced to understand that she was a person, a human being. Her bravery and presence of mind probably kept her alive.

Michael Sams, badger-faced, wooden-legged Michael Sams – by the following year, when Robin started at the grammar school and met Corinna, he'd become a playground bogeyman, the shadowy figure who offered you the bag of sweets, who shoved you into the back of a van as you walked home from the corner shop at twilight. *Michael Sams'll get you.*

And then, two years later, barely fifty miles away in Gloucester, came Fred and Rose West.

She and Rin were twelve turning thirteen by then: prime-time adolescence. It had gone on for weeks, the systematic taking-apart of the house at Cromwell Street where, over decades, Fred and Rose had together raped, tortured and killed young women, including their own daughters. White forensic suits on the news, day after day, week after week, another set of remains and another and another, in the garden, in holes dug in the cellar floor. Again her parents had tried to shield her but away from Dunnington Road, she and Rin had followed the news with a horrified fascination, reading the papers, watching the news at Rin's place when Di was at work and Will, babysitting, was doing his homework in the other room. There were few stories, thank god, as depraved as that. Rose was found guilty on ten counts of murder; Fred, charged with twelve, never stood trial. He committed suicide while on remand at Winson Green, HMP Birmingham, just a handful of miles up the road. Robin remembered: it was New Year's Day.

Two of the biggest crime stories of the decade, both local, both sexual violence against young women, a double whammy that happened just as she and Corinna became aware of the news, aware that they were – or soon would be – young women, and that monsters were not just in books but opening their car doors to offer you a lift in the rain.

It started with Stephanie Slater, her bravery as she lay alone in the dark, injured and terrified. To Robin, she became a hero, a symbol of strength, and when the Wests and their house of horrors came to light, Robin had an epiphany: that was what she wanted. She wanted strength. She wanted to be a hero. She wanted to break down the door and rescue the next Stephanie Slater. She wanted to be the one who followed the Wests home, kicked Fred in the bollocks, and pulled the girl away from the car, the teetering edge of the void.

That was what she told anyone who asked why she'd decided to go into the police. Over the years, she'd made it sound more and more ridiculous – *Behold the high-kicking, karate-chopping teen ninja girl! Marvel at the self-importance, the naivety!* – but it was true; it had been the first reason before she had another.

Maggie hadn't followed the Slater case in the news: she'd worked on it. Not immediately, on the original core team, but as soon as the investigation started to expand. Unsurprisingly, it loomed large in her memory. She'd kept quiet at Valerie's, of course, but in the car on their way here to the office, she'd brought it up.

'Kidnap for ransom? Really?' Robin was dubious. Nothing about the Woodsons' set-up said money, and Valerie's only real savings, she'd told them, were in a small private pension that wouldn't mature for another seventeen years.

'Remember the Slater case?' Maggie said. 'It was her *employers*, the estate agents, that Sams went after – he wanted their insurance money. Valerie might not have much but Becca works for a silversmith.'

Hanley's. Battered floral address book in hand, Valerie had given them the number. 'They make photo frames and candlesticks,' she said. 'Hip flasks and the like. Corporate gifts.'

'They'd have had a demand by now, wouldn't they?' said Robin. 'Thursday to Tuesday – five days?'

'Yes. Unless . . .' Maggie had glanced across. 'Julie Dart.'

Mentally shafted as she was, it had taken Robin three or four seconds to connect the dots. Then she did.

The investigation into Sams had expanded beyond Stephanie Slater. Based on similarities in the two cases, West Yorkshire Police believed that a year earlier, in Leeds, he had abducted another woman – if woman was the word. Julie Dart had been just eighteen when he'd taken her, a kidnapping 'dry run' that went wrong; she'd managed to escape from the coffin-sized box and he'd returned to find her desperately trying to get out of his workshop. He'd killed her.

'If there'd been a demand, we wouldn't be on the case, obviously – the police would be all over it,' Maggie said. 'But if something went *wrong*, he – or they – might not have got that far. He might have killed her, jettisoned the plan, like Sams did.'

'But if it *is* abduction, don't you think a sexual motive's more likely?'

'I do. But all lines of enquiry at this stage – everything's on the table until we get something solid. What else? There's a new notebook in the glovebox there; let's get some of this down.'

The list was on the table in front of Robin now, a spiral-bound page of parental pain from basic heartbreak to worst nightmare: she'd met someone and run away, upped and left; had an accident; overdosed; killed herself; been killed. The only good-news scenario, really, was that she'd needed to get away and had taken a break somewhere to clear her head. But then why not tell her mother, especially when they were so close? Why put her through this? And wouldn't she have taken *something* with her – a few clothes, her washbag? The only things she could see were missing, Valerie said, were the clothes she'd walked out in that morning.

And then there was her phone.

'Anything in her online stuff?'

Robin clicked back onto Facebook as Maggie stood and came around the table. The picture she'd been looking at was a social-media classic. Taken the Christmas before last, fourteen months ago, it showed Becca and Lucy with their heads together, big living-our-best-lives grins. Slight over-exposure made their line-less skin near-perfect. They were both wearing beanies – Becca's navy and studded with little silver beads, Lucy's dark burgundy with a scarf the same colour – and both had long wings of hair protruding from their hats like Afghan ears, Lucy's light brown, Becca's darker. In their hands were red cardboard cups, presumably the hot chocolate for sale at the stand behind them, beyond which, just visible, were the Palladian columns of the Council House in Victoria Square. *Christmas Market with my bestie!* Becca had written. *Love winter!*

Besties, BFFs – the terms hadn't existed when she and Corinna were that age. Not that they would have used them anyway – they didn't make a thing of their friendship like that. Even if she hadn't been up to her ears in nappies and revision when she was twenty-two, Robin doubted she would have been slinging her arms around her anyway, huddling in for photo after photo. Corinna might have made her do it occasionally – she was more of a cuddler.

She moved sideways to give Maggie a better view. 'Nothing that rings alarm bells,' she said. 'It's what you'd expect – pictures of her and her mates at parties and pubs, a couple of weddings, the occasional cat video or viral thing of someone doing something stupid. Nothing provocative, no bikini pictures or underwear-posing. I've been through all the comments for the past two years and there's no one creepy or over-keen, nothing that struck me as dodgy. Almost everyone appears in pictures from several different occasions, and I cross-referenced the less regular ones, who all seem *bona fide*, friends of friends, etc. I found Nick.'

'Show me?'

Robin scrolled back to September and a picture of a man in jeans and a maroon Adidas top. He was about thirty with curly hair cut short at the sides, left longer on top. Possibly – local pride – he'd been going for the *Peaky Blinders* look but it came

72

off more Gilbert Blythe in *Anne of Green Gables*. The darkness of it made his skin look slightly vitamin-deficient by contrast but he was attractive, tall and fit, muscle visible round the shoulders under the burgundy nylon.

'Hm. Is there just Facebook?'

'No, Instagram too.' Robin toggled to @BeccaWoods95's curated vision of the world. *Birmingham, UK. Food, books, fashion, design. 152 posts, 95 followers, 241 following.*

'The last thing was this, four days before she disappeared.' She moved the cursor over a picture of a bowl of spiced chickpea soup reposted from a cooking blog. 'About half of the posts are food-related, mostly photos of things she made, with little comments.' She clicked on a square captioned '*Sacher torte – worth every one of the 174,329 calories!*'

The rest was books and arty shots of silhouettes and trees, a few bits of interior design – nice chairs and rugs and kitchens – and then fashion, all pretty standard stuff. A woman in a green backless evening gown on a moonlit terrace was hashtagged *Goals* but the handful of reposts from fashion blogs were down to earth otherwise: women in superior combinations of boots, skinny jeans and enormous cardigans. It was a sort of rose-tinted, better-dressed version of real life. 'And only three solo selfies – nothing by prevailing standards.' A couple of weeks ago, in Shepherd's Bush, Robin had seen a woman pouting into her phone by the green veg at Tesco.

'Hm. What time did she say, again – Lucy?'

'Four.'

'I've just had an email from Roger Hanley; he can do four thirty at his office.'

The Jewellery Quarter. 'You take him, then; I'll take her?'

Maggie looked at her. 'I thought – just for now – we could work together.'

'Don't worry, I'm fully trained.'

'That wasn't why I—'

'It's fine. I'm fine. I'm not going to fall apart.' Brooking no argument.

Maggie hesitated, then sighed – *All right, against my better judgement.* She reached for her coat. 'I'm going to run down and get a sandwich. What can I get you?'

'Nothing. I'm okay for now.'

'Robin.'

'Something simple then – cheese and tomato. Thanks.'

Maggie shrugged the coat on. 'Will you be all right here?'

'For ten minutes, while you buy a couple of sandwiches?'

The door closed and Maggie's boots clomped down the steep wooden staircase towards the street door. The office took up two rooms on the third floor of a red-brick building at the nether end of Cannon Street, above a hairdresser, opposite a bridal shop and the entrance to the parking garage where they'd left the car. Coming in, Robin had seen the city centre shops she remembered of old, Poundland and Coral bookies, multiple outlets selling cheap sportswear, but just down the street, apparently, there was now a large branch of Jigsaw.

'Oh yes,' Maggie had said, 'we're getting proper posh. We've got a Jack Wills and a Muji within a two-minute walk now, get us. I'm very partial to the Japanese stationery, I've got to admit; I've bought all sorts of bits and bobs – little staplers and note-books and what have you. Can't resist it.'

Downstairs, the door slammed shut. Robin stood up. Her eyes were dry from lack of sleep and the hour and a half she'd just spent staring at Becca Woodson's life online. She stretched her neck and did a circuit of the dining table that dominated the main room. This was where Maggie took meetings, she said, and also where she did her desk work. The office had two laptops,

74

one exclusively Maggie's and an ageing Dell, which Robin would share with Lorraine, the woman who came in two days a week to do the billing and other paperwork. She was currently halfway through a fortnight in Lanzarote, Maggie said; she took a break in February every year, to help with her SAD.

A desk and a bank of filing cabinets were housed in a second, smaller room that led off this one and got its only natural light from the glass panels along the top of the dividing wall. A handful of large leather-leaved plants dotted here and there and that was it, her new place of work.

She took the kettle from its tray on top of the filing cabinets and carried it out to the miniature kitchen shared with the temp agency in the rooms across the landing. With some difficulty, she got it into position under the tap in the tiny sink and filled it.

Back in the office, she brought up the West Midlands Police's Twitter feed. She'd been checking it every ten or fifteen minutes, skimming over cycle safety and community policing notices to the frequent ones about serious crimes – another stabbing in Handsworth, a fatal hit-and-run in Balsall Heath, a slavery charge brought against two brothers in Lozells. There'd been a run of tweets with photos hashtagged MISSING. '*Have you seen Bill Scott? He's missing from West Bromwich and we're really concerned for him. Please call 101 with any information.*' She'd scrolled through them looking – hoping – for Josh; instead, with a jolt, she'd seen Corinna's face. *Murder enquiry launched following Edgbaston fire. Corinna Legge (pictured) sadly passed away yesterday.* Heart in her throat, Robin clicked on the link and read the short post on the police site but there was nothing new, still just the barest details of the fire, the search for *Josh Legge (pictured), believed to have been at the scene when the blaze broke out.*

All the local news sources had the story – the *Birmingham Post*, the *Mail* and *Midlands Today* – but again, none of them had a single new detail. Either the police were keeping information back or they didn't have anything.

Corinna Legge sadly passed away yesterday. She read the words again. They were ungraspable, completely surreal. Aliens land in the Bull Ring; Elvis spotted at Villa Park; *Corinna Legge sadly passed away yesterday.*

Yesterday – it was only technically still true. It was one o'clock, already almost thirty-six hours now since the neighbours had sounded the alarm, a day and a half. Rin was falling further and further behind, slipping away.

Robin reached for the notebook and turned to a new page. 'Assuming arson', she wrote, and underlined it. Quickly, she put down everything that came into her head, the earliest ideas – botched burglary; extortion attempt; feud with a third party; the road rage she'd mentioned off the cuff to the police – and the ones that, as the hours had started to stretch, she'd begun to have to entertain: someone Josh had crossed in business; something at Corinna's work; someone obsessed with one of them – a man or woman scorned, a bunny boiler; the partner of that person.

Revenge.

She read the list back. Burglary was still the only thing on it that seemed plausible. Rin and Josh woken in the small hours by a noise downstairs, investigating and confronting whoever it was they found, refusing to stand down. They would have tried to fight back, defend their home – yes, they would.

The rest made no sense. Josh's factory manufactured metal springs, and it had been going steadily for decades, probably a century at this point. People he did business with became family friends. Once, years ago, she'd been at theirs just before Christmas and he'd brought home six bottles of Scotch, all of them gifts from customers or suppliers. He'd shared another six between his sales manager and tool-maker. He was an old-fashioned manufacturer, making things that people needed and selling them, not some dodgy property developer, kicking tenants out of their homes, stiffing people on contracts.

And for another woman to feel scorned enough, Josh would have to be involved with her, surely. He was kind, a gentleman – what if someone had mistaken his kindness for attraction? If he'd been pursued, caught at a moment of weakness . . .

No. Robin would stake her worldly goods – the boxes behind the bedroom door *and* the ones now moved to the garage – on him being faithful.

You moved yesterday?

She remembered the look Thomas had given Patel. They were right, of course – she would have been all over that, too. There *were* such things as coincidences, but they were suspicious until proven otherwise, every time.

Her stomach turned over. *No*. She stopped herself. Just think: how else could that be connected?

Could Hinton be involved somehow? Was that possible? He was at large, whereabouts unknown – he could be in Birmingham. And he certainly had contacts here. But she was the person who'd let him go – she'd been fired for it, plastered all over the sodding *Mail* and the *Evening Standard*. Even if it hadn't been crystal to him that day, he'd know now. So – who? The person who had actually killed Farrell? An enemy of his?

No – it was too intricate, too massive a leap. Even if it was Hinton himself, which was unlikely enough, or Farrell's killer, why would they harm Corinna? And how would they even know she and Rin were friends? No one would find *them* posing together on social media. Plus, there'd been no threat, no claim afterwards – what would be the point of doing it if she, the target in this scenario, wasn't even aware? No, this was crazy stuff.

She bent her head, dug her nails into her scalp. What the fuck was going on? How could she find out?

Picking up her phone, she opened Contacts. Last night, she'd rung Di, Corinna's mother. She'd been ashamed of how relieved she'd felt to get voicemail. She'd left a message saying just that she was heartbroken, and heartbroken for her. 'If I can do anything, Di, anything at all, please let me know.' Just words, however much she meant them.

Will's number was underneath his mother's. Robin had it from group texts – photos of Peter, details for birthday parties and dinners – but she hadn't actually called him since the old days, when she and Rin were sixth formers and he'd used to pick them up from parties, sober as a judge in his little Peugeot. Will didn't drink, never had. 'Just not my thing,' he said but Rin told her it was deeper than that. He was afraid that if he started drinking, he'd never stop.

'Does he think that for a reason? Does he feel like he's an alcoholic?'

'No, but it runs in families; alcoholics quite often have alcoholic kids. He says he can't risk it.'

Will had been an adult since he was twelve, responsible and reliable as bedrock. While they'd been out getting smashed, he'd been studying. He'd done medicine at Edinburgh and he was a consultant neurologist now, at the Alexandra in Redditch. His wife, Lily, was an anaesthetist and they lived with their son and daughter in a snazzy barn conversion near Henley. Not bad for a bloke whose nickname at the boys' grammar, where irony was king, had been Thrill. But was he ever actually that boring? He was no Sean Harvey, tearing the place up with his delinquent tendencies and come-to-bike-shed eyes, but when you could hear what he was saying, Will was funny, which had become more apparent as, with the advent of Lily, he'd become more confident and thus more audible.

He answered almost immediately. 'Robin?'

They spoke at the same time. 'How are you?'

'I don't even know,' he said. 'Stunned.'

'How's your mum?'

'She's . . . not good. She's with Peter at the hospital, she was there all night.'

'The police came to talk to me yesterday – you probably know. They said he broke a lot of bones.'

'Yes, but the real issue's the lung. They keep calling it a puncture but it was more of a tear – the end of the broken rib tore the lung. They've operated, obviously, but now it's a waiting game. If he gets an infection, it could all just . . .' He trailed off into silence.

'What happened, Will? What are the police saying?'

'I don't know. Nothing. The same as yesterday.'

'You don't think Josh did this, do you?'

'No. I don't.' He paused. 'But I don't know what else to think, either. If he didn't, where the hell is he?'

Chapter Seven

Robin looked up. High overhead, above two encircling galleries of shops, an arching roof of white concrete beams and curved glass captured the last light from the sky and poured it down. In her day, anyone arriving by train at New Street had to exit the station via the Pallasades, a shopping centre of epic grimness, low-ceilinged and lit like a prison, its insides full of Woolworths and SockShop and crappy health-food stores, the outside decaying brown concrete. That was all gone – obliterated – and now, as if born in the light of the explosion, there was this, Grand Central, clean and white and imposing, like a modern cathedral or one of those Southern US mega-churches. A cathedral of commerce.

'I can't believe you haven't seen it yet,' Maggie had said when she'd told her where she was meeting Lucy. 'It's ever so smart.'

'Yeah, Rin's been boasting about it.' She'd stopped. Every couple of minutes she'd focus on something else, forget, then it body-slammed her again: Corinna was dead.

She was ten minutes early but when the escalator delivered her to the café at the top of the new John Lewis, Lucy was already waiting. She had on the same scarf she'd worn at the Christmas market, and her hair was down over the shoulders of a short black coat. Cheap black trousers, slightly scuffed high heels – career-dressing on a tiny budget. She worked as a PA for a firm of solicitors, she'd said on the phone. 'Family law – divorces, custody disputes.'

At close range, she looked barely older than Lennie. Under a ton of mascara, her eyes were round as a pre-schooler's. Though it had looked near-perfect in the Facebook photo, up close and unfiltered her skin was teenage: a smattering of acne dints below the cheekbones, an active spot half hidden by a lid of concealer.

'Lucy? I'm Robin.'

There was a hiatus, a moment in which the choreography felt off, a physical move missing. Of course: no badge, the extraction from the pocket, the thumb-flip that established her authority. Instead she took out the little Muji case Maggie had given her at the same time as a pay-as-you-go mobile. *Robin Lyons, Private Investigator, MH Investigation Services.* She watched the girl scrutinize the card.

'Shall we?' she said 'Tea? Why don't you find a table and I'll bring it over?'

Robin could see immediately why Rin had liked the café. Industrial spotlights and tiles, painted farmhouse tables and outsized lampshades – it was her taste all over. But that was true of John Lewis generally: not flashy or designer, but good quality, solid. It sold the illusion of a trustworthy, comfortable world. The idea made her want to put her boot under a table, send its cake-stands and shortbread flying. Lies.

Lucy had chosen a table by the window. She'd taken off her coat and was scrolling through her phone, which she dropped into her bag as Robin approached.

'Thanks again for meeting me.' She unloaded the tray and sat down.

'No problem – I wanted to. We're really worried – Harry and me,' she clarified. 'We were texting and calling but we kept getting voicemail. Then Valerie rang.' In the light, the wisps of hair at her temples showed hints of ginger, and her skin was pale, its underlying tone blue. Some Celtic heritage, probably – Scots or Irish. Her hands were graceful, the fingers long and elegant despite a clutter of silver rings, eight or ten across the two hands. 'We can't believe the police won't do anything. She wouldn't just disappear.'

'Okay. Before we start, I just want to say that as private investigators, not police, we – that's Maggie, my colleague, and I – we're not interested in getting anyone into trouble. We work for Valerie, and our job is just to find Becca.'

'You think she's all right?'

'Do you not?'

Lucy looked down. 'I don't know.'

'We've talked to Valerie, of course, but what someone tells their best friend is different from what they might tell their mum, right? I'm speaking for myself here, obviously.' She'd intended the line to be mildly funny, to put Lucy at her ease, but it had come out sounding weird, confessional. She cleared her throat.

'Basically, is there anything going on that she might have kept secret from her mum? Maybe something illegal – we know she used recreational drugs – or just something she didn't want her to know. We can be discreet about where we get information; neither Valerie nor Becca need to know you told us anything if you don't want that. For whatever reason. Okay?'

Lucy nodded.

'So, is there anything new in her life, or unusual? Even if you don't think it's relevant. Was anything worrying her? Has she been in any trouble?'

'No.'

'Does she owe anyone money?'

'No. I don't think so.'

Robin stirred her tea as if they had all the time in the world. 'What about men? Becca's lovely-looking, and her mum said she gets a fair bit of attention – was anyone bothering her?'

Lucy shook her head and her long silver earrings swayed, catching the light.

'How about Nick, her ex?'

'Nick?' Surprise. 'They broke up months ago and they didn't go out that long in the first place. He's with someone else now, from his work – we saw them shopping in the Bull Ring before Christmas.'

'How did Becca feel about that? Him having found someone else.'

'Fine. Not bothered. She was never *that* into him, she was the one who dumped him, and . . .' She stopped.

Robin waited, leaving the space for her to fill, but Lucy took a sip of her tea and looked out of the window. Through a fine mesh – to block sun on the plate glass, Robin guessed; there was optimism for you – their view was two multi-storey car parks and a Fifties flat-roofed office building. Beyond those, the grungy, slab-sided Holiday Inn was dwarfed by an incongruous tower of shining silver-blue glass. In the murk at street level, the lights were beginning to come on, the February afternoon already dimming towards evening.

'What about her new job, at The Spot?'

Lucy looked back. 'It's not that new, she's been doing it a while now. September – we went there for Ryan's birthday, another mate of ours. She'd been talking about going on holiday next summer – somewhere proper, you know – and she needed money. She said it looked fun to work there so she went in a couple of days later to ask. Have you been?'

83

'Not yet.'

'It's not just a bar. They do food and there's a club bit upstairs – DJs. The drinks are expensive, which is why it wasn't our regular.'

'*Was* it fun working there?'

'She said so, yeah, she liked the people. It doesn't shut 'til two so she was knackered if she had to do the close but it didn't seem to bother her, really. She just slept in at the weekend.'

'You never got the impression there was anything dodgy going on there?'

'No. Why?'

'Her mum doesn't sound keen on it.'

A small shrug. 'She thinks she'd be better off doing a college course, doesn't she? But Becca's not into it.'

'If it meant earning more in her day job, though? She could save for a holiday without having to work nights.'

Another shrug. 'Maybe. I mean, obviously she'd like to get paid more but it probably wouldn't be enough, the difference. And it would take too long. And it's still just working in an accounts office, isn't it?'

'She doesn't like it?'

'No, it's not . . . She *does*, and the Hanley family – especially Roger, her boss, she likes him a lot – but it's not setting the world on fire, is it? It's not what you dream of when you're a little girl: *When I grow up I want to process invoices.*'

'You think she had something else in mind?'

'Don't we all?' Lucy looked at her full-beam.

She knew, Robin realized suddenly. She'd told her her name on the phone – Lucy had Googled her and found the stories. Of course she had: what young person *wouldn't* Google a total stranger claiming to be a private investigator?

'I guess so,' she said. 'But she hadn't talked about it? Hadn't been making plans to go travelling sooner rather than later?' She remembered Becca's passport, still in the drawer.

'No. I'd have told you. And Val, when she rang me. She's doing her nut, isn't she? I wouldn't not say.'

'How's Becca's mood been lately? Has she been down at all? Depressed?'

'No. If anything, the opposite.'

'Really? Any reason?'

'I don't think so.' She looked to the window again, avoiding eye contact. Then, making a decision, she gave a short out-breath. 'I don't think it's relevant – it's *not* – but if this all goes . . . If something's happened to her, I don't want to be the one who didn't say something that might have led – only indirectly, it won't have anything to do with it at all, *at all*, but it's information and—'

'No one has to know it came from you, Lucy.'

'Look, why I'm freaking out – I know she wouldn't have just gone off somewhere because she had a reason to stay. A new reason.'

Robin felt it, the ratchet in her stomach that told her, *progress*.

'They think I don't know. And they're only not telling me because of some stupid idea about it affecting our friendship or me feeling left out or something,' she said. 'Which is ridiculous because I've got Cal – that's my boyfriend. Becca and Harry have started seeing each other. Well, not *seeing* – they've always *seen* each other. You know.'

'They've got together – they're sleeping together?'

'Yeah. I mean, I imagine. They're not telling me but they don't exactly have to. The way they are around each other – like, we've known each other since we were eleven, we're going to suddenly get *shy*?'

'When did it start?'

85

'Two or three months ago – December, the run-up to Christmas?'

'What changed? Why suddenly, after all these years?'

Lucy shook her head. 'I don't know.'

'What's Southside? Hoo, you *have* been away. It's what they're calling it these days – China Town, the Gay Village, the theatres, that whole patch. Rebranding, isn't it? Makes people see things differently.' Maggie pulled hair out of her mouth. Upstairs, without a tree in sight, Robin hadn't been aware of it but as she came down the long flight of steps to where Maggie had been waiting on the street, a bitter little wind had rushed to meet her, throwing her scarf in her face, whipping away body heat. She shoved her hands in her pockets.

A minute's walk from Grand Central, they were back in the old city centre, brutal concrete and grimy glass, the Holiday Inn like a punch in the eye, Smallbrook Queensway and the long curved slug of the Ringway Centre, a line of low shops under four floors of grim concrete boxes that looked like somewhere you might have been sent in pre-Glasnost Russia if you'd made political enemies.

On the pedestrian island, sandwiched between four lanes of thundering traffic, Robin turned her face to the sky. *Beam me up, Scotty, or god, or whoever. Just get me the fuck out of here.* 'All right?' Maggie mouthed over the roar. She nodded.

Once they were under the bridge, things improved marginally. There was a boarded-up nightclub, a fried-chicken place, a bookies, but the buildings were older and lower-rise, the concrete less dominant. After a block, a pedestrian zone had a handful of actual trees, red Chinese lanterns in their branches, and the Hippodrome where she and Luke had been brought every Christmas by Granny Lyons for the panto. Christopher Biggins wearing tights, pelting the audience with Fox's Glacier Fruits – good times.

The roar of traffic subsided. 'What did Lucy have to say?' Maggie asked, tucking her scarf back under her lapels. Her boots tapped briskly on the paving; Robin could hear them now.

'Well, she's sure something's wrong. Same as Valerie – she wouldn't just disappear, etc., etc. The main reason being, she'd recently got together with Harry.'

'Interesting. She hadn't told Valerie that.'

'They hadn't even told *her*. She guessed.'

'Did she know why?'

'They didn't want to mess up their dynamic, the three of them, she said.'

'You buy that?'

'Not entirely.' Robin stepped out of the path of a cyclist. 'Anything at Hanley's?'

'Don't think so. He comes across as a decent bloke, Roger Hanley. I liked him.'

'Lucy said Becca did, too.'

'He's old school, courteous. But not in that creepy, patronizing way, you know? Most of his staff have worked there for years, which tells you something – Becca's boss in accounts has been there twenty-two. She's really worried, they all are.'

'Nothing funny going on financially?' They'd discussed the possibility that Becca might have stolen from work, either money or stock, disappeared when she had enough or because she was afraid of being caught. If she'd needed money, stealing from Hanley's might have seemed like an answer.

'No. He got offended when I asked, went all knightly, like I was impugning her honour; talked about exemplary conduct, loyalty, "total honesty and trust".'

'Anything going on between them? An affair – a crush?'

87

'Didn't strike me – he seemed more dad-like. His own kids are the same age, not that that means anything. I'll keep an open mind but so far, he, Hanley's as a whole – not top of my list. So let's see about this place.'

The Spot was towards the end of the pedestrianized stretch, next door to a Chinese restaurant in a new build but itself a Victorian pub, high-ceilinged on the ground floor, the upstairs windows blacked out now to shield club-goers from passers-by, or vice versa. At street level, light poured out along with an early-evening buzz of voices, faint music, chinking glass. Robin entertained a momentary fantasy of installing herself at the bar, downing drink after drink until her brain short-circuited.

'Right, love, let's get this done so I can get you home.'

The website was all glinting bottles and spot-lit calla lilies, pairs of martini glasses sprouting sprigs of thyme alongside self-important talk about 'mixology' and 'small plates', but for once, photographic justice had been served. It was super-snazzy, the kind of place Adrian had used to take her, old and new combined, original iron columns, green tiles and age-spotted mirrors juxtaposed with a bar done in brushed steel. The two men behind it were twenty-something, cheek-bones and tans, both in navy shirts, sleeves rolled, collars undone.

They'd only been open a few minutes but the green-leather booths along the walls were all taken and ten or fifteen people lined the bar. Maggie perused a cloth-bound menu while they waited. 'Smart in here,' she said. 'Food smells good, too. *Trio of sliders*,' she tapped the list with a forefinger, 'I could murder those.' She looked away, mortified by her word choice.

'Ladies, what can I get you? Any questions?'

Australian. Robin grudgingly forgave him the tan.

'Not about the menu,' Maggie said. 'But I wonder if we could ask you about Becca Woodson.'

The easy smile faded. 'Becca? Are you police?'

'Investigators, working for her mother.' She put a card on the bar.

He breathed out. 'Jeez. For a moment I thought you were going to say she'd been found.'

'Found?'

'You know . . .' His eyes slid away.

Maggie glanced at Robin. 'Dead?'

'Yeah.'

'Is there a reason you'd think that?' Robin asked.

He looked at her as if she was thick. 'Because she's missing?'

'People go missing for all sorts of reasons. Not all of them sinister.'

'Well, yeah.' As if he were totally *au fait* with these things.

'How well did you know Becca?' Maggie asked. 'She worked three nights a week?'

'Normally. We're both here Fridays and Saturdays – I can't get a break on the roster. And we pulled a lot of extra shifts round Christmas and New Year's, it was all hands on deck. Bloody busy, no time to talk, but we used to sit down afterwards, have a few jars.'

'Was she on the bar?'

'Food, mostly. Or running drinks.'

'Did you ever get the sense anything was going on with her? Worrying her?'

'Me? No, but other people know her better – the girls here are thick as thieves. Look,' he said, 'David's in, the manager. I'll get him for you.'

He disappeared through a door at the end of the bar and about thirty seconds later returned with a man about Robin's own age, a little less tanned, slightly less Gillette-commercial, but still ready for his close-up. Black round-necked sweater, black-rimmed glasses, dark jeans – he looked cosmopolitan in a way no one who worked five minutes from the Ringway Centre had a right to. He came out from behind the bar and shook their hands.

'Justin said you're asking about Becca.'

He looked at Maggie's card then glanced at the doors as a group of five women came in, co-workers judging by the office clothes and the age range. 'Let's talk in the back room. Quieter at this time of day.'

They followed him through a wide arch into another room of similar size. More wrought-iron columns and antique glass but instead of a bar, there were tables for eating. The tiles were Moroccan, the booths along one wall full of patterned cushions. The vibe was darker, more intimate, candles in coloured glasses flickering on every table.

He ushered them to one in the far corner. At a serving station nearby, a woman in a white butcher's apron was steaming cutlery in a wine bucket, wiping it for watermarks and sorting it into a tray. 'Could you do that in the kitchen, Amanda? While we're open?'

'Sorry, David. Can I get you anything?'

He looked at them, eyebrows up.

'Not for us. Thanks.'

He waited until she'd lugged the bucket through the kitchen doors. 'So what's happening? Is there any news?'

'You talked to her mother on Friday, was it?' said Maggie.

'Yeah. Early – about seven? I've been feeling bad about it – I was probably a bit short with her. We were packed, and I was pissed off with Becca for not showing up. We had a party in that night – we've got a private room for events – and she was supposed to be doing it. I thought she'd just left us in the lurch.'

'Was that something she did often?'

'No. She'd never done it before. I try to run a tight ship so I don't have many flaky people – they don't last long, anyway – but Becca was reliable, she'd never pulled a no-show. And she was good – if someone else was off sick, she'd quite often work an extra shift for me at short notice. I thought if she was ill or whatever, she could at least have called so I could get cover.'

'Have you heard from her since you spoke to Valerie – her mother?'

'No. Nor's Arran, the deputy manager – he does the rota. He called a few times to see if she wanted to work this week – everyone gets one pass, shit happens, right? – but *nada*, just voicemail, and then her mailbox was full, he said. And then the police came.'

'So the police did come here?' said Robin.

'Yes. They wanted to know if she'd had any trouble with the punters. Pretty young woman, working in a club . . .' His hands were on the table and he moved them apart a little as if to say, yes, it was a reasonable question but what could you do?

'What did you tell them?'

'That she hadn't. Or nothing serious. There's always a bit of argy-bargy later on but . . .'

'Argy-bargy?'

'No, that sounds wrong. Just . . . flirting. Lairy lads, get a few drinks in them and suddenly they're Ryan Gosling, you know. *Come on, love, let me buy you a drink, your boyfriend won't mind. What, you haven't got a boyfriend?* Blah, blah, blah.'

'*Did* she have a boyfriend?'

The hands again. 'I'm not in the core gossip circle – being the manager has some advantages.' Playing for laughs; Robin kept

91

her face stony and saw it register. 'I don't know. There was a guy who came to meet her at the end of the night sometimes,' he said, 'but she introduced him to me as an old friend.'

On her phone, Robin scrolled to the picture she'd taken of the photo on Becca's mirror. 'This him?'

He took the phone and pinched out to enlarge Harry's face. 'Yeah.'

'So there wasn't anyone else – punter or otherwise – who'd taken a special interest? Sought her out, asked about her?' said Maggie.

He shook his head. 'The police asked the same, and I told them what I'm telling you. We're worried about her – she's got friends here. If we knew anything, or heard anything, we'd have been in touch.'

'Justin – is that his name? – he said the female staff are "thick as thieves".'

'They get on, yeah.'

'Could we talk to them – anyone who's here at the moment?'

He seemed to hesitate. 'Amanda's on but she's new, only started ten days ago, so she didn't really get a chance to know Becca. It's Tuesday so skeleton staff – we get an early rush, people having a quick one after work, a few people in the last hour or so, but it's not like later in the week. Becca worked weekends and Wednesday so her core posse aren't here. I can have a word with them again, in case anyone's remembered anything?'

'Thanks, we'd appreciate that.' Maggie stood up. 'This is a nice-looking place, by the way. We'll have to come again some time. For pleasure.'

'Yes, do.'

'Is it yours? Do you own it?'

He shook his head. 'Just manage it.'

'Who does?'

'It's a syndicate of investors – friends. They wanted to do something in Southside, regenerating Birmingham, you know?'

He walked them to the front door; either well brought up, Robin thought, or escorting them off the premises. In the box of space between the inner and outer doors, he shook hands again. 'As I said, we like Becca here. Will you keep me posted?'

Chapter Eight

'How was school?'

Lennie pulled her feet up and rested her chin on her knees, eyes fixed on the TV, where a dreaming Homer Simpson frolicked after a trio of rabbits in the Land of Chocolate. Ecstatic, he took a bite out of a lamppost and a chocolate dog before he was stopped mid-mouthful by a nasal white rabbit with a Mr Burns overbite.

Lennie shrugged. 'Okay.'

The Land of Chocolate morphed into a video game and the white rabbit bounced ahead up pink marshmallow platforms, taunting.

'What are the other kids like? Anyone you think you might get on with?'

Her eyes stayed fixed on the television. 'Maybe. I don't know.'

'What about the lessons – what did you have today?'

'Geography and history this morning, maths and physics this afternoon.'

'How were the teachers? Did you like any of them?'

Another shrug. 'I was just kind of getting through it.'

'I wish you'd stayed at home with Gran.'

'That would have made it worse. Doing nothing, I mean.'

'I know. Same here.' She reached out and put her arm round her daughter. After a moment, Lennie relaxed and shifted closer.

Homer's video game was quickly turning dystopic. The rabbit announced he'd slept with Marge and there was a crash on the other side of the wall as Christine dropped a pan. The lid did a slow drum-roll. 'B . . . Bother.'

'You all right, Chrissie, love?' came Dennis's voice from the tiny conservatory.

'Fine.'

Lennie looked at her. 'Not fine,' she mouthed.

Dennis's feet on the kitchen tiles. 'Ah, at least it's just water, sweetheart. Here, give me that, I'll do it.'

'Have you heard anything?' Len asked.

'Not about Uncle Josh. I spoke to Will and he said Peter's . . .' She hesitated. The urge to tell her that everything was fine, hunky-dory, not a cloud in the sky but she tried always to be honest with Lennie. 'He's stable. His injuries are very serious, as we knew, but he's had surgery and he's doing okay. Now we just have to wait.'

'Could he die, too?' Direct eye contact, nowhere to hide.

'With a big injury, there's always a chance something'll happen. An infection or . . . But he's being really well looked after. He'll have nurses with him all the time in Intensive Care.'

'Can we visit him?'

'I don't know. I'll ring Will again in the morning.' She gave Lennie a squeeze. 'What are you doing watching TV, by the way? You still have to do your homework.'

'I've done it.'

'Already?'

'There was hardly any – it only took twenty minutes. I did it when I got back.'

'Can I see?'

'Mum, I'm thirteen!'

'I know, I know. I'm not checking on you, I'm just curious. New school – I want to see what they give you.'

'It was maths.' With a display of weary tolerance, Lennie unfolded herself from the sofa and went to get her backpack. Robin felt a stab of guilt – yet another. Twenty minutes' homework – what the hell? It was at least two hours a night at Ravenscourt Park Girls and for her at the grammar school, too, back in the day. She'd spent hours hunched at the little desk upstairs, radio blasting in her ear, and Lennie had as well, back in London. That had been one of Robin's favourite things, coming home to find Len and Naomi, the sixth former who'd 'babysat' her after school, sitting at the kitchen table with their mugs of tea, earbuds in, so focused they hardly looked up when she came through the door. Naomi had been gutted when she'd told her they were moving – getting paid to do her homework, time away from her own place, tea and biscuits on tap: dream gig for a teenager.

Lennie handed her a file open to a page and a half of neatly drawn triangles. 'See? Geometry. I did all this last year – that's why it didn't take that long.'

'All right, clever clogs.'

Lennie stuffed the file back in her bag and sat down again. Homer woke on his sofa to discover it was all a dream and shook his fist at the unfairness of the world, eliciting a flicker of a smile.

'You talked to Adrian this morning?'

'Yeah.' A pause, eyes front. 'It felt too weird, him not knowing. He really liked Auntie Rin and I didn't know if you were going to call him.' She raised her hands then dropped them back in her lap. 'And I just wanted to talk to him.'

'It's fine. You don't have to feel bad – you can ring him whenever you want.'

96

'So can you.' A darting look. 'He said to say. No pressure – only if you want. He said to tell you that.'

Robin nodded. She thought of the last time she'd seen Corinna, the morning after the booze-fest. In the end, it had been a beer, hair of the dog, that got them over the hump, and one had led to another and then to talk of bad mothering – specifically, her own failure to provide Len with a father. Most of the time, she didn't worry about it more than fifty times a day – lots of kids were in the same boat and with worse, even less present mothers – but that afternoon, with everything screwed up and dark and magnified by alcoholic remorse, she'd wondered what kind of monster she was.

'Adrian loves her, Rin. He really does.' She hesitated. 'He said he'd ask if she'd let him adopt her formally if we—'

Rin's eyes went wide. 'Did he?'

'And she would – she'd say yes. She'd love him to be her dad.'

She remembered him standing at the railings on the Millennium Bridge, the dome of St Paul's lit up behind him as he stared down into the Thames, buffeted by the wind, hair blown back like a ship's figurehead. Weathering the storm – the storm of her. It had been a long time before he could look at her again, maybe two minutes. Sounded like nothing unless you'd stood through it, the wind making an X-ray of your bones as you watched the pain you'd inflicted on someone you cared about.

'But *you* don't love him.'

Robin let her gaze travel round the room. It settled on a pair of little boys enacting a violent scene with Lego figures at the corner table. 'Well,' she shrugged, 'you know me.'

'What does that mean?'

'You know what it means. It means my head's wrecked. It means I'm unfit for all that.'

'Is it him you're waiting for?'

97

'What?' She'd looked at Corinna, startled.

'Your phone. You keep checking it. Are you waiting for something from Adrian?'

'Oh. No. Gid, my DS. Former DS,' she corrected herself. 'I texted him earlier to see if there was anything new on Hinton so—'

'Right.' Bone-dry.

'What?'

'Nothing. Go on, drink your beer.'

'Delicious, Chrissie. Thank you.' Dennis reached for the spoon and gave himself another helping of cottage pie.

'Well, you must have been starving, love. It's nearly eight o'clock.'

'Oh, I was all right. No need to worry about me.'

'We have our dinner at seven. Normally.' Her mother loaded a neat little mouthful onto her fork, and glanced at Robin. 'Everyone's hungry after work and school, aren't they?'

'Sorry. We probably won't finish this late every day.'

'What were you doing? Surely these people aren't working after dark? Start early, leave early – you can't do building work after the light starts to go.'

'It's not just blue-collar workers who cheat the system. And Maggie does all sorts of different stuff, anyway. Doesn't she?'

Her mother looked at her, eyes sharp. In the car on the way back, Robin had asked Maggie if Christine knew about the other side of her work.

'Yeah, she's one of my best friends. And if I'm off somewhere – like last year, up in the Lake District after my bigamist – I like someone other than Nuttall to know where I am. Not having an other half. If I'm going to get kidnapped by some nutter, I'd like someone to notice within a twenty-four-hour period, you know?'

'Makes sense. I just can't believe she didn't tell me.'

'I asked her not to.'

'But in the last couple of weeks, when we were going to be working together?'

'Like I said yesterday, need-to-know.'

Robin had looked away. In the grand scheme, it was nothing, but it still pissed her off that Christine had known something about her job that she hadn't. Her work was *hers*, it was nothing to do with her mother. Yet another incursion, another erosion. And beyond that, what did it say that she'd kept her promise to Maggie rather than tell her own daughter something that might affect her? What was that, for Christ's sake?

'We're looking at a graphic designer,' she said now. 'We were waiting for him to leave the office where he's moonlighting so we could record his hours.'

'Today, of all days?' Christine's eyes widened. 'With everything that's—'

'Well, no harm done,' said Dennis quickly, putting his hand over hers. 'You're here now, aren't you, Robin? Teething troubles – it'll all settle down.'

She felt a surge of frustration. Teething troubles – as if this were the start of something long-term. She didn't *want* it to settle down; she didn't want to have to eat *when* her mother told her to, *what* she told her to. The powerlessness – the complete, stifling powerlessness. But then, said a nasty little voice, beggars couldn't be choosers, could they? And she who paid the piper – or made the cottage pie – called the tune. 'I was back at seven fifteen – it was hardly late.' She picked up her wine and took a gulp.

'I'm sure it seemed late to Elena. Do you usually drink on a Tuesday evening?'

'Yep.' She took another. 'Specially if my best mate's been murdered.'

It was a hand grenade lobbed onto the table – the word exploded in their faces, burnt the oxygen in the room, left their ears ringing. *Murdered, murdered.*

Christine put down her knife and fork and bent her head. It wasn't the sob but the genuine effort she made to stifle it that filled Robin with remorse. She was a monster – a real, vile monster. 'I'm sorry, Mum. I shouldn't have said that. I'm really sorry.'

Dennis gave her a terse nod – *Right. Now shut up* – and squeezed her mother's hand. 'It's okay, love. It's okay.' As if he was murmuring to a child. Lennie looked down, avoiding eye contact with any of them.

It was a minute or two before her mother got it together again, taking a tissue from the sleeve of her cardigan and blotting her eyes. She gave her head a little shake. 'Tell her, Dennis. You have to.'

He looked startled, shot a look at Lennie. 'Now?'

'Tell me what?' said Robin.

Under Christine's tasselled yellow lampshade, Patel looked as if the past thirty-six hours were beginning to catch up with him. Thomas, on the other hand, could have come straight from hair and make-up. Via wardrobe, actually: under the sharp coat, she had on a caramel round-necked sweater and another pair of immaculate trousers. It was nine o'clock at night, day two of a murder investigation – how the hell was she doing it?

Dennis hovered in the kitchen doorway then came forward to shake hands. 'Good to meet you. Well, not the circumstances. You know what I mean.'

Nervous. As far as Robin knew, his own dealings with the police were limited to filing a report twenty-five years ago when someone nicked his car radio during a children's birthday party at Solihull ice rink. Having a cop for a daughter, what he knew from her years in the job, meant nothing when it came to having detectives in his home, notwithstanding the fact that one of them looked like a sixteen-year-old tech nerd.

'Come through,' she said, taking control, but DS Thomas stayed put.

'Mr Lyons, it was just you who saw Corinna with the injury, is that right?'

'Yes.'

'Then it's you we need to talk to, okay?'

'Yes, of course.' A look of bemusement – *well, duh*, as Lennie would say – but then he got what she was driving at. 'Oh. Right.'

In they went and Patel closed the sitting-room door after them, looking Robin in the eye as if it was the sodding *Godfather*. The dramatic effect was undercut by the door being glass and because, in the kitchen, they could hear every word. Silently, without acknowledging what they were doing, she and Lennie took stools at the breakfast bar along the wall. Christine hesitated for a moment then sat, too.

'So, Mr Lyons.' DS Thomas's voice was totally clear; the wall might as well be cardboard. She and Patel were on the sofa again, inches away.

'Please, call me Dennis.'

'Dennis, Robin told us the rough outline, obviously, but we'd like to hear it from you. Tell us what you remember. Take your time.'

'Well, there isn't much more than what she said on the phone. I saw Corinna at the garage a couple of weeks ago. The Shell on Stratford Road, by Showell Green. I was on my way home – it must have been just after six, maybe quarter past. I was filling the car up. I might also have bought a Crunchie. Well, it was

101

two, actually. I stop in there quite often in the evenings, to be honest – I've got a bit of a sweet tooth.'

Christine huffed: on the way home to his dinner. Robin glared: *ssssh.*

'A couple of weeks ago – could you be more specific?'

Ask his wife when he didn't do a good enough job on his lamb chops.

'Um. I'll try. Well . . . Oh – the Crunchies. The reason I had two – I try to limit myself, normally – I'd just filed the VAT return for the quarter. A little reward, you know? I'll check the filing date, I can access the network remotely from here.'

'Thanks,' said Patel.

'Where do you work, Dennis?' Thomas.

'Meacham's, the hauliers. I'm an accountant. In-house, nothing too grand, obviously – glorified book-keeper, really.'

'Right. So, at the garage?'

'Yes. When I got there, Corinna was there, too. She was parked on the other side of the pumps; I only saw her car when I got out.'

'How were you sure it was hers?' asked Patel.

'I wasn't at first. She's got – had – an Audi like Robin's. Navy blue, really smart. It made me think of them both and I looked inside, just in case, and she was at the counter, paying. I was pleased – I always liked seeing her. You get very fond of your kids' friends when you've known them so long, all those birthday parties and sleepovers, all the kerfuffle over revision and exam results and teenage parties. Then suddenly, bang, they're gone – not just your own child but all her friends, too.'

The nerves were making him witter. *Come on, Dad, no need to be intimidated. Just tell them what you told me.*

'Corinna was special to us, though, because of what happened later. When Robin had Lennie, I mean, I – you know about that?

Chrissie and I were so grateful to her. We tried to get Robin to come back here so we could help but she wouldn't do it. She's . . . stubborn. Finds it very hard to accept help. At least from us. For some reason, she seems to feel she has to do everything on her own.'

'She's here now,' said DS Thomas, neutral.

'Never thought I'd see the day. When university started, she high-tailed it out of here like the place was on fire.' A pause. 'I'm sorry, that was a bad choice of . . .'

'When was the last time you'd seen Corinna before that evening?' asked Patel.

'Oh, months ago. Even though she lives just up the road. Robin didn't stay with her over Christmas this year so we didn't see her then. I don't think Chrissie even saw her this time with the cake. She was out; Peter was there with the babysitter.'

'The cake?'

'Chocolate cake. Corinna always loved the ones Chrissie used to make for Robin's birthday so as a little thank you for what she did back then, when Lennie was new, Chrissie used to make her one and drop it round there for *her* birthday every year. October time – Chris can tell you the date.'

Robin stared at her. What? How did she not know about that? Christine gave a little shrug. *So? Do I have to tell you everything?*

'Okay, right. So you saw Corinna inside, paying?' said Thomas.

'Yes. She didn't see me, I don't think, but when she came out, I called to her. It was odd. For a second she seemed really pleased to see me, she smiled and started to come towards me but then she stopped. She gave me a little wave, shouted "Hiya Dennis, sorry, got to go, mad rush," something like that, then backed away. It wasn't like her – she was a lovely girl, always had time for me before.'

'Backed away? In the car.' Patel again. Robin imagined him, pen poised earnestly over his notebook.

'No, walking. She was moving strangely – sort of sideways. Head down. I wondered for a moment if she'd done herself an injury, twisted her ankle or something. Afterwards, it made sense.'

'So how did you end up seeing it?'

'She had to drive past me to get out – there was a van at the pump behind, blocking her in. I saw it when she went by.'

'Could it have been the light – a shadow?'

'No. The place was lit up bright as you like – you know garages. It was a few days old, a lot of grey and purple in it – but it was definitely a black eye, a big one. No question.'

'Did she know you'd seen?'

'Yes, we made eye contact through the window. Just for a second, then she gave me a big, jolly wave, *All fine, nothing to see here*, and off she went.'

'What was your first thought when you saw it?'

'That it must have bloody hurt. Then I wondered how it happened, the accident.'

'Your immediate thought was she'd had an accident?'

'Yes.'

'You didn't think of Mr Legge?'

'No. I'd never had reason to think he'd raise a hand. Never. I've known him since he was a kid, sixteen or seventeen, and I never saw violence in him, even anger. He's a gentle man. When Corinna was down in London with Robin, he used to go down most weekends. He loved Lennie even when she was tiny – a lot of men that age wouldn't have known what to do with themselves.'

'Mr Lyons – Dennis. Obviously you knew about this yesterday – we spoke to Robin yesterday. Why are we only hearing about it now?'

'I didn't know whether I should say anything. I didn't want to pass on something that might look incriminating for Josh.'

'You wanted to protect Mr Legge,' said Patel.

'You're aware it might count as withholding evidence?' Thomas.

'Not *protect*. Just . . . not give people reason to think badly of him. Worse.'

'By "people" you mean the police?' Thomas again.

He hesitated. 'Yes. I suppose so. But others, too, if it got out.'

'Did Robin ask you to do that? Keep the information to yourself?'

'What? No. Absolutely not. She was the one who said we had to ring you.'

'We get the impression she doesn't believe Josh could have done it.'

'But you think he did?'

A moment of heavy silence. 'We follow the facts, Mr Lyons,' said Patel.

'Did you know Corinna in any capacity other than as a friend of your daughter?' Thomas asked.

'No. But as I said, you get to know your kids' friends very well. All that gang – Corinna and Josh, Samir later on.' He hesitated. 'Her core friends then.'

'Samir Jafferi?'

'Yes. He's done well in the police, hasn't he – we've seen him on the television quite a few times.'

'You've lost touch?'

'He and Robin had a big bust-up. We haven't seen him since.'

'What was that about, the bust-up?'

How is this relevant? Robin almost said out loud.

'Well, you'd have to ask her the finer points but they were supposed to go to London together, UCL, but Samir got cold feet at the last minute, stayed to do his degree here instead.

He was always close to his family so I wasn't totally surprised, but . . .'

'They were together, him and Robin. A couple.'

It wasn't a question; they'd spoken to him. Shit. She'd known they would, she'd told them to, but . . . *shit*.

'Romance of the century. No, I don't want to trivialize it. They were young, eighteen, nineteen, but they really loved each other. It was great – softened Robin up a bit, if I'm honest. They went backpacking together in their gap year, all round Europe, Southern Africa. Then he split up with her, just before university. She was heartbroken.'

Robin's face burned with humiliation. She could feel Lennie next to her vibrating with questions: *Why don't I know about this? Why have you never told me?* She kept her eyes down.

'Going back to what you said about Robin being here, Mr Lyons, living with you. If she wouldn't before, even with a new baby, why suddenly now?'

'She was under a lot of pressure,' he said. 'Financial, of course, without a salary. She isn't a saver so she didn't have anything to fall back on. Her rent in London must have been huge, not that she'd ever tell us. The job offer from Maggie was a life-line, and not just for the money.'

'Oh?'

'She's a funny one, my daughter. It's like she thinks she's not worth much unless she's constantly achieving – proving herself. Being fired by the Met's a disaster for her; she's at a very low ebb. She's always liked Maggie, she respects her – it was her who got Robin interested in the police years ago, when *she* was on the force. And the work itself – she's still investigating, isn't she, in a way?'

Robin pictured DS Thomas on the other side of the wall – sharp, put-together, employed – and closed her eyes with the shame.

'But also Corinna was here,' said Dennis. 'Mohammed couldn't go to the mountain this time, she had a husband and her son and a job, so the mountain had to come here. At crisis point, it's always been Corinna Robin wanted. Sometimes I think she was the only person she ever really trusted.'

Robin turned over, pushing the duvet off with her foot. Her mouth was dry again so she reached for the glass of lukewarm water on the floor. There was no middle way: she would either have to wake up parched – if she slept at all – or get up three times in the night to pee.

She lay back down, trying to find a cooler spot on the pillow. Overhead, Lennie was sleeping on her back – she could tell by the slight catch in her breathing. She focused on the gentle rhythm, tried to match it. In the gloom, the slats of the upper bunk were railway tracks, the lid of a box, the trapdoor over the *oubliette*. There was a line of old glow-star stickers along one of them, edges curling, luminosity years gone. She'd been looking at them for an hour and a half already; she'd come up as soon as she could after the police had left, needing a door between her and the world to try to think.

What she knew for certain: the black eye wasn't an accident. If it had been, Corinna wouldn't have hidden it. At the garage with Dennis, she'd have paraded it, made self-deprecating jokes: *Guess which bit of human plankton left the bathroom cabinet open?* But more than that, she'd have told Robin. Triumphs, humiliations – they'd shared everything. Corinna had seen her unwashed, lank-haired, wired up to the breast pump in a sports bra with the nipples cut out. Rin was protective of her dad, she didn't tell anyone about him, but she'd confided in *her* about the times he'd fallen down the stairs or puked at the dinner table; collapsed on the landing with his trousers round his knees. They shared the big stuff but also the small: a funny present for Josh's Christmas stocking; Gid's better jokes; Lennie and Peter's wobbly teeth, swimming badges, childish sayings – they'd gone back and forth every day. An accidental black eye would have been comedy gold.

So it was deliberate, she'd tried to hide it. But an accident was nothing to hide. Being mugged was nothing to hide. Getting lamped by a nutter who thought you'd looked at him funny was nothing to hide.

And if the black eye was connected to what had happened back then, if there'd been a warning like that, it would have been nothing to hide from *her*. With a dizzying shot of relief, Robin had realized earlier that if it *had* been connected, if someone had come after them, Rin and Josh would have told her straight away. Rin would have warned her – she'd have wanted to protect her. Thank god – thank god.

But then, what?

As any cop would tell you, victims of domestic violence frequently tried to hide it, for a multitude of reasons: the shame of having a violent partner in the first place; the shame of not leaving them. Everyone could talk the talk: easy to say that if your partner ever hit you, you'd be out the door before he could cradle his knuckles. Much harder to do it if you had no money and nowhere to go, children to house and feed and get to school on time. People covered for violent spouses to keep their own lives possible, to protect their kids, and because they loved them, at least to begin with. They covered bruises with make-up, lied to others, lied to themselves. They kept secrets.

Corinna was good at keeping secrets, Robin knew that. Had she been keeping this one? Close as they were, Robin knew that of course Josh and Peter were even closer. If Josh *had* hit her, Corinna *might* have lied to her to protect him.

But she still didn't believe it. So, again, what?

When they'd finished with Dennis, the police had called her in. 'Just a couple of extra questions.' Patel indicated the armchair, which had still been warm from her dad's behind.

'Robin,' said Thomas, 'I want to ask you again: have you ever had reason to suspect Josh was violent towards Corinna?'

'No.'

'Did you ever see Corinna with a physical injury she struggled to explain? Or whose explanation seemed suspect to you – unlikely?'

'No.'

'Do you know of anything Corinna was involved in that might have led to her incurring an injury like the one Dennis claims to have seen?'

She'd made herself meet Thomas's eye. 'First of all, he wouldn't *claim*. He's totally straight, my dad, so if he said he saw it, he did. Second, do you think I'd know about my best friend being beaten and let it go on happening? Not mention it when she's found dead in her burning home? And what would *lead* to a black eye? Martial arts classes? S&M? Fight Club?'

'We're asking you.' Complete patience.

'Well, as far as I know, she wasn't in Fight Club.' Robin stopped, took a breath. In her situation, she really couldn't afford a temper. 'I'm sorry. I want to be able to help you, obviously. I want to find out who did this and . . .' She shook her head.

'We're conscious, of course, of the fact that Corinna died on the day you moved back to Birmingham after – how many years in London?'

'Sixteen.'

'Can you think of a way in which the two things might be connected?'

She made eye contact again, held it steadily. 'No. I've been over and over it. I've asked myself everything, even whether it's Hinton. He's still AWOL, isn't he?'

'I can't say.'

Can't or won't? Thomas's face was perfectly neutral, of course. Why was she a cop? She'd make a killing at poker.

'For the sake of argument, then,' said Robin, 'let's say he is. He could be here in Birmingham – nothing to stop him. And he has contacts here anyway, old gangland ties. But how would he know *I* was here? That wasn't in the papers. And why would he come at me when I was the one who let him go? None of it makes sense.'

'Were you ever threatened by anyone you did put away?'

'Not seriously enough for something like this.'

Patel turned to a fresh page in his notebook.

'Robin,' Thomas said, 'you were – are – obviously very fond of both of them, Corinna *and* Josh.'

'Yes.'

'Has the relationship between you and Mr Legge ever been anything other than platonic, a friendship between—'

Robin surged to her feet. 'No. *No.* Absolutely not. Never.'

'Just so we have it for our records, Ms Lyons,' said Patel, 'where were you two nights ago, February thirteenth, between the hours of twelve midnight and two a.m.?'

Chapter Nine

Maggie lived a couple of miles away in Yardley Wood, in the left side of a pair of red-brick semis built in the Eighties, when armies of identikit Barratt and Wimpey Homes had colonized the Midlands. This must have been one of the least successful designs, because Robin had never seen it anywhere else. Despite acres of on-street parking, a double garage had been built into the centre of each pair of houses, taking up a huge chunk of the ground floor and confining the front doors and small windows to narrow strips of frontage on the outer edges. It seemed a high price for staying dry while you brought the shopping in but Maggie seemed to like it, or at least she'd never been bothered to move; she'd been here since her divorce, as long as Robin could remember.

As she pulled up outside, the eight o'clock news was starting on the radio and Maggie was letting herself out, double-locking the door behind her. Full-length fitted black coat today, with a large collar that she'd turned up around her ears, ruff-style. Big hair, half a stick of eyeliner – Siouxsie Sioux gets a day job. 'Hiya,' she said, opening the door and swinging her bottom into the passenger seat. She looked at Robin's face. 'Jesus, are you okay to drive?'

'I'm fine. I got more sleep last night.'

'How much?'

'Six, seven hours.' Three, maximum. Maggie narrowed her eyes, assessing; Robin pretended not to notice. 'Where to?'

'Office first, briefly. We'll park across the street same as yesterday then walk down. I need some exercise. Let's take Alcester Road in, change of scene. Left at the top here.' She pulled her collar round her throat. 'Bloody Baltic this morning – are these heated seats?'

The traffic was heavy through Moseley Village but that was fine by Robin. She'd stay in the car all day, given a choice. When she'd pressed the fob on Dunnington Road, the answering flash of the lights – *Here I am, let's go* – had almost brought her to tears. A pocket of her old life not yet snatched away. Dropping into the driver's seat, she'd remembered Luke's glee when he said she'd have to sell the car, and she'd gripped the steering wheel as if he were trying to wrest it from her. At this point, she *would* physically fight for it, and not just her fuckwit brother.

The village part of Moseley was posh. The Luftwaffe had let it off lightly, and the shops and pubs were the original Victorians and Edwardians, no mouldering Sixties concrete to contemplate throwing yourself off here. Big trees, a few nice-looking cafés and bars – even the chain restaurants were the better end of the spectrum.

'Any news?' Maggie asked.

'Well, the police were over again last night. Asking for my alibi.'

Maggie's head snapped round. In Robin's sleep-deprived state, the movement looked jump-cut, stop-motion animation with a skip in the tape. 'Yeah, among other things.' She told the story: Dennis and the black eye, the repeated questions about Josh's temper.

'Did your dad work out when he saw her?'

'January twenty-seventh. No doubt they'll check the CCTV at the garage if it still exists, to be sure he isn't making it up to exculpate me somehow.'

'They don't seriously think you're involved?'

'Not directly, as far as I know – I hope they'd credit me with sufficient brains not to do it the day I got back – but they like the timing. If not me, then something or someone connected to me.'

'You can see why. Careful, cyclist on your inside.'

Robin looked and saw a man in shiny blue Lycra shorts inches from the side of the car. Where had he come from? 'They wanted to know if I was sleeping with Josh. The theory being that I moved back here to facilitate our affair, which led to a showdown between them. Josh kills Corinna in the heat of the moment, burns the house down to hide the evidence – Peter's just collateral damage, too bad – then skips town.'

'Again, you'd want to eliminate it.'

'Yes, but not *now*, not *still*.' The cyclist swerved around the wing mirror then accelerated away, narrowly avoiding a van jumping the lights at the crossroad. 'Christ.'

Needless to say, she'd been awake at one thirty; she'd watched the red numbers on the desk clock come up like a losing spin on the slot machines. Forty-eight hours, done, finished, and they wanted to know if she'd been shagging Rin's husband.

'Maggie, you know I wouldn't ask this in any other circumstances but would you talk to your guy for me – Nuttall? I need some details. I don't even know if she was alive when the fire started.'

She'd woken at six, sweating, heart hammering, with an image of Corinna on her driveway wearing the orange canvas coat, the printed fern pattern warping suddenly, then starting to flicker.

She'd been there, too, in the dream, but she'd just been standing and talking, going on and on and on, and by the time she'd realized what was happening, Rin was in flames to the waist, trying to keep her arms above it, screaming.

'I need to know what they're doing to find Josh. What have they got? All this other stuff – was he violent? Was he sleeping around? – what are they actually *doing*? They must have some idea which way his car went. Even that – if I knew . . .'

'No.'

Robin kept her eyes on the road. 'Something's happened to him, too, it's the only explanation. If I had some idea what they're doing, I'd be able to—'

'Stop.' Maggie's voice was loud; on edge as she was, Robin nearly stamped on the brake.

For several seconds neither of them spoke. Maggie took a deep breath. 'Don't think I don't get what you're saying, don't think I'm not sympathetic. I know you're going through hell. But I won't ask Nuttall. You know you've done nothing wrong, I know it, but how's it going to look if you go fishing down back channels?'

Robin said nothing.

'Apart from anything else, Alan's not even on the case. He only rang me because he knows it's my area. It'd just be another distraction, something else to put you in the picture unnecessarily.'

'I wouldn't *do* anything with the information. You know I've got to stay squeaky clean. Any hint that I'd tried to involve myself with an investigation, I'd be screwed.'

'Permanently.'

'Which is why you can be sure I only want it so I know they're on top of—'

'Just don't.' Real sharpness now.

'What?'

114

'Don't think that because they're not the Met, they're not up to it. Just because this is the *regions* doesn't mean they're not fucking good. Don't ever make that mistake.'

Robin felt the rebuke like a slap. 'I didn't.'

Silence for several hundred yards. Eventually Maggie let herself sit back against the seat. It was a minute before she spoke again.

'At some point – at *this* point – you have to at least consider the possibility Josh did it.'

'No.'

She put a hand up: *Wait*. 'Sometimes – as you know, however hard it is to admit in this case – the simplest answer is the right one.'

Other cities kept a polite separation between their commercial and civic districts and the heavy industry; not Birmingham. Just two minutes and a flight of steps from the new Bull Ring and the space-age silver Selfridges building, they were into the grungy opening reaches of Digbeth.

After a blistering row one Sunday morning when Robin was thirteen or fourteen, Christine had ordered Dennis to get her out of her sight. They'd taken the little local train to Moor Street but instead of dragging her round the silverware at the museum for the nth time, he'd brought her here, local history freak that he was, on a sort of off-the-cuff walking tour of past industrial glories. 'Emphasis on past,' she'd said to Corinna on the phone afterwards. 'Now it's more like, here's a car park, here's a chip shop, here's the coach station.'

'Ah, the coach station,' Rin said. 'Did you see *my* dad?' and Robin had kicked herself. About six months earlier, the police had brought Mr Pascoe home when, off his face, he'd lurched behind a reversing National Express and got himself a concussion and a broken collarbone. She'd forgotten.

115

And the ennui was fake anyway. If she was honest, a day that had started off crappy – she'd cried, then been furious with herself for showing her mother any weakness – had turned into one she remembered as great now. Dennis had had a map showing where every German bomb had fallen in central Birmingham and they'd walked the streets matching the dots – red for incendiaries – to the buildings that filled the spaces left by Victorian factories and the pubs for their workforces. 'Just *imagine* what it must have been like before,' he'd said as if he were conjuring palaces. 'The stuff that was *made* here.' At six, he'd braved Christine's wrath and rung to say they wouldn't be home for supper. They'd had sausages and mash at a pub instead; she'd loved it.

Robin had expected some lingering frost from Maggie – a minor spat could lead to days of coldness from Christine – but as soon as they'd reached the office, it was as if nothing had happened. She was walking briskly now, getting her exercise, filling her lungs with exhaust fumes. The secondary gift of the German bombers, Dennis had told her that day: the Inner Ring Road, a strangling noose of dual and triple carriageways round the centre of town. They'd done the demolition work.

'What is it, the Custard Factory?' she asked, over the roar of three lanes of traffic.

'Exactly what it sounds like,' said Maggie. 'The old Bird's Custard plant. It was derelict for years then this developer bought it and gradually turned it into a kind of hub of hipster enterprise, all indie shops and start-ups, a little brewery, you know. Tattoo quotient: high.'

A little further on, a cluster of Victorian survivors loured at the day, red-brick seamed with a century and more of grime. The sky over them was crystalline, so blue it actually hurt her eyes to look at. Innocence and experience. When they rounded a college on the corner of Floodgate Street, a hundred-foot brick chimney painted with the image of a mustachioed man in a bowler hat hove into view. A cream building nearby wore a painted yellow tie three storeys high. *Here be hipsters.* 'Voilà,' said Maggie.

They turned off down a narrow street between spruced-up Victorian factory buildings painted raspberry and cobalt, emerald green. Strings of light bulbs criss-crossed overhead. There were shops at ground level, windows full of mannequins in edgy fashion, another that appeared to sell skate gear. For a moment, Robin felt old. Sometimes, between Lennie and the job, she felt like she'd missed her youth, fast-forwarded to a weird sort of pre-middle-age.

The street broadened into a courtyard where two life-sized model flamingos paddled in a big pink-painted pool. Further on, a Green Man that had to be forty feet tall loomed from a corner, wild-headed, sculpted from stone parts modelled in muscle groups. It was powerful – scary and strangely sexual at the same time. Plants curled from a lead box at his groin.

Maggie stopped outside the last building before the old brick viaduct at the end. 'This should be it.' She pressed the intercom and almost immediately a voice crackled, 'Hello?'

'Harry Norris?'

'Yes, hi. I'll come down.'

Thirty seconds later, they heard footsteps inside. When the door opened, Robin's first thought was that the man in the photo on Becca's mirror had done a Benjamin Button. The super-chill guy had gone; this one looked ten years younger and a lot less expansive. He was wearing black jeans and boots but just a blue chambray shirt on top despite the temperature. His eyes were widely spaced which, combined with ears that protruded slightly, made him look like Will Smith in the *Fresh Prince* era: good-looking, a bit goofy. No smiles, though – he looked drained. He shook their hands and put their cards carefully in his top pocket.

'Thanks for meeting us,' Maggie said.

'Thanks for coming. Lucy told me Valerie had hired you, she gave me your number, but then you rang me. I'm so worried, I . . .'

A door opened at the end of the hall and a man came out lugging a box of printer paper. Robin held the street door open for him, letting in a sweep of cold air.

'Come up,' said Harry. 'It's a lot warmer in the office, the guys have got the space heaters blasting as usual, forget the environment. Or the bills.'

They followed him up wide stairs past doors labelled with various vague creative-new-media-type names. The air smelled of fresh plaster and plastic, and Robin heard intermittent hammering – something fine, small-scale, not building work. On the second floor, funked-up bhangra came whirling out of an open door.

Outside Harry's, a mounted Perspex square read *Ragged Staff Digital Planning*. The space was a similar size to Maggie's office but lighter thanks to a metal-framed window almost the width of the room. In front of it a guy and a girl, Indian and white, both Harry's age, sat at laptops set up on a long trestle table. They were clearly waiting: when he opened the door, they were already looking.

The girl stood, pulling out her earbuds, and shook hands from inside giant baggy jumper-cuffs. 'Suzanna.'

'Jas,' said the guy. 'You're the detectives?'

'Private investigators,' Maggie said.

'Is there any news? We're really worried – we love Becca.'

Maggie glanced at Harry. 'Nothing yet, I'm afraid, but it's early days so . . .'

'Shall we talk in my office?' He gestured to a door at the back of the room. 'The timing's terrible – we've got a job to finish by the end of the week but we're finding it really hard to concentrate. Especially me.'

'What is it you do?' asked Maggie, as he showed them into a room with a glass table and three orange chairs. On the back wall was a pair of fierce graffiti-style illustrations of the Bear and Ragged Staff, the county symbol for Warwickshire.

'Digital marketing, strategy and design. The three of us do the strategy ourselves and we source the design from outside. This place has been good for that, there's a lot of good design happening here. A guy downstairs did these.' He tapped the frame of one of the bears. 'He's modifying this one into a logo for us.'

'How long have you been going? You seem very young to have your own business. And employees.'

'I've been lucky.' He ran a hand over his hair. 'Officially, we started in the summer, when I graduated, but really it was before that, at Warwick. Part of my degree – I did a project developing a digital marketing strategy, but then a friend's sister was launching an app, a kids' language-learning thing based on her PhD, and she didn't have much money for promotion so she asked if I'd help. That went really well so other people started getting in touch and it went from there. Jas and Suze were at Warwick, too. Different course – Digital Innovation. Jas and I shared a flat in Leamington; he recommended Suze when we needed a third person.'

'What was your degree?' Robin asked.

'International Business with Spanish.'

'You speak it?'

'Yeah, I'm bilingual. My mum's Dominican. We spoke both at home, growing up.'

'So obviously Jas and Suze know Becca, too?'

'Yes. She and Lucy used to come down for the weekend when I was at uni and since I've been back, we've hung out together here.' He glanced out into the main room. 'But they don't know that Becca and I . . .' he said more quietly. 'Lucy said she'd told you.'

Robin was surprised. 'You knew she knew?'

'I never talked to her about it but I guessed. I guessed she'd guessed.' A twitch at the corner of his mouth.

'In that case, why not just tell her?'

'She said, didn't she?'

'Because you didn't want to mess up your friendship, the three of you?' Maggie said. 'Yeah, but I don't know.' She shrugged. 'If you're such good mates, surely it'd withstand the two of you having a fling, even if it didn't work out?'

'It wasn't a fling.'

'All the more reason not to hide it.'

'What's she like?' asked Robin. 'Becca.'

Harry smiled for the first time. 'Lovely. I think she's gorgeous, obviously, but it's not that. She's got kind of an energy. She's really . . . *alive*, not just . . . going through the motions. She's funny, she makes things fun – her sense of humour's filthy.' He stopped. 'But she's also quite aware of people – she always knows if someone's upset, she's good like that. She listens. When you talk to her, she ends up knowing more than you actually say.'

'You met at school?'

'Yes. Grafton House. My mum teaches there – Spanish – so . . .' He sounded apologetic, as if he were embarrassed about having a private education.

'When did you first start thinking something unusual might be going on? She wasn't answering messages or . . . ?'

He picked up a paperclip and started to bend it apart. 'Friday.

I knew she'd left her phone at home on Thursday because she didn't reply to my texts so I called her at Hanley's. We spoke then and that was the last time.'

Last. Robin remembered the interview with Thomas and Patel, the realization that she'd sent her last-ever text to Corinna.

'Were there any signs she was thinking of taking some time away?' Maggie said. 'Has she seemed stressed lately, for example?'

'No. I've been racking my brains. There was no warning. I'd remember.'

'Was anything bothering her, that you're aware of?'

He shook his head.

'And how had things been between the two of you just before? Did she have any reason to be angry with you? Had you argued at all?'

'No. It was . . . great. Things were great.'

'Why were you really keeping it quiet, Harry?' Maggie sat back, crossed her legs. 'Why did it matter if people knew? What were you afraid of?'

'You're assuming it was me who wanted to keep it secret.'

'Wasn't it?'

'You want to know why I chose Warwick for uni, half an hour away on the train? It wasn't for proximity to my mother's cooking, believe me.'

'You wanted to stay close to Becca?' said Robin.

Samir got cold feet. Dennis's voice through the wall again, the kick in her guts even now. The humiliation – she'd never forgive Samir for that, the glorying look in Luke's eyes when he heard.

'You liked her all that time – what, three years?'

'Four, my degree was.' He shrugged. 'The long game.'

'But that must have been hard – you waited for years, you finally got together, and then she wanted to keep it secret.'

'Only for a while.'

'How long? Did she say?'

Silence.

'How did that make you feel, Harry?' said Maggie, softer.

'Fine,' he said, defiant. 'As you said, I'd waited four years – longer, actually, I'd always liked her. Even when we were kids, I thought she was special. If she wanted to take things slowly, that was okay by me.'

'Was it really?' said Robin.

'What are you implying?' he said. 'That I've got something to do with this? That this is my fault? No. I love her. And I know she loves me.'

'I'm not implying. I'm *asking* how you felt about being kept a secret.'

She watched his chest rise and fall. 'Hard as it is to believe, evidently,' he said, voice steady, 'I respected her decision to keep it between us until she was ready.'

'Okay,' said Maggie. 'Look, we're not suggesting you're responsible for whatever's going on. We're just trying to work out if you know anything, wittingly or not, that might give us a clue what that is. We're trying to find her, Harry.' She reached across the table and put her hand on his. Robin thought of the car outside Valerie's, how she hadn't been able to take her eyes off that giant turquoise ring. Harry seemed transfixed by it, too, eyes kept down for seconds after Maggie stopped talking. When he looked up again, they were shining.

'I feel like I'm going mad,' he said. 'I can't sleep, I feel sick all the time . . . I keep calling her phone just in case and I hear her voicemail message and . . .' He shook his head, looked down again. 'The worst thing is, I can't talk to anyone about it. I'm around Jas and Suze all day – fourteen, fifteen hours a day at the moment – and I can't tell them that actually, it's my girlfriend who's missing.'

122

'Why don't you? Becca would understand, wouldn't she, under the circumstances?'

'Because if I do, I'm admitting something real's happened.'

There was silence again for a moment. He broke it by pulling open a drawer in a filing cabinet and taking out a box of tissues.

'Can you think of anyone who *might* have a reason to hurt her, Harry? Did she have any enemies? Anyone she'd pissed off, that you know of?'

He blew his nose. 'No. She didn't have enemies.'

'Have you talked to the police?' Robin asked.

'I didn't have to. Valerie'd already done it.'

'You don't think your relationship might be relevant? You've just got together,' said Maggie, 'you'd been friends for years, you love each other, you've got to think it might work out. Don't you think that might tell the police that actually, she had a good reason – a new reason – to stick around?'

'I thought what her mum said would be enough. She'd told them how close *they* were, made it clear something was wrong. And to be honest, I didn't want to get involved unless I had to. Missing white girl, black boyfriend. I . . .' He shrugged. 'It didn't seem like a good idea.'

'You were afraid you'd be racially discriminated against? By the police.'

'Let's say I was afraid I'd get a lot of unwarranted scrutiny.'

'Maybe,' said Robin, 'your relationship's relevant for a different reason. Maybe by getting together with you, Becca pissed off someone else.'

'Who?'

'An ex of hers? An ex of yours?'

A pause, as if he were really thinking. 'No.'

'What about Nick?'

123

'Him? She never said anything. Anyway, how would he know? No one knows.'

'Lucy did.'

'She's different. She knows us better than anyone.'

'Was Becca in any sort of trouble, Harry?' Maggie with the soft voice again. 'We're not police, you'll get no judgement here. Valerie said she used recreational drugs; you wouldn't be betraying her if you told us . . .'

'Recreational drugs.' He made it sound ridiculous, old-woman-ish. 'Weed, some E now and again, a bit of coke if it was around but nothing regular and actually, not much lately at all. We haven't been *out* out, really, since she's been at The Spot and things have been intense here, too, so . . .' He tipped his head forward, covered his face with his hands. 'I'm wrecked,' he said. 'I keep imagining all the things that could have happened to her. Is she alone? Is she frightened?' He swallowed. 'I need you to find her. Please.'

They walked a little way back into town before talking, letting their impressions settle. As they passed the coach station on the other side, Robin thought about Corinna again, the eleven-year-old she'd been when they met, the later one who hadn't known where her dad was to tell him her A-level results or introduce him to Josh. Come *on*. The pressure was there in her chest, she could feel it, but she still couldn't *feel* it. Why the hell couldn't she cry? What was *wrong* with her?

'All right?' Maggie came alongside, stuck her arm through hers. 'Come on, give me your body heat, I'm older than you.' They waited for the lights then crossed the road. 'So, what did you make of him?'

'I liked him,' Robin said.

'Yeah. Me too.'

* * *

124

Valerie didn't have Nick's number but when Robin texted Lucy, she pinged it over straight away. Robin opened Becca's Facebook page and scrolled down to the picture of the man in the Adidas jacket, the short back and sides with the dark curls on top. She rang the number and waited.

'Hello?' Music in the background – sounded like Pearl Jam.

'Is this Nick?' She told him who she was. 'I wondered if I could talk to you about Becca Woodson.' It *was* Pearl Jam – 'Yellow Ledbetter'. Old school.

'Becca? Why?'

So he hadn't heard – or was pretending. 'No one's seen her for several days, I'm afraid. We're making enquiries, to see if we can track her down.'

'Several days? Is she all right?'

'Honestly? We don't know. We're still trying to work out what's going on.'

'God.' A few seconds' silence as he processed it. 'Why do you want to talk to *me*?'

'You went out together last year, didn't you? For several months.'

'Yes, but I haven't seen her since we broke up. October.'

'Why was that, if you don't mind me asking? The break-up?'

'She dumped me. She was nice about it, said she didn't have time after this new evening job she started.'

'Was that true, do you think?'

'Yes and no. Really, her heart just wasn't in it. I don't think mine was, now. I mean, I liked her, I don't want to play it off like I was totally cool with it at the time, but a lot of it was wounded pride, you know?'

'Did she ever talk to you about going away? Leaving?'

'I don't think so. No. I mean, why would she? She seemed happy with her life, as far as I could tell.'

'Did you ever meet Harry Norris?'

'Her mate with the business? Yes, of course. He's one of her best friends, isn't he? He fancied her, too, I thought.'

'Yeah?'

'He used to look at me all like, *I've got my eye on you*, you know?'

'But nothing had ever happened between them?'

'She said not.' He paused. 'For what it's worth, apart from the protectiveness, I thought he was all right. He's a decent bloke.'

'When was the last time you actually saw Becca? Or spoke to her?'

'I went round to her house once, a couple of days after we broke up, asked her to change her mind.'

'But she didn't?'

'No, and she was right. The thing is, not long after, I got together with Jules. We work together – she's in sales here. After Becca started at The Spot, I went out with the crew from the office a lot, Thursday, Friday nights, straight from here, and when we broke up, it just happened. I'd always assumed Jules was out of my league, to be honest, but luckily for me, she doesn't seem to think so.'

Chapter Ten

By the time Robin arrived, the daytime business of the hospital was over, the outpatient clinics and surgeries long emptied, late visitors to the ordinary wards on their way out. The corridors felt muted, drowsy, as if the ventilation system were pumping them with a gentle sedative. She followed the signs, pushing through one set of double doors after another, thinking of valves, a series of valves, taking her deeper and deeper towards the heart of the place.

Intensive Care didn't have visiting hours; people could come when they needed to, stay all night if they wanted, like Di had, Will had said on the phone, since it happened. She'd asked him whether Lennie could visit and his hesitation had been answer in itself. 'Why don't you see him yourself first then decide?'

She gave her name at the desk and waited for the receptionist to check the list. Worst nightclub in town.

The woman pushed her chair back. 'Wait here, please.' Rubbing her hands with sanitizer, she scanned herself through another pair of doors, making sure they locked again behind her before she disappeared down the pale corridor on the other side.

The only other person in the waiting room was a man in his fifties silently doing a crossword in the paper folded on his knee. A thermos flask protruded from a basket at his feet. A regular, she guessed, finding comfort just in being here, close to his loved one, protected by the order the place imposed on chaos.

The week Rin's dad's body had finally thrown in the towel, she'd told UCL she had a family emergency, stuffed a few clothes in a bag and got on a train. She hadn't told her parents she was back; she'd stayed with Di and Rin in King's Heath, sleeping on the sofa-bed, driving them to the QE in Di's car, making run after run to the café then the after-hours vending machine. How many hours had she sat in the waiting room that week? Twenty? Thirty? She'd come to know it well, to recognize newbies by the shock in their eyes, the long-haulers who came every day, living on crumbs of hope: a dose lowered by half a point, the movement of a hand.

The doors clicked open and the receptionist reappeared. Behind her was Di, who pulled Robin into a fierce hug, face against her shoulder, huge boobs crushed against her stomach. Twenty-five years on, Di's height, or lack of it, still took Robin by surprise. Whenever she hadn't seen her for a while, she forgot, because Di was not a small person in any other way.

She stood back, holding Robin at arm's length. She'd worn her make-up every day the week Trevor died – 'He liked to see me with my face on' – but not today. Di's face was round and even twenty years ago, it had looked pillowy, slightly puffy, as if she had a layer of water under the skin, 'like a water bed,' said Rin. The last time Robin had seen her, she'd thought she was ageing well, crinkling in a kindly way. Now it was as if a plug had been pulled, the water drained away, and her face looked pouchy, the skin swagged beneath eyes that were cried-out and tiny. She couldn't have washed her hair since it happened.

'Will told me you were coming so I waited,' she said.

'You shouldn't have. You must be exhausted.'

'I wanted to see you. *You* haven't slept, have you? You've got to try and sleep, Robin.' Ever the nurse.

'You too.'

'Tonight. I'm going to try, anyway – they've given me something. I wanted to stay again but I've got to keep myself together for him, haven't I?' She glanced towards the locked doors. 'I can't go to pieces; he'll need me.'

'Is there any change?'

'His blood oxygen's slightly better tonight but . . . There's such a long way to go. Will told you they're keeping him in the coma for now?'

'Yes, he did.' She hesitated. 'Di, have you heard anything from the police?'

'Have *you*?' Her focus sharpened.

'No. But I'm probably the last person they'd tell.'

A moment's confusion. 'Ah god, love, I forgot. She told me about your trouble, of course. Corinna.'

The name hung in the air between them.

Di's chin trembled. 'They've found his car,' she said.

Robin felt herself startle. 'Have they?'

'This morning. They rang this afternoon.'

'Where?'

'Warwick Parkway. The car park at the station.'

'Did he get on a train?'

'They don't know yet. They're going through the CCTV. He didn't use his card – they're trying to see if he bought a ticket with cash.'

Robin didn't ask; she didn't have to. Di had fought it, she

didn't want to believe it and yet, as the hours passed and he wasn't found, didn't come forward, she too was asking: why not?

Most of the ward was open, the beds divided by curtains, but built down one side were four separate bays with walls and closing doors. Robin knew without being told that Peter's was the one furthest from the entrance. The police guard outside was in plain clothes, visitors here had enough to worry about, but she'd recognize the posture a mile off. 'In case he comes back to finish the job,' Will said on the phone. The unnamed he.

The lights had been dimmed for the night, the lamps at the nurses' station angled down. From behind curtains came the gentle push-and-suck of a machine, a series of low beeps as another demanded attention. A pair of rubber soles squeaked on lino.

The blind in the internal window of Peter's room was drawn, the door pushed to. 'Robin Lyons, the family friend,' murmured the nurse who'd walked her back. 'Di vouched for her.' The guard looked at her then nodded the go-ahead.

The bed was positioned in the centre of the room, raised like an altar, covered in white. The shape of it was odd, boxy – there was some sort of structure under the sheets to hold them away from his body, she realized, making a tent to keep him warm without touching him. The bank of monitors around the head of the bed cast an otherworldly glow, faintly green, as if this wasn't a hospital but some sort of alien laboratory.

She approached. He was lying on his back, the head of the bed raised as if to put him on display, their prize. A band across his face held tubes in place in his nostrils. The first three inches of his hair had been shaved around a gash that stretched over his forehead and across his scalp. He looked like a prisoner, shaven-headed and beaten. His face on the pillow was so small.

It was him, of course, but it wasn't. This Peter was purple-lidded, sombre, bird-fragile. Their Peter had been born hilarious, a sprite – his ears were even slightly pointed at the top, kinks in the cartilage. They'd come from his great-grandfather on Josh's side, Corinna said, a recessive gene; there was a photo on the wall at Russell Road. The shape of his face, though, had come from her – along with his eyes, which were like five-pence pieces, round and silver-grey.

At the desk in the corner, the nurse finished making a note, pushed her glasses back on her head and stood up. 'Hi, I'm Rachel,' she whispered. 'I'll be with him 'til the morning, little man. Here.' She lifted a chair from a stack in the corner of the room and brought it up to the bedside. 'Don't be afraid to hold his hand. And talk to him.'

'He's on a ventilator?' Will hadn't told her.

The woman nodded. She looked at the machines, checked the levels in three pouches suspended from a rolling stand behind the bed head. 'All under control. I'm going to nip to the loo, give you a moment.'

Robin heard her whisper a few words to the guard outside then the soft *tap-tap* of her shoes as she receded through the ward. She stood for a moment, then sat down. Peter's left arm was at her eye level now, the hand protruding from a cast that reached to his shoulder. She looked at his fingers curled on the blanket. He was ten, for fuck's sake.

'*Look, Rob.*' Corinna's voice in her ear, full of wonder. Against her palm she'd held Peter's newborn hand, a wrinkled pink starfish, nails like mother-of-pearl washed tissue-thin. She'd been crying tears of painful joy, riding the tidal wave of maternal

131

hormones. 'God,' she'd said, trying to laugh, 'how could I have made something so perfect?'

'You I understand,' Robin had said. '*Him*, though?' She'd tipped her head at Josh, sitting across the bed. He'd been half laughing, half crying himself.

She reached between the rails and slipped her fingers under Peter's. She hoped that deep down, wherever he was, he might sense her, curl his hand round hers, even if it was only an automatic motor response, like a baby's. Nothing – the fingers stayed inert. 'Pete, sweetie, it's me, Auntie Robin. I . . .' Her throat seized up. She remembered the way the skin had folded on his tummy when he was new. Like one of those Japanese dogs with the faces like wrinkled plush blankets, and just as soft. She remembered Rin bending over him at the changing table, singing 'How Much Is That Doggie in the Window?' as she eased his legs into a fresh suit, Lennie standing solemnly by to watch, the big girl at nearly four.

The rhythm of the ventilator: *beat beat suck; beat beat suck.* She'd been lying to herself when she'd said she'd understood the situation, even on a superficial level. She hadn't at all.

The pressure in her chest was intensifying – she tried to take a breath and couldn't. She coughed and then she started to keen, a sound dragged from the bottom of her lungs. Her chest heaved as if she'd been sprinting. She pushed the chair away from the bed, buried her face in her knees, covered her mouth. She tried to bring it under control – *head down, steady your breathing, Steady Your Breathing* – but she couldn't do it; the sound, the movement, were whooping, self-perpetuating, like the states Lennie had used to get into as a toddler, when nothing worked except crying herself out.

The bar of light from the doorway widened then narrowed again – the guard, the nurse, she didn't see. *Stop it!* Christine's

132

voice, hissing, shaming. *Stop it, Robin. Get yourself under control! What will people think? You're hysterical!* Could Peter hear her? Or the other children on the ward, injured and ill, scared by this crazy woman weeping in the night?

She should have known – why hadn't she? The black eye – there had been a warning. It didn't matter that Corinna hadn't told her; she'd always known when something was going on in Robin's life, she hadn't needed to be told. But when *Corinna* had needed *her*, Robin hadn't been there.

She was aware of movement in the room now and again, a rustle of paper, wheels as a monitor was rolled closer or further away. At some point, the nurse lowered the rail and she dropped her face into the blanket. She flinched at a hand on her shoulder but it stayed there, steadying.

She cried for Peter, she cried for Corinna and Josh. She cried for herself. Finally, exhausted, she stopped and let her eyes close.

She jerked up to find herself drooling, the pristine blanket smeared with mascara. How long had she been out? Minutes? Hours? She pulled up her cuff and scrubbed at the marks, trying not to disturb Peter's arm.

'It happens, don't worry about it,' said a voice from the gloom behind the bed. The nurse, replacing one of the bags on the IV stand. 'It'll be changed in the morning, no harm done. Better that you let some of it out.'

Robin stood up. Her back and neck ached, and her legs were stiff. She backed away a few steps as if she'd just staggered off a boat.

'Take care of yourself,' said the woman quietly. 'Go home and get into bed.'

As she let herself out of the room, the guard on the chair

turned and gawped. He'd heard it all, of course, every hooting, snotty moment. She stumbled back up the corridor towards the waiting room, wanting a drink more than she ever had before in her life. *Saying something*, said Corinna. She'd get a taxi, a black cab from the rank outside, screw the money. She needed to be alone, to get herself under some sort of control before she walked into Dunnington Road.

The doors wouldn't open. She tugged at them, gently at first, then harder and harder until a nurse came out from a curtained bay and hit a release button on the wall. Robin muttered a thank you and plunged out as if she'd been underwater.

The waiting room was empty bar a man on the same row of chairs against the far wall. She glanced over, expecting the cross-word puzzler with his flask and air of silent forbearance. No – it wasn't him. Sitting forward, head bent over his hands, was a younger man, broad in the shoulders, black coat, blue-black hair cut short against the nape of his neck.

Samir.

In one of the weird jump-cuts that had been happening all day, he seemed to be across the room in a second, pinging up in front of her like a spring-loaded target. She jumped and he reached out to steady her arm before quickly pulling his hand back.

'Sorry, I didn't mean to startle you.'

She met his eye with a jolt of recognition. 'You didn't,' she said, looking away. She brushed a brisk hand under her eyes, one then the other. 'It was the first time I've seen him. It was . . . a shock.' Her throat was thick.

'I know. I saw him yesterday. The last time, before, we had a kick-about in the garden.'

His voice was the same: soft, rounded-sounding, no hard

edges. It was posher than hers, less of an accent, even though he'd lived here far longer than she had now. She made herself look at him and was disorientated a second time, as if the jump-cut just now had swallowed a decade rather than a couple of seconds. Or she was nineteen again and looking at an e-fit projection of him sixteen years into the future, grey shaded in over the ears, fine lines bracketing his mouth and fanning from the corners of his eyes. He'd filled out. The Samir she'd known had been willowy despite the broad shoulders. This one was solid; he took up space.

'Can we talk for a moment?'

Now, after a decade and a half? 'I should get back – it must be late.' She scanned around, looking for a clock. 'Lennie'll be waiting for me. My daughter.' She shook out her jacket, shoved an arm into the sleeve.

'I know who she is,' he said gently. 'It's half eleven – she'll already be asleep, won't she? A couple of minutes. It's about Rin.'

She looked at him: really? What else would it be about? 'Fine, a quick one, but let's walk. I need to get out of here.'

He followed her into the corridor. It was wide and empty, lights reflecting blankly off lino and gloss-painted walls, but Robin could feel the hospital around them, a huge engine humming in the night, like a cross-Channel ferry, or a giant animal, warm and slow-breathing, protective. They walked for a moment, putting distance between themselves and the ward. Their footsteps echoed.

'You knew I was here,' she said, stopping. 'You're on this, aren't you?'

'The case? No.'

'But you're Head of Homicide.'

'The SIO's a guy called Webster. He's very experienced; he—'

'*DI* Webster, yes, I saw him on the news. It's not a domestic.'

He took a breath. 'Do you think I'd give it to someone who couldn't handle it? Not just handle it – do it well.'

'*Do* you think it's being done well? DS Thomas asked if I was sleeping with Josh. Yesterday.'

The words stole the oxygen between them for a moment, and she felt blood rush to her face. He broke the eye contact, looked away. Up ahead, the double doors swung open and a porter came through wheeling an empty bed. They waited for him to pass.

'I heard what your father saw,' he said. 'Rin with the black eye. You told Thomas and Patel yourself he's a reliable witness.'

'Husbands aren't the only people who hit women.' Her cheeks were burning.

'No, but most women who *are* hit are hit by their partners.'

'You really think he hit her? Come on.'

'You really think she was getting into fights?'

'I don't know.' She shrugged. 'It's not impossible, she could be fierce. She could fight if she wanted to. And who said she was hit, even? There are other ways to get black eyes.'

He stopped. 'Look, Robin, I don't *want* to believe this. I really don't. That's why I'm here. I'm asking you to help us. Me.'

She met his eye and for a moment, she had the feeling she was looking into a palimpsest, layer after layer of shifting memories, moving over each other like slides loose in a box.

'Please,' he said. 'Even if for some reason you couldn't tell Thomas and Patel, tell me. Tell me something that'll help us prove Josh didn't do it.'

'I can't,' she said.

'Can't or won't?'

'You think I'm withholding information?'

His turn to shrug, but with a strange half-smile. 'That's how mad this is. If it meant we could prove my friend didn't kill his wife, I would actually hope you are.'

If I told you what I know, you'd be sure he did kill her.

She looked down quickly, hiding her eyes as if he'd be able to read the thought in them. *Jesus.* 'Look,' she said instead, gesturing back in the direction of Intensive Care. 'Look where we are. This wasn't Josh.'

He took another deep breath. 'Not the one we knew.'

We? 'What are you saying?'

'We think – Webster and his team, I mean – that he had a breakdown.'

'Why?'

He looked at her as if she were an idiot of the first order. 'Because of the factory.'

'The factory?'

He frowned. 'Are you being serious?'

'What about it?'

He was staring at her now, eyebrows pulled together. 'You don't know? She hadn't told you?'

'For Christ's sake, Samir – told me what?'

'It was about to go under. Bankrupt.'

She pulled her head back. 'What? Why?'

'All the usual reasons – cheaper imports, rising costs. They couldn't compete any more. One of their biggest customers went bust, apparently, about two years ago. That was a big blow.'

'But . . .'

'He'd been under a lot of pressure for a long time. Months – years, actually. They'd borrowed.' He glanced down the empty corridor. 'It wasn't just the money. Mr Legge senior – Gerry – told Webster Josh felt like he was destroying generations of the family's work, that he was responsible.'

The words tumbled in Robin's brain, a set of phrases that wouldn't arrange themselves properly.

'And the lay-offs were another thing. He'd had to get rid of people who'd been there thirty years, who his dad had taken on when he was a kid. Men in their fifties who'd been on the shop floor since they were sixteen, women who relied on the flexible hours.'

Yes, it made sense, he would have hated that, firing people – been tortured by it, actually. Josh had an old-fashioned sense of his duty towards his workforce; he looked after them far beyond any legal requirements, Rin told her. The factory hadn't run on huge margins at the best of times but when one of his long-standing van drivers had cancer, he'd paid him his full salary plus Christmas bonuses for three years while he recovered.

'So that's one thing,' she said. 'What other lines is your man Webster pursuing?'

'Robin. Apart from anything else, you know I can't talk about it.'

'Di told me you've found his car.'

'And that doesn't change your thinking at all?'

'Not about him *killing* her. There's something going on, he was involved in something – at this stage, I know that – but no.'

His phone buzzed in his pocket. He took it out, looked at the screen and rejected the call. 'You're a good friend.'

She snorted. 'Not very good. My best mate is dead.'

'That's not your fault.'

'Tell your team. They asked for my alibi last night.'

'I know. But I told them I didn't like you for it.'

For fuck's *sake*. Robin felt a sudden, dizzying urge to throw everything in the air, jump off the cliff. 'Well, what if you're wrong?' she said. 'Maybe your judgement's off. Maybe I *was* sleeping with my best mate's husband then got tired of it all and killed the pair of them.'

She glared at him, daring him to say something, but the look of astonishment on his face cut her dead. The burst of whatever it was evaporated in a second, and she felt herself wither inside. What the fuck was wrong with her?

Self-disgust, bitter, and with it, a memory of Corinna's wedding.

It wasn't the worst day of her life, but it was top five, even now, probably top three. That had been her fault, too. Rin had tried to protect her – more than tried. In the week before the invitations were posted, she'd gone on and on about it, ringing, sending emails, *'in case it's easier to tell me like this than over the phone.'*

'I just want to make sure you're totally okay with it,' she'd said. 'Josh and I are fine – completely fine – if you'd prefer him not to be there. He's a friend, a good friend, but you're my matron of honour.'

Some stupid impulse had made her insist it was fine – completely fine – if he was there. She wanted to show everyone that he hadn't hurt her at all; she'd walked away without a scratch. But more than that, she'd wanted to show *him* her life. *Look at my amazing daughter and my degree and my fast-track job at the Met. I did it! Ha! Without you!*

Six weeks before the wedding, however, Rin had turned up on her doorstep in London. 'There's been a development,' she said. 'He wants to bring someone.'

Everything that had happened in between – the tarting around; the advent of Lennie; her degree; starting at the Met and the unholy logistical hell of just trying to keep it all together – fell away.

'It might not be serious,' Corinna said. 'It's only new.'

If it had been anyone else, she would have told her to bugger off: why would she care if it *was* serious? What was he to her? Old history, water under the bridge, bad rubbish. Instead she'd sat on the scratchy sofa with her arms round her knees, silent. Corinna had sat with her.

'This is not about me,' she'd said eventually.

'What?'

'It's not about me. It's your wedding day. You're my best mate; he's one of Josh's best mates. Samir and me – it was over years ago. *Five* years. I've got time to get used to the idea of him having a girlfriend so I'll deal, okay?'

'No, I don't think it's a good—'

'He's coming and he's bringing his girlfriend. End of story.'

Arrogant as she was, she'd thought she could handle it. She was Robin Lyons, single mother by night, scourge of the crims of Ladbroke Grove by day (schedule highly susceptible to change); what did she have to fear from an old boyfriend who'd proved himself unworthy?

When the day came, she'd spent it with her guts on fire. The register office had been manageable – short, structured; with a lurch, she'd seen him fleetingly outside but he hadn't seen her – but the reception was something else.

They'd had it at Josh's parents' place in Edgbaston, a marquee pitched on the lawn, Hilary's flowerbeds wild blurs of colour in Van Gogh brushstrokes, the sky a limitless kind of blue that Will, *in loco parentis*, referenced twice in his speech as a portent of things to come. The temperature had been in the high eighties but even with all the sides pinned up, it must have been a hundred in the tent, and completely airless – as she listened to Will, seated next to her at the high table so it felt as if everyone was staring at her, Robin had

140

felt sweat gathering in bands around her middle. The Coast dress she'd had to open a store card to buy had seemed like a good idea in March – it had fitted then, too, before another three months of post-shift, exhaustion-driven takeaways – but when she stood up, sweat had seeped through the satin and made salty white lines. Upstairs in the bathroom mirror, the pouch of flab above her C-section showed so clearly she might as well have hired a town crier. *Oyez, oyez, slut and unmarried mother; oyez.*

He'd said four words to her that day – 'Hello, how are you?' – then moved away before she could reply. He hadn't even looked at her. All afternoon and through the evening her eyes had found him in the crowd over and over but not one time had he been looking back. She'd moved into a different world: their lives had diverged completely. He was still young, here with his girlfriend; she was a *matron*, fast-forwarded to an adult world of nap schedules, childcare, Child Benefit. Responsibility.

Liz was tall and lean – Robin heard later that she'd played squash for the Leeds university team – with thick brunette hair that had slowly undone itself from some sort of up-do over the course of the day. She might have been sweating like crazy but she had on a funky patterned dress that wouldn't have shown it if she was. She looked good but in a realistic way, not tarty or over-made-up, nor the opposite and annoyingly natural. Robin couldn't even console herself that she was thick: she was going to be a lawyer, Corinna had reluctantly told her; she'd just finished a CPE.

'I don't know what to say, Rob,' she'd said when she was back from her honeymoon. 'I want to tell you she's vile – I want to hate her for you, I *do* hate her for you. But she isn't vile. If she wasn't going out with him, you'd like her. She's . . .

141

all right.' She must have been: the following summer, he'd married her.

Corinna's wedding was when she'd finally realized it was over. Done. Through everything that had happened, even having Lennie, some part of her believed that what they'd had, that level of connection and engagement – sympathy, actually, in the literal sense of feeling things in the same way – was too strong just to cease to exist. She'd allowed herself to believe, at least on some level, that there must have been something else at work, that something had happened to Samir which for some profound reason, he hadn't been able to tell her. That day, she'd understood – at last – that that final sustaining scrap of comfort was false. A lie. She'd been kidding herself: there'd been nothing profound about it; she'd just been wrong.

When he'd broken up with her, she'd been devastated. She'd been open with him, unguarded in a way that she'd only ever been with Corinna, before or since. She'd let herself be vulnerable because she'd trusted him and he'd turned round and thrown it in her face.

That had been bad enough but what troubled her even more – the secondary gift – was that her judgement had been so off. If she'd been wrong about that, what else was she wrong about? It had taken a long time, years actually, to come back from that. Rin might say she never had.

'I'm sorry. That was really stupid – I don't know why I said it. I'm exhausted, I'm frustrated, I . . .'

'We should go, anyway,' he said. 'It's late. How are you getting home?'

'Cab.' Emphatic. Highly unlikely he'd offer her a lift, especially

142

after that, but just in case. The idea of being stuck in a car with him.

On the other side of the doors, she stopped. 'I'm going this way.'

He glanced at the wall. 'Are you?'

She looked up and saw a sign for the Renal Outpatients Unit.

'Robin, look,' he said. 'I have to back my team. I chose Webster to lead, now I have to trust him to do the job. It's one of the hardest parts of having a senior role, you know that. Especially with this case.'

She opened her mouth to say something – *Oh, sod off with your 'senior role'* – but he wasn't finished. 'I wanted to say to you – I've been trying to say – I was really sorry to hear what happened at the Met.'

By the time the cab turned into Dunnington Road, it was twenty past midnight. She'd told Lennie she'd be back after she went to sleep, and Christine and Dennis were usually in bed by half ten so it was a surprise to see the glow of the standard lamp through the downstairs curtains. What fresh hell? She paid the cab and let herself in as quietly as she could.

Dennis was in the armchair, the *Post* on his lap, a rerun of *QI* muted on TV. She closed the internal door behind her. 'What are you doing up, Dad?'

'Oh, I wanted to make sure you got back okay.'

'I catch dangerous criminals, remember? Or used to.'

'You're still my daughter.' He dropped the *Post* on the little table and stood up. 'Do you want a drink? I'm going to have a Scotch.'

'Really? Yes, please.'

He padded to the kitchen, where she heard him get the stool

to reach the top cupboard. Wine and beer could live at eye level but Christine kept the spirits tucked away up there, as if their corrupting power were too strong for casual exposure.

He returned with the bottle under his arm, holding a finger between the glasses to stop them clinking. Sounds like that reached her mother like bat signals. 'How was he?' he said.

'Bad. Worse than I thought. Will told me but I hadn't really . . . He's on a ventilator.'

'Good god. That poor little thing.'

'I went to pieces.' She gestured at her face, as if he might not have noticed. Dennis handed her a glass and sat down next to her. 'Then Samir showed up.'

A flicker of alarm crossed his face. 'Why?'

'Basically to beg me to tell him something that meant Josh didn't do it. They all think he did.'

'They?'

'The police. Him. Will and Di.'

Leaning against the upper bunk, head on the mattress, Robin listened to Lennie's breathing. *The best thing I ever did* – she said it so often, and meant it every time, but tonight the knowledge was physical, a knot in her stomach. Gently she put an arm over Len's chest, pressed her nose against the back of her head. A surge of longing – she wanted to grip her, lock her in her arms so she could never get away. She was okay for the moment, Lennie didn't want to get away, but she was thirteen, well into adolescence. A couple of years ago she'd demanded a starter bra, one of those T-shirt-material harness things, and last year, just before Christmas, she'd started her period. She was growing up – soon she'd want if not to get away, with luck, at least to *go*, be independent, an adult.

She'd only been eight years older than Lennie was now when

she'd had her. Ludicrously young – what had she been thinking? And yet, hadn't she guided herself right that time? Hadn't she made the best decision that day on the bus when she shoved the sensible thing aside? She'd trusted her gut and she'd never regretted it. It was time to do it again.

Chapter Eleven

It was light, more or less, but in the shade of the portico, the carriage lamp was still on. Along Russell Road just now, the streetlights had been hazy balls of orange, the trees and bushes that screened the deep front gardens just silhouettes. Robin pulled her jacket round her, the leather cold against her neck, and rang the bell a second time.

Soft footsteps inside then the door opened a crack, stopping at the extent of the chain. A vertical strip of Kath's face, wary-eyed.

'Hi,' said Robin.

The door closed, chain rattling. It opened again but still only partway. Kath was barefoot in pyjamas, arms crossed over the cardigan she had on top.

'I should have rung, probably, but I wanted to talk to you face to face.'

'The bell – everyone's in bed. Dad's been up all night; he's only been asleep a couple of hours.'

'I'm sorry, I didn't think.' There was a pause, as if now she'd acknowledged her, Kath expected her to turn and go. 'Can I come in?'

Another pause but then Kath stood aside.

Robin followed her back to the kitchen. She'd always loved this room, the sheer scale of it; you could fit the footprint of her parents' whole house in here. It was a room you could breathe in: wide and high-ceilinged, with a view all the way down the garden. When they were teenagers and Josh's mother, Hilary, had still been alive, a pair of double doors had led out to a crazy-paved patio almost hidden by the rampant greenery from a horde of mismatched pots. When she'd died and Kath and Gareth had moved in, they'd completely redone the kitchen, replacing the back wall with bi-fold doors and taming the garden. That had been after Josh and Corinna's wedding; Hilly had been there for that. She'd been especially kind that day, telling her how lovely Lennie was in her tiny flower-girl dress, how much she admired Robin for working and bringing her up alone. As if she'd been able to see the demolition job going on inside her.

Kath stood with her back against the island unit, arms tightly folded. On Josh, the high cheekbones and long straight nose were combined with their father's round face so that at certain angles – especially if he hadn't been running for a while – he looked like an anthropomorphized moon in a Victorian children's book. Kath's face was narrower, more like their mother's, and the cheekbones gave her a warrior look. As Robin had confessed to Corinna a few years earlier, she found her slightly intimidating.

'Really?' Rin'd been fond of her; they went shopping together, out for dinner.

'Well, not *really*, but she's not one of those teachers who leaves their authority at school, is she?'

'Rich, coming from you.'

But Kath commanded respect, always had. Even at eighteen, she'd been self-contained and certain of how she was going to negotiate the world. She'd inherited this lovely house just off Cannon Hill Park but in everything else, she was naturally abstemious and self-disciplined. These days, she biked the boys to their school, Rin said, then carried on to her own, where she taught upper-school maths. She took modern classics on holiday – 'There's me with my *Gone Girl*, and Kath's ploughing through Umberto Eco' – and the boys, Al 'n' Ed, could apparently take or leave screen time. She made Robin feel frivolous.

She was staring at her over the cheekbones now: *Come on then, let's hear it.* As if Robin were a kid caught smoking on the school bus. With a flash of something like déjà vu, though, Robin was reminded of Valerie, the way she'd stood in front of her and Maggie like a rabbit in the headlights, and it dawned on her: Kath wasn't being aggressive; this was defence.

'I've told the police everything,' Kath said. 'There *isn't* anything else. I know she was your best friend but she was *my* friend, too. Imagine how *I* feel, knowing people think my—'

'Kath – stop.' Robin's voice was louder than she'd intended, taking them both by surprise. 'I haven't come to pressure you.'

A small snort.

'I don't think it was Josh.'

She gave a bitter shrug. 'You mean, you think he had a breakdown.'

'No. I don't think he did it.'

Kath looked at her, assessing, then her eyes filled with tears. Robin havered. Should she go over there, put an arm round her? Would that be good – was Kath a hugger? Probably not, with people she wasn't close to. She felt a guilty wash of relief.

Kath gulped and reached for the kitchen roll on the worktop, hands trembling. 'I'm sorry.' Another painful-sounding swallow. 'That . . . You took me by surprise.' She pressed the paper against her eyes. 'I thought you'd come to have a go at me.'

'What? No.' Robin was taken aback. What kind of person did Kath think she was?

'It's just . . . Someone besides me and Dad who doesn't think he's a monster. Or – best-case scenario! – he lost his mind.'

Robin took a breath. 'I'm not saying I think he was totally innocent.'

Her eyes: *Please don't hurt me.*

'I don't know what happened – at all – but I think it's possible he was mixed up with something that got out of control. Or someone.'

'Why?'

Your instincts tell you? The memory of Freshwater's scorn launched a spasm of self-doubt: what if she was misleading Josh's sister? 'At this stage it's only a theory, I don't want to give you false hope.' She looked Kath in the eye. 'Did you hear what happened to me?'

One nod. 'Josh told me.' A tiny pause. 'And I saw it in the paper. They get the *Mail* in the staffroom.'

'I'm completely out of the police for now, maybe for good. I could be wrong about that case, Jamie Hinton, I still don't know, and I could be wrong about Josh. I want to be totally upfront about that.'

Another nod.

'But the fact that there's no sign of him yet, three days in. That he hasn't given himself up or been found. If it had been a moment of madness, I think one way or another, he would have been found by now.'

Kath's eyes were fixed on her.

'Then last night I heard the factory was going under.'

She frowned. 'You didn't know that before? Didn't Corinna tell you?'

'No. Did she talk to *you* about it?'

149

'Yes. But I'm family, I knew anyway, so . . . She really didn't tell you?'

Something – pride – stopped Robin answering again. 'Can *you* tell me?'

'Not the real minutiae; I'm not a shareholder, I never look at the books, I just know the gist. You know that's how they split things, when Mum died, to avoid inheritance tax later? We got the house, me and Gareth, with Dad living here as long as he wants to, and Josh got the business. He and Dad are the only shareholders. Dad still has thirty per cent, which'll be shared between the grandchildren eventually, or would have been, so they had meetings here, over dinner. It's a family business, there's no secrecy about it.'

'When did the problems start?'

'Some time ago – three or four years? More? It's not new, they'd been bumping along for a while. There are always ebbs and flows, anyway – when we were kids Dad had two or three hairy periods, the recessions at the start of the Eighties and the Nineties. This was different, though – business moving overseas, globalization. Then Novamat went to the wall, which was a real blow.'

'Was that about two years ago? Samir mentioned a big customer.'

'Yes, that's them. There were cash-flow issues, too – people weren't paying on time. Couldn't, themselves. Anyway, you know my brother, he pulled out all the stops. First he cut his own salary in half, then for a few months he didn't take one at all and they lived on Rin's income and a few bits and pieces of savings. Gareth and I took a loan against the house to help but then they got a big order from Poland and he paid it back. We tried to stop him but he insisted. He was expecting another order, he said, the same again, but in the end, it didn't happen. The customer got a cheaper quote from China.'

'When was that, your loan?'

'Three years ago – about that.'

'And then what?'

'He started laying people off. Which he found really hard.' She paused. 'He got depressed – anxious. Both.'

'Did he see anyone about it?'

'His GP. She gave him antidepressants – an SSRI.'

'Did they help?'

'Seemed to. He coped better.'

'And the police know about that?'

'Of course. We've told them everything. But they're interpreting it as *proof*, evidence of instability, rather than him dealing with it. They talk like it was way more than it was, a major depressive episode. It wasn't – I would have known.'

But *she* hadn't known at all, Robin thought. Corinna hadn't told her.

Kath ran her hands through her hair, pulling it back against her skull. 'I've been over and over it, we all have. The only thing that stands out is something he said at Easter last year. He mentioned a cash injection. We were washing up after lunch. I asked him about it and he got a bit flustered – as if he hadn't meant to say anything and it'd slipped out. All he'd tell me was he'd borrowed against the machines. I said it sounded like a risk – if he couldn't pay it back, he'd lose them – and he said yes but he'd had to.' She shrugged, the gesture so like his she could have been acting out the memory.

'He wouldn't say who the loan was from?'

'No. I asked, directly, but he went off on a tangent, started talking about how when things got going again, he'd replace some of the machines, have an overhaul, get costs down. It was deliberate – I remember saying to Gareth he didn't want to tell me.'

'Who do you think it might have been, if you had to guess?'

'I don't know.'

'A bank?'

'No. Not a bank.' Kath looked her in the eye. 'He would have told me. At the time I worried it was one of those dodgy pay-day loans places with the exorbitant interest. Now I don't know if it was even that legitimate. What if it was a loan shark, he couldn't pay them back and . . . ?'

'You've told the police about this, obviously?'

'Yes. They said they'd look into it but we haven't heard any more.'

'Okay. Can you think why he might have gone to Warwick?'

'You mean his car?'

'If it was him who took it there. Does he know someone there? A friend, a business associate?'

She shook her head. 'No one we know.'

'Kath,' Robin felt her heart begin to beat faster, 'had either of them ever been involved in something in the past that could have caught up with them?'

'Like what?'

'I don't know. An accident, maybe – a hit-and-run?'

'No. No way. They'd never do that, either of them. If they ever hit someone, they'd have stopped.'

'I know.' Her cheeks were burning. 'I just want to be completely thorough.' She tried to sound reassuring. Credible. 'Did they still have their after-school babysitter? Ana?'

'Yes. They'd cut her hours down, she was only doing two afternoons a week, but yeah. They were sharing her with another family at Peter's school, she went to them the other three days. That was purely to save money – Josh did pick-up on those days.'

'Have you spoken to her?'

'No, but the police have. I don't know if she told them very much – apparently she was very upset.'

'Have you got her number?'

Kath's look sharpened.

Here we go. 'I want to make some enquiries,' Robin said. 'Independently.'

'You don't trust the police.' Not a question, a statement.

Careful, careful. 'It's not that. But I think there's a chance, knowing them as well as I do, Rin and Josh, that I might pick up on something the police would miss.'

'Would you tell them you're doing it?'

'No.' The word echoed. 'More than that, Kath, I'd ask *you* not to. I can't risk it. I'm going to appeal my dismissal and if the Met get wind that I've been poking around in a case . . .'

Kath eyeballed her. 'And if you find something?'

'Then I'll suck up the consequences and take it to them straight away. At that point, they'd go easy on me, I think. I hope.'

On her way out, Robin paused at the bottom of the stairs, her eye caught by an angle of greenish light slanting through a door across the hall. Back then, the room had been Gerry's study, the strange underwater light made by a big laurel outside the window. On Rin's wedding day, she'd entrusted Lennie to Hilary and hidden in there for a few minutes to let the rictus drop off her face. It had been cool and serene, she remembered, fitted book-shelves and minimal furniture, just an armchair, a standard lamp and the table Gerry used as a desk, its top covered with papers. She'd found it steadying that day, a reminder of the real world, the refuge of work. *This, too, shall pass.* She remembered some-thing else. 'Kath, do you still have that wall of photos?'

'Yes, of course. Do you want to see it?'

'Can I, quickly?'

Kath opened the door. 'It's still Dad's study, probably hasn't changed much since the last time you were here. Though he's taken up genealogy in a major way since he retired so excuse the piles and piles of bad photocopies. If you need to know what we were doing during the Civil War, he's the man to ask. Though if you've got any kind of boredom threshold, I wouldn't.'

The furniture had been moved since the wedding, to maximize light, Robin guessed: the desk with its messy heaps of paper was by the window now, the armchair positioned directly under the lamp. It was instantly recognizable as an old person's workspace, and not just by the magnifying glass on the mousepad and the dated desktop computer. Here were the treasures of a lifetime: a framed photograph of Gerry and Hilary somewhere hot, another of Kath and Josh as blunt-fringed Eighties toddlers in a paddling pool on the lawn. A pebble paperweight painted with a childish snail, a home-made *papier mâché* matchbox cover.

The photographs took up an entire wall, thirty or more in various sizes arranged in five rows, one per generation. The shape they made was Christmas tree-like, branching down from a single picture at the top into three progressively broader rows, and ending – the trunk – in three pictures of the present generation. Josh.

'Dad did it years ago,' Kath said, 'when I was seven or eight. It was a big project, all the copying, framing. We were warned about the genealogy, I suppose.'

The picture at the top was a formal photograph of two men standing shoulder to shoulder, stiff in three-piece suits and sharp white collars, watch-chains, clipped moustaches. They were probably about thirty but the formality made them ageless. *George & William Legge, founders of Legge Bros Springs, Bishop St, Birmingham*, said the handwritten caption. *1889*.

In the next row down they appeared again but visibly older, late fifties maybe, flanked by two younger men – a son apiece, Robin guessed. This time they were outside, in front of a brick building with wide wooden doors.

On their own, maybe ten years later, the sons stood proudly either side of a long-bodied, open-topped car. Kath pointed at the man on the left.

'Edward. He was killed in the First World War. At Passchendaele. He hadn't had children so the business came straight down our side of the family. George was my great-grandpa.' She tapped the glass over another picture, a man standing with a posse of ten or twelve cross-armed men in shirtsleeves: *You and whose army?*

'In the second war, the factory was making parts so our grandpa had a reserved occupation. He was in the ARP, so he was up on rooftops at night, as well, watching for bombers. This is him in the Sixties, with Dad. And look at Dad in this one.' She pointed at Gerry in a brown suit and cream shirt with long collars. 'Fashion by *The Sweeney.*'

Robin bent her head to look at the last row. In the middle of the three pictures, Josh stood with his dad in the same spot by the wooden doors where his great-grandfather had been pictured with the car eighty-odd years before.

'That was his first day,' said Kath.

He'd been twenty-two, Robin knew; he'd started the summer he'd graduated from Aston, she'd just finished her first year at UCL. He looked so young now but at the time, it had seemed incredibly mature, working, earning a salary, training to take over a business one day. Like his dad and his dad before him, he'd started on the shop floor then moved through each of the various departments, the tool shop, packing, sales, learning it all from the bottom up. In the picture he was smiling broadly, a hand over his eyes against the sun, shirt and jeans. 'He was so excited,' she said. 'I remember.'

'Following in Dad's footsteps,' Kath said. 'Growing the business for the next generation. It's all he wanted to do.'

She'd arranged to meet Maggie at the office so from Edgbaston, Robin drove straight into town. The puny February sun hadn't broken through but there was some light behind the cloud now. For the first time in weeks – since the confrontation with Freshwater, in fact – she felt, if not positive, at least not completely adrift.

From the car park across from the office, she texted Lennie. She'd been asleep when Robin had left; she'd put a guilty kiss on her cheek and slipped out, afraid that if she woke her, she'd miss Kath. It was quarter to nine now, she'd be starting school as Robin typed.

Sorry to sneak out this morning – didn't want to wake you. Good luck today – see you later on. Love you.

When she reached the top floor, legs buzzing from the stairs, Maggie was on a call. She raised her eyebrows and pointed animatedly at the phone: *Got something here.*

Robin listened while she checked West Midlands Police's Twitter feed. Burglaries, pursuit of a stolen car on the M42, an early-morning warrant in Yardley with cannabis and weapons recovered – nothing that seemed relevant to either case. She searched for Corinna, nothing new, then typed in 'Joshua Legge'.

'Were you in the Warwick Parkway area in the early hours of 13 February? Did you see this man?'

The photo was the same one of him by the fire, glass in hand, eyes half closed, the smile more and more vampirical the longer she looked at it. He was barely recognizable as the man she'd just seen on the wall at Russell Road.

'Right, no,' said Maggie behind her, 'that's not how I roll. I gave you my word.'

The tweet had been posted late last night not by West Midlands Police but Warwickshire. In the past, before West Midlands was created, Birmingham had been under Warwickshire's jurisdiction but it was a neighbouring force now, wrapped around the city to the south and south-east. Clearly they were sharing information.

'Of course. Yes. And likewise. You've got my number.' Maggie hung up and sat back in her chair.

'Who was it?'

'Friend of Becca's, if friend's the word. Bloke called Stevo – Steven Cotton. He says he did morphine with her.'

Robin did a double-take. 'Morphine?'

'Started as a curiosity thing, he claims. His gran died and when he was helping clean up her house, he found her medication.'

'Alternative translation: he knew his gran was on painkillers so when she died, he hot-footed it round there. When?'

'She died in June.'

'And Becca got involved how?' Robin pulled out a chair and sat down.

'They bumped into one another when they were out one night. They knew each other from way back but they hadn't seen each other for a while. He told her he had it, she was curious, she went back with him.'

'How did you get this?' Robin gestured at the phone.

'Lucy. She rang about twenty minutes ago. She spoke to him last night, she said, went round to his place. No love lost there – she told him if he didn't speak to us, she'd go to the police instead.'

Robin frowned. 'She didn't mention it at all when I met her.'

'Yeah, she said. But she mentioned that when you spoke to

her, you told her what Valerie said about drugs. Yesterday she spoke to an old school friend who told her Stevo was using. Becca had spent some time with him last summer, Lucy said, so she wondered if two and two made four and went round there to find out.'

'"Spent some time with"?'

'They had a thing for a few weeks. Clearly the drugs were his classy way to get into her knickers. Haven't looked him up yet but I'm willing to bet he wouldn't have fancied his chances otherwise. It was just sex, though, it sounds like – Lucy said Becca likes her boys bad on that side of things. Apparently Harry's a bit of a departure.'

'Did this Stevo say *how* they took it?'

'His gran's stash was pills so they were crushing them then snorting the powder, but they tried injecting later. Just once, he claims, before she kicked him to the kerb. His expression.'

They looked at each other as a new range of possibilities branched around them, cracks in the ice under their feet: had Becca been using, too? Had she overdosed? Was she lying some-where alone, undiscovered? Or maybe she'd been with someone else and they'd panicked.

'Little scrote,' said Maggie. 'If I was Valerie, I'd cut his fucking balls off.'

Maggie rang Nuttall first. Hard drugs were a significant vulner-ability factor for a misper; they'd review Becca's status now. 'He'll raise it at the management meeting this afternoon,' she said, hanging up. 'If they change her status, we'll have to see where that leaves us. In the meantime, on we go.'

'Is this why she needed the job at The Spot? To pay for it? Stevo's granny died in June; she started there in September. How much could his gran have stockpiled anyway?'

'Two jobs, a boyfriend, friends, her mother, social media – you wonder how she'd find the time to get wasted. Though she obviously *was* feeling the pinch time-wise – when I asked if she'd ever seen Becca under the influence, Lucy said she'd actually barely seen her this year. Three times, she said – once when they went to the sales together, like Valerie said, then twice with Harry, cinema and drinks.'

'Has she told *him* about the morphine?' asked Robin.

'No. She's happy to delegate that to us.'

'He knew about Stevo generally, though? That Becca had had a thing with him?'

'She says not.'

'Really? The "besties"?'

'That's what I said. But apparently she kept her flings quiet as far as Harry was concerned. If she was actually going out with someone, she told him, obviously, but not the casual things. She cared about that, Lucy said; she didn't want him to think she was a slapper.'

'Well, you have to hand it to her,' said Robin, 'she's good at information control. Do *we* tell him?'

'Maybe not, if we don't have to. Why hurt him any more?'

On the table between them, Maggie's phone rang again. She looked at the screen then at Robin. 'I'll go in the back office so you can ring Harry. Wish me luck.' She closed the door between them. 'Valerie,' she said. 'How are you doing?'

Robin waited for the squeak of the desk chair then brought up Harry's number. He answered on the second ring. 'Robin. Is there any news?'

'Have you got a moment? You're at the office? Okay. Lucy rang Maggie this morning. I don't know whether she's been in touch with you, too?'

'No.'

159

'That's all right, Maggie said we'd call you.' She took a breath. 'They've been talking to a guy called Stevo – Steven Cotton. Do you know him?'

'*Of* him. I've met him once or twice over the years, not a lot. Why?'

'He says he gave Becca prescription painkillers last summer. Morphine.'

Harry was silent.

'Did you know?'

The panic was gone. When he answered, his voice was flat. 'No.'

'Did you ever see it, do you think? Did you ever see her with pills or did she ever seem out of it? Or anxious?' Silence at the other end. 'Or did you ever get the impression she was trying to hide something?'

'Could you hold on a second?' Sounds of movement then a door closed. He'd moved into the smaller office. 'What do you mean by "out of it"?'

'It'd be similar to heroin, the effects – they're both opioids. In fact, quite often people who start on prescription painkillers move on to heroin because it's easier to get on the street. And cheaper.'

More silence. 'A couple of times,' he said slowly, 'over the summer, late summer, like, August, September, I did think she seemed . . . spacy.' His voice was quieter again. 'Nothing extreme, just, like, somewhere else mentally, you know? Distracted. But actually, she stood us up a couple of times, too – me and Lucy. Once she was supposed to come out and we were sitting in the pub waiting for her and she just didn't show up, no text, didn't answer her phone. She said she'd fallen asleep.'

'How about recently?'

160

'She's been wiped out, sometimes, knackered, but I put it down to her working so much, I didn't think anything of it.'

'Have you seen any physical signs, Harry? On her body.'

Another long pause, then, 'You're asking if she was injecting, aren't you? Is that what you heard?'

'We don't know,' she said. 'I wanted to ask you.'

'I never saw it,' he said. 'But I wouldn't necessarily know if I did. Track marks, that kind of thing – I've seen it on TV. In real life, though, or anything subtle . . . This guy – Stevo. What the *fuck*?'

When Maggie emerged from the back office, she was pulling a whiteboard about six foot by four foot on its long edge. 'God almighty,' she said. 'If it wasn't so early, I'd have a drink.'

'She didn't take it well?'

'She did not.'

Robin helped her slide the board over to the window. 'Where did this come from?'

'Behind the filing cabinets. I don't use it very often but I thought we could put up what we've got so far, make a plan of campaign. Thought an investigation board might make you feel at home. Here, let's rest it on a couple of chairs, for a bit of height – if you grab that one.' She took markers and a lump of white tack out of her pocket then went back to the little office, returning with a handful of print-outs. 'Okay.'

In the centre of the board, she stuck a black-and-white copy of a photograph Valerie had given them. Lucy had taken it last year, she said, May or June, when the girls had done a day trip to London. They'd had lunch in a park, and the photo showed Becca at a picnic table, a big pot of salad in front of her. The sun was shining, and she was wearing a V-neck T-shirt, grey in the copy, pale green in the original, and a chain with a silver feather that hung over her sternum, its tip pointing down into the groove between her breasts. Her sunglasses were pushed back into her hair and you could see she was about to laugh, her lips pressed together in a way that looked urgent. There was a bottle of lemonade in her hand – she had her mouth full and was struggling to swallow before she laughed and sprayed it everywhere. 'That's her,' Valerie had said. 'Her spirit.'

'Friends and associates.' Maggie stuck up smaller pictures of Harry, Lucy and Nick, then drew another line and wrote 'Steven Cotton, aka Stevo'. She circled it, wrote 'morphine' underneath.

On the left side of the board, she wrote 'Hanley's' and 'The Spot' then stood back. 'So.'

'We need to find out how far into it she was, obviously. Where she was getting it if it wasn't from Stevo, who she was doing it *with*, if anyone.'

'Yep.' Maggie wrote, marker squeaking.

'Whether this was why she was working at The Spot – for the money. Or if there was another connection there – someone she was buying from or with.'

'The Spot generally,' Maggie said, turning. 'The past six months since September. So she starts her job there, apparently to start saving for a holiday, but it's a pretty hard-core way of getting a bit of money together, don't you think? Three shifts a week plus the extra ones at Christmas the Aussie barman mentioned – that's a lot when you've got a full-time day job. How much money did she need?'

'Lucy did say she wanted to go somewhere proper.'

'Bali, at that rate.'

'*If* she wasn't spending it as fast as she was earning it.' Robin bit a hangnail at the side of her thumb. 'But I agree – The Spot feels significant. It was why she told Nick she had to break up with him, and the Aussie said the girls were close, right?'

'"Thick as thieves".'

'Yeah. Was she hanging out with them instead of Lucy because of the drugs?'

Maggie was writing quickly.

'I'm also still interested in the fact that Becca wanted to keep the Harry thing secret. Maybe I'm the weirdo here, maybe other people would be as chilled as he claims to be, respecting her decision and all that, but I don't know.'

On the line between him and Becca, Maggie wrote *Secret*. 'Definitely bears further questioning.'

Robin looked at the word. 'Though are we being daft?'

'How so?'

'Was it really true that no one knew? The guy at The Spot, the manager, he said Harry used to come and pick her up sometimes, right, at the end of her shifts? They close at two. Even if they hadn't actually told anyone they were together, you don't pick someone up at two in the morning when you're just an old friend, do you?'

'Unless there's another reason,' said Maggie.

'Like what?'

Robin looked at her. 'Protecting her? Keeping her safe?'

Chapter Twelve

'We've got to tick off a bit of the other stuff,' Maggie'd said when they'd finished. By then, they'd been sitting side by side on the table, feet dangling. 'Becca's the priority, obviously, but the other clients pay the bills and they'll get restive if we let things slide. Given that The Spot's not open 'til this evening, how do you feel about getting some insurance fieldwork done this afternoon? Divide and conquer – work solo, we can cover twice as much?'

'I feel good about it.' She paused. 'Maggie . . .' Sitting there in front of the whiteboard, ideas pinging between them, she'd felt momentarily back in the game.

'Hm?'

'Thank you. Again.'

'For what?'

'Everything. The job – all of this.'

'Oh, give over.' She'd slipped down from the table, brushed off her behind. 'I'm already dreading you sorting your appeal and leaving me. Maybe I won't let you.'

Now, after an hour parked down the street from a nail salon in Ladywood, Robin felt that brief sense of engagement ebbing away, along with any residual body heat. She'd lost sensation in

164

her toes twenty minutes ago. Sod it – she turned the ignition on and cranked the heater up. She'd just have to risk drawing attention to herself, though frankly, she'd be surprised if her target, the co-owner of the salon, would connect a woman in an Audi with her boyfriend's dodgy insurance claim. Possibly she didn't even know about it. Maybe she'd been thrilled when Tony gave her his 5 Series when he traded up, never dreamed he'd reported it stolen and put in a claim for it along with a brand-new set of golf clubs previously unbeknownst to the insurers but nonetheless in the boot, apparently, at the time of the alleged theft. If she really *hadn't* known, Robin hoped she could prove it: she could be looking at a fraud charge otherwise.

Who knew, what did they know, and why: the questions she spent her life asking.

A few years ago, too weak with flu to change the channel, she'd seen a daytime TV programme about a woman who covered large plates with mosaic designs. Through the mental fog, Robin had watched her tweezer in the glass tiles, gluing each one carefully before going back to a heap for another. She hadn't marked out the designs beforehand but worked from a template that the camera hadn't shown, so that only towards the end, as she finished, had the viewer seen fish and reeds and silver eddies in water. It was like her job, Robin had thought, except the pictures *she* was left with were even uglier. And there were no tiles until she'd extracted them one by one from people who, on a scale from hesitant to kill-to-avoid-it, didn't want to give them to her.

She checked her phone again. Just after getting here, she'd texted Lennie to ask how it was going but there'd been no response. Maybe she had a double lesson, hadn't seen it yet.

Why hadn't Corinna told her the factory was struggling? Or had she? Had she, Robin, just missed it? Three or four years ago, around the time the trouble at the factory had started, she now remembered, Rin *had* mentioned issues – customers slow to pay, competition from China – but then she'd stopped talking about it. Was that because Robin had never really engaged? Because she hadn't, she admitted. She hadn't taken it seriously because she thought they'd sort it out. They'd be fine, the factory would be fine, because, in the end, it always had been, hadn't it?

But why hadn't Rin told her about Josh's depression? She'd never even alluded to it. Had he asked her not to out of some ridiculous sense of shame? Surely they were way past that, the three of them? And even if he *had* asked her not to, Corinna knew she could talk to Robin in total confidence.

A buzz on the pay-as-you-go, a text from Maggie: *Nuttall checked back with hospitals: nothing.* Good news, maybe: no one fitting Becca's description had been admitted with an overdose. On the other hand, if she *had* overdosed, she hadn't been brought in.

Movement in the rear-view: a silver 5 Series BMW cruising up the road behind. She kept her eyes down as it passed, looking up again once the driver was out of sight. They hadn't bothered to change the plates. Seconds later, she heard the engine go into reverse, and the woman backed into an empty spot across the road, two car-lengths ahead. Pretending to text, Robin filled the phone with pictures: the car; the woman getting out, pressing the fob, looking back briefly as she tottered across the road to the salon, expensive-looking handbag hooked on her forearm.

She texted Maggie, *Ladywood done.*

Great, came the reply. *Want to try Selly Oak?*

Wilco.

Robin locked the phone and dropped it onto the passenger seat. She fired up the engine, feeling guilty. When Maggie had suggested working solo, she'd jumped at it because it gave her an opportunity. Thursday was one of the two days Ana had picked Peter up from school, Kath had told her, so if normally she would have been with him, maybe she'd be at home now. Catching her might be a challenge otherwise: she seemed to work round the clock, cleaning and cooking somewhere 'til mid-afternoon, babysitting in the evenings, too, quite often, after she'd finished with them. She had a son of her own back in Slovakia who was in a tennis academy; she'd come to the UK to pay for it.

Kath hadn't had Ana's number but she'd had her address in her SatNav: she'd dropped her home from babysitting one night when they'd been out, the four of them, and she'd been the designated driver. They'd got back after midnight, and she hadn't felt comfortable putting Ana on a bus or on her own in an Uber. Robin remembered Gamil, Maggie's friend at the bakery. He'd seen Becca get out of an Uber or a private cab, hadn't he, some time just before dawn in October. She'd looked wobbly – he'd thought she was drunk. Had she been using then? She made a mental note to add it to the board.

From Ladywood, her own SatNav brought her out through Selly Park and Stirchley to a cul-de-sac off Allens Croft Road. She parked round the corner and walked.

At first glance, the close looked pretty decent. It was separated from the main road by a bushy hedge on both sides and several tall trees, another complete row of which formed a backdrop for the houses at the far end. In the summer, it was probably very green. The houses themselves looked decent, too, steep-roofed semi-detached Fifties builds in red brick, patches of front garden shaped and sized according to their position round the tarmac bulb. As Robin got closer, though, the initial impression began to tarnish. One of the houses had been awkwardly converted into flats, two identical front doors jammed side by side and,

167

behind the wall, the garden next door was just a square of cracked concrete knotted with dog shit. A caravan parked further along had had its wandering days.

Ana's house was at the end of the bulb, furthest from the main road. It was mid-afternoon now, just after three o'clock, but the curtains in the ground-floor bay were drawn. Weeds covered the lawn, and a plastic trough of rain-flattened earth by the step was full of groundsel.

The intensely patterned glass in the front door made it hard to be sure, but a moment or two after ringing the bell, Robin thought she saw a shimmer of movement inside. She waited then rang again. Nothing. No movement in the window; the curtains were undisturbed. She glanced around then lifted the letterbox. 'Ana,' she called, 'it's Robin, Corinna's friend. Peter's friend. We've met before.'

Still nothing. Either she'd been mistaken or whoever it was really didn't want to come to the door. She was about to take the alley round to the back when, with a thud, a panel in the window overhead was pushed open. A blonde head leaned out enough just to look down. Ana.

The window shut again and seconds later, there were feet on the stairs. A chain rattled but when the door opened, Robin saw that she'd been fastening it, not taking it off. Ana stood behind it with the same wary expression that Robin had seen on Kath's face earlier, though that had been directed only at her. Ana's pale eyes scanned the close behind her, too.

'Thanks for coming to the door.'

A little nod. 'How did you know I live here?'

'Kath gave me your address. Josh's sister.'

'Is Peter – bad news?'

She loved him, Corinna had told her. 'She doesn't sit there on her phone, she *plays* with him – hours and hours of cards and football and Stardew Valley on the PlayStation. She cooks from scratch for him, too; he sits at the counter and talks to her. He won't eat broccoli when *I* make it, but for Ana . . .'

'No more bad news, no,' Robin said. 'He's the same. Have you been to see him?'

She shook her head. 'No. I want but . . . I'm not the family.'

'But you're a good friend. I can let Will know you want to visit, Corinna's brother; I'm sure they'd be pleased. Or I can give you his number.'

She seemed hesitant. 'Okay. Thank you.'

'Look, Ana, can we talk?'

Raised eyebrows.

'I've got a few questions. I . . .'

She pulled back. 'Questions – why? I already talked to police.'

Robin lowered her voice. 'This is not for the police. It's different – private. I'm trying to find Josh. For Peter's sake – his father. Please.'

Ana hesitated again but then, with another glance out into the close, she slid off the chain and opened the door enough for Robin to slip through.

Inside it was chilly but the air carried the mixed scents of a citrus detergent and something warm and oniony. After the front garden, she'd expected neglect but the place was orderly, the strip of hall carpet old but recently vacuumed, the mail on a little table stacked neatly next to a vase of pink silk peonies. The mirror above it was spotless.

She followed Ana into the kitchen at the back of the house where she was surprised to see another woman of about their age sitting at a small Formica table eating rice and stew. The back of her fleece said *Tesco, Fruit and Veg Team*. 'Marta,' Ana said, 'my friend. She lives here, too. This is Robin, friend of Corinna and Peter.'

169

The woman nodded, solemn. 'We are all sorry. Very sorry.'

'Thanks.'

From the window ledge by the back door, Ana picked up a pack of cigarettes. 'No smoking in the house. We talk outside – okay?'

The back garden was almost entirely shaggy lawn. At the end, about fifteen feet away, a damp bench was pushed back against wooden panel fencing, behind which were the tall leafless trees Robin had seen from the road. Ana stayed on a strip of crazy paving immediately outside the door, pointing at her feet: slippers. She lit a cigarette and blew out a cloud of smoke. Inside the house, Robin saw the other woman bring her plate to the sink by the window. Water gurgled down the drain.

'Is it just the two of you?' she asked. 'You and Marta?'

'Here? No. Four. Four women. Two sisters – they share a room.' She took another puff on the cigarette. 'We're all the same: work, send money home for children and old parents. Sick parents.'

'It must be hard to be away.'

'I miss my son. My mother. But I have friends here. Peter.'

'Visit him, Ana – really. We don't know if he can hear us but if he can, I'm sure he'd like to hear *you*. And see you when he wakes up.'

Ana gave her a frank look, as if to say, don't bullshit me, don't tell me he'll get better if he won't. 'You want to ask questions. You're not police? Corinna said you're police in London.'

'Not any more. We live in Birmingham now. We live with my parents in Hall Green, Lennie's at St Saviour's. I work for a friend – here, look, this is my card.' She took one from her pocket and handed it over. Ana eyed it.

'But coming to see you, this is just me, on my own.'

170

'The police came here in the morning when it happened. I answered all the questions. I don't know anything else.'

'What did they ask you?'

'Why you ask that?' A slight narrowing of the eyes.

'I'm trying to work out what they already know. I have to find out what they *don't* know – what they've missed.'

'Why you don't ask them, if you were police?'

'I was on a different force, they wouldn't tell me anything. And I was fired so they don't trust me.'

Again, the look: don't try and spin me any lines. Then a shrug. 'They asked me, was there trouble in the house? Fighting.'

'What did you say?'

'I said the truth. Two years ago, one year and a half, some fighting but not now, for a long time. It's better. Corinna and Josh – they were . . . good. Strong.'

'Yes. That's why I don't believe what the police think, that Josh did this.'

Ana looked at her but said nothing.

'What were they fighting about, two years ago?'

'They didn't fight with me in the house but I felt . . . In the air – atmosphere? And Peter told me.'

'What did he say?'

'Mum and dad shouting. Doors slamming. He was scared, thought they get divorce – his dad move out to different house, not see him.'

'Did he say what they were fighting about?'

'No.'

'Did he ever tell you about any violence – hitting?'

'No. He said one time Josh throw a glass.'

'At Corinna?'

'No.' She pulled back, looking actually offended. 'On the floor. Just to break it, make big noise.'

171

'Ana, a few weeks ago, my dad said he saw her with a black eye. Is that right?'

'Yes. She had black eye – all . . .' She described a semi-circle with her hand, temple to mid-cheek.

'Did she tell you how she got it?'

'I said to the police when they come second time: she told me she fall on the stairs holding big hard books, from the library.'

'Did that seem right to you?'

'Yes. I didn't see fighting, all happy. She told me stairs and books, I believed her.'

'Did you ever see them fighting with anyone else? Was anyone angry with them or threatening them? Did Corinna or Peter ever seem scared?'

Ana took a long final drag on the cigarette then took it to a plant pot by the step. A sizzle as she dropped it in. 'No. Like I told police, all was fine. Happy family.'

'How about you? Did *you* ever feel scared at the house? Did you ever feel like something was wrong there?'

A hesitation so fleeting Robin almost missed it. Ana shook her head, emphatic. 'No.'

Kevin Young had been one of those kids who got his adult face years ahead of schedule. Christine used to say that you could look at him at ten and know exactly what he was going to look like at forty. At the time, Robin had had no idea what her mother was talking about but when she'd gone on the website this morning and seen the picture of 'Our MD Kevin', she'd remembered straight away. The defined nose above the short upper lip, the chubby cheeks – it was the sort of face that, depending on context, could belong to a Tory MP, smooth and pink, or a pub landlord. For a while in their teens, people had called him Crafty, after the darts player Eric Bristow, the 'Crafty Cockney', whom he actually *had* looked a lot like, even then. 'Fair enough,' he'd said. 'Except I'm not a bloody Cockney and neither's he, now – he lives in Leek, don' he? Up the road.'

Crafty had been an ideal name for Kev. He wasn't at all devious, she'd never known him do anything dishonest, but he'd been naughty in inventive ways. The other boys had traded in things like rubber dog shit and putting worms in people's trainers but Kevin's stuff had always been ingenious – like the time he'd got his dad to distract Mrs Bucknell at drop-off while he rigged an elaborate marble-run down the stacks of books on her desk. It had been brilliant, run around her stapler, the ruler in her pen pot, weights and elastic bands, the whole thing triggered by a length of string he'd attached to the back of her top drawer. Mrs Bucknell's eyes had followed the marble round her desk like a spectator's at doubles tennis. He'd planned it for weeks, he said, when she'd made him demonstrate it to the class.

Kev and his dad, little and large, partners from the off. Kev and his sister Kelley, who was almost exactly a year younger, had been late children, arriving just when Mr Young senior – Morris – and his wife had given up hope, Kev said. As children, they'd had crazy-extravagant parties, always shared because their birthdays were days apart – one year when they'd been eight and nine, or nine and ten, Mr Young had got a mate to set up bumper cars, a shooting range and a candy-floss machine in their back garden. It was like going to a party at Willy Wonka's. Until a few years later, Robin hadn't understood Christine's disapproval about the whole thing or linked it to the muttering to Dennis afterwards about 'gyppos'.

The Youngs weren't gypsies but they weren't petit bourgeois, either, not interested. 'We are what we are,' Mr Young had said, when Kev had passed the eleven-plus but they turned down a place at the grammar school. 'I'm not having that in our family, kids looking down on their parents. My boy's my boy.' So Kev had gone to Savvy's, which was how, five years later, Robin had met Sean Harvey and had fun putting the wind up Christine for a little while. She and Kev had always got on well, shared a sense of humour and an appreciation of boundary-pushing, and because he only lived a few roads away, they'd stayed in touch after she went to the grammar. They'd never so much as kissed, they'd never fancied each other, and then she'd introduced Kev to Corinna. Nothing had ever happened between them, either, but not for lack of trying on Kev's part. Full credit to him, though: when Rin had finally had to give him a definitive 'no', he'd taken it on the chin. 'Out of my league,' he'd said. 'Fair enough.'

Kev's dad had been the second MD of Young's Metals and Kev was the third. The yard was where it had always been, over in Bordesley, the slogan in the wrought-iron arch over the gates – *Make Your Old Metal Young's* – unchanged. Even on the website, however, she'd seen Kev's influence. He might not have gone to the grammar but he'd always been ambitious. The old Portakabin his dad had worked in was gone and in its place was a single-storey office building of some size and – for a scrapyard – style. Inside, there were two receptionists behind the desk. There'd been a lot of talk on the website about overseas partners and services for high-volume business, and the yard was twice as big as she remembered, whatever had been next door back then – a factory, was it? – long gone.

She hadn't known if he'd even recognize her, she hadn't seen him since Rin's wedding, but as she walked across the yard behind the offices, following the receptionists' directions, she saw him notice her then do a double-take. He said a few words to the bloke he'd been talking to then strode across the mud towards her, coat flapping.

'Christ's sake,' he said and put his arms round her. A

174

rib-bending hug and the smell, disconcertingly good, of what was definitely expensive aftershave. The coat was expensive, too, the wool lapel soft against her face. It was like being cuddled by a full-sized, nicely perfumed bear.

He put her down and looked at her. 'Jesus, Rob.'

'You've heard then?'

''Course I have. I'm gutted. That lovely, lovely girl. Can't get my head round it.'

'Me neither.'

'You must be hurting.' He shook his head. She remembered that about him, the way he'd never been ashamed to be frank about emotional stuff, never worried it made him look weak to feel.

'It's like I'm on the moon,' she said.

Another nod. 'How long you been back? I heard you were coming.'

'Less than a week. Sunday. Feels like months, with all this.'

'Yeah. It must do. You don't come back a lot, though, do you? Didn't. When did I even see you last?'

'Rin's wedding.'

'Really? Bloody hell. How's your little girl? She can't be that little any more.'

'Thirteen. She's great. She's at Savvy's, actually, started on Monday.'

'Savvy's?' He looked surprised.

'Moving mid-year – we missed the test for the grammar,' she said with another stab of guilt. As she'd parked the car, she'd had a response from Lennie at last. Two words: *I'm okay.*

'But Savvy's turns out *some* decent people, doesn't it?' she said. 'When did all this happen?' She gestured round her at the enormous yard. Behind them, a field of dead cars stretched as far as the eye could see, supervised by the giant claws that would lift them to the compactors. As she'd come round the side of the offices, she'd seen skip after skip of industrial cast-offs, sheared metal sharp as razor wire. They were standing in a clearing between giant heaps of old radiators and iron spools, lengths of copper pipe and odd lozenge-shaped little tanks.

'Catalytic converters,' he said, following her gaze. 'Oh, we've built it up gradually over the years, expanded next door. We make a good team, me and Dad.'

'He's still working?'

'Oh, yeah. Mum keeps on at him but he'll never retire. We strike a balance – he does as much as he wants, consultant role, you know.' He smiled. 'Mum wants to go on a cruise but I'm trying to convince her mates to take her instead – girls' trip. I think it'd be the death of him, all that sitting around. Either that or he'd be buying up their old liners, making salvage deals left and right. Can't let him loose round the Med – not bloody safe.'

Robin wondered about that. When they were thirteen or fourteen, Morris Young had done time for fencing. The yard was the perfect front for it, of course: plenty of margin for error in the books, lots of cash-in-hand business, at least back then – she'd seen the signs up front about the change in the law. In 2012, it had been made illegal for dealers to buy scrap cash-in-hand, a reaction to the boom in metal theft after the crash of 2008, when people had been dragging in whatever they could get their hands on – copper wiring, drain covers, lead roofs. His dad being away had been the one thing Kev wouldn't talk about, but they'd all seen how it affected him. It had been like a part of him was missing. That had been the only time Morris had been inside, as far as she knew, but the rumours about his connections had died hard back then.

'Who told you I was coming?' she said.

'Rin. I saw her, what, three or four weeks ago? Walked into

a place up town, restaurant, and there she was, her and Josh.'

'How were they? How did they look?'

'Like they always did. Good. They definitely weren't fighting.'

'Had you heard anything about them?'

'Like what?'

'Like, Josh was going under. The business.'

'Yeah, I knew about that.' Matter of fact, no surprise.

'*I* didn't know. Corinna didn't tell me.'

'You serious?'

'So obviously I wondered why not – if there was some reason.'

'Not that I know of.' He put his hands in his pockets and did a sort of turn on his heels, looking round. To anyone watching them, Robin thought, he'd look like a man surveying his domain. 'Between you and me, I knew about it 'cause I helped Josh out a bit.'

'How?'

'Bought his scrap – stainless, largely. He did a big clean-up at the factory, brought down what he had, I gave him a bit of money. Cash. But I don't want you thinking it's something I do, all right? You remember when my dad was inside? Not fuckin' happening to my kids. So it was a one-off, only for him. Well, for her, really, if I'm honest. Never went out a hundred per cent, that candle. They were in a tight spot, I did what I could.'

'Did you lend them any money?'

He shook his head. 'It was just that one deal, a couple of grand. Paid slightly over the odds but, you know, special circumstances, like I said. It's what I could do for them – my thing. What have you heard about a loan, then?'

'It was something Kath said – Josh's sister. She said seven or eight months ago, he mentioned a cash injection. That couldn't have been your cash, could it?'

'No, it was longer ago than that. A couple of years – more, probably, by now. Also, two grand? Helpful, always, but it's not going to stop the tide going out, is it?'

'She's wondering if he went to a shark.'

'And you're here to ask if I've heard anything on the vine.'

She looked at him. 'Yeah.'

'Like I said, it's not fucking happening to my kids. Which means that all this – me – we're legit. No funny business, nothing – apart from that one thing with Josh – off the books. Whatever people want to believe about my dad, *I'm* not connected.'

'Right. And presumably, if Rin told you I was coming back, she told you why?'

'She did.'

'So I'm not connected, either. This – asking some questions, trying to work some things out – is what *I* can do. *My* thing.'

'Right you are, then,' he said.

Chapter Thirteen

From the cab window, the dome of the Central Mosque was lit up white against the night sky. The final prayers of the day must just have finished, and a ribbon of men was unfurling down the pavement, alone or in knots of two or three. Quick, get home, Robin thought, you've got to be back here again before dawn. Not for the first time, she wondered what it was like, living a life so regimented. The feeling of claustrophobia almost over-whelmed her but then she wondered if it might be liberating: when your presence was required five times a day by god, there had to be a limit to how much anyone else could expect of you in the interim.

The pay-as-you-go buzzed in her hand. *'Booth-thing in back room, on right.'*

Half an hour ago, Christine had turned from washing up the dinner things, incredulous. 'Out? *Again?* When are you ever at *home*? It wasn't even light this morning when you left. Poor Elena, if she—'

'I know, it's a lot. But it's work. With Maggie.' She gave her mother a meaningful look – *Remember the secret stuff?* – but if

179

she got it, the idea of a woman in jeopardy apparently didn't mitigate the disruption to her evening.

For her own part, Robin was delighted to go out again. When she'd arrived back at Dunnington Road earlier, Luke's car was parked outside. Maybe he was just popping in, she'd hoped, but no, the dining-room table was set for five and there he was, cosily ensconced at the kitchen counter while Mummy made his favourite roast chicken.

'Natalie gone to Zumba without leaving you any dinner, has she?'

Bitch, he mouthed then looked at Christine with puppy-dog eyes: *See how mean she is to me?*

'Robin,' their mother had said, stern. She'd turned back to the stove but not before giving Luke an undeniable look of sympathy. 'Luke quite often comes over in the week,' she said. 'Whether he wants to or not.' She'd given him another look – this one, if Robin wasn't mistaken, to see if she'd raised a smile. 'Imagine if Lennie left home and never came to see you.'

'Give it a few years and you won't have to,' Luke said, sipping his tea. 'Poor kid. I bet she's counting the days.'

'Well, at least I . . .' Robin had stopped, swallowed the retort and walked away. Luke wasn't worth her emotional energy today. Any day, actually.

She'd found Lennie reading, huddled into a corner of the sofa, feet tucked under. 'Hi lovely.' She'd sat down next to her. 'What's the book?'

Lennie held up her paperback copy of *The Owl Service*, bought a couple of years ago at the Oxfam on Marylebone High Street, dog-eared even then.

'Eighth time or ninth?' Robin asked, trying to put a smile in her voice. At times of crisis, Lennie was a comfort reader, going back to the same handful of books again and again. She must have wanted this one a lot: the boxes of her books, mummified with packing tape, were on the very top shelf in the garage to keep dry.

'Tenth. Maybe.'

'How was school today?'

'Okay. We had PE.'

'What did you play?'

'Netball.'

'How was that?'

'Okay.'

Not quite blood from a stone, Robin had thought, but close. 'Have you had English yet?'

'This morning.'

'Who's your teacher? What books are you doing?'

'One book.' She'd paused. '*Lord of the Flies.*'

Robin's heart had sunk. They'd done that last year at RPG. She thought of the maths homework, too. Would Lennie just be going over stuff she already knew? She'd get bored, lose interest, and this was an important time, thirteen, fourteen; if she disengaged now, she could . . . No – Robin had stopped, told herself to calm down. It was too early to panic and Len liked to work, she'd never had to be compelled. 'So you've got a head start,' she'd said.

Len had shrugged. 'I was up for something new.'

Over dinner, the mother–son love-in had nearly put Robin off her food – it made her sick how Christine pandered to him. *Would you like more potatoes, Lukey? Another beer?* No wonder he was so bloody stunted.

Worse, though, was that – of course – he'd heard her conversation with Len through the wall. 'So how are you doing at Savvy's then, Lennie?' he'd asked through a mouthful of chicken.

181

The one thing you could say for Natalie was that she was a civilizing influence on him.

'Okay. It's only my first week.'

'Must be a bit of a culture shock after that place in London. I looked it up online – very smart. Like bloody Hogwarts, those buildings.'

'Luke,' Dennis had warned.

'What? I'm showing an interest,' he said. 'It must have cost you a fortune, Rob – no wonder you're skint.'

She gave him a scathing look. 'Actually, Lennie got a scholarship. And you went to private school yourself, didn't you?' She'd stopped, the triumphant riposte dying on her tongue. He *had* gone to private school – because he'd failed the eleven-plus for the grammar. Her parents had paid for him to go private precisely to avoid the automatic default: Savvy's.

On the whiteboard this morning, Maggie had tapped *The Spot* then underlined it. 'So, what's going on? Drugs is the obvious question – is someone dealing there?'

'Especially with the club bit upstairs. Though, do you remember,' said Robin, 'when we went in, the manager – David – said he was pissed off the day Becca didn't show up because she was supposed to be doing an event in a private room, a party?'

'Hm.'

'This syndicate he mentioned, the owners – is the place a front for something? Gambling? If they were running illegal betting there, it got out of control, Becca saw or heard something . . .'

'If the police *had* got wind of anything, they'd be taking this more seriously.'

'But if they've managed to keep it on the down-low . . . "I run a tight ship" – remember?'

Maggie'd nodded.

'And the police did go there. He told us. He said they'd wanted to know if she'd had any trouble with the punters. Possible he was trying to deflect us, point us towards the clientele rather than The Spot itself.'

She'd nodded again. 'Yep.' Turning to the board, she wrote *Drugs? Gambling?* 'Right. I'll get on the blower to some of my peeps round and about, see what I hear. Why don't you see what you can find out online? About the owners, too. That word, syndicate – I never like it.'

Robin had spent the rest of the morning waiting for Lorraine's decrepit Dell to load web pages, one by agonizing one. She'd almost been able to feel herself ageing. To think she'd ever moaned about the Met's hardware.

And it wasn't just the hardware. At the Met, she'd have been able to check in a moment whether any of them had previous, but as a private investigator, she had no access to that information. Even to check her own police record, she'd have to apply by post, with copies of her passport and birth certificate. The only way to check someone else's was if you were a company thinking of hiring them for work in health or childcare, and even then you had to be certified.

She'd started the glacial-pace Googling with The Spot itself. The first hit after its own website was a piece in the *Post* from when it opened. The photo showed 'David Lawrence, manager' at the bar with Tom Harris, Rob Wilson and Iain Ferguson, 'three of the directors of New Avon Holdings, the syndicate of friends behind the new venture.' Three suits in three different shades of grey, ties in silver and navy and an ill-advised mauve. Salt-and-pepper hair, softening jowls. The fug of middle-aged-male self-congratulation coming off it had got the back of her throat.

From there, she'd gone to the website for Companies House, where she'd got the other directors' names – there were another three, apparently, six in total – their birthdays and postal addresses. In one of Maggie's A4 notebooks, she'd allotted them a page each then started work. The whole thing was an object lesson in frustration: on top of the agonizing lack of speed, not one of them had an unusual name. Two of the three not pictured were called Steve – Baker and Perry – and the sixth was called Paul Smith, for Christ's sake, which would mean scrolling through hundreds of pages of hits just to get past the fashion designer.

In the end, she'd texted Gid: *Could you run a couple of searches for me? Not Hinton-related, promise.* To her surprise, her phone pinged moments later: *No. And stop asking.*

She'd decided to look on the bright side: at least he hadn't blocked her number. She'd begun to wonder.

There was a man on the door this time, headset and all; she felt his eyes on her before she was even out of the cab. When she reached the front of the line outside, however, his frank up-and-down was followed by a brief nod. If he'd been told to look out for her, he hadn't recognized her. Or he had, and he'd been told to let her in.

He opened the door on a wall of noise. It was just before ten, Thursday night, and the front bar looked like a rush-hour Tube carriage, people crammed in back to back, bags between their feet, drinks held at shoulder level to give them a fighting chance. At the bar itself, the crowd was four or five deep, everyone yelling to get themselves heard. Some were still in office gear, straight from work, others dressed for the night in jeans and shirts or strappy tops. A perfume cloud hung in the air, people out to get lucky.

Five bar staff tonight: the Aussie they'd talked to, Justin, plus two other blokes and two women, all in their early to mid-twenties, all wearing the navy shirts, all good-looking. She took a line through the crowd that looped her far enough away to make it hard for Justin to see her, and edged her way through to the back room, dodging drinks and bags, catching snippets of bellowed conversation: 'And I said to her, you've got to tell her it's not on; she just can't do that, who does she think she is?'; 'You going next Saturday, mate?'

Maggie had stayed in town so she'd sent the cab for Robin. When she'd phoned to tell her, they'd had a brief catch-up. She'd spoken to two contacts on the city centre team, she said, a sergeant and a PC, neither of whom had heard rumours about anything illegal going on here. She'd also spoken to a friend, Sara Kettleborough, who was a journalist at the *Post*. 'Word is, it's kosher, she says. Last year, apparently, the manager found out that one of their weekend doormen had a little sideline in blow and fired him immediately, called the cops. Same for a couple of punters they caught with pills upstairs. Zero tolerance.'

'*Methinks the lady doth protest too much?* Deliberate tactic, so they look lily-white?'

'Maybe. Either way, it doesn't get us any further.'

It was the same with the syndicate so far. Via Google, she'd managed to glean details on two of them, Iain Ferguson and Steve Perry, both of whom had decent legitimate income sources, Ferguson being an estate agent and Perry owning a nursery out near Evesham – plants, not babies. Perry had organized a sponsored walk of the Cotswold Way last summer and in 2014, Iain Ferguson had run the London marathon and raised twenty-three thousand for the hospice where his father had died. The photo in the *Dudley News* showed him and his twin daughters, aged ten, posing outside with a giant cheque. If either he or Perry had had trouble with the law, they'd managed to keep it off the Internet.

She hovered a second on the threshold of the back room, locating Maggie in a nook on the right as advertised, then plotting a path that avoided the three waiting staff she could see. All were young women, all dressed in tight-fitting black under long white butcher's aprons. This room was packed, too, but with everyone at tables, minus a bar, plus soft furnishings, it was a degree or two quieter, a little easier to navigate. She glanced around as she made her way over – couples, groups of friends in their twenties and thirties, a table of three blokes in their forties who looked slightly out of their element, possibly on a post-divorce pick-up mission. At another table, a guy of about thirty-five was drinking with two much younger women. He was moderately attractive, light brown hair cut almost as short as his stubble, a black leather biker jacket that looked expensive. The girls were both bottle-blonde and pretty in an over-made-up way, eyebrows plucked to near-extinction. As Robin passed, the man made a joke she didn't quite hear and both of them laughed as if something depended on it.

A candle in a green glass cast Maggie in a witchy half-light. 'I've just ordered a glass of vino,' she said as Robin sat down. 'And that trio of sliders.'

'Haven't you eaten? It's nearly ten.'

'Oh, I've had *dinner*,' she said, dismissive. 'Thanks for the Ladywood pics earlier, by the way. How did you get on in Selly Oak?'

'Nothing,' said Robin, full of guilt. 'No-show.'

'Happens all the time. As you know. Glass of wine?' She held up a hand and caught the attention of the waitress, who came straight over.

186

'Good evening. What would you like?'

What was her accent, Robin wondered, Italian? She was eighteen or nineteen and very pretty, with large wide-set brown eyes under a pale forehead and a full lower lip. Her hair was in a graceful, plaited kind of up-do, as if she'd come direct to her shift from a Renaissance fresco.

'Red? Your friend ordered the Malbec. Would you like the same one?'

'Yes, that's fine. Thanks.'

Maggie waited until she'd retreated. 'So,' she said quietly, shifting closer. 'Nuttall called just after I spoke to you. They're *not* changing Becca's status.'

'Really?' Robin frowned.

'I know. Other more pressing cases, resources, the usual. He'll keep checking in with us and obviously we'll let him know anything pertinent ASAP.'

'How did Valerie take it?'

'I haven't told her. She knows I've told him about the pain-killers but not that they reviewed her status. What good would it do? I think it's because *she* said she didn't know about it, that Becca wasn't off her face all the time, that they can justify stalling.'

'How long have you been here? Seen anything?'

Maggie tipped her head from side to side. 'About ten minutes. Keeping my eyes open.'

'Guy over there with the girls.'

'What are you thinking?'

'Nothing, really. Could be posing as some kind of "modelling" scout? But probably just a common-or-garden douchebag. Should we try and get a look upstairs?'

'Definitely, if we get a chance. Speaking of mothers, by the way, I just had a narky text from yours.'

187

'You're kidding me.'

'No. And before you say anything, this time I think she *was* pissed off I was dragging you out again.' She glanced at a waitress with dyed pink-and-silver hair cut into a fringed bob, waited until she'd passed. 'But she's worried about Lennie, too.'

'I know. Which is reasonable. I hate being so absent. Even when I'm there – mentally, you know.'

'I was thinking, unless something urgent comes up, why don't you take the afternoon off tomorrow? Friday – go and meet her from school, do something together.'

'She doesn't like it,' Robin said before she'd even consciously thought it. 'Savvy's.'

'She told you?'

'No. She wouldn't want to make me feel bad.'

'Hm. Well, I wouldn't worry yet, it's so early. I'm surprised she's even going this week.'

'She was adamant. I told her she could take the week off, start again on Monday, but she wouldn't.'

'How strange.'

Robin made a face: *ha ha.*

'You know,' Maggie said, turning the candle between her fingers, 'there's a difference between dwelling and giving yourself a chance to acknowledge that something major's happened in your life.'

'I *have* acknowledged it.'

Maggie's eyebrows flicked up, sceptical.

The waitress arrived and carefully unloaded the glasses from her little tray. 'Here you are.'

'Where are you from?' Robin asked. 'I'm trying to place your accent.'

'Milano. Italy.'

'Ah. Nice.'

188

Maggie waited until she'd gone again. 'Don't draw attention to us 'til we've had the sliders, will you? I've been thinking about them since Tuesday. But going back to Lennie – seriously, her feet can't have touched the ground. It's too much for anyone to process, let alone at thirteen. Give her a chance on the school front, she'll start to settle in.'

'I don't fucking *want* her to settle in.' It burst out, sounding way more hostile than she would have chosen.

Maggie looked at her, eyebrows now all the way up.

'I'm sorry. I don't mean *here* – Birmingham.'

'Yeah, you do.' She sipped her wine.

'Maggie, I . . .'

'You can't always be in control, Robin. Sometimes things happen. What you've got to do is find a way to live, be comfortable – or at least not constantly chafing against it all – until you can sort things out.'

'But . . .'

Maggie put a hand up, *Wait*. 'Nothing's forever. Take some time now to get your breath back, recuperate a bit.'

The waitress returned, bearing the sliders. 'Gorgeous,' said Maggie, eyes following them down to the table.

'They're very good – my favourite,' the girl said.

'What brings you to Birmingham?' asked Robin.

'I'm sorry?'

'Why are you in Birmingham? I'd rather be in Milan, given the choice.'

'Oh, no – Birmingham's good. I like it here. I'm studying – I'm doing an exchange programme, to improve my English.'

'It sounds very good already.'

She smiled. 'Thank you.'

Maggie shoved the second half of the little burger into her mouth.

189

'How long have you been working here?' Robin asked. 'The Spot, I mean.'

'Since the summer.'

'You like it?'

'Yes. It's a good place, nice people.'

Over the girl's shoulder, Robin saw that the silver-haired girl had paused by the serving station and was watching them. She had a sudden sense that their time might be limited. 'Do you know Becca Woodson?' she said.

Instantly the girl's face turned serious. 'Becca? Yes. You know her?'

'You know she's missing?'

'Yes, of course. We're all very . . . stressed. Worried. How do you know her?'

'We're helping her mother, trying to work out where she might be. We want to find out if anything was worrying her – if she had any problems. Did she ever mention anything like that to you?'

The girl shook her head.

'She had a boyfriend, right? You met him?'

'Boyfriend? No. She had a friend, Harry, but I don't think . . .'

'Did she ever have any trouble here, with other men? She wasn't frightened of anyone, that you know about? Scared? Customers or maybe someone more directly involved here . . .'

The silver-haired woman had put her plates down and was heading their way.

'God's sake,' said Maggie under her breath. 'Give me indigestion, why don't you?'

'Hi there, is everything all right?'

She was twenty-six or -seven, Robin guessed, slim in her tight-fitting black gear, hands armoured with silver rings, nose pierced with a glinting pink stud clearly chosen to match the pink strands that framed her hair, the silver-grey bulk of which made her look strange and other-worldly, as if she came from a future where people had worked out how to get old without getting wrinkles. Local or local-ish, by the accent. 'Cecilia?'

'They're friends of Becca,' said their waitress, 'trying to help her mother.'

'That's right,' Maggie said. 'You know her, obviously – she worked here?'

'Of course, yeah. How can we help?'

Less a genuine question than a veiled *Get lost* but Maggie feigned blithe unawareness and explained.

'You were in yesterday, weren't you?' The woman shifted her weight to the other foot. 'David said. You're investigators.'

Again Maggie ignored the tone. 'So he told you the kind of thing we're trying to find out? It's really only background. Just if anyone here thought there was anything going on with her, anything bothering her. Did she have any issues with alcohol, that you know of, or . . .'

'Didn't he talk to you about this yesterday?'

'Briefly, yeah, but—'

'He's in now, I'll get him.'

'Well, that's torn it,' Maggie said *sotto voce*, watching her weave quickly away. 'Bugger.'

A minute or so later, the woman reappeared, bringing David with her. Another black sweater, this one slightly V-necked, black jeans, the black glasses – again more French graphic designer or architect than Birmingham city-centre club manager.

No handshake today. 'May I?' He pulled out the chair on the opposite side of the table and sat down. 'So you're back. Is there any news?'

'Unfortunately, no.'

191

'Can we see that as good news? In a way?'

Maggie tipped her head. 'If you want. I don't think we can see it as anything at the moment. As I said to . . . ?'

'Lisa,' said the woman now hovering at his shoulder.

'To Lisa, this is really just another fishing expedition; we haven't got much further since we spoke yesterday. But you mentioned then that Becca had good friends here, especially among the other girls.'

The manager looked at Lisa. 'Yes, that's true,' she said.

'Was there anyone she was particularly close to, would you say?' Robin asked. 'Someone she might have confided in?'

'No,' said David.

'Tarryn,' said Lisa.

Robin looked between them.

'She's not on tonight,' he said. 'Tarryn's Aussie, she's here travelling. She's taken a few days off. Edinburgh, is it, this time?' Again he looked at Lisa.

'Yes,' she said. 'I'm section head in the back room, so . . . It's what she does – works extra shifts and saves up a bit then puts her time off together and visits a new city. She's been more places in the UK than I have. *I've* never been to Edinburgh.' She looked at David as if it were his fault. 'Or Liverpool. That's where she went last time.'

'When did she leave?' asked Robin.

'Monday?' said David.

Lisa nodded.

'Do you have a number for her?'

'Of course,' he said, 'but if you're asking for it, the answer's no. I'm not going to start handing out employee information to anyone who's not police. I'll also ask you not to come in again like this. We're a business, you can see how busy we are, it's disruptive, and it's intimidating for my staff. I don't want them

192

or anyone else thinking that whatever's happened to Becca is connected to The Spot. All right?' He looked at their glasses and Maggie's burger plate, empty now bar the salad garnish. 'These are on us. Lisa'll close your tab.'

When she got home, Dennis was up again. He silenced the TV as she dropped onto the sofa. 'How'd you get on, love?'

'All right.'

'Maggie's got a lot of work on at the moment, hasn't she?'

'Yeah. I'm surprised she's managed on her own 'til now.'

'Well, as you know, she's a very competent woman.' Her dad had always been frank in his admiration of Maggie, which had confused Robin when she was younger. Didn't Christine mind? Didn't she feel threatened, Maggie being different to her in basically every way? *She'd* have read criticism into his praise of someone so opposite. The pair of them, Dennis and Maggie, were far more alike than he and her mother. On bad days, she'd wondered what life would have been like if Maggie had actually *been* her mother. As a child, without Christine's restraining hand, she'd have been twice the size, for sure; Maggie and Dennis were a bad enough influence on each other, goading each other on to second helpings and desserts. God knows what they would have fed a child, left to their own devices.

'Speaking of which,' he said now, 'competent women, I mean – I wanted to say, go a bit easier on Luke, will you?'

'What?'

'Your mother said you were at each other's throats again from the moment you walked in tonight. You're too old for this behaviour – you're thirty-five, love.'

'He's thirty-*seven*.'

'Come on, you're making my point for me. *Both* of you are too old but I'm asking *you* to be the bigger person.'

193

'Why?' Petulant-sounding, even to herself.

'Because you are,' he said, simply. 'Or you could be.'

For a moment Robin was lost for words.

'Think about it. Do you think it's easy for Luke, being your brother?'

'How hard can it be? I've barely been here for the past decade and a half.'

'That's probably not a good thing as far as he's concerned, whatever you might think. And look at it from his point of view – he could say that you've spent your whole life showing him up: you went to the grammar, university, you've got a great career; he's . . .'

'*Had* a great career.'

Dennis gave her a look. 'And you've got Lennie.'

'He's got Natalie. Though that's not necessarily a win, is it?'

He shook his head. 'No. Stop it. I'm asking you to be kinder to him. If not for his sake, then for mine.' He turned back to the TV for a moment then picked up the remote again and turned it all the way off. 'Also, I've been thinking. I've got a little pension that'll mature next month, on my birthday, and—'

'No.'

He held up a hand. 'I know you're working all hours with Maggie to get some money together but why don't you let me help you out, just this once? It would only be speeding things up, just get it all moving a bit quicker. You could get your own place, start working on—'

'I can't,' she said. 'I can't take your money.'

'So don't *take* it – think of it as a loan, pay me back when you can.'

'Dad. I appreciate it, really, but I can't. I need to sort this out myself.'

He sighed. 'Well, if you change your mind, you know where

I am.' He stood up and turned to plump the cushion, setting it back in the chair the right way up, zip side hidden, straight. 'One other thing,' he said. 'I know you think your mother's some sort of indomitable force but she's not, you know. She's a human being, too. Fallible and vulnerable, just like the rest of us. Will you try and remember that? Give her a chance. For me?'

As she cleaned her teeth, Robin stared at her reflection in the mirror and was punched by a fist of memory so sudden and hard she choked.

They'd been standing just here, side by side, she and Corinna, getting ready for the party at Monica's house to celebrate the end of A-levels. It was June and hot, they'd been out in the park all day getting strap marks and slightly drunk on white wine they'd decanted into a thermos, demob happy, giddy about the future that had just yawned open in front of them, limitless in its school-free liberty.

Rin had elbowed her out of the way to do her cat's eyes and, laughing, she'd elbowed her back, bodging her arm so that Rin had drawn a big whisker of kohl into her hairline. They'd fallen about, laughing like lunatics until Luke, sour-faced, came to make sure they weren't laughing at him. After he'd gone, Rin had caught her eye in the mirror. She'd tipped her head sideways until it had bumped against Robin's. *'Love you, you know.'*

She'd just rolled her eyes.

Now she looked at the space beside her and saw the reflection of the pale pink wall and the thermo-nuclear heated towel rail behind her. Corinna was gone.

She swiped her eyes as the grief was overtaken by anger.

Why didn't you tell me, Rin? What could be so bad you couldn't tell me?

Something. Whatever Josh had been involved in, it had been so bad, so shaming, they'd kept it secret even from her, the person who'd kept *their* secret, the three of theirs, for nearly twenty years.

Chapter Fourteen

Breakfast on the fly didn't happen at Dunnington Road. As kids, she and Luke had come down every day to find the kitchen table laid, butter in a dish, the tea already brewing. In winter, Christine, messianic about hot food, had done them porridge or a boiled egg with buttered soldiers. Seeing the one she'd made for Lennie this morning caused Robin a stab of feeling, not all of whose strands she could identify. Guilt and frustration, obviously – yes, *she* should have made Len breakfast – but there was something painful, too: Lennie had Robin's old egg cup, a stretch of china wall with Humpty's two stripy legs dangling, the cup part formed by the top of his trousers.

Because of the late finish, Maggie had told her to come in at ten. 'Great, so I'll drop Len off,' said Dennis. 'You and your Mum can have a coffee before you go, Robin.'

She opened her mouth but was silenced by a look. *For me.*

Hard to know who was more uncomfortable. She assumed her mother would sit back down to finish her toast but after seeing Lennie and Dennis off, she chucked it in the bin and started clearing the table at warp speed, as if now her husband was gone, her own right to eat had expired. The milk was back

197

in the fridge, jam in the cupboard, taps running before Robin could carry a pair of plates to the sink. 'She makes me feel so lumbering,' she remembered telling Rin. 'Like some kind of . . . pachyderm.'

Christine washed and Robin dried, the draining board filling faster than she could clear it. On the windowsill was a vase of daffodils, new since yesterday. 'Those are nice,' she said to break the silence. 'Bright.'

'I thought we all needed something hopeful-looking.'

Robin turned, her hand reaching for the cupboard automatically, the order of the house so deeply ingrained in her that, even now, sixteen years later, she had a whole neural pathway for her parents' toast rack.

Her mother carefully cleaned the egg cup, rinsed it then handed it to her.

'Gran gave me this for Easter years ago. You had it all this time?'

'You never said you wanted it, so . . .'

'No, I mean, you kept it. You didn't throw it away.'

'I wouldn't.' Christine looked startled. 'It's yours.'

'You don't have to keep stuff if it's cluttering up your house.'

Her mother gave her a strange look, as if she were being deliberately thick, then plunged a pan into the water. Puzzled, Robin turned and put Humpty back where he'd always lived, next to Luke's egg cup, which was shaped like the bottom half of a chicken, a white cup supported by claw-like yellow feet. The strange, tender feeling still lingered, and to get rid of it, she thought of getting his cup out, asking Christine if it reminded her of Natalie. But then, she thought, even if it did, her mother wouldn't be mean enough to say so. Unlike her.

Christine pulled the plug, rinsed the sponge and started cleaning the work surface in neat stripes.

She's a human being, too. Will you try and remember that?

She should try and talk to her, shouldn't she? That's what people did with their mothers, shared what was on their minds.

Give her a chance.

'Mum,' she said, 'I don't think Len likes Savvy's. Has she mentioned it to you?'

Christine tapped the toaster and swept the fallen crumbs into her cupped hand. 'No. She's more likely to talk to you, though, isn't she?'

'I don't know. Normally, yes, but in this case, I'm worried she doesn't want to make me feel bad.' A swoop in her stomach at the leap of faith: usually she'd do anything to conceal vulnerability from her mother.

'Well, it must be very hard for her, don't you think? Going from that lovely school with playing fields and a swimming pool to an inner-city comp? It's not much above a sink school, really, Savvy's. That's why we had to send Luke private, even though it meant a lot of sacrifices.'

Robin thought of Kev in the middle of his enormous scrapyard, king of every rusting heap he surveyed. 'They do have successes, though, Savvy's. Kevin Young . . .'

'Kevin Young had a family business to go into.'

She took a deep breath. 'That's true. But he's grown it – it's huge now.'

Christine said nothing, her back turned as she straightened the salt and pepper grinders, scrubbed at a spot Robin couldn't see.

In for a penny. 'What would you do, if you were me?'

A pause, unremarkable unless you'd seen it a hundred times before. Her mother seemed to gather herself, as if she were drawing on a malign energy source, undergoing a transformation. When she turned, her eyes were hard. '*I* wouldn't be in the situation in the first place,' she said. 'The job I can't talk about but Adrian – we thought he was a nice man. The twice you let us meet him.'

'Yes, I know. He is.'

'What are you looking for, Robin? That's what I don't understand. Wasn't he good enough for you?'

Why do you think you deserve better? What makes you so special?

'He's good-looking, he's gentlemanly. And he loves Lennie, obviously.'

Robin thanked god she'd told no one bar Rin what he'd said about adoption. Christ, if her mother knew.

'He's got a good job, hasn't he?' said Christine. 'Well paid?'

'What's that got to do with anything?'

'If you'd got married, he could have helped with the school fees. And you wouldn't have had to move back here at all; you'd be living with him, wouldn't you? Elena said he's got a lovely house, a garden, and—'

Robin felt blood rush to her face. 'What are you suggesting, Mum? Apart from that this is all my fault.'

'I'm not *suggesting* it's your fault, Robin. Who else's fault could it be?'

For a moment, she didn't trust herself to speak. Yes, of course it was her bloody fault. But again, when you were an actual agent in the world, that was how it worked: you made the decisions and you lived with them; good or bad, they were yours. Much easier to let someone else take responsibility. 'So,' she said, 'you think I should have married Adrian to bankroll my life? To get a house and have him pay my child's school fees?'

'Why do you have to do that? Why do you have to make everything sound so . . . vile?' her mother hissed. 'He loves Lennie – don't you think he might have *liked* to have done that for her, got pleasure from it? Don't you think he might have enjoyed sharing his life with you both? But no, you *don't* think like that, do you? It's all you, you, you – what *you* can achieve, how *you* can do it all by yourself.'

'So I should have sold myself, you're saying? Done a deal? Let him pay for everything because he loves me. Isn't that prostitution? Safely middle-class, socially acceptable prostitution.'

They stared at each other, Robin's chest burning with feeling. So much she wanted to say, to ask: *I've worked so hard, Mum, to provide for Lennie, to make a success of things. To prove to her that we – women – can. Even if you disapproved when I had her, isn't that something? An achievement? Aren't you proud of me at all?*

Her mother huffed, a short jet of air from the nose, then turned her back.

'Go to work, Robin. Please.'

Five minutes later on Wake Green Road, Robin stopped the car and rested her forehead on the steering wheel. Her head was pounding, the start of a monster headache. She took a couple of Anadin with a swig of stale-tasting water from a bottle in the door. Screwing the lid on, she saw pronounced veins in the backs of her hands. Maybe she'd have a stroke – that felt like a logical next development.

She had to get out of Dunnington Road, she couldn't live like this. But how? She couldn't take Dennis's pension, even if it *was* a loan, even if, as she suspected, he'd laid a breadcrumb trail of little pensions all the way through his sixties. At her age, taking her dad's money wasn't much better than taking Adrian's. But what other options did she have? Could she get a bank loan at this point? Perhaps if she asked Maggie to support an application, confirm that she was employed and . . .

201

She stopped suddenly. Corinna had offered to lend her money, too, hadn't she? That hungover day in London, she'd offered to lend her the deposit on a place.

'No, don't get funny, I'd like to. I'll even charge you interest if it would make you feel better.'

A month's rent. Or a month and a half. How could she do that if she and Josh were broke?

Had she had money salted away? Rin, who'd grown up with very little, was careful. Saving was so second nature to her, she hadn't thought that Robin wouldn't do it. But no – when Josh had stopped paying himself, Kath said, they'd lived on Rin's salary and her savings. Given how much he hated laying people off, they surely would have used those up first. Unless she had a secret account – but then, why would she?

How much had Rin earned? Since Peter was four or five, she'd been selling advertising space for a group that published local magazines. Her base pay was modest, she said; most of it was commission. She'd liked the challenge, claimed it kept things interesting. She'd never told Robin how much the commission came to but it couldn't be a lot. They weren't talking *Vogue* here – the magazines had names like *Solihull Life* and were distributed free around dentists' offices and hotel lobbies. The advertisers were local restaurants, salons, florists. She'd be surprised if Rin had made thirty grand. Which sounded all right, liveable-on, but as the sole income for three people, the mortgage on the snowman house, two cars, childcare? Forget it.

What about the supposed loan against the machines? That would be just like Corinna, lending money from a loan *she'd* needed. If you were part of her gang, she'd give you her shoes even if she was standing on hot coals, too. But the loan had been Easter last year, ten months or so ago – how much had it been?

She did some rough calculations. Say Rin *had* earned thirty thousand. After tax and National Insurance, that would be somewhere around twenty, roughly, say twenty-two for the sake of argument. Less than two thousand pounds a month take-home, either way. Would that even cover their mortgage?

She'd got Ana's number yesterday on the pretext of arranging a visit to Peter but she rang it now, doing more calculations while she waited. She didn't know the going rate in Birmingham but in London she'd paid Naomi seven pounds an hour for after-school with Lennie. Naomi was sixteen so say ten an hour, for an adult. Two afternoons – three o'clock 'til seven, at a guess. Eight hours at ten pounds an hour – £320 a month. Even at eight pounds, it was £256, a significant chunk of two grand.

And then there was evening babysitting. They'd gone out to dinner at least once with Kath and Gareth, and Kev had seen them out on their own, too. Quite apart from the babysitting, there was the cost of the dinner itself. Given Kev's set-up these days, Robin doubted the place had been a dive, either.

'Hello?' Ana's voice sounded distrustful, reminding Robin of her wariness at the door.

'Hi, it's Robin,' she said. 'I haven't spoken to Will yet but I'll let you know as soon as I do, okay?' She'd have to text him next. 'I've just got a couple of other questions.' Don't ask if it's okay; why give her the chance to say no? 'You only worked for them two afternoons a week now, is that right? Two for them, three for another family. They'd cut your hours?'

'Yes, from September, two afternoons. In the holidays a bit more. When no school.'

'Did they pay you on time?'

'Why you ask?'

'I've heard that Josh's business wasn't doing so well – I wondered if they were struggling for money.'

'They paid me on time,' she said, defensive, as if Robin were throwing shade on their honour. 'Always.'

'How? I mean, did they transfer money to your account or . . .'

'Cash,' she said. 'They paid me in cash. Okay?'

In the office, they sat on the table looking at the board. Maggie drained the last cold mouthful of her coffee.

'I'm sorry,' Robin said.

'For what?'

'Diving in too quickly, drawing attention before we could get more of a sense of the place. Or go upstairs.'

Maggie shrugged. 'We got a couple of new things.' She pointed the marker at *The Spot*, under which it now said *Tarin?*

'One thing, technically.'

'Well . . .'

'Though,' Robin said, 'we also got confirmation of a kind, didn't we?'

'How so?'

'Both times we started talking, we were referred to the manager, David, almost straight away. The barman did it and Lisa did last night. Also, she was watching us. As soon as we exchanged more than a few words with our waitress, she was over.'

'Hm.' Maggie was listening.

'Policy, do you think? Everything through him? And is this since Becca disappeared or has it always been like it? Either way, what does that tell us? I mean, it's just a bar, isn't it, a club, not the bloody Foreign Office.'

'Though you could be forgiven for thinking that,' Maggie replied, dry. 'The Italian, two Australians that we know of.'

'Seriously, though, Maggie, why does this "ship" have to be so tight?'

* * *

'Harry? It's Robin.'

'Hi.' Trepidation – what was she going to tell him now?

'It's okay,' she said, 'nothing alarming. I wanted to ask you about a woman called Tarin. She works at The Spot, we heard she and Becca were friends. Have you met her?'

'Yeah, quite a few times. She's cool, Becca likes her a lot. She's Aussie, two or three years older than us. She's over here travelling.'

'You wouldn't have her number?'

'I don't, sorry.'

'Do you know her surname?'

'No.' A pause. 'Why?'

'Nothing specific, we're just following up with anyone Becca might have talked to recently. Tarin's away at the moment, taking a few days off, and obviously The Spot don't give out staff numbers.'

'Try Instagram – she's got an account for her travelling pictures, she showed us one night. And actually, Becca showed me some of them too, independently.'

'Do you know what her handle is?'

'I don't. But they followed each other, if that helps.'

'Okay, great. Thanks. Harry – one other quick thing. You used to go and pick Becca up from The Spot, is that right? When she finished – quite late?'

'Two o'clock, when they closed. Friday and Saturday, mostly. We'd have a drink then she'd come and stay at mine.'

'So you picked her up so you could spend the night together? No other reason?'

'Like what?'

'You weren't ever worried about her safety at The Spot?'

'Why?' His voice quickened. 'Should I have been?'

'Not as far as we know at this stage but we need to cover all the angles.'

'I didn't like her finishing so late,' he said. 'I liked picking her up because I didn't feel great about her getting Ubers on her own. Even Ubers were a compromise – she wanted to get the night bus. God – was I worrying about how she got home and all the time, the danger was *there?*'

Punch-drunk as she'd been when she'd trawled Becca's social media, Robin did now have vague memories of cross-referencing an Australian woman's account somewhere. She found Becca's page and went through the pictures one by one, scanning the comments for a likely-sounding username. A photo dated October showed Becca and Lucy at Sarehole Mill, Hall Green, according to the location stamp. *Birthday outing to Middle Earth – love a Hobbit!* Becca had written. *@OzTarrynTravels – The place I was telling you about, Tolkien's inspiration!* Bingo.

Robin clicked on the tag. @OzTarryn's circular profile picture showed a cold-looking but grinning woman with a surfboard on what looked like a beach in North Devon. Grey water, grey sky, leaden sand – Bondi, eat your heart out. *Aussie girl taking time out from the 9 – 5 to see the world,* said the bio line. *Current location: Workshop of the World, UK, aka Land of the Ancestors.*

'Got her,' she said to Maggie.

The first two rows of pictures, posted only an hour earlier, were location-stamped Edinburgh, and a couple would have been recognizable anyway: the castle on its crag, a view down the Royal Mile. One posted yesterday showed a slightly tatty-looking café with a jumble of wooden tables and wheelback chairs. *Where it all began,* Tarryn had written. *The Elephant House! Birthplace of Harry Potter!* Never met an exclamation mark they didn't like, these girls. Robin ran her eyes down the comments hoping for some return fantasy-fiction fan-girling but alas, no @BeccaWoods95.

'She's not *in* any of these Edinburgh pictures, is she?' asked Maggie, over her shoulder.

'No. Would have been nice, wouldn't it, to show Valerie Becca posing around among the bagpipes with her new bezzie mate?'

'Can we get in touch with her on here? Tarryn?'

'If I create an account. I'll do it now.'

In the couple of minutes it took to do that and come back to the page, another picture had appeared, this one an iron cage over a grave in a moodily twilit churchyard. *Last night at Greyfriars Kirk . . . Mortsafe – to keep out the body-snatchers!*

Robin clicked to comment straight away – maybe she could catch her online. *Hi*, she wrote, *I'm trying to get in touch with @BeccaWoods95 and heard that you're friends. Really appreciate if you could DM or email me. Thanks.* She gave the Hotmail address she kept for mailing lists and online shopping and opened that account in a new window.

While she waited, she went back to her deep dive on the syndicate of investors. After an agonizing process cross-referencing Facebook and the photograph from the *Post*, she had isolated the right Tom Harris from about a hundred others and identified him as the owner of a chain of seven local shoe shops: Droitwich, Shirley, Perry Barr, Redditch. He was forty-nine, went to Catholic school then university in Lancaster before moving back to Brum and opening the first shop. What had made him choose shoes, of all things? Like Iain Ferguson and Steve Perry yesterday, though, he seemed to be an upstanding member of society; three of the four little articles she found were to do with the twenty pairs of shoes he gave away in September each year to children whose parents would otherwise struggle to afford them.

The Dell's fan laboured as she toggled back to Hotmail then

Instagram. Nothing from Tarryn yet though there'd been no new pictures since the mortsafe, either.

Robin turned to Steve Baker's page in her book with a sinking feeling. Steve Baker – for crying out loud. To torment herself, she typed the name into Facebook and scrolled through screen after screen after screen of hits. This time she didn't even have a photograph. Without much hope, she Googled the name and the first line of the address she'd got from Companies House. To her frank astonishment, up came a link to a Facebook page dedicated to campaigning Birmingham City Council for a pedestrian crossing. Baker and his wife, Frances, were tagged in a photograph showing a petition with pages of signatures. From what Robin could tell, the son of a family friend, a teenager, had been hit by a car while crossing their road.

She clicked through to Baker's own page. He was younger than the three who'd been pictured in the *Post*, not much older than her, probably – yes, born 1979 said his profile. KES then Durham for university, and now he was a property lawyer. She scrolled down through pictures of him, Frances and their two young daughters at Christmas and in Halloween costumes, on a beach holiday in Corsica. Below those was a large group photograph, a crowd of men in suits all looking up towards the camera, congregants before a pulpit. *Class of '97 reunion!*

Robin stopped. Josh had gone to KES. He'd been three academic years ahead of her and Corinna, and they'd left Camp Hill in 2000. And he'd been to a reunion last summer; she remembered the story of the hangover.

She double-clicked on the photograph, enlarging it to fill most of the screen. Baker was in the second row and then – yes. There he was. Middle left, turning to talk to his neighbour just as the shot had been taken: Josh. Robin sat back in her chair.

They must have known each other. There were, what, seventy

or eighty men in the photo? KES wasn't enormous – if they'd been there together, in the same year, at the very least they'd have been aware of each other. Had they been friends? She hadn't ever met him but Josh hadn't met all their school friends, either. She didn't remember him talking about a Steve Baker but, again, a name so unremarkable would go in one ear and out the other. Her first impulse was to text Corinna – she actually reached for her phone. When the shock subsided, she stood and carried the laptop round the table.

Maggie peered at the screen. 'What am I looking at?'

'Steve Baker, just here, he's one of the syndicate, and then here . . .' She pointed.

'Is that . . . Josh?'

'KES reunion, class of '97. Taken last year.'

'They knew each other?'

'Not that I was aware of, but I wouldn't have known all his school friends, necessarily, and maybe they'd reconnected since then, recently even. He's stayed local, too, this guy. Maggie,' Robin chose her words carefully, 'the police think Josh had a mental breakdown because the factory was struggling.'

Maggie frowned. 'Was it? Did you know that?'

'No. Samir told me.'

'Samir?'

'He was at the hospital when I went to see Peter. Rin hadn't said anything. I mean, two or three years ago, she mentioned there were some issues – fewer orders, slow payments – but I had no idea things were so rough.' She paused. 'There's some suggestion Josh had another source of money.'

'Samir told you that, too?'

'Kath, Josh's sister. He'd got a loan, she said, but he wouldn't tell her where from.'

Maggie put her elbow on the table, tapped her fingers

against her lips. 'Had you ever heard them mention The Spot?'

Robin shook her head.

'It's probably just a coincidence. It's not a big city when you move in certain circles. But check it out.'

She searched the Net for other links between Josh and Steve Baker, and then for any between Josh and the other investors. After twenty-five minutes she came up empty-handed. 'Nothing online,' she told Maggie. 'I think I'm going to ring him.'

'Okay. Gently does it, though.'

Baker's law firm was on Colmore Row, five minutes away on the other side of the cathedral. She dialled the main number and waited for the receptionist to put her through.

'Steven Baker, good morning.' He sounded delighted to be a provincial property lawyer on this dull February day. 'How can I help?'

Robin introduced herself. 'I'm a private investigator,' she said, 'but I'm also a friend of Josh and Corinna Legge.'

'Oh god,' he said, 'I'm sorry.'

'You've heard about what's happened?'

'Of course, yes. Dreadful – just . . .' He tailed off, and she pictured him shaking his head.

'Obviously time's passing now,' she said, 'so I'm widening the circle and talking to anyone who might have known him. You were at KES together, is that right? Were you still in touch?'

'No. I saw him last summer, June or the beginning of July, but that was a school reunion. We said hello – we were on the rugby team together back then and I always liked him, he was a good bloke, but we were never close. We were in different groups.'

'Mr Baker, we're following up every possible connection – I understand you have an investment in a bar in Hurst Street, The Spot?'

A momentary hesitation. 'Yes. How did you hear about that?'

'Did Josh have any connection to The Spot, that you know of?'

'No. Certainly not a financial one, if that's what you mean. I wouldn't know if he'd ever been there, of course, but . . . What . . . ? Hang on a moment, I'm confused. What's the link to The Spot?'

Robin felt suddenly foolish. Yes, what *was* the connection, apart from her and her desperate need to make any kind of progress?

'I'm sorry,' she said, 'I don't mean to imply there is one at all. As I said, at this stage, time being what it is, we're just following up on any and every detail.'

'Because if you *are* implying there's anything criminal going on at The Spot,' he said, all jollity gone, 'I'd advise you to be very careful. It's a reputable business, owned by a group of reputable people, run by a very capable manager. As I'm sure the police would be happy to confirm.'

At half past two, Maggie stood, cleared their sandwich packets off the table and tossed them into the bin. 'Right, I'm kicking you out. Go and see your daughter. Give her my love.'

'I'll let you know if I hear from Tarryn,' Robin said, putting her jacket on.

'Yep. And I'll keep you posted from this end. Otherwise, see you Monday.'

Across the street in the car park, Robin took a moment to think. It was earlier than she'd expected, school didn't finish until three forty-five, so as long as she didn't hang about, she had time for a detour. She opened Google Maps, worked out a route round the one-way system and fired up the engine.

Bishop Street was directly behind the wholesale markets, ten minutes' walk, if that, from the Selfridges building with its spotted silver skin. They'd come this way, Digbeth, to see Harry but this time she turned off on the other side of the road, by a mean-looking building painted with a giant leprechaun and signs for Carling Black Label, its windows blinded with cardboard. A pile of boxes on the steps had been someone's bed for the night.

After a few hundred yards, the road divided and since no one was behind her, she slowed down. The buildings here were classic small-scale industrial, two or three storeys of red brick, the better-looking ones Victorian, the modern ones built as basically as possible, plastered with garish signs. An engineering works and the printing company next door looked lively, as did a place selling sheet plastic, but next to a car-repair shop was an abandoned warehouse, its wooden despatch doors padlocked and peeling.

The pub on the next corner was boarded up, too. The buildings beyond it were low and ugly, whatever businesses they'd once housed long gone, sheets of chipboard rotting where the windows had been. Others had been knocked down to make litter-strewn parking spaces, not that there was any shortage of either. No wonder Josh had needed antidepressants – how had he managed so long without them?

She pulled in across the street from Legge's and let the engine idle. As she knew now, these were the premises that the first brothers Legge had bought back in the 1880s, the sturdy Victorian two-storey remaining a constant as the generations photographed outside it elapsed. Every working day since Victorian times, a Legge had opened these doors, greeted the workforce, set about selling their springs. So much history, and then the older history of the city underneath. She knew from Dennis that this area had been the start of Birmingham, where first the markets, then the workshops had sprung up along the little river Rea that ran right

underneath here somewhere, tarmacked over now, gone underground like some Brummie version of the Styx.

She'd been inside two or three times, years ago, before Peter
was born. She and Rin had come to meet Josh for lunch one
day; another time they'd got a ride back with him from town.
He'd given her a tour, showing her the workshops on the ground
floor where huge bits of machinery spun greasily, overseen by
men who stuffed away copies of the *Sun* as they approached,
and wooden crates of finished springs in copper and stainless
steel waited to be packed for despatch. The offices were upstairs,
a long room with six or seven old-fashioned desks, Josh and
Gerry's at one end, at the other the secretaries and the book-
keeper who'd made a huge fuss of Lennie, she remembered now,
feeding her pretty much a whole pack of Tesco mini-muffins.

She'd expected the factory to look shabby now, the failure
inside reflected on the out, but they'd been keeping up appear-
ances: it was the best-kept property by far on this stretch of the
road. It was shuttered, of course, the grille down over the loading
bay, all the blinds drawn, but the narrow strip of yard out front
had been swept and the navy-blue paint on the door was glossy.
Even the windows were clean.

The history, that sense of continuity, had surrounded Josh like
warmth in the folds of his coat; it was one of the many things
Corinna had loved about him. She'd spent her first decade
moving from one place to another according to whether her dad
was on the wagon and employed, or AWOL, last seen en route
to the off-licence with Di's purse. It wasn't until she was twelve
and Di finally gave up on Trevor that she'd lived anywhere for
more than a year. Even after the divorce, their first landlord in
King's Heath had sold the flat out from under them. Josh's family
could trace their history on this patch for hundreds of years.
They didn't rent, they owned.

Would he ever walk into the factory again? One way or another, she doubted it now. After five days, it was getting harder and harder to believe he could come back physically unharmed from wherever he was. And even if he was still alive, there'd probably be criminal charges to face.

He'd done something, she was sure of it now. That sense of continuity, solid ground under his feet, had a flip-side: a stupid sense of responsibility, a compulsion to share his security with other people – Corinna, Peter, his workforce. He'd wanted to keep them safe. Robin felt a sudden burst of rage – she wanted to grab him, bodily shake him, *You idiot, you idiot – what have you done?*

A memory of the scream, shrill, heart-stopping, and she was back in that yard, the brick wall behind them, the alleyway disappearing in darkness. A half-ring of streetlight. His face. *I don't know. I don't* know.

The sound of an engine yanked her out of it. Heart beating fast, she saw a silver saloon coming down the road behind her. Two men in the front seats, visors down against the sun which already, at barely three o'clock, seemed to be making its excuses. Too late to move: it would only draw attention. She lowered her head, tried to meld with the seat.

They indicated and pulled in just in front of her. Robin kept her eyes down, avoiding meeting the driver's in his mirror. She heard the slam of doors, the double beep of the lock.

They crossed the road towards the factory without speaking. Even if she hadn't already recognized one of them, she would have known they were CID. Both wore suits, the younger one's slate-blue, the other's grey with a green wax jacket over the top, like travelling salesmen who'd left their briefcases in the car but for a masked watchfulness, a state of physical alertness she knew back to front because she had it, too. What were they doing here? Had they got something new?

The younger one stepped forward to ring the bell then turned to say a couple of words. A moment later, the door was opened by DS Thomas, who stood aside to let them in. She'd got away with it, Robin thought, but then, just before he stepped over the threshold, the older of the two men turned to look at her. DI Webster. He caught her eye and gave her a single nod.

Chapter Fifteen

Doing things quickly was not one of Lennie's strong suits, so it was a surprise to see her among the first out of school. She stalked across the playground with her head down, on a mission. Behind her, kids foamed through the double doors like a pot boiling over, a bubbling hormonal mass of blazers and backpacks. If part of the point of school uniform was to render teenagers as unattractive as possible, Savvy's – shapeless black trousers, white shirt, shiny black blazer – was an unequivocal success. The white kids – boys *and* girls – looked like third-rate snooker players from the Eighties, basically translucent after years without natural light, raised on chips. At RPG, most of the girls looked as if they spent the summer on yachts off St Tropez and some of them probably did. At least that pressure was off. She'd wanted the top-notch education for Lennie but not the nagging sense they were poor relations tolerated because Len was bright. Or what she thought of as the Octavia von Country-Estate factor: *'Henrietta tells me you're a detective. How very . . . exotic!'*

Lennie opened the door and dropped into the seat next to her. 'Hi, Mum.'

'Hi, lovely.'

'Can we go? We're right outside. I thought you'd wait round the corner like Gran does.'

'Sorry.' She started the engine and indicated to pull out just as a coach cruised alongside, blocking her in. 'How was your day?'

'Pall Mall.' It was one of their in-jokes, Del Boy French – 'Bonnet de douche, Rodney!' – but it was a half-hearted effort.

'What do you fancy doing? We could go for a walk, have a hot chocolate . . .'

'Do you mind if we just go home?'

'Really?' *God.* 'No, of course not. Probably a good idea.'

Lennie wrapped her arms round her knees, feet on the seat. Robin thought about telling her off then decided against it.

'What do you think of your new teachers? Anyone good?'

'Too early to tell, really.'

'How about the science ones – chemistry? Biology?' Ms Rosetti, the biology teacher at RPG, had been Lennie's favourite.

She shrugged. 'I don't know. Not sure.' She turned to the window and rested her head against the glass. For a couple of minutes they drove without talking, Robin's guilt now laced with a sense of rejection that even she knew was unreasonable. Suddenly, though, Len lifted her head.

'Why have you never told me about that guy?'

'Which guy?'

'The one Grandpa told the police about.'

'Samir.' Amazing, she hadn't said his name in years and now it felt like she couldn't stop. 'I have.'

'Yeah, you told me he *existed*. Not that you *loved* him.' For a level-headed kid who'd always been more dinosaurs-and-fossils than dolls-and-clothes, Lennie was weirdly sentimental. Too much Disney at a formative age, probably, all those big-eyed princesses on the weekend afternoons when it was raining and

217

Robin's will to drag her broken body off the sofa after a week of fourteen-hour days had failed. Despite the example in front of her, Lennie believed in Love with a capital L – The One, the happily-ever-after.

'I *did* say that. Or I thought you'd probably . . . read between the lines.'

Lennie shook her head, not buying it. 'Grandpa said he broke your heart.'

Christ alive. 'Well, he kind of did. We made plans – promises – and he broke them.'

'How? What plans?'

'You know we went travelling together, him and me? We talked about it all the time then, all the way round Europe and Botswana, Zambia, South Africa.' Spinning dreams at street cafés by ferry ports on Greek islands; on a flat-bed truck from Lusaka to Victoria Falls. Eight months. 'We had this whole plan for our lives. We were going to go to London together – UCL like I did, he had a place, too – get our degrees then join the Met together. But then, like Grandpa said, just like that,' she snapped her fingers, 'he bailed.'

'Why?' The million-dollar question. 'Grandpa said it was because of his family. Staying close.'

No lies to Lennie. 'That's what he told me.'

'But you didn't believe it. So what was the real reason?'

'When it boiled down to it? He just didn't love me as much as I loved him.'

Lennie frowned. 'Poor Mum.'

'Oh, I was all right. After a bit. Takes more than that to crack me.' She reached across and squeezed Lennie's nylon-clad thigh. 'And if it *had* all worked out between him and me, I wouldn't have had you, would I? He did me a *big* favour. Massive. Biggest ever.'

Lennie nodded slowly, not agreeing but absorbing, taking it in.

The traffic was thickening, Friday afternoon. The weekend stretched bleakly ahead: no school, no work, no distraction from the grim reality of their situation.

'Has Gid rung you this week, Mum?'

'No.'

'Have *you* been in touch with *him*?'

'On Monday, before I heard the news about Rin. I texted him.'

'Mum.' Lennie took a breath. 'I know things are really crap at the moment and you must feel like . . . I don't know what you feel like but it must be a hundred times as bad as I feel and that's *crap*.' Another breath. 'And I know things are going to be bad for a while, really bad, and we'll always be sad about Auntie Rin, that won't ever stop, but I wanted to say . . . Just, don't forget about our other life. Our *real* life. Please. This is only temporary, isn't it? You said. We live in London – we're going back. But you have to get things going. You've got to keep the pressure on.'

What pressure? All she had were her texts to Gid, and those were like fly-fishing: long, speculative lines sent glancing out across the distance, gossamer-weight.

And here was Lennie in a hideous shiny blazer on her way to spend the weekend at her grandparents' stifling house, a hundred miles from all her friends and her old haunts, everything she'd known for the thirteen years of her life so far.

'Len,' she said, making a flash decision, 'how do you feel about going to London tomorrow? I could go and see Gid, try and get things moving; you could get in touch with Carly and Emma, see if they're around?'

Lennie's face brightened instantaneously. 'Really?'

As soon as they got through the door, Len raced upstairs to get

219

changed. Robin fiddled with her phone as long as she reasonably could then buckled up and went into the kitchen. Her mother was sitting at the counter where she looked up stagily from the *Daily Mail* crossword.

'Hi.' Robin dropped her jacket onto a stool then quickly picked it up again. 'Mum, look, I'm sorry about this morning. When I was talking about money and . . . relationships, I didn't mean to imply anything about *your* life. I just . . .' Christine raised her eyebrows and the words dried up. 'Anyway, I'm sorry.'

'Is it okay if I put the TV on, Gran?' came Lennie's voice as she passed the doorway.

'Of course, love. Would you like a biscuit?'

'Yes, please.'

'You sit on down, I'll bring you one in.' She stood up and got the tin out of the cupboard. 'Let's not say any more about it, Robin. We're different, we do things differently. We know that, don't we, after all these years?'

And there it was again, the drawbridge, chains clanking as her mother pulled it up, leaving her stranded on the other side. 'No, please, can't we . . . ?'

'I mean, I just wish you'd try and be a bit less . . . brutal.' She took a knife from the block and decapitated a packet of chocolate digestives. 'I expect it's a good thing to be hard in your line of work but it isn't very attractive. Your attitude towards your brother . . .'

'*My* attitude? Do you ever think about what it's like for me, your favouritism? Always taking his side in a fight, always taking his word before mine . . .' Justifying his crapness while she found the negative in everything Robin did that was good.

Christine paused then seemed to come to a conclusion. 'Luke came over last night,' she said, 'because he and Natalie are having a tough time.'

Something in her tone stopped the glib response on Robin's tongue. 'Why?' she said. 'What do you mean, tough?'

'They thought they were expecting but it was a false alarm. They're both very disappointed, obviously, and things got a bit . . . heated. Your brother needed a bit of support.'

And now she felt like a cow. Great. 'Just for the record,' she said, 'I came in here to apologize.'

'And there you go. Why do you always assume I'm criticizing you?'

'Weren't you?'

'I'm trying to help you.'

'By what? Telling me I'm hard?'

'By telling you that storming around bickering and pushing people away all the time isn't going to make you happy. It's no wonder you can't hold down a relationship. This idea you seem to have that relying on anyone else is a sign of weakness or in some way against your feminist principles . . .' The usual disdain at the phrase, as if she wished she had her rubber gloves on.

Somewhere in her jacket, Robin's phone rang. 'It'll be the seventeenth century, I expect,' she said, 'wanting their worldview back.'

'Mum, Gran,' came a plaintive voice from the other room, 'could you please stop fighting?'

They stared at each other, the phone ringing. Christine turned away and took a side plate from the cupboard. 'Are you going to get that?' she said, cold.

Robin dug it out of the jacket pocket and looked at it: *Number withheld.* She hesitated then went out into the tiny hall. 'Hello?'

'Robin? It's Samir.'

Oh, for fuck's *sake.* 'Hold on.' She reached back into the kitchen for her jacket then let herself out of the front door, an instant temperature-drop of about thirty degrees. 'Right,' she said, jacket on, 'let me guess. You're calling because Webster saw me in Bishop Street?'

'Correct.'

'I was in my car, didn't even get out. I wasn't doing anything.'

'Apart from putting yourself in the frame. Do you want him to think you're involved? Is that the idea?'

'Of course not.' She kicked a loose stone and sent it skittering all the way past Christine's mini-roses to the pavement. The houses across the street looked back unimpressed.

'So . . . ?'

'You asked me to tell you something that proves Josh didn't do it. I'm trying.'

'Robin.'

'*You* can't tell *me* anything, I know that, but I can tell *you*. Ana, their babysitter – she's nervous. Why? And if Josh basically didn't have a job any more, why did they even *need* a babysitter? If they were getting by on Corinna's salary, how were they paying her? I know they paid her in cash but where were they getting that? It must have been a couple of hundred a month at least, and—'

'Hold on, hold on. Just stop a minute.' When he spoke again, his voice was quieter. Was he at work? 'We're on the same side here.'

'Are we?'

'I understand where you're coming from, I do, but . . .'

'What's Ana frightened of, Samir? Because she is. Both times I've talked to her – when I went there, she was afraid to open the door. Why, if it was a domestic?'

'She saw something? She's a witness?'

Robin said nothing.

'Okay, look,' he said. 'She's nervous because she's here illegally. In the UK, I mean.'

'How? She's Slovakian – we're not out of the EU just yet.'

'She's not Slovakian, she's from Serbia, which, as you'll know, has never been *in* the EU.'

Oh. 'She told Rin she was Slovakian.'

'I know, she said. But she was lying, for obvious reasons. She's scared now because she doesn't want to get removed. That also tells you why they were paying her in cash, by the way.'

'Why but not *how*. Where were they getting the money? How about the loan against the machines – have you got anywhere on that?'

'How do you *know* about that?'

Robin considered obfuscating but decided against. 'Kath.'

'You spoke to her, too?'

'She's a friend.'

A pause long enough to let her know he didn't accept that. He knew how she'd felt about Kath back in the day. 'Well, obviously,' he said, 'she told us about it as well, and Webster's team have been looking into it.' He hesitated and in the background at his end, she heard a distant scream, not fear but excitement – a kid's scream, part of a game, the exhilaration of being chased, nearly caught. Was he in a *playground*? Or at home? If he was on his own phone, he either had it set to withhold his number automatically or he'd done it specially for her.

'Don't do this,' he said. 'Don't involve yourself. You've got too much to lose.'

News to me.

'If word reaches the Met, you'll screw up any chance of an appeal.'

'How do *you* know about *that*?' Ha.

'If it's what you're thinking of doing,' he said smoothly. 'If there's a chance you can still sort it out, don't wreck it.'

What was it to him? Unless he wanted her gone, of course,

223

safely back in London and off his ground. Which was a strong possibility.

'I'm asking you to trust Webster and his team,' he said. 'My lot. Me. I understand that it must be very hard.' For five or six seconds, there was silence on the line, the unspoken drowning them out. 'So I'll tell you two things. First, DS Thomas has been following up on the loan. She's excellent, as I'm sure you saw when you met her, and she's found no evidence that Josh had outstanding debts, kosher or otherwise.'

'But . . .'

'Second, we've had the PM back.'

Robin's heart made a single hard beat, like a kick on the inside. 'And?'

'You promise this'll go no further? I can trust you?'

'You've always been able to trust *me*, Samir.'

The scratch of shoes on a rough surface, a soft fabric crumple. She imagined him on a bench, leaning forward, looking at his feet. ''Rin was dead before the fire started. I wanted you to know that so you didn't have to imagine . . .'

'How?'

'Head injury. Blunt force.'

She closed her eyes. 'How many blows?'

'Just one, at the temple. It matches the shape of the brass table lamp they had in the sitting room, the square base. Robin, there's just no evidence that anyone else was involved.'

She turned to go back inside but when she reached the front door, she sat down on the step instead. Chest aching, eyes unfocused, she stared unseeing at the same bit of the path until Lennie came to find her. 'Mum, you're frozen! Come in.'

Should she tell her about the post mortem? Could she stand to let her imagine the violence, Josh swinging a table lamp at

Rin's head? But then, what was she imagining now? Rin burning alive, in agony?

She told her, and Christine, too, who was folding sheets in the utility room, and whose expression went from tight disapproval through apprehension to pained horror in the few seconds it took to say it. 'Oh, love.' She dropped the sheet into the laundry basket and took a step forward. For a moment, Robin thought she was going to hug her but then her mother reached out a hand and gave her a sort of pat, a double-tap on her shoulder, *there there.*

As soon as she decently could, she went upstairs. Christine had vacuumed during the day, and the nap of the six-by-four patch of carpet was brushed into stripes like the lawn at a stately home. Robin sat down at the small white desk. How many hours had she spent here back then, the little radio blasting in her ear, *Let's all meet up in the year 2000*, Robert Smith keeping her company from the side of the wardrobe? All the messing around, Rin and Josh and Kev, Samir, that was what she remembered when she looked back but actually, the truth was, if she was at home and she wasn't asleep or eating, she'd been here at this desk with her eyes glued to her files. She'd been driven then, really driven, and it had paid off. She'd blown her A-levels out of the water.

She needed that drive again now, that same intense focus. She reached for the laptop, opened Google and typed in 'Farrell Hinton'. The list of hits appeared, the *Mail* piece number one, right at the top: *VIOLENT GANGSTER FREED BY ROGUE MURDER COP.* She moved the cursor over it then swung off quickly and opened Hotmail in a new tab instead. Five new messages, four of them spam offering her Viagra, Cialis and money off at Nando's – now *there* was an evening. One of them, sent an hour earlier, wasn't spam.

Hi Robin, thanks for your message. Yes, I'm friends with Becca and I'm really worried about her, of course, so if there's anything you think I can help with, let me know. Tarryn

Robin hit 'Reply'. *Hi, thanks for getting in touch. I'm an investigator working with Becca's mother, Valerie. We're following up on a couple of things and it'd be great to talk to you. I'm happy to ring you or, if you prefer, you can call me.*

She gave her number then went back to the *Mail* piece.

The photograph was one of the worst of her ever taken. Whoever had leaked the story to the *Mail* had given them either her address itself or enough information to find it, and the photographer had lain in wait outside until she'd put on her rattiest coat and trainers. No make-up, no sleep – she looked like she'd spent the night carousing in an underpass. By comparison, Hinton looked like an upstanding citizen or at least a City banker. If you didn't know the photo had been taken outside court, you'd think he was on the steps of a particularly smart office building or his country pile. His suit and hair were impeccable, his inner pit bull chained up for the day so that here, unalloyed, was the suave, charming Hinton – Jamie, so innocuous-sounding – the one whom Freshwater, in that final showdown, had actually suggested she fancied.

The photographs captured the spirit of the piece entirely: look at the slobbish, morally bankrupt woman the Met set against this sophisticated criminal mastermind. No wonder she didn't have the chops to get him – or had she even been under his sway? He was good-looking, charismatic, persuasive; she was an unmarried mother forced to earn her own living, no doubt desperate to be financially supported . . .

Hinton, said the *Mail*, was a slippery bad apple, ripe for the picking – *actually in police custody* – until this un-made-up slattern whose highlights needed redoing wilfully let him go.

Robin looked at Hinton. Of course he was bad but when it came to the murder of Jay Farrell, that wasn't the issue. However much Freshwater – who seemed to believe that all crims were mentally a crowbar short of the full house-breaking kit – wanted it to be true, Hinton was too switched on by a factor of about fifty.

Her *hypothesis – Get me, Patel!* – which she hadn't had time to prove before being kicked out, was that a rival, as yet unidentified, was trying to frame him, picking off Farrell, who wasn't really in the life, to limit their own exposure to comeback.

Now, with the severely limited resources currently at her disposal, working solo from a hundred miles away, she had to find out who that rival was. It didn't help that she'd pissed off her guy at Central Task Force at the end of last year, either, killing any hope he'd help. He was a bit of a jobsworth, though, she consoled herself; he probably wouldn't have anyway, knowing – because who didn't? – what had happened to her.

She clicked off the *Mail* piece and went back to the page of hits. They'd been through reams of this stuff before, both her team and, in the first mad days after she'd been booted out, she herself, staring at the screen until three in the morning, barely able to keep her eyes open. But maybe with so much else going on, the tornado in her head, everyone else certain they'd got their man, they'd missed something.

Her phone rang on the bed behind her. She leaned back on the chair and managed to scoop it up without standing. She didn't know the number but when she picked up, the voice was Australian. 'Hi, is this Robin?'

'Yes. Tarryn? Thanks for calling.'

'No problem. Like I said, I'm so worried. I've been away for a few days and no one from work knows anything. Is there any news? Has anyone heard from her?'

'I'm sorry, no. Not yet.'

'You said you're an investigator – are you with the police?'

'No, I work with a small private agency. We have police contacts if we need them and we're ex-cops, we're trained, but we're not police, no.'

'Okay.'

Robin thought she heard a note of relief. 'Is that a good thing?'

'No. I mean, not as far as I know. Except that if the police aren't involved and it's just private, it's less worrying, you know? From the point of view of her being safe, I mean, not . . .'

'Not . . . ?'

'Hurt. Or worse.'

'How long have you known Becca – you don't mind me asking a few questions?'

'No, that's fine. Whatever, if it'll help.'

'Did you meet at The Spot? My colleague and I were there yesterday and Lisa, is it, who runs the back room?'

'Yes.'

'I can't remember if she said you two had known each other before.'

'No, we met there. I've been there a bit longer, I started in July, and I'm full time so I helped train Becca and we worked together quite a bit. We just hit it off, she's fun. Actually – she's a couple of years younger than me – she reminds me of my little sister.'

'In what way?'

'She's funny, kind of self-deprecating. Ironic one-liners, generally at her own expense. She's good on a night out – likes a few drinks, likes a dance, she'll always come for a kebab with you at the end of the night. And she's kind. She knew I was missing home round my birthday so she made me this amazing chocolate tart – it was like something from a patisserie in Paris but she'd done it herself, all these decorative curls. She's the only person who's been shown a photo of the KP's new baby.'

'KP?'

'Kitchen porter. Pot-washer, vegetable-peeler. She talks to him – or tries anyway, his English isn't great. She says hello, brings him a lemonade from the bar, you know?'

'Right. So she's popular?'

'Definitely.'

'Any of the blokes ever shown an interest? Or customers?'

'A bit – there was some flirting but nothing major. And even if they had, they wouldn't have got anywhere.'

'Why?'

A little pause. 'Have you met her friend Harry?'

'Yes.'

'They're going out. Seeing each other.'

'Did she tell you that?'

'Yes.'

'You didn't guess or work it out?'

'No, she told me.'

Interesting. 'I'm sorry, that probably sounded a bit weird but I wanted to be sure. You're the only person we've come across that she actually did tell.'

'I know,' she said. 'How's Harry doing? Is he okay?'

'Not really. Tarryn, do you have any idea why they were keeping it quiet? He said it was because of their friend Lucy.'

'That's what she told me, too, yeah.'

'Did that strike you as strange at all?'

'Honestly? Yes. But, you know, she and Harry have only just got together, it's new, and the three of them have been friends for years. She said she wanted to give it a bit of time before she upset the dynamic. And people *are* strange, aren't they? I think

229

that all the time. They do things totally differently from how you ever would.'

'What did you make of her? Lucy.'

'I thought she was all right. Sweet. Straighter than Becca.'

'How so?'

'Just . . .' Robin imagined her frowning on the other end of the phone. 'It's hard to put a finger on. She came out with us a couple of times, she was always fun, but not . . . I guess she just felt a bit more . . . conventional.'

'Becca isn't?'

'Not in the same way. She still lives with her mum, obviously, and all that but she has her wild side. It's not even that wild, to be honest. Just . . . freer. Less limited. I don't know, it's hard to describe. I guess it's just a mind-set thing, attitude.'

Robin got the impression she was choosing her words carefully. 'Tarryn, I don't want you to feel like you're betraying her confidence but we heard that Becca was using prescription drugs.'

She'd expected her at least to hedge but instead she said frankly, 'I knew she did a bit last year, yes, she told me. But she wasn't doing it any more.'

'Really? When did she stop?'

'Some time in the autumn. October? Yes, it was – "birthday present to myself", she said.'

'Do you know why? I mean, what changed?'

'She bumped into the friend she did it with the first few times and she said he looked like shit, excuse the language. Like he was letting it get out of control. That wasn't the road she wanted to go down, so she stopped.'

'Just like that? Morphine, opioids – they're extremely addictive, as I'm sure you know. Just to be able to stop . . .'

'She said she'd smoked a lot of weed to compensate.' A little snort, half a laugh. 'That's what I mean about her being different.

230

She's – surprising. When I met her, I wouldn't have guessed she'd be someone who'd even try painkillers in the first place but she said she was curious – she wanted to know what it was like. Then, like you say, how many people can just stop? That's the thing about her – she's got a will of iron.'

Chapter Sixteen

Glancing across at Lennie in the passenger seat, Robin caught her eye and got a smile. When she'd come downstairs this morning, she'd found her breakfasted and ready to go, earnestly wrapping a stack of Christine's biscuits in a piece of tin-foil. 'For the car,' she said. 'So we don't have to stop.' It had been another of those moments when Robin felt she'd been shown a glimpse of the future, a fleeting premonition of what life would be like in not even five years' time. Len looked nearly grown-up today, in her boyfriend jeans and favourite T-shirt, a grey one with a black glitter lightning bolt across the chest, quite rock 'n' roll, and she was tall, already five five. Robin was relatively tall though, at five seven, and Len's father had been tall, too, so that wasn't surprising.

'*How tall?*' said Corinna's voice suddenly. She'd always leapt on the slightest new detail about him.

'*Six two, six three – something like that. Don't know, he was lying down.*'

'*Slapper.*'

She took a silent breath, pushed the pain away. 'You're okay to keep going?' she said. 'You don't want to stop at Oxford for a drink, or the loo?'

'No, I'm okay.'

'It's the memory of that Burger King, isn't it?'

'Yeah. I'm scared you'll force-feed me another one and this time I'll burst.'

Robin smiled. The M40 moved past them on either side, ribbons of grey, busy even on a Saturday morning. It had been planned in the Sixties to link London and Birmingham, which amazed her now she thought about it – the *Sixties*. The part linking London to genteel Oxford had been made first, of course, but the last bit between Oxford and Birmingham had only opened in the early Nineties, not even thirty years ago. The capital and the country's second city, that huge engine of industrial prosperity, with no direct link until then. Hard not to see it as an insult, as if London were leery of an open conduit for anything other than the money Birmingham generated.

'Mum, do you miss Ade?'

Ade?

'Adrian.'

'I know!' She made a face. 'I know who *Ade* is. God, Len, I'm not senile yet. It was just the change of subject that—'

'It wasn't a change of subject. So do you?'

No lies – with the rider that if it was small and white and it would protect Lennie's feelings, and no harm could come of it, very occasionally it was all right. 'Yes. Of course I do.'

'*I do.*'

'I know, sweetheart.'

Robin looked at her hands on the wheel and remembered that night on the bridge, how Adrian had gripped the rail as if he'd been afraid the Thames churning blackly below would surge up and pull his feet from under him. Alongside the guilt at hurting him there'd run another feeling, one she hadn't identified until hours later, lying alone in her own bed, head pounding.

He'd taken her for supper at Swan on the South Bank, next to the Globe Theatre. His treat, he insisted. They'd been there on one of their early dates when he'd still been so bizarrely formal, offering to pick her up (she'd always refused, and she'd usually been coming direct from work anyway), dropping her off and asking the cab to wait until he'd seen her safely inside. She'd found it hilarious, the kid-glove treatment: as if she didn't spend her days dealing with killers.

Their table was a small round one in the corner of a banquette so they sat at right angles to one another, knees bumping. Ade had his back to the window to give her the view, the darkening Thames and the myriad sparkling lights on the other side, the white dome of St Paul's rising over them like some vision of Ancient Rome. The first time they'd come, she'd loved it but that night, the whole thing had stuck in her craw. Three years earlier, they'd split the bill, she'd insisted, but she couldn't do that any more. This time, the chic minimalism, all the natural wood and leather symbolized a cosmopolitan world that was no longer hers, and the popping corks were ironic – *Oh, well played, Robin!* This was for other people now, successful people. She'd watched Adrian hand over his card with a stone in her stomach, felt a wash of relief when the door snapped shut behind them. As the evening had worn on and the other tables had grown louder, she'd started to feel they were laughing at her.

Up on the bridge, she'd stopped to look at the city downstream, the Walkie-Talkie, Tower Bridge, the bright tip of One Canada Square far in the distance. It was the third week of January and the lights looked like decorations left up when the party was over. She was leaving.

He'd turned to face her. 'Marry me.'

It had been so windy she hadn't really heard him, or she told

234

herself she hadn't. She brushed the hair off her face and pulled her beanie down. 'What?'

He'd had a weird look on his face, half laughing, half frightened, like a child about to do something forbidden. 'Will you marry me?'

She'd felt her mouth open. Eventually she said, 'Now?'

'Well, not *right* now, obviously – there's paperwork to do, and I'd like to invite a few people . . .'

Paperwork? It took her a moment to understand he was joking.

'Robin.' He reached out and touched her face as if she were someone different. 'I want to be with you. Properly. I want us to live together, be a family. I love Lennie – I think she loves me, too. If you agreed, I'd ask her if she'd let me adopt her formally. I want to be her dad – it would be a privilege.'

For some seconds, she couldn't speak. They stared at each other and she'd watched his expression change from hysterical daring to suspense.

'I can't,' she said.

'You can.' He smiled but she could already see withdrawal in his eyes, defensive retreat. 'Unless there's something you haven't told me? You're already married or . . .'

'No. No, I'm not married. Adrian – I just can't.'

'Why?' A note of aggression.

How to explain? The wind had shoved her, a hand on her chest, and she'd taken half a step backwards. The disconnect was dizzying – she had been sitting there feeling humiliated, cast out, and he'd been thinking of *marriage*? What the hell? Wasn't that reason enough? That they could have dinner together and be in such totally different places in their heads? What chance did they stand? Her life was in free-fall, she was Wile E. Coyote off the edge of the cliff, feet scrabbling at the air, and he was thinking about who to invite to their wedding.

And yet, she'd thought in the days afterwards, waiting in the sitting room while he silently collected his things from the bathroom and loaded various bits of kitchenware into a box, it was her fault. She'd given him the impression there was a chance. She'd liked him – enjoyed being with him. He was clever, he made her laugh. She liked his taste in music, the smell of his skin.

'What's the catch?' she'd asked Olivia six weeks after they'd met. Olivia, her favourite mum from RPG, had introduced them; Ade was an old university friend of hers. 'I like him. He's funny, handsome, likes books and *The Wire*, and he knows a lot about London history.' *Good in bed.*

'None – no catch.'

There really wasn't. In three years, there'd never been a deal-breaker – no hidden nasty streak or penny-pinching, no roving eye or porn collection. And yet. And yet. For a long time, she'd waited for it to kick up a gear – to fall in love, as Lennie would say – but it just hadn't happened. Knowing that it would be good for them all, she'd tried to compel it, put the full force of her will behind it, but nothing. Perhaps it was too easy. Perhaps she needed grist to engage, to get traction.

He'd known, of course. The imbalance had been so obvious. He loved her, after a couple of months she'd seen it; after three, he'd told her. At that point she'd just about been able to fudge it – it was happening, she said, he was just ahead of her – but after a year, shamefully, she'd had to lie. *Was* it really lying, though? Maybe this *was* her version of love now. Maybe what she'd felt with and for Ade – respect, affection, comfort – was her real deal. She'd told him about Samir; that was how much she trusted him.

Which was why, when he proposed, she'd been angry. Not angry – furious. Hadn't he understood? No, it was worse: he had. He'd known that under normal circumstances, at full strength, she wouldn't have accepted. He'd waited until she'd lost her job and run out of money. He'd waited until she was defence-less, to give himself a fighting chance.

Lying in bed at the flat that night, seething, she'd had to stop herself ringing him. What happens next, in your mind? she'd wanted to ask. I become the beta to your alpha, the unemployed woman living in your house, on your money? Did he want them to have a baby – quick, she was thirty-five? Do that first, time is of the essence, sort your career out later, when the kids are bigger. We've got enough on my salary, no need for you to work.

She gave herself a little shake: stop it. That was all over, finished, done.

Lennie had already gone out to the car when Christine had pulled Robin aside. 'Here.' She'd reached for her hand and pressed a loose roll of notes into it. 'To tide you over.'

'Mum . . .' She hadn't known what to say.

'Well, you can't go down there to London with nothing, can you?' said Christine, abrupt. 'It's ridiculous. Go on, you're keeping poor Lennie waiting.'

Outside, when Robin looked, she saw that she'd given her a hundred pounds.

Two and a half hours later, they stopped for the lights at the roundabout on the raised section of the Westway over White City. Robin looked at London laid out in front of them. Once, in her early twenties, she'd stopped just here on a day when the sky had been high and sheer, Lennie asleep in her car seat, thumb in, the city shimmering in the heat. *I've done it*, she remembered thinking, *I've made it*. Now, twelve years later, here she was again with her tail between her legs, spat out by London like a piece of gristle.

She circled Shepherd's Bush Green then came round to Wood Lane, where she pulled over as close as she could to the long flight of steps outside Debenhams. 'There you are, madame: Westfield, your oyster.'

'Thanks, Mum.' Len reached for the handle.

'Wait, hold on.' Sending her a silent thank you, she took Christine's notes from her pocket and gave her daughter two twenties. 'Here.'

'Really?'

'Have fun – make sure you eat something. Say hi to the girls for me.'

'I will.' She reached over the gearstick for an awkward hug. 'See you later.'

Robin waited until Lennie had disappeared from view then found the address in her SatNav and headed back to the Westway. Gid lived in Ruislip, on the western edges of London, miles back the way they'd just come. It would have made far more sense to visit him first, on their way in, but she'd wanted to be alone, Lennie safely off with her friends rather than forced to witness her straw-clutching.

It took nearly another half-hour to reach the house but that was okay. As ever, the car was a cocoon and today she had time to kill: she wasn't picking Lennie up from Carly's house 'til seven, and she only had two people to see. The other one was at three o'clock, across the city. Unlike Gid, he knew she was coming.

Over the six years they'd worked together, she'd been to Gid and Efie's several times, for Christmas parties – the cost of the cab back into town was a nightmare – and the annual summer barbecue, when their modest back garden became a sort of mini-carnival, half-barrels of charcoal cooking all afternoon and into the night, tables of salads and fruit, deckchairs for the adults, a paddling pool and a water slide set up for the children where the grass sloped gently down to the conifer hedge at the end.

Both Gid and Efie were second-generation Brits; their respective sets of parents had come over from Freetown in the late Sixties, and they were that rare thing: committed Christians who didn't make her want to punch them. There wasn't a scrap of sanctimony about either of them, they'd never even tried to talk to her about Jesus or the Word or any of that crap, and the booze always ran freely at their parties, hence the cabs. They were just moral, community-minded people who tried to live good lives. Pulling up across the road, she realized – again – how much she missed working with Gid, his solidity.

Their street wasn't dissimilar to Dunnington Road, two facing lines of semis built to look identical back in the Fifties, since customized in a hundred different ways. The pairs either side of Gid and Efie's were unpainted, the pebble-dash around the upper windows aged to the grim brown of mushrooms left too long in the fridge but their house and the one attached, which belonged to Mr T, a widower, were painted white. Efie gardened for him, too, Robin knew, and their son, Mark, who was twelve, had started mowing his lawn last summer. It was a whole world, one whose details she hadn't realized until now she'd enjoyed hearing about, a super-gentle soap opera where nothing bad ever happened. Apart, of course, from in Gid's work life. She'd wondered about that a lot over the years, the disparity between the peace here and the bloody mayhem that was their daily stock-in-trade.

She ran through her opening gambit a final time then got out of the car. Like Christine, Efie had planted her front garden with roses but hers were full-size, not the prissy mini ones. Robin rang the bell and waited. From behind the house came voices, the springy thwack of foot meeting ball. If he'd had a whole weekend off, Gid came to work knackered on a Monday, run ragged by Mark and Seth, the younger one.

Movement behind the glass. The door opened to reveal Efie, as she'd guessed it would. 'Robin!' She gave her a hug, catching her hoop earring in Robin's hair as she pulled away again. 'Come in. This is a surprise – Gid didn't tell me you were coming. I thought you were in Birmingham.'

'Yes, just back for the day, tying up a few loose ends.'

'Come through. I was having a quiet few minutes while they were out there.' She pointed through the kitchen window to the garden where Gid was indeed playing football with the boys. They watched them for a moment, Gid's long legs covering the lawn in about four strides, the boys weaving round him like dancers round a maypole, showing off their fancy footwork.

'I'm sorry,' she said, 'I didn't mean to barge in.'

'No, no, you're not at all.' Leaning over the sink, she rapped on the glass and motioned to Gid to come in. 'How are you, Robin?' There it was, the grave tone that had started to fill that question in the past six weeks.

'Oh, you know. It's a big adjustment. Not sure how much longer I'll be able to live with my mother before Gid's sent to arrest me.' A startled expression reminded Robin that Efie had a tendency to take what people said at face value. Not something she and Gid had in common, thank god: he wouldn't have lasted an hour in Homicide. 'Only joking,' she said. 'My mum's lovely. I'm just not sure anyone should live with their parents past the age of eighteen, you know?'

'Totally,' said Efie. 'Coffee? I'll bung the kettle on.'

From the corridor came the sound of the back door opening and the thud, thud of shoes coming off. Feet padded in their direction.

Gid's face arranged itself into happy surprise but not before she'd seen the momentary *Oh, no.* Fuck, Robin thought.

'Hi,' he said. 'How are you?' A brief hug.

'Doing well,' she said. 'Scaring your wife that I might commit matricide but otherwise good.' She'd made the decision last night not to say anything about Corinna. Gid knew her best mate was back in Brum and that, along with Maggie, she'd been one of the things that made it bearable to go back for a while, but he'd never met her. Homicide would know about the case, given that Josh was wanted and suspected to have left the Birmingham area via a station with a direct line to London but – unless DI Webster and his team had contacted them about her, which, she'd admitted to herself with alarm, was very possible – they wouldn't know about her connection to it. If she could stop those two circles overlapping, she'd do it.

'The boys are getting so big,' she said, looking out to where Mark and Seth were now taking turns to kick the ball into a netted goal. 'Seth was four when I met you.'

'I know, it's crazy, isn't it? How's Len?'

'Okay. Shopping with her friends – or actually, drinking cappuccinos and gossiping, I expect. Thirteen going on twenty-five.'

They chatted about anodyne stuff – how the boys were doing at school, a reading scheme Efie had set up at the children's home where she volunteered – until the coffee was made and poured. Then Efie took her mug and pointed to the window. 'I'll go and see how the boys are getting on, give you a moment.'

Robin waited until they saw her go down the steps to the lawn. 'Sorry for showing up like this,' she said. 'I was coming to London anyway and I—'

'Where's Lennie doing her shopping?'

'Westfield,' she admitted.

241

'So you made a special trip back out here.'

She considered a cover story but it was futile. 'I wanted to talk to you.'

'And you thought that by showing up here, you'd put me on the spot. Or get more out of me than if you just phoned.'

She smiled. 'You're a good detective.'

'I know,' he said. 'Which is why I'm not going to jeopardize myself – and our living – by doing what you're asking. Even if I wanted to.' He took a sip of his coffee, an excuse to break eye contact. Too hot – he winced.

'This isn't right, Robin,' he said. 'Coming here to my family home when you know what you're asking me to do could get me disciplined. These texts – *Any news? Could you run a couple of searches for me?* – they've got to stop.'

She felt a sudden sense of abandonment, a tug at her knees like a wave ebbing, leaving her stranded. 'I thought you were on my side.'

There was a charged silence, broken by a mechanical shudder from the fridge.

'I am,' he said. 'Which is why I'm trying to help you. In the right way.'

'Come on, Gid, you agreed with me. You don't think he did it either, so why . . . ?'

'You still don't get it, Robin, do you? It's not *about* Hinton and Farrell, it doesn't *matter* whether you're right or wrong.'

She snorted. 'Now you sound like Freshwater.'

Gid paused. Like her mother, he had these moments sometimes – she'd seen them numerous times – when he halted mid-conversation and gathered himself. Where Christine seemed to be drawing on negative energy, though, Gid appeared to tap into some extra reserve of calm.

'At the time, I agreed with you about Hinton, yes. Now, I'm

242

not sure. But either way, like I said, it doesn't matter. It's irrelevant.'

'Have aliens stolen your brain?'

'The problem,' he held up a long-fingered hand, 'is your attitude to Freshwater. To the team. I know a lot of other people feel the same as you – and I'm not saying I don't – that he's a careerist, that he's petty and vain and only cares about how he comes across in the media and to the brass but that doesn't change the fact that he's the guv'nor. You can't just do your own thing when you're part of a team, Robin. Even if you don't respect him . . .'

'And why would I?'

'Even if you don't,' he said, ignoring her, 'you have to respect the office. We, your team, respected your position; you had to respect his. That's how it works, the Met – any serious organization. The structure is there for a reason. If you just take things into your own hands, no one knows where they stand. You respect the office because if you don't, everything falls apart.'

From Ruislip, she drove back to Shepherd's Bush, found a metered space in the knot of residential streets off Uxbridge Road – cheaper than parking at Westfield, look at her being sensible – then walked to the Underground station. She could have driven again but who knew what the traffic would be like trying to get back out later, and parking would be a nightmare over there. And to be late for Lennie today would feel particularly crap, much as Len'd probably enjoy the extra time with her friends.

The Central Line took her all the way, stations clipping by one after another, people getting on, getting off, all purposeful, three-dimensional, while she felt to herself like a wisp, less and less substantial by the minute. Sodding Gid – scratch what she'd said about sanctimony, another thing she'd been wrong about.

Sitting there lecturing her – what the hell was that? A spark of outrage glowed behind her ribs; she blew on it, encouraging. Yes, how dare he? Talking to her like that, as if grasping the concept of 'team' was somehow beyond her intellectual reach. The ember of fury glowed – better. That was what it was, wasn't it, the emptiness behind her ribs? Disappointment. Gid had been her right-hand man; she was disappointed because he'd turned out to be a fake like everyone else, setting aside his principles – who cares if Jay Farrell's real killer goes free if it means we can get Hinton? – for a pat on the back and a quiet life.

And how dare he suggest *she* was the one with a problem with the system? Like Freshwater, he seemed to have forgotten that it wasn't the police who decided who was guilty or not. Why bother with a judicial system at all, judges and juries, due process, when the police could administer justice? Just sling the crims in jail, cut out the middle-man – think of the money it'd save. Actually, why not go one further and dispense with the police, too, devolve responsibility to roving squads of vigilantes?

By the time she came through the ticket barrier at Liverpool Street, she felt substantially better, galvanized. She bought a Twix for some energy and ate it Maggie-style, three bites per finger.

The café was a couple of minutes' walk away, tucked off Bishopsgate in a little arcade. It was busy, and she was still in the queue when Boz appeared briefly in the doorway, blond hair with the light behind it, the same boxy build. He materialized momentarily at her side. 'Mine's a big latte, takeaway cup. Oh, and one of these.' He handed her a wrapped brownie from the shelf then wove his way back through the room to where, she saw, he'd spotted a couple of suits getting their coats on.

Boz, she'd thought before today, was like the anti-Gid. They'd met at work, they'd been borough CID together, she DS, he a constable, but where she'd moved up, making inspector, joining

Homicide, he'd made a sideways move and joined the other team. He'd been working on a case involving the fringes of a local gang when he'd met and fallen in love with the sister of one of the suspects, from whom, idiot, he'd accepted money to suppress a key piece of evidence. The sister, Lauren, had visited him regularly while he did his time and when he got out, he'd married her and gone to work with the family business. Boz had grown up in care; Robin suspected that the Ryan family, both huge and tight, gave him the sense of belonging he'd originally hoped to find in the Met.

She paid for the coffees and carried them over. 'And your brownie, sir.'

'Cheers. So, how are you doing? How's tricks?' No patronizing note in the question this time, thank god; she felt a rush of good-will towards him. She'd always liked Boz, could never muster the wherewithal to blame him for what he'd done. A large part of her had actually been glad for him. The few bits he'd ever told her about his childhood had sounded like hell; he'd been overdue a bit of happiness, and she'd been there in the early days of Lauren, when he hadn't been able to keep the smile off his face. Robin had been a character witness at his trial, in support of a lenient sentence.

She shrugged now. 'So-so. You?'

'Good. Lauren's expecting again.'

'Is she? Congrats.'

'Thanks. Hoping for another girl, don't tell her. Everyone keeps going on about maybe we'll get a boy this time but I love my girls and I want another one.' He opened the brownie and offered her some.

'I'm all right, thanks.'

'So, to what do I owe the proverbial?'

'You've heard about Jamie Hinton, have you?' The Ryans

weren't particularly big-time themselves, nor violent, but they knew a lot of people.

'Of course, yeah. I mean, I saw it in the newspaper,' he said. 'Sorry about your job. Are you looking for an in on the dark side?'

'I'm probably in enough trouble for now but if it comes to that, I'll give you a call. No, I wanted to ask you if you'd heard anything about him or Jay Farrell.'

'Guessed as much. Sorry, no, I haven't. Only what I've read.'

'I still don't like Hinton for Farrell. I think it was a set-up, that either someone heard about the theft of the drugs and saw an opportunity to incriminate him, or, alternatively, it was a case of two birds with one stone.'

'Someone with a beef with both of them, you mean?'

'Maybe.'

'Hm.' He tipped his head from side to side, considering. 'I'll put some feelers out for you, but I haven't heard anything, sorry. I'm not saying I would have, necessarily, but word gets around. Leave it with me but just don't get your hopes up, all right?'

'That's the one mistake I'm not making at the moment.'

Chapter Seventeen

'Morning,' said Maggie, getting into the car. 'How was your weekend?' She had her black coat on again, collars up, a purple scarf hanging either side of her neck. Coming down the path just now, she'd looked like the priest from *The Exorcist*.

'Okay. Yours?'

'All right. Had Sunday lunch with a friend, sat around. What did you do?'

'Len helped Mum and Dad in the garden yesterday morning, planting some bulbs – agapanthus, apparently, whatever they are – then we all went for a wander round Sarehole Mill in the afternoon. I remembered it after seeing Becca's Instagram – Len's read *The Lord of the Rings* about twenty times, I thought she might be interested.'

'Was she?'

'Yeah. It all looked a bit muddy outside, being February, but she liked the exhibition. And the tea shop.'

'Good to show her some of the local stuff, while you're here. What did you do on Saturday?'

'Went to London.'

'Did you?' Sharp eyes from the passenger seat.

'To cheer her up. And for something to do, to be honest.' She saw Maggie's eyebrows flick up, sceptical, but chose to ignore it.

'Any news on Josh?'

Robin hesitated. When she'd called on Friday night to say she'd spoken to Tarryn, she hadn't told Maggie she'd also spoken to Samir; she'd needed time to absorb what he'd said first. She knew she could rely on Maggie to keep it to herself, though. 'Samir called me,' she said. 'They've had the post mortem back. She was already dead when the fire started. It was a head injury, a single blow to the temple with their table lamp.'

Maggie squeezed her eyes shut. 'Oh, Rob.'

'They're not looking for anyone else.'

Maggie took a second, choosing her words. 'How do you feel about that?'

'I don't believe Josh would set the house on fire if he knew Pete was upstairs. I never will. Even if he'd lost it with Rin, which I also struggle to accept. But his child . . .'

'How *is* Peter?'

'That's why we went to the Mill yesterday – a distraction. I'd been texting Will about taking Lennie to visit but he called to say not to. He's got a respiratory infection.'

'What does that mean?'

'Well, family visitors only – they want to minimize his exposure. From a recovery standpoint . . . It was one of the things they were most afraid of.'

As they climbed the stairs to the office, they heard the landline ringing. It stopped just as Maggie got the first key in the door. 'Bugger.' Five seconds later, though, Robin's pay-as-you-go rang. 'Harry?'

He seemed not to hear her. 'Robin? It's Harry.'

248

She closed the door behind them. 'Is everything all right?'

Maggie stopped, halfway out of her coat.

'Valerie just came barging in here. She's saying I killed Becca.'

'I was here early – I don't know how she'd even know I'd be at the office at eight. Jas and Suze are round the corner, by the way – I told them to come back in an hour.' He took another turn across the floor, trainers squeaking. He looked younger again today, a T-shirt and soft navy hoody taking the place of the chambray shirt. 'She buzzed downstairs so I went to let her in, obviously. She seemed okay then, shaky but okay, so we came up here to talk. As soon as I closed the door, she . . . went nuts.'

'Tell us what she said, as close to her actual words as you can.'

'She said she knew I'd given Becca painkillers, that I'd got her addicted to pills so that I could "have my way" with her. Sleep with her, control her.'

'Control?'

'If she needed drugs and I was giving her them, she'd keep coming back to me.'

'But you've been friends since you were kids, Valerie told us that herself. Why would you need to?'

'That's what I said. But she said *you'd* told her Becca was sleeping with the person who gave her the pills.' He stopped pacing and looked at them, Maggie then Robin.

They glanced at one another. Shit. 'I'm sorry, Harry,' Maggie said. 'That is true. We didn't tell you because Becca didn't want you to know, and—'

'When?'

'Not when you two were together, obviously. June, maybe a week or so into July. It was a flash in the pan, a fling. Nothing meaningful.'

'How do you know that?'

Robin glanced at Maggie again. 'Lucy told us.'

'Great. So now I can't trust her, either.'

'I think you should interpret it as knowing you can,' Maggie said gently. 'Becca asked her to keep it under her hat so she did. Becca didn't want you to think badly of her. She cared about that – a lot.'

He dipped his head and turned to the window.

'Harry,' said Robin. 'Steven Cotton's irrelevant.'

'Hardly.'

'She spent a few nights with him, under the influence.'

'A few nights during which he got her hooked on painkillers.'

'Actually, he didn't,' said Maggie. 'Or we don't think she was really hooked. We've heard she wasn't doing it any more. She'd stopped.'

He sniffed, rubbed his hand over his face.

'I got hold of Tarryn on Friday night,' Robin said. 'Via Instagram, like you suggested. She said Becca told her she'd stopped using. She'd bumped into Stevo in town and, I'm quoting here, "He looked like shit". She had a moment of clarity, decided to pack it in.'

He turned. 'When?'

'October. Around her birthday. On the phone, I asked you if you'd ever seen any physical signs of it. You said no, right? And that lately she hadn't been flaky or unreliable, just knackered? She was working a lot – that makes sense. And if she'd been injecting regularly, it's unlikely she'd have been able to stop.'

'That's major, Harry,' Maggie said. 'Good news.'

'Tell us what happened with Valerie.'

He pulled out a chair and sat down. 'She assumed *I* gave Becca drugs because I'm black.'

Maggie shook her head. 'Let's not jump to conclusions. I know you're angry, and that's completely understandable, but try to give her the benefit of the doubt if you can. Her daughter's missing, she's under a massive amount of strain – you know what that's like. It's probably our fault. We had to tell her about the two of you seeing each other, and we also told her Becca was given drugs by someone she'd had a fling with. She put two and two together and got five.'

A snort. 'Is that why she called me a fucking black bastard?'

Robin saw Maggie stiffen. 'Did she?'

'She came barging in here, into *my* office, *my* business, and told me she knew what I'd done, that I was a "fucking black bastard" who'd given her daughter drugs, shagged her then killed her.'

'Harry, I'm so sorry.'

'It was like – I don't know what it was like. I've always thought she was weird. I didn't know if it was just me or if she was like that with everyone. I said to Becca a couple of times I didn't think she liked me.'

'And what did she say?'

'Not to be daft, I was imagining it. She said her mum was just shy and people took her the wrong way.' He shook his head. 'I think she would have hit me if it hadn't meant actually touching me. She said I'd been "sniffing round her daughter" for years, she'd seen the way I looked at her. As if I was some kind of animal. As if I wasn't fit to be Becca's friend, even, given what I am. Which, by the way, is mixed race – my dad's white. She might have said more but I opened the door and told her to get out.'

'What was Becca's own relationship with her like?' Robin asked.

'Close. You know about her dad? She was eight at the time and it made them super-tight. It was just the two of them all those years, looking out for each other.'

'What did Becca say about living at home?' asked Maggie.

'Not a lot – she didn't really talk about it. Occasionally she made a throw-away comment about living with her mother but I think it was just to stop people teasing her. Her mum did her washing and ironing, looked after her like that. And it made financial sense. Even sharing a place would have cost a few hundred a month, and she doesn't earn much at Hanley's.'

'From what we've heard, she's a bright girl, sparky. She didn't want to go to university?'

'No. She *is* bright, definitely – she's quick, very sharp, it's one of the things I like about her. But she was never particularly into academic work. She did all right at Grafton, she didn't struggle, but it's not a specially academic school. It's one of their things, a range: they have the academics for those who want it but it's not all about that. It's not a pressure-cooker.'

'What did she get for A-level?'

'An A and two Cs.'

'What was the A?'

'Home Economics. Not that it's just cooking but she's really good at it. Properly good – Lucy and I keep telling her to apply for the *Bake Off*. And swimming. She was captain of the school team but she only does it for fun now. Did.'

'Did?' said Maggie.

'I mean, she stopped doing it competitively after school. She didn't join a local team, which she could have done. Recently she hasn't even had time to go to the pool.'

'Harry, when Valerie said you'd killed Becca,' asked Robin, 'what do you think she meant? Exactly. Was she just talking about drugs or was she accusing you of actually *murdering* her?'

He shook his head. 'I honestly don't know.'

* * *

As they walked back through the Custard Factory, Robin's personal phone rang. *Kevin Y.* She hesitated.

Maggie looked at her. 'Are you going to answer that?'

'Here.' Robin handed her the car key. 'You go ahead; this'll only take a second.'

'It's okay, I don't mind waiting.'

'No, it's chilly. Go and get the motor going.'

With a quizzical look, Maggie took the key. The phone stopped before she was out of earshot; Robin waited a moment then hit redial, moving away from the café she was standing outside when she glimpsed Jas and Suze through the window.

'Hiya,' said Kev. 'Thought I'd missed you.'

'Sorry, I was just finishing something.' She glanced ahead. Maggie was turning the corner onto the main road, out of sight. 'How are things? Have you got news for me?'

'I have,' he said, 'but I don't know if you're going to like it. Or maybe you will – depends what angle you're coming from.'

'Hit me.'

'So I asked a couple of friends to ask friends of theirs if they'd heard anything on the vine, like you asked.'

'Thanks, Kev, appreciate it.'

'Word is, Josh *did* borrow money.'

Robin felt a swell of something unfamiliar: hope. 'When?'

'That's the thing. Two and a half years ago, more or less – September 'fourteen.'

'Who from?'

'Hold your horses. The thing is, he *did* borrow, and no doubt at hair-raising rates, but—'

'How much? Do you know?'

'Twenty grand.'

'Hm. But . . . ?'

253

'He paid it back, Rob. All of it. The debt was settled fair and square, pleasure doing business with you, sir. No one knows of anyone who was out for him on that score.'

She didn't like it. Of course Josh could have borrowed from someone else, too, unknown to Kev's friends of friends, it could be anyone, but it was another dead end. When Kev hung up, she stood for a moment, bereft. She hadn't realized how much she'd been counting on it, her last iron in the fire.

But as she started to walk it dawned on her that if the loan had closed off one avenue, it had opened another, or at least raised a new question: *how* had he paid it back? Had the Polish order Kath mentioned covered this twenty K as well as the loan she and Gareth had given them? Robin stopped at the top of Gibb Street to send two messages, one after the other. By the time she reached the car, she had replies. *Our loan was 3 yrs ago, paid back 6 months later w money from Polish order.* Then, *No inheritance or insurance pay-outs. Don't think they had anything worth 20K to sell.*

She opened the door and got in, giving Maggie a nothing-to-see-here smile.

She eyed her. 'What are you up to?'

'Me? That was school, about Len's inoculations paperwork.'

A single upward move of the head, *Sure.*

Robin started the engine. 'Valerie's?'

'Yep.'

As she pulled onto the main road, the new pieces began to arrange themselves. Josh had repaid Kath and Gareth and taken out the shonky loan at the same time. Had there been a Polish order at all or had he taken the loan at punishing interest to pay back his sister? But how had he repaid *that*? The couple of grand Kev had given him for the scrap might

254

have covered a payment – ten payments, two grand a pop plus interest? But he must have been in a tight spot to go to Kev in the first place, it occurred to her now: Josh was proud and he knew Kev had held a torch for Corinna. He must have bristled to some extent at having to go to him cap in hand. And assuming that had dealt with one payment, what about the other nine?

'Just be careful,' said Maggie suddenly. 'Listen to me on that at least.'

Valerie had clearly been expecting them. She burst into tears the moment she opened the front door and she led them down the hall to the kitchen without a word. She looked terrified, dark eyes wide, shoulders hunched as if she were about to spring into a defensive ball, hedgehog-style. The room had changed since the first times they'd seen it. It wasn't filthy but standards were slipping. A dirty milk pan had been left on the hob and the work surface around the kettle was now patterned with Spirograph tannin circles.

'So I'm guessing you know why we're here,' said Maggie.

Valerie looked at the floor. 'You've spoken to Harry.'

'We've just come from his office.'

'I'm sorry,' she said, with a sob. 'I didn't mean . . . I'm in such a state. I . . .'

'What did you say to him, Valerie?'

She bowed her head, her chin almost touching her chest. 'I called him a black bastard,' she mumbled.

'He said you also accused him of giving Becca drugs.'

'But *you* said that! You said she'd got them from who she was . . . sleeping with.'

'Valerie,' said Maggie, a little more softly, 'you told us yourself that Becca played the field. I distinctly remember telling you we

255

believed she'd started taking morphine last summer – early last summer. And you told us – and we've confirmed – that she had a whole relationship between then and now with someone other than Harry. Nick. Who, by the way, also had nothing to do with the drugs, just to eliminate any confusion there. So I don't accept it was a mistake.'

'I'm sorry,' she said. 'I said I'm sorry.'

Maggie ignored her. 'I want to be clear: I'm taking this very seriously. I won't tolerate racism, and no amount of worry is an excuse. Do you understand me?'

A quiet 'Yes.'

'Valerie?'

'Yes.' Slightly louder.

'Another hint of it, we'll resign from your case immediately, we won't hesitate.'

Silence.

'I'll also tell you that if I weren't genuinely worried about Becca, I'd do it right now.'

A barely audible 'Thank you.'

'Don't thank me yet.'

'Harry said you accused him of killing Becca,' said Robin.

Valerie looked up, button eyes shining. 'With the drugs, that's all I meant.'

'Are you sure about that?'

'Yes.'

'Did you accuse him of giving her drugs in order to control her?'

'Yes,' she said again, looking back down. 'He's always liked her. Don't forget, I've known him and Lucy since they started at Grafton House. She's never got involved with him before – why now? And why, just after she did, has she gone missing?'

'You know, Valerie,' said Maggie, shifting her weight to the other foot, 'given what you said today, people might think *you* had a motive for killing her.'

'What?' She stared, aghast.

'Did the idea of your daughter with a man of colour disgust you so much that you killed her?'

'No!'

'It's a question people could reasonably ask. You need to consider that.'

Valerie blinked, sending parallel tears down her cheeks.

'Right. So, tell us, have you got any concrete reason for thinking Harry has anything to do with Becca's disappearance?'

'No.'

'Don't say it just because you think it's what we want to hear. Are you *sure* you've never had reason to think he might hurt Becca?'

'Yes.' Valerie hesitated, grappling with something. 'He loves her.'

'All right.'

Valerie turned to get a tissue from the box on the table and Maggie looked at Robin. She shook her head slightly: *incredible, isn't it? In the twenty-first century.*

Blotting her eyes, Valerie crumpled onto a chair at the little table. She coughed and blew her nose. 'I really am sorry,' she said. 'I don't know what came over me. I wasn't planning to . . . launch into him. I just wanted to talk, to ask if she'd said or done anything that would explain . . . I . . .' She shook her head. 'I've always been bad with people. I get things wrong, I don't trust myself around them. I feel like everyone else knows how to handle themselves in the world and I don't.'

'Everyone feels like that,' said Robin.

She looked up, sceptical. 'You?'

'Are you kidding?'

'I should apologize, shouldn't I? I should tell him I'm sorry – ring him or . . .'

'To be honest,' said Maggie, 'the best thing you can do now is keep away from him. We'll tell him we've spoken to you, that you regret it and send your apologies but just leave him alone. Tensions are running high – no one's at their best.'

'Do you think we can forget this, you and me? Put it behind us?'

'It's not us you need to worry about. And we need to focus on Becca.'

'We had some good news for you this morning, before this,' Robin said.

'Really?' The sudden hope in her eyes was painful to see.

'We don't think Becca was using morphine any more,' she said. 'Opioids generally. It sounds like she'd managed to stop some months ago.'

Valerie's body relaxed, her shoulders visibly dropping. Almost immediately, though, she tensed again. 'But what does that mean? If it's not that, what's left?'

The car doors slammed, shutting out the street. Robin remembered how they'd left Valerie's house the first time. A week ago today – it felt like months.

'Christ on a bike,' said Maggie, putting on her seatbelt. 'Bring back the insurance fraudsters.'

'*Could* she actually have done it, do you think? Killed Becca accidentally in a rage, disposed of the body, constructed all this to divert attention?'

'Would she have hired us? She'd have had to go to the police, it'd raise suspicion otherwise, but investigators? Seems unlikely.

Also, she'd never have been able to lift the body so how *would* she have disposed of her?'

'Maybe that was why the kitchen was so spick the first time: she'd just done a big clean-up. Messy business, dismembering someone.'

Maggie rolled her eyes. 'Come on, sicko, get moving.'

The street was empty so Robin did a U-turn and headed them back towards Stratford Road. At the end, however, instead of turning left towards town and the office, she indicated right.

'*Qué?*' said Maggie, looking up from her phone.

'Quick detour. While we're here.'

Robin watched as with the tip of his knife, Gamil arranged the kite-shaped pieces of kaju barfi into a seven-petalled flower then, in a deft sequence, whipped a length of ribbon from the dispenser, tied it present-style around the box and curled the ends. 'You're sure that's all? You see how many different kinds I have.' He swept a hand through the air over the pastel array. 'These, with pistachio, they're my favourite – try one.'

'No, honestly, that's perfect. But please let me pay for them.'

The hand again, this time waving her away.

'Thank you.'

'My pleasure. So what did you want to ask me this time?' He looked between them. 'Is it the same girl?'

'Becca, yes,' said Maggie. 'Rebecca Woodson.'

Robin brought up the picture she'd just taken of the photo-graph on the fridge, Valerie and Becca in Torbay after Becca's GCSEs, Becca in her cut-offs and strappy top, Valerie in Clarks nun-sandals and a mid-length skirt, their squinting smiles. She handed it to him.

'We wondered if you knew her mother at all?'

'She lives locally?' he asked, pinching out to enlarge her face.

'Yes.'

'I don't, I'm sorry.'

'She's not a customer? She doesn't come in?'

He shook his head. 'No.'

Chapter Eighteen

Robin's head slipped along the glass; she jerked awake. Ten past four – shit, she'd been out for at least twenty minutes. No wonder: the car was like the tropical house at Kew. She turned off the heater and opened the window, letting in a slap of cold air.

The view was doing nothing to keep her awake, either: a trading estate in Hockley; specifically, the warehouse where Michael Dixon, forty-two, was working a fifty-hour week packing shipments for an online electrical-parts supplier while also claiming Jobseeker's Allowance. Allegedly. Hollow-cheeked and dull-eyed, his picture suggested he hadn't had many lucky breaks in life. Maybe today was an exception: if he left work at four, as they suspected, she'd just slept right through it.

No missed calls. Good, at least she hadn't been caught napping by Maggie, and she hadn't missed Tarryn.

She'd left a message for her at lunchtime. When they'd spoken on Friday, the significant information seemed to be that Becca had stopped using, but now Robin wondered if she'd missed the point entirely. At least twice during the call, she'd had the impression, hadn't she, that Tarryn was choosing her words carefully? She also remembered her relief when she'd said she was a private investigator. Her explanation had made sense – if the police weren't involved, they didn't know Becca was hurt – but she could think on her feet, she was clearly an intelligent woman. A bit of Internet research this morning had unearthed a history degree from the University of Sydney, and she'd been working in marketing for a big media group before she'd come travelling.

Becca trusted her; she was the only person they'd found in whom she'd confided about either Harry or the drugs. And Tarryn worked at The Spot.

The phone vibrated in her hand – was it her? No. *Mum mobile.*

'Robin?' Her mother sounded anxious. 'Is Lennie with you?'

'No. Weren't you picking her up today?' For a moment, she doubted herself – god, had *she* been supposed to? – but no, she remembered Christine telling Len she'd see her in the usual spot.

'Yes, I was – I am. I'm outside school now but I've been here twenty-five minutes and she hasn't come out. I'm parked where I always do, just round the corner.'

Robin thought of Friday afternoon, how she'd fled the place as if it was on fire. 'Have you tried ringing her?'

'Of course. There's no answer.'

'Did you leave a message?'

'Yes but obviously she hasn't replied or I wouldn't be calling you, would I?'

'Okay, sorry. Stay on and I'll call her from my work phone. Just a minute.' On the pay-as-you-go, she keyed in Lennie's number. 'It's ringing,' she said but then it stopped and went to voicemail.

'Hi, Len,' she said, 'it's Mum. I'm just on the other line to Gran, she's waiting for you outside school. Obviously there's crossed wires about pick-up. Could you give one of us a call?

Either this number or my usual – whichever, doesn't matter. Speak in a mo.'

'No answer?' said Christine.

'Have you spoken to Dad? Could he have got her?'

'No. I don't think so. He had a meeting with the sales director at four. I'll try him, just in case. Call you back.'

Her mother hung up. A lorry went by, too fast for the little road, metal doors clanking. The quiet that flooded in afterwards felt deeper, absorbent. The commercial buildings across the road were all in use, there were twenty or more cars parked in the yard out front, but she couldn't see a single human. She imagined pale men moving behind the mirrored windows, invisible but watching.

The phone. 'It's me,' said her mother unnecessarily. 'Your father's at the office. He hasn't heard from her.'

'I'll ring the school. Maybe she's in detention or—'

'Detention? Lennie?'

Robin felt a bizarre defensive instinct: yes, Lennie. Was her daughter so blandly obedient she'd never get into trouble? 'Well, she's not taking to the place like a duck to water, is she? Perhaps someone tried to push her around and she retaliated, or maybe she saw someone else being picked on. She wouldn't stand for—'

'Wouldn't they tell you if she was going to be late?'

'I don't know. I don't know their systems yet. The number's on this phone, Mum. I'll ring you back.'

The call was answered almost immediately. 'St Saviour's.'

Robin recognized the school secretary from when she'd been registering Lennie. Pam Travis – she'd been no more inspired-sounding then. 'Hello,' she said, 'this is Robin Lyons, Elena Lyons' mother. Has she been kept back at school for any reason? My mother's waiting outside to pick her up.'

263

'Hold on,' the woman said wearily. 'I'll check the detention list.' A huffing breath suggested she'd had to stand up. Robin heard shuffling papers. 'Here. Lyons?' Another breath, this one closer to the phone and heavier, as if the effort was tiring her out. 'No. Sorry.'

'Is there any reason she'd be this late out? She couldn't be talking to a teacher or working on a project somewhere?'

'Does she do chess club?'

Robin hadn't known they had such a thing – she was surprised. 'No.'

'That's the only after-school on Monday, sorry.' The woman took another stertorous breath then seemed to soften. 'Give me your number and I'll go down and check, just in case.'

Before calling her mother, Robin took a moment to think. Where could Lennie be? She didn't know Birmingham well enough to have favourite spots and even if she did, she knew she wasn't allowed – she was thirteen, for god's sake, she couldn't just wander off on her own. *No, don't get cross, concentrate.* Maybe she'd needed a bit of space, walked home – she'd used to walk from RPG. But that was always with Naomi, never alone, or if she was going home with Carly and Emma, they all took the bus together. She didn't have a friend from Savvy's to walk with yet, or if she did, she hadn't told them.

Could she have gone into town? To have a look around, drift about some shops? Or the hospital to try to see Peter?

Quickly, she called Will. No reply.

She Googled the number for the hospital and asked to be put through to Intensive Care. 'Peter Legge?' said the woman. 'No, there's no visitors with him at the moment, and I've only got adults in the waiting area, sorry.'

Christine called on the other line. 'She's not in detention,'

Robin told her. 'The secretary's gone to see if she's joined chess club without telling us.'

'Would she?'

'I don't think so but I don't think she'd just wander off somewhere, either. She's not with Peter, I just checked. Though she could still be on her way there. Maybe she got the bus into town – she's got money, I gave her some on Saturday. I'll call her again, hold on.'

Voicemail again. 'Hi, Len, it's me. Give me a ring as soon as you can, we're just a bit worried. You're not in any trouble, nothing to worry about, just want to make sure you're okay.' She paused. 'I love you.'

'Now what?' said Christine.

'Could you drive the route home, see if she's walking?'

'What are you going to do?'

'Go to Corinna's.'

The snowman house, where they'd spent Christmases and weekends, where Len had been doted on by Rin and Josh and played for hours with Peter, the closest thing she had to a cousin or in fact any family her own age. Poor Lennie, what kind of childhood was it, the single child of a single workaholic mother, no father, no family nearby until now and only then under duress. *Mum, Gran, could you please stop fighting?*

The school run had shaded seamlessly into rush hour. Edgbaston was almost halfway round the city from Hockley, north-west to south, light after light after light, traffic solid. Both phones were on her lap, ringers on maximum, but her eyes kept going to them anyway. *Come on, Len.*

There would be a simple explanation, she told herself. But Lennie had never done this before – she was reliable, she'd never gone off on her own. But then, she'd never been uprooted before, had she, never been pulled out of a school where she'd been happy and had a ton of friends, separated from a man who'd wanted to be her father, dragged off to a city she'd only ever visited in order to share a room with her mother and have someone she'd loved be violently killed.

Lennie, I'm sorry – I'm so sorry.

And what if the explanation wasn't simple? What if she hadn't just gone off?

Feeling sick, she faced it: if Lennie had been taken, it would be her fault. Her work, either Hinton and Farrell or Becca, would have made her a target. Because even if Becca had been abducted at random – a pretty girl coming home in a unlicensed cab in the small hours, alone, tired, possibly drunk – the likelihood of the same applying to Lennie – taken in broad daylight, in the two hundred yards between the school gates and the door of her grandmother's car – was nil.

And then there was the other possibility. With another nauseous swell, she thought of that night. If Corinna had been killed for that . . .

The car in front baulked at an amber light, forcing her to stamp on the brake just as the phone rang through the Bluetooth.

St Saviour's.

'Mrs Lyons? It's Pam Travis at the school.' She was breathing as if she'd just finished a spin class. She wasn't radically unfit, Robin realized suddenly, she was *asthmatic*. Years ago, a bloke she'd arrested had had an asthma attack on the way to the nick. Even after they'd got him an inhaler, his breathing had sounded just like this: laboured, hard work. God, why was she such a bitch?

'I went down to the gym for you, to chess club.' She paused, took a painful-sounding breath.

'Thank you so much.'

'No problem. Elena wasn't there.' Wheeze. 'But on the way back, I bumped into Mrs Shah, who teaches Chemistry.' Wheeze. 'She was supposed to have had her this afternoon, she said – Elena's class had double chemistry at the end of the day – but she wasn't there.' A cough. 'So I checked the register for the lesson before that, French, and she wasn't there, either. We think she left school at lunchtime.'

By the time she made the turn into Corinna's road, Robin's nerves were jumping. Lennie wasn't at Dunnington Road – Christine had called when she reached home. She'd even checked Dennis's tiny shed.

The snowman house was about halfway down, its position marked now by a break in the line of cars parked at the kerb. Robin scanned the pavement. No Lennie. She pulled in opposite the house, as much as the police cones allowed. No one sitting on the wall or huddled among the bushes.

The uniform was still at the gate. He gestured at her to move off; she ignored him. She made herself look properly. First the garden – the white forensics tent was still there, its pointed top just visible over Rin's huge rhododendron – then the house itself.

Even though she'd seen it on TV, even though she'd conjured those images on the way here to prepare herself, it was horrifying. Nightmarish. The black sockets of the glassless windows, the soot stains like ghoulish make-up. The hole in the roof was covered with a large blue tarp now and the edges flapped in the wind. She could hear the snapping even in the car, like flames, crackling.

A rap on the glass an inch from her ear. She jumped then lowered the window.

'Miss?' The uniform stooped, bringing his face into view. He was in his late forties, sandy, avuncular. 'You can't park here, I'm afraid.'

'I'm looking for my daughter.'

'Sorry?' A look of alarm.

'Her name's Lennie – Elena. Corinna and Josh were friends of ours.' She pointed at the house. 'I wondered if she'd come here to . . . see. To grieve.'

'Oh. Right.' He looked at her and narrowed his eyes slightly. 'How old is she?'

'Thirteen.'

'Have you got a picture? I've been here all afternoon.'

Robin showed him and he shook his head. 'No. Sorry.'

She drove back to Hall Green sick to her stomach, eyes landing on everyone she saw: not her, not her, not her. Why wasn't she answering her phone? She thought of Becca's phone in its sparkly mint-green case, fallen from the bed, out of sight. Had Lennie left hers somewhere – dropped it?

A text from Will: he hadn't seen her; keep him posted. Christine phoned again: she wasn't in the little local branch library round the corner, either, but it was half past five now – places would be closing, wouldn't they, shops and cafés? Maybe wherever she was would shut and she'd make her way home?

As Robin turned into Dunnington Road, her own phone rang again. A spike of hope that collapsed as soon as she saw the caller ID: *Adrian*. Seriously? Now? She waited for it to ring out. Almost immediately, it started again: *Adrian*. Was he pocket-dialling? Or had he called back to leave a message this time? It rang out and she waited for a voicemail notification that didn't come. It rang again: *Adrian*. Oh, for fuck's sake. She hit the button.

'Robin?' The familiar voice filled the car. 'It's me. I just got home from work and found a very shaky Len on my doorstep.'

Her mother wouldn't let her go until she'd sat for half an hour and drunk the hot chocolate she made her. 'For the shock. I can see your hands shaking, Robin. I'm not having you on the motorway until you've calmed down a bit.' She'd started to remonstrate then gave in. Alone in the bathroom, she dropped her head into her hands and felt her whole body trembling.

The M40 again, this time alone, the tail-lights ahead streaming in the dark, road signs looming: London, London. The supper Christine had packed for her – 'All finger-food, I know you won't stop' – sat untouched on the passenger seat. She was buffeted by waves of emotion: fury at Lennie for scaring her; relief so profound it felt almost religious; guilt; fury again.

When she reached Shepherd's Bush and pulled up behind Adrian's BMW, she leaned back against the seat and closed her eyes for a moment, collecting herself. Rain pattered onto the bonnet from the branches of the lime tree. Her legs were still shaking as she climbed the front steps.

Lennie opened the door, face apprehensive. Robin pulled her into a hug so tight that after a few seconds she wriggled loose. 'Ow, Mum, too hard.' Then she laid her cheek back against Robin's shoulder. 'I'm really sorry.'

'It's all right, it doesn't matter. Just don't do it again or I'll murder you with my own bare hands, okay?' She laughed but the lump in her throat made it come out wrong.

As she'd known she would, Len disappeared the moment Adrian handed Robin a glass of wine. She had no energy to refuse it if she'd wanted to; the adrenaline that had been coursing through her since the phone call in Hockley was gone, wire cut. From the sitting room came the sound of voices; Lennie had turned on the TV.

'You look shattered,' Adrian said. 'Sit down.'

She pulled out a chair, making its wooden legs screech on the slate floor. It was an effort not to put her head on the table; she felt like she'd just got out of bed after surgery. 'I can't believe she came all the way here on her own,' she said.

'Independent woman. Where does she get it?' A twitch in the cheek, half a smile.

Adrian's kitchen. How many hours had she spent in here? They'd both always liked it more than the sitting room, gravitated here naturally, stayed at the table long after they'd finished eating. It looked its best in the evening with the glow of the lamp on the sideboard and the reflected gleam of the spotlights over the steel counter. If Lennie had designed the lighting herself, just for tonight, she couldn't have done a better job. More indirect light shone through the glass panels over the table – the couple next door were putting their children to bed. They'd never actually lived here, she and Len – Adrian had asked but she'd said no, of course – but they'd been here so much that they knew the rhythms of the place as well as the ones at their own old flat. The so-called guest room upstairs had been full of Lennie's things, the bed always made up with the candy-striped sheets Adrian had taken her to choose at Peter Jones.

He poured himself a glass and took the chair across the corner of the table from her, two or three feet of space between them. Soft grey shirt, black tie – still in his work clothes. He didn't need lamplight to look good but it didn't hurt. It played up the planes of his face, the long straight nose between the wide-set brown eyes, the cheekbones. When he frowned, deep lines appeared between his eyebrows and his lower lip protruded. She'd found that strangely compelling back in the day. Sultry.

'I'm sorry all this is happening to you,' he said.

She took a swig of wine. 'I brought it on myself.'

'Corinna?'

'The rest.'

He didn't deny it, she noticed. 'Are the police getting anywhere?' he said. 'I didn't want to ask Len. I keep searching online but I can't find any news.'

'There isn't any. They're not even looking for anyone else any more. They're convinced it was a domestic. She and Josh had a fight, he whacked her over the head and killed her, probably a moment of madness, then set the house on fire.'

'Josh? No way. I can't believe that.'

She felt a rush of affection for him, had to stop herself reaching out and rubbing his arm. 'Thank you,' she said instead.

'For what?'

'Thinking the best of my friend.'

'I liked him. Like him. You know that – I always have. Have they got any idea where he could be?'

'Not as far as I know. The last I heard, they hadn't got further than finding his car. They probably think he's taken himself off to end it all.'

He frowned again, deeper. 'Wasn't your guy on West Midlands friends with him, too?'

'He's not my guy,' she said pettily. 'But yes.'

He shook his head, bemused. 'I don't get that.' He took a mouthful of wine then put the glass down, sliding his fingers either side of the stem.

'Adrian, did Len talk to you at all?'

'A bit, over pizza. She didn't want to say anything disloyal but . . . She's having a hard time. You know that.'

Robin's cheeks were hot. 'Did she mention anything specific?'

'She says you fight with your mum a lot.'

271

'She's doing my head in. But I'm trying. Anything else?'

'Not really. It's kind of . . .' He shrugged. 'All of it, I think. Basically, apart from Corinna, she's just homesick. She wants to come home.'

Robin felt a burst of frustration. 'D'ya think?' She pulled her best gormless expression: *Is that why we're here, in London? In your kitchen?*

'Robin,' he said.

The look on his face pulled her up short. 'What?'

'I know I'll never be Samir.'

She stared.

'But I'll never be *Samir*. I'd never let you down. I'd never do that to you.'

She couldn't get the sodding lump out of her throat. 'I know,' she said eventually. 'I do know that, Ade. And I wish I . . .' She shook her head. 'It's not enough.'

Defeated, Lennie cried as they drove away, big tears running down her cheeks in the strobing amber streetlight. Robin felt sick with self-loathing. Inflicting pain on herself was her prerogative, and Adrian was an adult, he'd known for a while what he was dealing with, the masochist, but not Lennie. 'There aren't enough sorries in the world to tell you how bad I feel, Len,' she said, 'but I am so sorry.' *Sorry for not loving the right person, for not being able to pretend. Sorry for what I've done to you. For what I am.*

Lennie said nothing. She turned her face towards the window and wiped her cheeks with her fingers. The network of little streets around Ade's house – Robin had driven them a hundred times, knew the shortcuts, where the metered parking was, the all-night corner shop. Windows glowed, the people behind them having late suppers, watching the news, accepting without a second thought that in a bit they'd go upstairs to their own rooms, their own beds.

As they approached the Fuller's brewery on the roundabout at Chiswick, Lennie shifted her body in her seat suddenly and glared at her. 'You said you missed him.'

'What?'

'Here. In the car, on Saturday morning when we were driving. I asked you and you said yes.'

'No, I didn't. I . . .' She stopped. Yes, she remembered, she did. *If it was small and white and no harm could come of it.* Despite everything, she felt a flare of frustration – Jesus, could she not get a break? Could she not get away with one single, well-intentioned thing? 'I'm sorry,' she said. 'You're right, I did say that. And I do. He's a lovely man and I miss that. But I can't pretend, Len. It wouldn't be fair to any of us. It would be cheating. It would be cheating him.'

Lennie said nothing. She shifted her body again, turning her back.

The dashboard clock read 11.52 when they reached Dunnington Road. The downstairs lights were on, Dennis up again. Lennie had fallen asleep on the M25, head against the glass, but she'd woken up as they'd left the motorway and now she took off her seatbelt, picked up her backpack and got out without a word. The slam ricocheted down the street.

Glancing up as she locked the car, Robin saw her mother backlit in the doorway. She must have sat up to keep Dennis company; she'd known he wouldn't go to bed before they were safely home. She saw Lennie hug her tight, their two bodies becoming a single silhouette. *Help me, Gran, save me from my horrible, selfish cow of a mother.*

They disappeared and Robin felt a stab of abandonment. Weird:

273

did she really care if her mother didn't give *her* a hug at the door? But as she came up the path, Christine stepped back into the light. The look on her face.

Robin stopped. 'What?'

'Love, Peter had a heart attack.'

'I didn't want you to know while you were driving,' Christine said, Lennie curled in next to her on the sofa. She turned the glass of Scotch between her hands, the crystal catching light from the standard lamp. 'I rang Di to see if I could bring her some things for the fridge but I didn't get that far. I knew straight away something was wrong. More wrong.'

'Where was she?'

'With Kath, on their way back to the hospital – they'd only just got the call. Kath rang half an hour ago with the update, I told her we'd be up. Thank god they managed to resuscitate him.'

'What did the doctors say? Could it happen again?'

'Apparently there's no way of knowing. It's the infection in the lung, Di said – his body's under so much strain and it's just not responding to the antibiotics like they thought. They're going to add another one but after that, it's just a matter of hoping.' She paused, put her arm around Lennie. 'They've been told to prepare for the worst.'

The words settled round them, toxic dust.

'But he could still be okay, couldn't he?' Len's voice sounded so small.

Christine pulled her closer. 'We don't know yet, sweetheart. He's very, very poorly.'

They sat up for half an hour or so then began the slow process of rotating four people through one bathroom. Robin went last, in no rush: she knew she wouldn't sleep for a while. Lennie climbed the ladder to her bunk without a word, said nothing when Robin said goodnight.

She lay alone in the dark, duvet pushed back, window open, sweating.

The day she'd brought Lennie home from the hospital, it had been Corinna who picked them up. She'd arrived at Charing Cross carrying the detachable part of the car seat like an Easter basket. Robin had been terrified of hurting Lennie's tiny neck so after she'd put her little socks on – less frightening but still scary – it was Rin who'd lifted her into the moulded plastic shell with its grey velvet lining, strapped her in. She'd had to carry her, too, as Robin, white with pain, did the C-section shuffle through the corridors to the lifts. She'd felt deranged, bent in half, staring wide-eyed at normal people, who seemed to have withdrawn from her behind an invisible but impenetrable wall. Her pregnancy bump had deflated quickly – stress, probably, said the midwife, ripe with judgement – and her maternity dress hung off her like a shroud.

It was freezing, a blue-skied knife of a December day, the frost still on the ground at lunchtime. Corinna had salted the stone steps down from the street. On their front door, she'd stuck two tinsel sparklers and a banner with big gold letters, CONGRATULATIONS. When she unlocked the door, Robin smelled beef stew and burst into tears of pathetic gratitude.

The emergency C-section had been all her own fault: by racing to finish as much of her dissertation as she could before Lennie arrived, she'd given herself stroke-level high blood pressure, bringing Len's arrival forward two weeks. 'So that backfired,' Rin had said, dry, from the vinyl chair at her bedside on the ward. They'd started laughing, Robin clutching her abdomen, trying to hold her stitches together, begging her to stop.

Love you, you know.

And I love you. I wish I'd told you. I wish I'd said it at the time. Do you think I didn't know, you emotional retard? Get a grip!

Robin grinned as tears slid sideways into her hair. What would Corinna do? If the roles were reversed and she was dead, Corinna the one lying here in a freaking bunk bed while Lennie lay dying in hospital, what would she do?

As if she even needed to ask.

Chapter Nineteen

This time, she drove into the close and parked right outside the house. Enough: if there was someone here to be afraid of, she wanted to see them. The dog whose sordid patch of concrete she'd noticed last time was at home today, a huge German shepherd that lunged to the extent of its chain as the car passed. Its guttural barking, barely domesticated, echoed around the close, trapped under the marbled sky. The light felt sharp, tinted a queasy yellow that promised the snow Christine said was forecast.

The curtains in the downstairs bay were drawn again. As she rang the bell, she felt eyes on her and turned to see the front door three houses further round shut silently. The barking continued, alarm at the prison perimeter, doing nothing to allay her unease. She'd been calling Ana all morning, six times in total, leaving two voice messages, the second, an hour ago, apologizing if she was being alarmist. 'Could you text, Ana, just to let me know you're okay?' No response.

She rang the bell again, shaded her eyes and peered through the hectic patterned glass. A pale blur at the top left corner, moving – she stepped back. A tug on the chain, the clunk of the deadlock, and the door opened on a woman in a light-blue dressing gown, her hair in a towel turban. Not Ana but her friend, Marta. Just as Ana had, though, she scanned the close over Robin's shoulder.

'Sorry to disturb you. I hope I didn't get you out of the bath.'

No answer. The door stayed at the same narrow angle, the chain at chest level between them.

'Is Ana in?'

The woman shook her head.

'Is she at work?'

'I don't know.'

'Marta – that's right, isn't it? I've been trying to reach her but she's not answering her phone. I think something's going on. I'm worried.'

Marta's brow furrowed, but strangely, it made her look younger. In her Tesco fleece, glancing up from her stew at the table, she'd looked the same age as Ana – as her: thirty-four, thirty-five. Now, bare-faced, pink from the bath, she didn't look more than late twenties. She hesitated a moment then slid off the chain. When Robin was inside, she locked the door behind them.

Unsettled, Robin followed her to the kitchen. The smell of citrus detergent was unmitigated by food this time, adding another dimension to the austerity of the room, which now looked bare as a barracks kitchen, the worktops empty apart from a disposable set of salt and pepper shakers by the hob and a cheap electric kettle in the corner. There was nothing on the windowsill or the table; the only thing to suggest anyone actually lived here was a corkboard by the door that bristled with paper: a flyer from the council, menus from a Chinese and the fish and chip shop, a couple of photographs. Her card, the one she'd given Ana.

As subtly as she could, Robin assessed the back door. The little bolt at the top was on; the light coming round the lock said the latch and dead-bolt were, too. She doubted she'd be able to kick it out if she had to, certainly not quickly.

'When did you last see her?' she said. 'Today? Was she here last night?'

Marta pulled the lapels of her dressing gown over her collarbone. The room was very cold, her feet bare. 'No.'

'Has she got someone she stays with? A boyfriend?'

'No.' Slight indignation. 'She has husband at home.'

'When was the last time you saw her? Or spoke to her?'

Silence.

'Marta?'

'Saturday.'

Robin's own call to Ana, when they'd spoken, had been Friday morning. It was Tuesday. 'Has she been home since then? You just haven't crossed paths?' The woman looked confused. 'I mean, you haven't been here together – you were at the house at different times?'

'No,' Marta said. 'She's gone. She put things in suitcase, call taxi, gone.'

'Did you see her go? Yourself – with your own eyes?'

'Yes. I was here. I saw. She hug me, get in taxi, go.'

'Was she alone? Was anyone with her?'

'Alone.'

'Where did she go?'

'I don't know, she didn't tell.'

Ana had introduced her as her friend, hadn't she? Friend, not housemate. It might have been a question of language but Ana's English was pretty good.

'*Why* did she go?'

A moment passed but then Marta said, 'She is afraid.'

'Of who?'

279

'Police. They find out she is Serbian.' She jerked a thumb over her shoulder, *Out*.

'But they told her she was safe for now. While Peter's ill, they're turning a blind eye – I mean, not worrying about her status. They want her to be able to visit him.'

She shrugged. 'Maybe she not believe.'

'Is that true? Is that what she said?'

'Is what she said to me.'

Robin tried to meet her eye but couldn't. 'Look,' she said in frustration, 'I'm not police. I don't care about anyone's immigration status, I don't give a toss. I'm not going to cause any trouble like that for Ana, for you, anyone. I'm just trying to find out what happened to my friend and her family. Her little boy's ten. *Ten*. He had a heart attack last night – he nearly died. There's every chance he still will.'

A look of consternation crossed the woman's face.

'Someone *did* this to them and now Ana, who worked for them, spent time at their house, has disappeared, too? Afraid of police who told her not to be afraid?'

Marta looked at her, unblinking. Did she understand?

'Who is she scared of, Marta? Tell me.'

'I don't *know*.'

'Is it Josh? Corinna's husband – Peter's dad?'

Not a flicker. 'She told me, scared of police.'

The frustration turned to anger. 'And *I'm* telling *you* that's total shit.' She moved into Marta's space; Marta took a step back, against the cupboards. 'Tell me where to find her. Otherwise, I'll go to the police and tell them Ana didn't just *know* what happened, she was involved – she was part of it and you're covering for her. Accessory to murder.'

'I *can't* tell you,' Marta said, fierce. 'I can't. She didn't tell.'

'Then where do I start looking? Where did she work?'

'I don't know. Cleaning, other family for babysitting – I don't know address.'

'Did she tell the police? Or shall I ask them myself? Shall I say you sent me?'

Marta looked as if she wanted to spit in her face. 'Church,' she said. 'Serbian Orthodox church. Sometimes she goes.'

The door slammed behind her, setting the dog off again full-throated. As she reached the pavement, it leapt, half choking itself as the chain yanked it back. Further enraged, it leapt again, then again as she rounded the back of the car. She snatched the door shut after her, locked it. If it pulled the ring out of the wall and got free, it would have gone for her and who would have dragged it off?

She turned out of the close onto Allens Croft Road, heart thudding, the reek of burning bridges in her nostrils. If Samir heard about this, she was in deep shit. Well, so be it.

'Nearly two hours for lunch?'

'I know. Sorry.' Robin sat down and made a show of prodding the computer back to life. She'd taken some deep breaths before coming upstairs, tried to normalize for re-entry, but the energy was still humming off her, she could feel it.

Maggie sought eye contact and held it. 'Where were you?'

She hesitated. 'I went to Ana's.'

'Corinna's babysitter?'

Reluctantly, Robin told her about the conversation with Marta, omitting mention of her physical intimidation and threats to the woman, or her information about the church.

'She definitely knew the police were turning a blind eye?' asked Maggie.

'Yeah.'

Elbow on the table, she tapped her fingers against her lips in the way Robin was coming to know well. 'Is *she* Serbian? This Marta?'

'I don't know.'

'Might be why she was frightened at the door?'

'It didn't feel like it. And I told her I didn't care about her status.'

'Have you told Samir any of this, Robin? Or Webster, is it?'

'Not yet. I will.' At some stage.

'Do. Then leave it alone – leave it to the people whose job it actually is. Please. There's no point anyone trying to help you if you're hell-bent on self-sabotage.'

'I'm not. I—'

Maggie held up a hand then pointed at the laptop. 'That's all. Now, work – *our* work. How are you getting on?'

'Nothing. I've been through all six of the syndicate now and the worst I can see is a year's ban for drink-driving.'

'Which one was that?'

'Rob Wilson. The accountant from Kidderminster.'

'How about the one in the picture you showed me? The school reunion.'

'Steven Baker.'

'I'm assuming that came to nothing, the connection to Josh? Just a coincidence or you would have told me, wouldn't you?' Her expression said it wasn't a rhetorical question.

'Of course I would. He did know Josh, he said, but purely from school. That was the only link between them.'

'Right. So what about the manager, David?'

'Not a lot so far. He used to run a place in Leeds, apparently, which gets good reviews at first glance. I'm going to poke around a bit more, see if there was anything there. His Facebook's almost all *Top Gear*-style reposts about cars, and him and his mates getting hot under the collar about entertainment systems.' It was a bit disappointing, actually, given the suave appearance; she'd hoped for evidence of an actual inner life. 'But I'll keep going. There's something at The Spot, there has to be.'

'Have you spoken to Tarryn again?'

'Trying. I left her a message yesterday lunchtime but she hasn't called me back. I'll give her another go now.'

It was amazing, Robin thought, that you could grow up in a city, live there for eighteen years, and still be oblivious to an entire, apparently vibrant subculture a handful of miles from your doorstep. If you'd asked her yesterday, she'd have thought of the Serbian Orthodox church in Ladbroke Grove, her old turf in London, before she'd ever remembered one in Bournville.

But according to its website, this had been the first in the UK, built in the Sixties by Serbs displaced during World War Two on land sold to them at a special rate by the philanthropic Cadbury family. The Cadbury name was all over Bournville, of course, because they'd founded it, moving their chocolate factory out from the city centre in Victorian times to what had been fields then, building their model village for the workforce. The family was Quaker and even now, you couldn't buy booze here.

The village had become a suburb long ago but it was still green and open, liberally scattered with trees. The church was set back from the road on a slight rise, standing proudly on its corner like the symbol of resilience it was. She'd been weirdly moved by the story of how the displaced Serbs had built it with their own hands, doing their paid work at night so they could labour by day, living on very little while they scratched together the money to pay for it. The building seemed to embody the story: its footprint was small, the walls just brick, but it reached twice as high as the houses across the street, cresting in a complicated roof of arches and multiple levels, a high copper-clad dome.

The entrance was round this corner, opposite the medical centre whose small car park she was in. Twenty minutes ago, a bald, dark-bearded man had driven up to the gate to the church compound, unlocked it then driven through, out of sight. After a couple of minutes, he'd reappeared on foot, stocky in a charcoal suit, and opened the double doors of the church itself. Good, Robin thought; even if Ana arrived and left by car, she'd enter the building this way, and she'd have an opportunity to approach her.

As far as Maggie knew, Robin was back on the trading estate in Hockley having another crack at Michael Dixon, but his luck had held for a second day. She felt guilty, of course, especially after the two-hour lunch, but what could she do? She'd had to come; after this, Tuesday, there wasn't another service until Saturday morning.

Vespers started at five. At ten to, a silver Nissan Micra turned off Cob Lane and indicated into the church drive. A man in his sixties, probably, alone. A moment later, a couple arrived, the woman's grey hair just visible under a green patterned headscarf. Then, within a minute, the trickle became a flood, relatively speaking, twelve or fifteen cars appearing at the mouth of the little lane, making the sharp turn onto the church grounds. Unsurprisingly, given the time, a lot of the congregants were retirement-age but a couple in their twenties walked up, holding hands, and she saw two men in their forties, another of thirty or so, shaven-headed and smooth-faced.

But by five past five, when the doors were shut, only three women between twenty-five and forty had walked through them, two of them together, friends, the other with a man who looked like her dad. None of them was Ana.

A car pulled alongside and a pregnant woman got out and unbuckled a little boy of about eighteen months from the back. Robin watched as he toddled inside the medical centre, holding his mother's hand, then Googled 'Serb Orthodox Vespers service length' on her phone. Nothing formal but a couple of people on chatrooms suggested somewhere around forty-five minutes.

She took the photograph from her pocket, her thumb finding the short tear made by the drawing pin as she'd pulled it from the corkboard. It had been taken in the garden at Ana's house, she recognized the bench and the fence, the backdrop of tall trees. Four women smiled for the camera, their arms around each other, all squinting slightly against the late-afternoon sunlight pouring over the roof of the house in front of them, Marta on the end, then Ana next to two women who looked alike – presumably the sisters she'd said shared a room.

It was a risk but again, what choice did she have? There'd be no more leads from Marta, and Will said Ana hadn't been in touch about visiting Pete. Just in case it was specifically *her* whom Ana was ignoring, Robin had called her using the office landline when Maggie went to the loo and then from a phone box round the corner before she got in the car. Nothing. Each time, the phone rang then went to voicemail.

The energy of the encounter with Marta hadn't completely subsided; it would be a challenge to sit still for three quarters of an hour. In an effort to distract herself – and assuage her guilt at bunking off surveillance of Michael Dixon – she tried to do some Internet research on her phone but she was too wired for painstaking work on a tiny screen. After a few minutes, she gave up and opened Games instead.

At twenty to five, Solitaire was swallowed by an incoming call. She did an actual double-take at the caller name then glanced

285

up. Across the road, a blond man, one of the forty-somethings, was pinning the church doors open.

'Gid?'

He was walking, soft sounds of movement layered against a background of passing cars, a distant siren. 'Robin? It's me.'

Yes, they have this thing called number recognition now, she nearly said, before some vestigial scrap of self-preservation yanked her back. 'Hi.'

'Look, I'm sorry about the weekend. I mean, I know you wouldn't have done it – shown up like that – unless you were under pressure, so let's forget it, okay? No hard feelings?'

'Well, I wouldn't go that far.' She'd intended it to sound jokey but it didn't and actually, good.

Across the road, the bearded man who'd unlocked the gates had come outside and was standing by the door, his suit now covered or replaced by black vestments – was that the word, the long black frock? He was getting ready to greet his congregation as they left, she realized, and as she watched, an elderly couple emerged, the woman holding her husband's elbow on the steps.

'Gid, I'll call you back. I can't talk now.'

'Just a second. We've had a break in the case – I thought you should know. We've got CCTV of Hinton the night Farrell died.'

The central beam of her appeal case came crashing down. Freshwater was right, she was wrong. Fuck. *Fuck.* The deflation quickly became annoyance: so why was Gid calling? To rub it in, tell her that actually his holier-than-thou monologue had been on point but he could still find it in his loving Christian heart to forgive her?

'It's definitely Hinton on the tape, no doubt,' he said.

'Okay, Gid, I get it.' Ten or twelve people stood in front of the church now, the old couple talking to the priest, others waiting their turn, chatting in groups of two and three. The young couple came out and then the women she'd guessed were friends. They didn't linger but headed straight to wherever they'd all left their cars, round the back. Robin's hand went to the door.

'No,' said Gid in her ear, 'you don't. The tape's from a club in Newcastle. Hinton wasn't in London when Farrell died.'

'So he got one of his goons to do it, went out of town to give himself an alibi, made sure he was seen out and about. We talked about that, remember – he tried it in his GBH case?' The priest was talking to a different couple now, touching the man's upper arm for emphasis. The three of them laughed silently.

'Yes,' said Gid, 'we discussed it this morning, too. We don't know – would he do that again? Especially when it didn't work last time. And we didn't *get* the tape – it came in by post, anonymous, wiped for prints. It feels like something else is going on.'

'Like what?'

'We're not sure.'

Across the road, the group was breaking up, people separating themselves off and moving away. The priest shook hands with a small man in a grey suit then stepped back towards the door, ready to go in. The young couple headed down the driveway.

'Gid, I've really got to go. Anything happens, let me know, okay?' She hung up, shoved the phone in her pocket and cranked the door open.

The woman had covered her head with a paisley scarf for the service but she pushed it backwards as Robin approached, letting it fall around her neck like a scout's neckerchief, knotted under her chin. Both she and her boyfriend had mid-brown hair and pale eyes, his behind a pair of steel-rimmed glasses. He stepped forward slightly as Robin approached.

'Sorry to bother you.' She addressed both of them. 'I wondered if you could help me?'

'If we can,' said the girl in a Brummie accent.

287

Robin took the photograph out of her pocket. 'I'm looking for the woman second from the left, with the blonde hair. Her name's Ana – do you know her?'

The guy shook his head. 'Sorry.'

'Can I?' The woman took the picture from her, angled it to the light.

'I was told she worships here sometimes,' Robin said.

'She's Serbian?' The woman looked again. 'Yes, I've seen her but only a couple of times. But yeah, she's definitely been here.'

'Have you ever spoken to her?'

A head-shake. 'No.'

'Is there anyone here you think *might* know her?' Robin gestured back towards the rapidly shrinking group in the yard. There were only seven or eight people left, most of them elderly and slow-moving.

'I don't know. You could ask.' She handed the picture back.

'I will. Thanks.'

She felt their eyes on her as she strode up the drive and through the church gates. To her relief, the priest had gone inside but she saw the group tense as she approached, a small but unmistakeable tightening. One of the old men moved closer to his wife. God, did she really look that bloody scary?

She chose the guy with the shaven head who, up close, had a kind-looking face, brown eyes under an impressively cliff-like forehead that suggested either years of rugby or blackboards' worth of equations. 'Sorry for barging in,' she said, addressing the group at large as much as him.

They waited.

'I'm looking for a woman who your . . .' *Co-worshippers? Colleagues?* '. . . friends,' she gestured back towards the road, 'your friends said had been here. I really need to get in touch with her. I wondered if you knew her.'

She handed the photograph to the shaven-headed man. 'The blonde one,' she said. 'In the blue T-shirt. Her name's Ana.'

He shook his head.

'Anyone else?'

He handed the photograph to a woman in a tweed jacket who scrutinized it then said no. One by one, it went around the little group. A tiny woman who looked about eighty said in rich Brummie that she'd seen her at a liturgy in December but she hadn't spoken to her. 'Pretty girl,' she said. 'On her own.'

'Why are you looking for her?' A voice from the back, deep and male, heavily accented. One of the men she'd put at forty or forty-five stood slightly apart, tall anyway but elevated further by his position halfway up the steps to the church door. He had a full head of salt-and-pepper hair and a black overcoat over dark trousers. Robin thought briefly of Kev.

'She used to work for a woman who died. Corinna Legge. I need to talk to her.'

In a second, the group parted, even the tiny woman on her cane moving at surprising speed. He came towards Robin, pulled up to his full height, shoulders back, occupying as much space as he could. Her turn on the receiving end of the intimidation.

'Are you police?'

'Yes.' She fronted it out. *So don't even think about trying anything.*

'Your ID?'

'In the car.'

He snorted, derisive, then came closer, bringing his face so near to hers that she could smell old coffee on his breath as he uttered a string of words as incomprehensible to her as their intent was absolutely crystal. He waved a hand towards the gate as if he was flicking crumbs off a tablecloth. 'Go – get out.'

The rest of the group stared at the ground as if trying to render themselves invisible.

'No one here will talk to you,' he said, following her gaze. 'There is no point for you to stay.'

Robin looked at the elderly woman. Her eyes were bright, taking it all in, enjoying the drama. She wasn't intimidated by the big guy, she was out beyond his reach, too old to be beaten or scared by bully-boy tactics, seen it all before and didn't think much of it then.

'What did he say to me?' Robin asked.

The woman smiled, revealing a set of perfect pearly false teeth. 'He said, you're not police, you're a pimp.'

Chapter Twenty

Robin had to hand it to Lennie: she was very good at keeping a mood going. 'Way better than me,' she'd said to Christine, back down in the kitchen. Maybe Len got it from her father – who knew? She'd opened the bedroom door just now to find her curled over the desk like a question mark – how had she never noticed how bad the ergonomics were, with that chair? The door was eighteen inches from Len's elbow so she had to have known Robin was there but nonetheless, when Robin touched her shoulder, she'd jumped and given her a look of pure outrage, as if she'd deliberately set out to creep up on her. With an air of long suffering, she'd taken out one earbud. 'What?'

'I came up to say hello – I've just got back. How was school?'

'I'm doing my homework,' she said. 'Unless dinner's ready?'

'Not yet.'

She'd put the earbud back in. Robin thought about pushing it, then turned and left.

'I've always liked that about you,' said her mother now, adding a half-teaspoon of low-sodium salt to a pan of potatoes. 'You never let things drag on, just do your shouting and get it over with. Luke's a good sulker but you never have been.'

'I haven't got the self-discipline.'

Christine moved the chopping board and knives to the sink. 'There's wine in the fridge door. You've caught me out – I thought you'd be back later so I've only just put the chicken in the oven.'

'Let's hope it's one of Dad's two-Crunchie days,' she said and her mother actually smiled. What the hell was going on?

Whatever it was, she was grateful. Any more aggro today and she'd go over the edge. Maybe her dad had had a word. Apart from the glowering presence opposite, dinner was almost harmonious, if subdued. Just before Dennis arrived home, Di had called to thank Christine for the vegetable lasagne she'd left in her porch during the afternoon. 'She said Peter's had another rocky day,' her mother told him now. 'Not the heart, thank the lord, but they've been taking blood every few hours and there's no sign that the new antibiotic's doing anything. Now they're worried about the dreaded S-word.'

'What's the S-word?' Lennie asked.

'Sepsis,' said Robin.

'Gran?'

'Like your mother says.'

'What is it?'

Christine glanced at Robin. 'It happens when you're very ill, when you've got an infection. Your body tries to fight but it can't. It's like poisoning – blood poisoning.'

'Can you die from it?'

'Yes, love.'

Lennie put down her knife and fork and looked at the table.

Robin floundered. Should she go to her, give her a cuddle? But Lennie was so angry with her, she'd probably push her off.

'It was kind of you to take the food, Mum,' she said. 'Thanks.'

'It feels like so little – I wish I could do more.'

292

'Did you know she was vegetarian, by the way, or was that just luck, the lasagne?'

'What? Oh – no, I did know.' She took a sip of the half-glass of wine she'd let Robin pour her over an hour ago, surely the temperature of bathwater by now. 'Di and I have had lunch together a few times over the years. She's a good soul – I've always . . .' She stopped, stiffened. Robin listened and heard it, too: footsteps on the path. A moment later, the doorbell.

'I'll go.' Lennie pushed back her chair.

'Are we expecting anyone, love?' Dennis asked Christine.

'I don't think so. Robin?'

'No.'

Silence apart from the sound of Lennie doing the locks, everyone waiting. Who came to the door unannounced in this day and age? At night.

'Hi.' The questioning rise at the end – someone Len didn't know.

'You must be Lennie,' he said. 'You've grown a bit since I last saw you. Is your mum around?'

'Er – yeah. Come in.'

A couple of seconds later, they appeared in the archway, Len wide-eyed, behind her Samir. It was half past eight but he was in work gear, dark trousers and a pale blue shirt under a grey three-quarter-length coat. She met his eye with the same jolt of familiarity.

Dennis stood and dropped his napkin onto the table.

'Mr Lyons.' Samir stepped forward a little. 'Sorry to intrude, especially while you're eating. I didn't mean to disturb your dinner.' He held out his hand.

Robin watched as her dad looked at it, pausing just long enough to be sure Samir noticed. In that second she felt a burst of love for Dennis that brought her almost to tears. That was for her.

Her dad had always liked Samir – so much, in fact, that she'd had to persuade herself back then that it wasn't a disqualifier – but the pause, the momentary question of whether he would take the hand or not, was his way of telling him, I haven't forgotten. I haven't forgiven the way you treated my daughter.

Samir dipped his head slightly, as if he were acknowledging this, then turned to her mother. 'Mrs Lyons.'

'Samir. How are you?'

'Well, thank you.' He looked back at Robin. 'I wondered if I could talk to you for a couple of minutes?'

Dennis, Christine and Lennie were all looking at her: what was going on? She thought of how they'd perched on the stools next door to listen in on Patel and Thomas, how Dennis had almost certainly taken her place when she'd swapped in. The chance of having a private conversation anywhere in the house was nil. Even if you weren't actively listening, you couldn't help hearing. She still needed therapy for the first time their parents went away for a weekend and Luke had Natalie over.

'Let's go for a walk,' she said to him. 'I need to stretch my legs anyway.'

She got her coat off the peg, hyperconscious of him behind her. She wondered if he felt them as well, the echoes of all the other times they'd stood exactly here while she put her coat on, his car waiting outside, already warm from the drive over to pick her up. She sensed him on the back of her neck, as if he were bringing up the small hairs there. She took her keys from the dish on the side-table. 'Come on then.'

The temperature drop was startling, the evening air so cold after the incubator that she felt it crackle in her chest. Living at Dunnington Road might actually kill poor Pam Travis, the school secretary, she thought, all these radical climate changes.

As usual, the street was empty, everyone back in their boxes,

294

even the traffic on Stratford Road sounding distant. She waited until they'd rounded Terry Willett's redoubtable Ford Transit, out of view from the house in case Lennie or Christine were watching from a window. She was careful to stop before they reached the little playschool at the end of the stretch. That was an echo too far – it was where they'd used to say goodbye before Samir got the car. She had a sudden sense-memory of the cool railings against her bare shoulders on a night that summer, that strappy cotton top she'd had, left by accident in a hostel in Windhoek eventually. Gnats weaving in a cone of streetlight, his hand behind her head, fingers in the fine hair at the base of her skull.

She shut it down. 'So,' she said, 'what do you want to talk about?'

He put his hands in his pockets, looked at her. 'The incident room got a call earlier from the Serbian church in Bournville,' he said. 'You wouldn't know anything about that, would you?'

Robin said nothing.

'Apparently, there was a woman there this afternoon menacing the parishioners. Mid-thirties, brown eyes, brown hair tied back in a scruffy bun, black leather jacket and jeans? Drove away in a navy-blue Audi?'

'Nope. Doesn't ring any bells.'

'For Christ's sake, this isn't funny.' He spoke through his teeth, jaw gritted.

'Who's laughing?'

'Not me. You bloody idiot – impersonating a police officer!'

'I didn't – I didn't *impersonate* an officer. It was only because this massive bloke started getting heavy – talk about menacing. He asked me if I was police; I said yes to stop him lamping me.'

Samir's eyes were glittering. 'I'm supposed to be at parents' evening at the moment, Robin, at my son's school. Instead, here

I am, racing over to Bournville to pour oil on troubled waters, try and contain the fucking mess you've made. They were threatening to file a police harassment complaint.'

'Harassment? Oh, please. I was there once, for five minutes – not even. I showed them a photograph, asked if they recognized someone, that was it.'

'Did it occur to you that Webster might have sent people there, too? Or did you think that was beyond his ken, that only *you* could fathom a connection between a Serbian woman and a Serbian church?'

The great Robin Lyons.

'Corinna's gone, Robin. I don't want to be cruel but that's the reality – she's dead, there's nothing you can do for her. Why can't you just leave it alone? I've asked you – I've *told* you: leave it.'

She felt it go, like a twig-snap in her head. Anger surged through her, filled her stomach, her chest, her arms. Pressure on her temples, like a thumb and forefinger, pincers. 'I can't.' The words came out in a growl. '*I can't.*'

'Why?'

Another surge. *Stop*, said a brain cell that still had a grip but she was past caring, past control. 'Because,' she said, 'it's not just about Corinna. It's about Peter – *he's* not dead. Not yet. And Josh – remember him, your friend Josh? He saved my life, Samir – *saved my life*. If he's dead, I need to know why, I need to understand. And if there's any chance he's still alive, however small, I'm going to take it. I need to find him. For Peter, so he has a dad. To clear his name.'

He was staring at her, irises almost black in the streetlight. 'What do you mean, he saved your life? Him and Corinna – when you had Lennie? Looking after you?'

She stared back. He knew? He knew that Rin had lived with

296

her in London, that Josh had come most weekends? In her mind, when she'd gone, got the fuck away from here, she'd imagined that she'd gone from his mind, too. That was certainly the impression he'd given her that night, when he'd told her he wasn't coming to London after all, he suddenly – drop of a hat, five days after they got back from travelling – just didn't feel the same any more. Of course he'd heard the big stuff, like her being pregnant, actually having Lennie, but it hadn't occurred to her – why hadn't it? – that he'd know more than that, the domestic details, how they'd helped her, kept her going. That of course Lennie had never had a dad to go to *her* parents' evenings.

She could do it – she was right on the edge but she could still pull back. She looked him in the eye. 'No,' she said. 'Before that. Years ago. Here, in Birmingham.'

'What are you talking about?'

Stop, ordered the voice. *Stop*. She looked around – the street was still empty. She lowered her voice anyway, right down. 'When we were seventeen,' she said, and as the words left her mouth she felt weirdly light, disembodied. As if she were smoke, rising. 'We went out one night. Me, Rin and Josh. We got very drunk – I don't know why, we were just having a good time.' A static mental image of green baize, balls scattered over it like Christmas decorations. 'We got drunk at happy hour and just carried on. Then Josh said he'd heard about a new club in the Jewellery Quarter and we wanted to dance so we went there.'

Samir's eyes hadn't moved from her face.

'We were staying at Rin's, Di had gone to her sister's for the weekend, no one was waiting up for us.' The whole thing was a blur, snatches of memory here and there, a collection of pictures she'd never been able to put in order. 'It was late, I don't know what time – one o'clock, two? Josh went to the bar and I looked around and I suddenly realized I couldn't see Rin.'

297

Here the sequence in her mind was clearer – a little. Was Rin okay? She'd gone looking for her. Was she throwing up? She remembered lurching towards the loos, a strip of little lights along the floor like the emergency exit path on a plane. The door to the ladies – almost falling through it as someone opened it from the other side. Calling her name – nothing – then looking under the doors for Rin's feet, losing her balance, putting her hand in something wet. Lurching out again. 'This girl came after me, asked if I was looking for my friend. She said she'd seen her, she was in a state, her boyfriend had taken her home. I knew it wasn't Josh – I'd just seen him at the bar, they'd never have left without me.'

'What happened?' His eyes still hadn't moved.

Robin looked up and down the street. 'This bloke had got her. Taken her. He must have been watching her. He waited 'til she was way too drunk, almost out of it.' The feel of the night air on her face, half running, half falling out of the club onto the pavement, suddenly dead sober. *Which way did they go?* She should have asked for help – why hadn't she asked for help, the bouncer, anyone?

'He'd dragged her round the corner, into this yard off an alley. I never would have seen them but I heard him over the wall, this kind of . . . grunt. When I got there, she was lying on the ground. He was pulling her jeans off.'

Samir looked sick.

'I went for him.' *Behold the high-kicking, karate-chopping teen ninja girl.* 'I started hitting him, kicking him, trying to pull him off her.' Rin trying to crawl out from under him but she was so drunk, pinned on her back, she couldn't turn over. 'Then I kicked him in the face and he pulled my legs out from under me, just put his arm out and . . .' She mimed, the single sweep that had brought her crashing to the tarmac. 'I hit my head, really hard

– the next thing I knew, he had his hand . . .' She put her fingers round her throat.

'Then suddenly Josh was there.' His face over the man's shoulder. 'He'd come looking for us – he'd heard me fall. Josh stopped him. If he hadn't, he would have killed me, Samir. Throttled me. I don't know if he was high or psychotic – the look in his eyes. There was a skip right by us – Josh grabbed a bit of pipe and smacked him.'

Samir's face. 'Why didn't you tell me?'

Stop, the voice was screaming now. *STOP.*

'Because he killed him,' she said.

Samir closed his eyes briefly, covered his hand with his mouth. A car went past, a couple, the woman in the passenger seat. Robin caught her eye and she looked away, superior: a lovers' tiff in the street, at their age?

'It was defence,' Samir said. 'You know that. He might not even have been charged. He saw you two being attacked, he fought him off.'

'I know that *now* but we were seventeen, Corinna and me, we were still at school. We were scared out of our minds.' She paused. The street felt like a stage-set, unreal. After all these years – to say it. To say it and be done. 'And it wasn't just defence.'

'What do you mean?'

'It was, then it wasn't. The first time he hit him, he knocked him unconscious. Out cold.' His eyes had gone blank above her, and he'd slumped sideways onto his shoulder, then his back. 'But he kept on hitting him.' The arc of the pipe from high over his head, two-handed, again and again. 'Three times – maybe four. Then Rin screamed.' That scream – shrill, animal panic. She'd remember it for the rest of her life. 'It stopped him – it was like she'd pulled him out of a trance.' The pipe had dropped to the pavement, ends ringing off the tarmac one then the other, slow motion, a spinning coin coming to a stop.

'No one came?'

'No. The scream was so loud I thought someone would have to. But no.'

'What did you do?'

'We walked away. Home, to Rin's – all the way.'

'The pipe?'

'Josh hid it in his coat and we dropped it in the canal off Newhall Street.'

She looked around in vain for somewhere to sit. She felt hollow, emptied out suddenly. As if she'd been carrying the story in her stomach all these years like a stone, a giant tumour, and it had finally been cut out.

'We sat up the rest of the night in Rin's room,' she said. 'Josh and Rin both threw up. We were all trembling, shaking like . . .' She held her hands into the light.

'Josh told us that when he was twelve, they'd gone on holiday to France, and his mum had made friends with this other English family at the campsite. They had kids the same age, they went down to the beach together, had barbecues. He said one night he'd got up to go to the toilet block and he saw the man, the husband, forcing himself on her.'

'His mum? Hilary?'

'He'd got his hand up her skirt, he said, he had her pressed up against a wall, she couldn't get his weight off. He'd gone running, Josh, stopped it, but Hilary made him swear never to tell his dad. Or anyone. As if it was she who'd done something wrong.

'The look in his mother's eyes, he said, her terror – he'd never forgotten. The man had his hand over her mouth, he said, and there were just these silent tears streaming down her cheeks.'

300

'*Making her powerless. Violating her. My mother.*' She saw Josh on the end of Rin's bed, sweating, white. That airless room, the smell of vomited alcohol. '*And I was just a kid. Twelve. He was a man, he was strong – I couldn't do anything. I wanted to beat his head in. I wanted to kill him. But he just walked away. Scot free.*'

Samir's eyes were locked on her face again. He was completely still.

'When he saw the man with me, he said, his hand round my throat . . . He said he didn't even remember hitting him.'

'Was he telling you the truth?'

Robin pulled back. 'What?'

'Josh,' said Samir. 'Did you and Rin believe him?'

She remembered the look on his face as he saw the pipe in his hand, the man on the ground. Incomprehension. Then comprehension. Disbelief. Horror.

'Yes. Of course we did.'

She and Corinna next to each other on the floor, curled as small as possible, arms gripping their knees. 'I can't describe it,' she said. 'It was like an actual nightmare. That night, weeks after. The fear – my heart was pounding constantly, I was nearly sick whenever the phone rang. It was in the paper, the *Post* – man attacked in Jewellery Quarter, left for dead. We kept waiting for a witness to come forward – the girl who told me Rin had left, one of the bouncers. We talked about going to the police ourselves, just to make it stop.'

'So why didn't you?'

'We were going to, we'd made up our minds, but then he was identified. In the paper, I mean – obviously the police knew before. He had previous, two rapes; he'd only been out three weeks. We talked about it for hours then we made a pact to keep it secret. He'd raped before, he wasn't an innocent guy having

301

some kind of mental breakdown, and even if Josh hadn't been charged, the story would have followed him round forever: *That's Josh Legge; he killed a man.'*

Samir's face was a confusion of shock and disbelief and – yes, she wasn't mistaken – anger. 'Why didn't you tell me?' he said. 'Now, I mean, in the past week. At the hospital – I asked you. Even if you couldn't tell anyone else, remember? Eight days, Robin, *eight days*, a whole line of enquiry, a *major* line, that we've known nothing about.'

'Because it's not relevant.'

He stared. 'Not relevant? Corinna – your *friend* Corinna? – she's dead and her husband's killed someone before and it's not *relevant*?'

'Because it *isn't*. If it's about that, why hasn't whoever hurt them come for me? I didn't tell you, Samir, because I knew this is exactly what you'd think. I was there, I was involved, too. I know it's not what's at the bottom of this.'

He threw up his hands. 'How? How can you be so . . . obtuse? How can you miss the point that's staring you in the face?'

'What?'

'But no, actually, you're not. Are you?'

'What are you talking about?'

'You didn't tell me because you didn't want me to know Josh was – *is* – capable of murder. Because *you* don't believe he did this, killed Corinna, you took it on yourself to suppress information that made him look guilty.'

'Because you'd have stopped looking for anyone else! The real killer.'

'*Josh* is a real killer.'

They stared at each other. For the first time, Robin understood – really understood – that it was true. Josh *was* a killer. He'd killed a man – she'd seen him do it with her own eyes. Whether

302

or not she understood why, whether or not she was grateful to him for saving her life, it was true: he'd been so overcome by anger – rage – that he'd lost control and killed a man.

In Samir's eyes, she saw her shock reflected. He was doing it, too, trying to understand how the Josh he'd known – kind Josh, loving Josh, his friend – had taken another man's life.

He turned away from her, faced back the way they'd come. She watched his shoulders rise and fall, the clouds of his breath. 'I can't . . . I need to think about this. I need to think what to do.' He spun around again. 'Don't tell anyone else what you told me, all right? No one.'

'Obviously.'

'And don't – repeat, *do not* – talk to anyone else about their case. Are you listening? Because if you do, I'll arrest you, I mean it. I've got the grounds. Impersonating a police officer at the very least – I don't have to tell you that's a crime. Let alone anything to do with this other . . . Jesus Christ.'

He turned and walked away. He'd gone a handful of steps when he stopped again. For several seconds he said nothing. Then, 'When it happened, were we together? You and me.'

'Yes.'

'Where was I?'

'Cambridge. You'd gone to visit your sister for the weekend.'

'And where was I when I came back?'

'What do you mean?'

'You were living with this, going through this "nightmare" and you didn't tell me? How did you keep it from me, Robin? How *could* you? Something so massive. When we were so . . . close.'

'Mum?' In the dark, Lennie's whisper seemed to float down from the top bunk. For a second Robin thought she'd imagined it. 'Are you okay?'

303

'Yeah,' she whispered back. Then, because she wanted to acknowledge the olive branch, 'Yes, I'm all right.'

'What did he really want?'

When she'd come back in, she'd said he'd wanted to check a couple of things, ask her opinion on Rin's state of mind. 'He told me to stop interfering.'

'But you're not.' Indignation.

'I am. A bit. I can't believe they haven't got anywhere – I was trying to work out what they're missing.'

'Is that all?'

Oh, god: had she sneaked out somehow and listened? No, she'd checked behind them, she'd kept checking. And Lennie couldn't have come close enough to hear without *them* hearing *her*. Robin's stomach lurched – the idea of her daughter knowing. Even thinking about it in the same room as her now, as if the poison could seep out, get airborne.

'When you came in, you seemed . . . upset.'

Robin flailed.

'Was it a shock? Seeing him again?'

She hadn't told her, had she, that she'd seen him before? 'Yes. It has been. I saw him at the hospital, too – briefly. When I went to see Peter.'

'You didn't say.'

'It didn't seem important.'

'Really?' Lennie let the word hang.

It dawned on Robin what she was driving at. 'Oh, Len, no. It's not – no. That's ancient history – like, pre-history. Cavemen. Dinosaurs.' Quick, humour: the old deflector.

'That's not why – Adrian?'

'No. I promise you, one hundred per cent. Samir's married, he's got kids, and *he* dumped *me* back then, remember? And it doesn't matter what he thinks, it wouldn't matter if he got down on his knees and begged because I would never . . .' She stopped but it seemed this was the night for truth-telling. The genie was out of the bottle – out on the town, actually, with its mates. 'He really hurt me back then. Deeply hurt me. It was more than just splitting up with a boyfriend.' She paused again, felt the weight of Lennie's listening. 'The rejection – I felt like he'd rumbled me. I felt like there was something wrong with me and I'd got away with it for two years, managed to hide it, but then he'd finally seen the truth and reared back in horror.'

She thought of him three hours ago, turning his back, walking away.

Overhead, Lennie was very still. 'What truth?'

The thought was out of Robin's mouth before she knew she'd had it, before she knew that it was what she'd ever – always – thought. 'That when it came down to it, basically, I wasn't worth loving.'

'What?' Shock in Lennie's voice. 'Why would you *think* that?'

Because I'm the kind of person who has this conversation with her thirteen-year-old daughter? Because I'm a wrecking ball? Because there *is* something wrong with me and I don't know what it is and I can't stop it?

She swerved away from the edge, got her hands back on the wheel. Jesus. 'I don't think that *now*, obviously.' She tried a laugh, stopped when she heard how nuts she sounded. 'It was just an age thing – it's hard, that time. Trying to work out who you are and negotiate the world. Finding your people. Not for everyone, though – you're going to be completely different because you know how much you're loved, right?'

A small voice said, 'Yes.'

'I wasn't nearly as sorted as you, or as clever. But I got there in the end.'

There was silence overhead for several seconds and then a

whole-body shuffle. Lennie's feet appeared on the ladder, the creaking incredibly loud in the stillness of the house. She lifted the edge of the duvet and lowered herself in.

They lay on their backs, shoulder to shoulder, looking at the curling edges of the glow-stars in the light from under the door. 'I think you're worth loving,' Lennie said.

Chapter Twenty-one

When she opened her eyes, the room was filled with weak light. She waited for her brain to load, reopen the files on the desktop, but then, with a wash of pure panic, she remembered: she'd told Samir. She lay rigid, heart pounding. After eighteen years, someone else knew. Not just someone: the Head of Homicide.

And Josh was a killer. A *real* killer.

Lennie had fallen asleep with her but she was on her own now. 'Len?' No answer. She reached up to press the bottom of the mattress through the slats and felt it lift too easily. 8.22 said the desk clock.

She came out onto the landing with the tentative step of someone assessing the damage after a blast. She had the surreal feeling that while everything looked the same, it was fundamentally undermined and would crumble at a touch. But no: the floor stayed solid, the railing round the top of the stairs supported her weight. Her dad had been last in the shower and the air on the landing was humid with Old Spice. Down in the kitchen, someone was buttering a slice of well-done toast.

She showered and dressed quickly, not bothering to dry her hair. It felt essential to be out and ready, to get ahead of things.

She checked her phone again as she came downstairs but of course Samir wouldn't leave any kind of message, nothing that could be used as evidence that he knew.

'Morning, love.' Christine looked up from pouring a cup of tea.

'Hi. It's late – why didn't you wake me?'

''Cause you've basically slept ten hours total since we've been here?' said Lennie, mouth full of bran flakes.

Robin took her wallet from the counter, put it in her jacket.

'Aren't you going to have any breakfast?'

'I said I'd be at the office at nine. I'll get something on the way.' She rounded the table and squeezed her daughter from behind the chair, kissing the top of her head, breathing her in. 'Love you. See you later on.'

'Have you heard?'

Maggie was waiting for her, standing in the narrow strip of carpet between their whiteboard and the table, radiating energy, collars up like antennae, bangles chiming.

'What?' For a vertiginous moment Robin thought she was going to say that Josh had killed a man.

'They've found a body.'

She stared. 'Is it him?'

'What?' Maggie looked confused. 'No – god, no, sorry. No. A woman – it's a woman's body.'

Robin reached for the back of a chair as her blood pressure went through the floor. 'Who?'

'I don't know. Sara – Kettleborough, my mate who works at the *Post* – she only rang five minutes ago, not even. I knew you'd be here any second or I would have called you.'

'Where?'

'Tyseley, old engineering works. She didn't have any details beyond that, it'd just come in, she was on her way there. I'm on the police Facebook page, see if . . .' She tapped the keyboard, refreshing. 'Yes, here. It's just gone up.'

Robin went to look. At the top of the feed, accompanied by a generic picture of a PC by a squad car, were four short paragraphs posted two minutes ago.

A murder enquiry has been opened after the body of a young woman was discovered in a disused factory in Tyseley this morning. The woman had sustained multiple knife wounds. Her identity is yet to be established.

The area has been sealed off while forensic examinations are underway.

Detective Inspector Lara Morton from the Homicide Unit is leading the investigation. She said, 'The investigation is in the very early stages but my team and I will do everything we can to ensure justice for this young woman.

'I would ask anyone with information to contact us on 101 or anonymously at Crimestoppers.'

'I've emailed Nuttall,' Maggie said. 'He'll tell us if it's her.'

Her? Which one? Maggie meant Becca, though, of course, not Ana. Or Tarryn, even – where was she? Why hadn't she answered her calls?

On the table in front of them, Maggie's mobile rang. *Valerie Woodson.* They looked at each other.

'She couldn't have seen it already? It's just gone up.'

'I'm surprised it's taken her so long.' Maggie took a fortifying breath and picked up. 'Valerie?'

Robin heard a sob.

'No wonder they always had you on family liaison,' Robin said, when she hung up.

'You mean it wasn't just because I'm a bird?'

'Well, that too, obviously. But you're really good at it.' In five or six minutes, without giving her false hope, being careful to say that they had to be prepared for it to be Becca, Maggie had managed to talk – and listen – Valerie back from the brink of hysteria. By the time she said goodbye, the voice on the other end of the line sounded almost calm.

Maggie slumped in the chair and let her head drop back. For a few seconds, she looked her age, the skin around her eyes tissue-thin, throat creased above the smooth disc of tiger's eye on her necklace. 'How not to start the day,' she said. 'Lorraine's back from Lanzarote, she's coming in to do the books, so I've been here since seven doing paperwork.'

'Are you going somewhere?'

'What?' She opened her eyes.

'Skirt.'

'Oh. Yeah. I've got a meeting at Hargreaves & Partners at eleven.' On the desk, the laptop pinged: incoming. She sat forward again and clicked in to her email. 'Nuttall.' She looked up. 'It's not Becca.'

Lorraine arrived at ten. Her fortnight's holiday had evidently been spent on a sun-lounger; she was tanned to a shade Robin wouldn't have thought possible for a blonde, the blue of her eyes almost supernatural by contrast. Tall and athletically built, she was wearing a pale pink crocheted cardigan that looked like a newborn's matinee jacket knitted on a giant scale. If Maggie's element was silver, though, Lorraine's was evidently gold, multiple fine chains around her neck and a load on her wrists, which rattled on the desk in the back office as she sat down with the Dell, requisitioned with unwarranted jealousy as soon as the introductions were over.

'You're a devil for the detail, aren't you, Lorraine,' Maggie said.

310

'Invaluable. Though there's not much invoicing to do, unfortu-nately, darl.' She extracted an old-fashioned ledger from the filing cabinet. 'Just the three reports I was finishing before you went. I'm halfway through another, if I get a second, but we've been busy. We've got a case on the other side of things.'

Two very plucked eyebrows went up.

'Becca Woodson, twenty-two. Missing from Sparkhill. We've actually just had a bit of a scare – there was a body found in Tyseley this morning. Not her, thank god.'

'Do they know who it is?'

'Not confirmed yet – Nuttall said he'll be in touch. Right, Rob, hand me that kettle and I'll get it on. I need a coffee before I go. Are you still on your herbal whatnot, Lorraine?'

'Here, I'll do it.' Robin took it from her.

'Thanks. On the subject of invoicing,' Maggie said, following her out to the front office, 'how did you get on with Michael Dixon yesterday? Any joy?'

Michael Dixon? Oh, yes. 'No,' she said. 'Afraid not.'

'Really? Again?' Maggie frowned. 'Have I got my wires crossed? Or maybe it's a different one – it's possible, isn't it, two Michael Dixons? But I was pretty sure I'd got the right one.'

'I'll try again this afternoon.'

'Well, maybe. Let's see how we get on. I'll be back by lunchtime, we'll make a plan of campaign. Have you heard from Tarryn?'

'No. I've texted and emailed, and I sent her another note on Instagram, too.'

They looked at each other. 'Has she posted anything since Monday?' said Maggie.

'Not the last time I checked. Can I?'

'Of course.' Maggie slid her laptop across the table. 'Use it while I'm out. If you're going to be with us for a while, we'll have to get another one. Maybe two – replace the Dell.'

'Needs it. It'll pay for itself in what you save in man hours.'
She opened Instagram in a new tab and went to Tarryn's page.
'No, nothing. Her last post was Sunday morning.'

'Could you make a start on these?' Maggie handed her a sheaf
of papers. 'Two new cases from FCI, came in last night. Mysterious
shed fire that totalled a ride-on mower and a list of power tools
that looks a bit extravagant for someone who's not building a
full-size replica of the Eiffel Tower in their back garden. Also,
two TAG Heuers, insured a month before they went missing.'

'Subtle.' As Maggie pulled away, Robin caught a whiff of toothpaste. 'Have you just cleaned your teeth?'

'What? Oh – yes. Coffee, you know.' She got out her lipstick
and applied a top-up coat, checked it in a little compact mirror.

Robin looked at her more closely. 'Maggie, are you . . .
blushing?'

'No, I am not.'

'Ooh, are you meeting Richard Hargreaves?' came Lorraine's
voice from the back.

'God almighty, it's like the bloody Spanish Inquisition.' Maggie
zipped her bag then went to the broom cupboard and got out a
pair of heels. She stuffed her feet in and hustled out of the door
like she was under fire.

Robin listened to her going down the stairs, usual clumping
muted. When she heard the street door slam, she clicked back
to the police Facebook page. Nothing new there, and the Twitter
account echoed the same bare details. The *Birmingham Mail* site
had the story now but nothing new. A photograph showed a
dilapidated factory building, the entrance taped off.

Maggie had left her email open, Nuttall's message three from
the top in her inbox. Robin glanced towards the back office,
checking she was out of Lorraine's eye-line, then clicked on it.

No ID yet but checked for you, def not Becca. More ASAP.

She went into Maggie's sent messages, searched for ones she'd sent to him and read six or seven to get a feel for the style. From her own phone she emailed Maggie a picture of Ana's photograph, copied it quickly onto the desktop and then deleted the email before – fingers crossed – Maggie could see it on her phone. Then she went back to the inbox, opened his message and hit 'Reply'.

Couple of others (attached & below). Would be great to eliminate if poss?

She pasted in a link to one of Tarryn's Instagram selfies, attached Ana's photo and sent the email before she could hesitate. Then she deleted it from the Sent box, moved the picture to the trash folder and emptied it.

Twenty minutes later, she had a reply. *No to both – good news?*

Maggie returned at two, the toothpaste on her breath replaced by white wine, cheeks definitely pink. 'Say nothing,' she said, picking up the laptop.

'So you had lunch then?' Robin couldn't resist.

'Just a sandwich.'

'Well, as long as it was just a *sandwich*,' said Lorraine, sticking her head round the door.

'Right, that's it. One more word, and I'll drive you both to the Job Centre.' But when she turned away to hang up her coat, she grinned.

Three quarters of an hour later, Maggie's mobile rang. 'Al?'

Robin stiffened.

'What's the latest? Have they?' Maggie stood and went to the window, looking out over the tiled roofs opposite. 'Shannon Harris – Shannon like the river?' She turned and mimed a scribbling motion. 'Right.' She covered the phone with her hand,

313

mouthed *prostitute*. 'Okay, of course, will do. Thanks, really appreciate it.'

Robin let her shoulders drop – she'd got away with it – and at the same moment she remembered the man outside the Serbian church. *Pimp*.

'What's that?' said Maggie. She was still on the phone; she hadn't hung up. She listened for a few seconds and Robin, deliberately looking down, was aware of her turning round. She felt her neck prickle. 'What?' Maggie said, confused. 'No. Oh – yeah, of course. Sorry, senior moment. No, definitely good news – thanks again.'

She hung up and walked slowly back to her desk where she made a few clicks on the laptop. Looking at her Sent messages, Robin thought with cheeks aflame, checking the trash folder.

'Is this how you worked at the Met?'

Chapter Twenty-two

There was no bench on this stretch of the pavement, just some bollards outside Ladbrokes to thwart ram-raiders and a litter bin with a lip meanly designed to deny anyone a three-second perch. Robin loitered between them, so intent on her own watching that it was a couple of minutes before she realized that *she* was likely being watched, someone inside Ladbrokes at this very moment monitoring the CCTV, wondering when she was going to come in and stick them up for the takings on the 2.20 at Doncaster. She crossed the road again and took another turn on the pavement outside a large Chinese supermarket she hadn't noticed when they'd been here before.

Until this afternoon, she'd never thought literally about the expression 'tear a strip off' but now it described exactly how she felt: strip-waxed, the top layer of her skin ripped away. Maggie's anger had been all the more blistering because it had been contained at first by Lorraine's presence. Robin had felt her across the table seething, gathering steam. After twenty minutes she'd said, 'Let's pop out for a second.' As they'd gone downstairs, her body heat had seemed to radiate, scorching.

They'd gone round the corner onto Corporation Street, where

she'd stopped short. 'It's not *what* you asked him. I'd have asked him *for* you if you'd asked me.'

You wouldn't, Robin thought. Not Ana.

'Tarryn,' Maggie said, as if she'd read her mind. 'I'm not going to help you dig your own grave, poking round Corinna's case.' She was so worked up, she didn't register the turn of phrase. 'It's the sneakiness – deleting the messages, emptying the trash.'

'I'm sorry,' she said. 'I'm desperate, I wasn't thinking straight.'

Maggie had given her a hard look: not good enough. 'He's my best contact – you nearly made me look like an idiot. And you can't say you weren't thinking straight, I don't buy it, because this is hardly the first time, is it? Taking matters into your own hands?'

For a mad moment, she thought Samir had told her. No, paranoid, no, of course he hadn't. Of course he hadn't, for fuck's sake.

Maggie's lips had been a pale line. 'Let me just say this: at the moment, I'm seeing things from your man Freshwater's point of view.'

The *Get out of my sight* subtext was hard to avoid but it'd been a relief anyway when, as soon as they got back, Maggie had despatched her to Hockley again in pursuit of Michael Dixon. And of course, being both bodily there and awake this time, she'd got him. She'd emailed the pictures back and received a terse *Thanks* in reply. Two minutes later: *Now go home, get a proper night's sleep and sort yourself out.*

Instead, she'd driven back to the city centre, parked the car and come here.

The Spot opened at six; she'd been in position since half past five. David had already been in; a couple of minutes after she arrived, one of the Gillette barmen, not Justin, had rung the bell and from her spot behind a small van, she'd watched him open

316

the door. Lisa and another woman she hadn't seen before were next, let in by the barman, and soon after that, two more women. None were in the tight black gear, the leggings and ballet wraps; if they were waitresses, they clearly changed on the premises.

Quarter to six, ten to. Was Tarryn coming? If she was around, surely she would be – she'd just had a break, how much more time off could she have? But then, if she *was*, why hadn't she replied to Robin's messages? In the twenty minutes between emailing Alan Nuttall and getting his response, her lack of contact, the absence of any new Instagram posts, had seemed more and more significant. But maybe she'd resigned, Robin had reasoned. She was travelling, wasn't she, and that's what you did – stayed somewhere for a little while, moved on. She hadn't mentioned it when they spoke but why would she, it was none of Robin's business. Maybe she'd had some kind of family emergency back home in Australia. Or maybe she just wasn't very well – maybe she had a cold.

When Shannon Harris was identified, the sense of unease had dissipated, but now, as Robin waited, it started to creep back. Six o'clock – five past. Where *was* she? She was almost startled when a minute later, she glanced up and saw Tarryn under the trees in the pedestrianized area, walking at speed. Relief, followed by the usual weird disconnect between seeing someone you'd never met but looked at in scores of pictures. It was like seeing someone famous. Before she could get any nearer The Spot, Robin strode across the street and put out a hand. 'Tarryn?'

She stopped, frowning. 'Yes?'

'I'm Robin, we spoke on Friday on the phone. I've left you several messages – I was starting to worry.'

'Why?'

Robin was confused for a second. 'Becca's missing – I thought . . .'

317

'Oh. Jeez, sorry. No, I'm fine. But I'm late – my shift started at six, I'm not changed.'

'I'll be quick. Why *didn't* you reply to my messages? Are you avoiding me?'

'No, of course not. No.' She pressed her phone, lighting the screen. 6.07. 'Look, I've really got to go.'

'A woman was found dead this morning, Tarryn. Murdered. I thought it might be you.'

'What? Why?'

'I checked with the police – I even sent them your picture.'

'But she was a prostitute.'

Robin stopped. She frowned. 'How do you know that?'

'What?'

'How did you know she was a prostitute?'

'I . . .'

'That information hasn't been made public yet.'

Tarryn looked down the street as if she was thinking about making a run for it. Robin grabbed her arm. 'That woman was someone's friend. Someone's *daughter*, just like you are. If you know something, tell me.'

She glanced round then focused on Robin's face, eyes narrowed. She was trying to gauge her, get her measure.

'Can I trust you?' she said. 'How can I be sure?'

'I don't know,' said Robin, frank. 'I give you my word. I used to be police.' How lame that sounded. 'And if it matters, which maybe it does, I'm not police any more.'

'Because someone I care about, a friend, could get in serious shit if . . .'

'With the law?'

Tarryn shook her head quickly, dismissive. She looked around again then lowered her voice. 'This friend – I want to help her

318

but I don't know how. She was the one who told me about the woman. She made me promise . . .'

'It's not Becca?'

Another head-shake.

'Okay, look. Whatever you tell me, I won't do anything to endanger your friend. I promise. You can count on that. On me.'

Tarryn gave her another appraising look then nodded in the direction of the trees. They moved back a few feet, away from the road and the flow of foot traffic.

'When I came here, Birmingham, I got a room in a flat-share,' she said. Her voice wasn't much above a whisper now; close as she was standing, Robin strained to hear. 'One of the girls there worked at The Spot. That's how I found the job here, she recommended me.

'One night, we were at home watching TV when the door went and these two blokes forced their way up the stairs. Rough blokes – really scary. They were from a collection agency – my friend had a pay-day loan and she couldn't make the repayments. She was scared shitless, she's only twenty-three. They went into her room, went through all her things, her dressing table. She started crying, she thought they were going to take the jewellery her mum left her, we were all begging them, but then one of them looked at her and muttered to the other one. He laughed – I don't know if it was that horrible at the time or because of what happened after . . . Then they left – just like that. Dropped everything and went.'

Robin waited.

'But they were back the next day. Only one of the first guys but he'd brought his boss. I wasn't there, I had a shift, but I could tell something had gone on the moment I came through the door. All he'd done was talk, she said, and look at her and tell her how difficult it was to pay money back once you'd got into trouble, the interest going up and up and up. He'd said he could help her.'

A couple walked by. Tarryn waited until they'd passed.

'She said the boss had made some comment about liking them young, and the next day, he came back on his own. Basically, what it came down to, he'd "look after her" while she worked it off. She'd actually pawned her mother's necklace in the morning – it had a tiny diamond on it – but he wouldn't take the money. He went with her to the shop to buy it back, made out like he was doing her a favour.'

'Why didn't she call the police?'

'Because she was terrified. Completely out of her depth, terrified. A couple of days later, he came into The Spot, him and two others. They weren't doing anything you could say was actively threatening, just looking, making their presence felt. I thought she was going to have a breakdown.'

'Why didn't *you* call the police?'

'Because when I cornered her in the kitchen, she begged me not to. Pleaded. He'd told her that bad things happened to people who did.'

'Did anyone else notice, or say anything? The manager – David?'

'Yeah. He asked her what was going on, why was she so upset, but she just made up some cock-and-bull story.'

'And he believed it?'

'No. He went to talk to them, sat down with them, and a couple of minutes later, they got up and left. They left a fifty-pound tip.'

'He didn't go to the police either, though, obviously. Why not?'

Tarryn glanced towards The Spot. 'I talked to Lisa about it – she runs the back room, where I work, they're together. She said he'd had some trouble in the last place he worked, in Leeds. She wouldn't tell me what but that's why he's so careful.'

'Trouble with people coming in, or trouble himself?'

'She wouldn't say exactly. I think she wanted me to think it was people coming in but . . . Anyway, as far as David was concerned, it didn't matter after that because the problem evaporated. She didn't work here again. She went to work for *him*.'

'Where?'

Tarryn looked sick. 'Massage parlour.'

'Do you still share a flat?'

'No. She moved out.'

'When did you last speak to her? Today, I'm guessing.'

'This afternoon.' Even quieter, 'She rang me because she knew the woman who died. Shannon.'

Progress. Robin felt an exhilarating surge of adrenaline. 'How? Through him – the massage parlour?'

She nodded. 'She said Shannon was his girlfriend, too.'

'Did he kill her?'

'She thinks so. Yes.'

'What's his name?'

'I don't know, she won't tell me. At the beginning, he said to call him Robbie but it's not his real name.'

'I need to speak to her. No one has to know. Anything she tells me – I can find a way to pass information on without anyone tracing it back.' A man lingered nearby, lighting a cigarette. She glared at him until he moved off. 'Stop it happening again, Tarryn,' she said, 'to someone else. To your friend.'

'I don't know if I can – if she will, I mean. I'll try. She won't go to the police. I doubt she'll say yes but I'll ask.'

'Thank you. And I'll do whatever I can to help – please tell her that. Make sure she knows.'

'I will.'

Robin nodded. 'Did they know each other, she and Becca?'

'No. They didn't overlap here. And I've never introduced them.'

321

'You're sure?'

'Yes. Becca's not working as an escort, I promise you.'

She realized at once she'd made a mistake. 'I've really got to go. I'll lose my job if I'm any . . .' She moved away but Robin stepped in front of her.

'You mean, she's doing something else. You know what she's doing.'

She tried to dodge but Robin moved again. 'Just tell me. Valerie, her mum – she's out of her mind with worry; she's a wreck, exhausted. If—'

'It's her mum who's the issue.'

From the car park, she rang home to say she'd be late. 'How late?' said Christine.

'Very. Midnight, even.' Robin braced herself for the protest but none came.

'Okay. Lennie's upstairs doing her homework. Do you want me to call her?'

'No, don't interrupt her. Will you tell her I'll ring in a couple of hours?'

'Righto. Robin, whatever you're doing – and I won't ask . . .' a pause long enough to tell her she got it, this was Maggie's secret-squirrel work '. . . be careful? Please?'

'I will.' She hesitated. 'Thanks, Mum.'

'Right, now off you go.'

From Birmingham, Bath was more or less a straight shot, the M5 with a dog-leg east at Bristol, about a hundred miles in all, according to the SatNav. Of course, it was the latter half of rush hour – when was it ever *not* bloody rush hour? – but by the time she reached the Bromsgrove exit, the traffic began to thin and she picked up speed.

Robin had to hand it to Becca, she'd planned her exit like a pro. The first rule of disappearing: don't go where people would think to look for you, nowhere you have friends or family or ties of any kind. She'd been clever because the tie to Bath wasn't hers, it was Tarryn's: the friend from Sydney she'd originally come travelling with was assistant manager of a hotel there.

'So Becca's staying with her?'

'No, working with. Or for. She's got a job in the kitchen there, as a sous chef. She's going to train – it's what she's always wanted to do. She started this week.'

'What's the name of the hotel?'

Tarryn had shaken her head at the position Robin was putting her in. 'All this – she worked so hard to set it up. All the hours she did here, saving up, figuring out how to do it. Leaving Harry. I promised.'

'All Valerie needs to know,' Robin said, 'is that she's safe.'

The hotel was just to the north of the city centre, halfway up a sloping street lined with Regency terraces in yellow Cotswold stone, a mixture otherwise of discreet offices and private houses. It was quarter to nine now, and along the length of the road, expensive curtains filtered golden light. As she and Lennie had driven away from Shepherd's Bush, the lit windows had seemed to symbolize everything she'd lost but tonight they were warmer, reflecting the glow of the breakthrough, the relief that Becca was safe.

She locked the car and walked back up the street. Passing just now on her way to the parking spot, she'd thought the hotel looked small, but from the pavement, she could see that behind the façade, several houses had been knocked together. The town-house door was painted glossy navy, the brass letterbox and carriage lamp were newly polished: your extremely aspirational home-from-home. A brass case displayed the evening's menu, handwritten, two plaques directly above it signalling the restaurant's listings in international travellers' guides. Robin thought briefly of Natalie, her pride in Birmingham's Michelin stars.

No formal reception desk, just a little nook inside the front door, a man on the telephone. He held up a finger – *With you in a moment* – but she shook her head, *Don't worry*. 'The bar?' she mouthed, and he covered the handset.

'Across the hall, left.'

'Thanks.'

Whoever had done the interior design had made an excellent job of it. The aesthetic was second home on a banker's salary, colours muted and no doubt Farrow & Ball, original modern art on the walls, carpets that swallowed her footsteps on contact. Blousy flowers filled an urn in the central lobby, where a wide staircase disappeared up with a sort of musical flourish, the banister a mahogany treble clef.

Just around the corner, a sign pointed the way to the restaurant, and the brasserie scents of roasting beef and garlic grew stronger. She heard voices and clinking cutlery and then, as she rounded another corner, a waiter with plates up each arm crossed the hallway ahead and backed through a door at the far end.

Through its glass panel, Robin saw a large kitchen, eight or ten androgynous figures in hats and whites. She swung the door open and went in.

Movement and noise – plates, pans, barked instructions, roaring fans. As she approached, she could feel the heat of the spotlights over a service counter where two men were working with complete concentration. The older one swabbed the rim of a dish with a tea towel, double-checked his four plates. As he straightened to hit the bell, he saw her.

'Can I help?' He looked at her street clothes. 'You can't come in here, I'm afraid – we're in the middle of service.'

'I'm looking for Becca Woodson,' she said, and at a counter against the far wall, she saw a figure in a white jacket and baggy checked trousers flinch.

'Is it an emergency?'

'No.'

'Then she won't be able to talk for another half an hour or so.'

'That's okay,' Robin said. 'I'll wait.'

At the bar, she paid for a small celebratory glass of wine with her credit card. She'd have to fill the car up, too, before she got back on the motorway but her anxiety at spending any money was slightly leavened this time by the idea that in a few days' time it'd be the end of the month and she'd be paid, albeit pro rata and on a much lower salary. She took an armchair in the corner with a view of the room and rang Lennie to say good-night.

At half past nine, a figure appeared in the doorway and there she was, Becca Woodson, her dark hair tied back, any make-up she'd had on before her shift long sweated off, but still clearly recognizable as both the girl on her mother's fridge at sixteen and the one about to spray lemonade all over a London picnic table.

She glanced around the room, nervous. For a moment Robin thought she was looking for police but then realized she just didn't want to be seen in her kitchen gear by guests at other tables. She stood up and went over.

'Becca?'

'Are you Robin? I've just got Tarryn's messages.'

Robin took a card from her pocket with the usual pang for

her badge. She remembered the first time she'd felt it, when she'd met Lucy outside the John Lewis café. It seemed like a decade ago. 'Can we talk for a couple of minutes?'

'Not here – staff aren't allowed.' She gestured at her whites. 'There's a yard at the back.'

Robin followed her down the hall and out through the kitchen, where the focus of activity had shifted to a counter at which two figures were spinning clouds of sugar over dishes of pale mousse. Two or three people glanced up as they passed.

A fire door led to a fenced-off bit of space at the back, about half a house's worth of original garden. There were small trees along the line of the terrace, and white garden umbrellas mushroomed over the larger part of the garden reserved for guests. The lit windows of the houses behind gave the space an intimate, tenement feel.

Becca's plastic lighter glowed briefly, neon pink. It had been years since Robin had smoked, usually even the smell turned her stomach these days, but she felt a momentary yearning for the little ritual of it, the camaraderie.

'Private investigators.' Becca exhaled, shaking her head. 'I mean, I knew she wouldn't leave it but I thought she'd just keep badgering the police.'

'She's been really worried.'

'Out of her mind, probably. I know. And I feel horrible – shitty. But I just couldn't do it any more.'

Robin channelled Maggie, her gentle voice. 'What was going on, Becca?'

'Taz said you promised you wouldn't tell her where I was.'

'Yes, I did.'

She took a deep breath. 'Mum relies on me,' she said. 'Relied.' Her eyebrows flicked up. 'Always has, since I was little.'

'She said you're very close.'

326

'We are, I love her – I mean, she's my *mum*. But I can't . . .'
Fleeting expressions crossed her face, one then another, as if she
were conducting a silent argument with herself. 'This is what I
can't stand,' she said. 'The guilt. Constantly feeling like I'm not
doing enough, like I should basically give up having any kind
of life of my own. It probably *still* wouldn't be enough if I did.'
She looked away.

'Why do you feel guilty?'

'My mum's agoraphobic,' she said. 'Technically, I don't even
know if she is because she's never actually seen anyone about it
– she refuses. Either way, she's a shut-in. She doesn't go outside.'

'Why?'

'She's scared.'

'Of what? Did something happen to her?'

'No. Or not that she's ever told me. She's just always been like
it, as long as I can remember – petrified of the world and other
people. When I was a kid, after Dad died, she didn't have a
choice, she had to interact to some extent. Just now and again,
you know – one school event out of every two or three, just
enough to stop people getting suspicious. If she hadn't, someone
would have noticed and I probably would have been taken away
or something. Then she would have been totally on her own and
she would have been stuffed.'

'How so?'

'She couldn't even go shopping without me – I was doing the
weekly shop on my own by the time I was ten. And as soon as
I left school, that was it, overnight – she went into the house
and hasn't been out since. Like she'd been tortured and it was
finally over.'

Four years. Robin remembered her that first day in the hallway,
her currant-bun eyes in the dark. Then she thought of Gamil.
After the episode with Harry, she'd assumed Valerie didn't use

327

the bakery because it was Indian-run but actually she didn't use *any* shops.

'The Internet's been a lifesaver for her. And for me – if she couldn't order from Tesco online, I couldn't have left.'

'You went to Devon, though, didn't you? A week's holiday, when you were sixteen. There's a photo on the fridge.'

'The place was *booked* for a week. We were there one night. Mum had a panic attack when it got dark and we had to get the first train home in the morning.'

'What about work?'

'She doesn't.'

'How? I mean, financially . . .' Mentally, all of it.

'Dad's life insurance and some other investments he had. They'd only had a little mortgage, they bought the house from Mum's parents, and she paid that off straight away. The rest covered school fees and our living costs but it's running out. No, it's *run* out.' She hesitated. 'I've been supporting us both since I left school. Not very well, we haven't had much – my job didn't *pay* much, especially for two people to live on. It would have been impossible if we'd had a mortgage. So I got the job at The Spot and that's where it all fell apart. Or came together, depending on how you look at it. Or who you are.'

'What do you mean?'

'I started there for the money, it was tough being so broke all the time, but then I got to know the other people who worked there and I looked at their lives and . . . I had this moment in the back room one night when I just thought – what the fuck am I doing? Loads of them – like, half – are over here travelling, seeing the world, and I just . . .' She shrugged. 'I saw my life and what it was going to be like and I . . . didn't want it.'

'Living at home? You wanted to travel?'

328

'Yeah, that, but not just . . . I realized I wasn't *doing* anything. I was just messing around. It was like this whole . . . syndrome.

'It's like I'd convinced myself that going out and having a good time and messing round with drugs and blokes . . .' She lowered her voice. 'I was telling myself that's where the adventure is. But it's not, is it? That's just stupid stuff. I looked at the others – especially Taz but there's this Polish girl I like, too, Agata. And Ceci. She's only nineteen, she's Italian and she's over here working, learning English, and it's . . . brave. I thought I was daring but actually, all that stuff is just crap, isn't it? You'll probably think *this* is stupid, like naive or something, but I was inspired. They inspired me.'

'I don't think it's stupid.'

'*I* want to do something brave. The wild behaviour – I was actually just avoiding what I really wanted. Because I was scared.'

'Tarryn said this is what you want to do.' Robin gestured at the kitchen behind her. 'Cooking professionally.'

Becca smiled. 'Yeah. I know you've seen my Instagram so you know I'm really into it. And Mum probably told you.' She dropped the cigarette, crushed it underfoot then dropped the butt in a bucket of sand by the wall.

'Pretty much everyone did.'

'I've only been here a few days, obviously, and I'm totally bottom of the pile – like, arranging side salads – but I feel like this is it. This is the adventure. Hard as it would have been in some ways, staying would have been the easy way out. I'd have used Mum as an excuse not to take the risk. But I'm going to do it – I *am* doing it. I want to work in Paris one day, that's my dream. I took a bit of a risk, taking my passport from home, but I've promised myself, as a reward, I'm going to save up for the Eurostar and go for a weekend. I've never been before.'

'Good for you,' Robin said, and meant it.

'But I've hurt my mum. Who knows how badly – very. Even paying for this, you – she must have sold something. But I had to. She'd have made me feel so selfish, I would never have been able to.'

'What about Harry?'

Becca opened the packet again and took out another cigarette. 'I love him,' she said. 'I have for years. Always. But I knew Mum wouldn't like it.'

'Because he's mixed race?'

'Yeah. When I had my moment of clarity at work, that was part of it, too. I suddenly realized that instead of this lovely bloke who I liked and who liked me, I was messing round with losers because I was scared. Scared of what it would mean to get into something real – serious. And scared of Mum's reaction. Does she know?'

'Yes.'

She nodded, resigned.

'He's gutted, Becca.'

'I know. I mean, because I am – I knew he'd be the same. I feel so bad, the last thing I want is to hurt him, he's done nothing to deserve it.'

'Why didn't you just tell him?'

'Because he wouldn't have let me go, either. Not in the same way as her, with the guilt – though he'd probably try a bit of that if he thought it'd get results,' she smiled. 'But he'd try and convince me that it was enough – you know, being together. But he's got his business and so he feels like everything's sorted, he's not missing anything. I was.'

'Do you want me to tell him you're okay?'

Robin expected an immediate yes but Becca shook her head. 'Not yet. I've got to feel like I'm really going to do this. I've got

330

to get my roots in so that no one can talk me out of it. When I know I've done it, I'll get in touch with him. I don't know if he'll forgive me. I've been asking myself if I would and I don't know. You've spoken to him, haven't you?' She sharpened. 'What do you think?'

'I'm not sure. I know he loves you and he's frightened for you.' But that might work the wrong way, against her; the breach of trust might be too huge. 'He's extremely loyal,' she said. 'He didn't even hint at your mum's situation.'

'He doesn't know. I've never told anyone except Tarryn.'

Robin frowned. 'Really? Why not? And why her?'

'Because she's on the outside. She doesn't know her – she's never met her. It felt too . . . disloyal to tell Harry or Lucy.'

'But if it helped you? All those years, when you were a kid . . . Even if it hadn't made a practical difference, wouldn't it have made you feel better, knowing someone else knew what was going on in your life?'

She shook her head. 'I had to look after her.'

I think you're worth loving.

'Please don't tell anyone,' Becca said. 'I've hurt her enough.'

'If you don't want us to, we won't. I promise. But you know, if it helps with the guilt, maybe, in the end, it'll be good for her, all this.'

'What do you mean?'

'It's not true any more that she hasn't been out. She went to see Harry.'

Chapter Twenty-three

It was quarter past midnight but as she'd hoped, the light in the front bedroom was still on, another sign that for now, the tide was at least standing rather than racing out, taking everything she had with it. She'd done it, she'd found Becca, and she had a way to make things up to Maggie, atone. And maybe, she'd thought, alone on the motorway, if she could speak to Tarryn's other friend, get a lead on the Shannon Harris case, she might be able to pull something back with Samir, too. Some respect, she thought, grimly, if not leniency.

It had taken real self-discipline not to ring from Bath but she wanted to deliver the news in person, for maximum impact. With the hum of the motorway still in her ears, she pulled in, and picked her phone off the passenger seat.

Are you up?

Almost immediately, *Why?*

I'm outside. Can we talk?

Outside??

V quick one – good news.

A few seconds later, the landing light came on and then the one in the hall. 'I'm four hundred and ninety-three years

332

of age,' said Maggie, opening the door. 'Are you trying to kill me?'

It had to be twenty years since Robin had seen her without make-up, and it was shocking, frankly. Scrubbed of the Jack Sparrow kohl and hidden behind glasses, her eyes looked very small. Her hair, that triumph of engineering, hadn't moved since the office but without the rest of the look – the make-up and the silver, the black gear replaced by a tightly belted towelling bathrobe – it was more psychiatric ward than punk.

'Nice slippers.'

Maggie looked at the pair of furry white rabbits, their three-inch ears lined with pink velvet. 'Present from Alissa.' Her sister's daughter. 'Don't push it.'

'Can I come in?'

'Briefly.' She stood aside.

Robin managed to wait until she'd closed the door but only just. 'I've found Becca.'

'What?' Maggie's eyebrows drew together.

'Yes. And she's fine, absolutely fine. She's left Birmingham and she's working in a hotel. I've just been there, hence the time. I saw her – I've spoken to her.'

'Where?'

Robin hesitated. 'I promised her we wouldn't tell anyone.'

'Where?'

She felt a strange resistance, as if it were her own secret. 'Bath. It's a great hotel – she's got lucky. Or done well. She's got a job as a sous chef. She's always wanted to cook professionally, she's going to start training.'

'How did you discover all this?'

'Tarryn.'

'So she contacted you in the end?'

'No,' she admitted. 'Maggie – this afternoon, Alan Nuttall. I felt really bad, I shouldn't have done it, and I'm sorry. I wanted to find a way to make it up to you so I went to Hurst Street and waited up the road to see if Tarryn was working. I was worried about her – we both were, weren't we? – and . . . It's a friend of hers who helped Becca get the job, she said, an Aussie. She's the assistant manager of the hotel.'

'Why did she do it – Becca? Did she say? Why the cloak and dagger, scaring her mother half to death like this?'

'She said she felt trapped, or about to be. Get this: Valerie's a shut-in.'

'A shut-in?' Maggie's forehead corrugated.

'Or was. An agoraphobic, or something like it.'

'I know what a shut-in is.'

'Everything frightens her, apparently. Until her jaunt to Harry's, she hadn't left the house since Becca left school. *Four years.* Becca was supporting them both. What she told Lucy wasn't true: she didn't get her job at The Spot to save to go travelling; she was struggling to make ends meet for the two of them on what she was earning at Hanley's. Ironically, going away was the result.'

Maggie said nothing.

'And it wasn't just Valerie,' said Robin, growing self-conscious under the intensity of her focus. 'She felt like she was about to get trapped by her relationship with Harry, too. Not because of anything he did but because it was the real deal.'

Somewhere around Gloucester services, Robin had had another realization. She'd actually startled in her seat. 'Remember she told us that Becca's passport was still in the drawer?' she said now. 'Not true. She took it with her. Valerie *knows* nothing's happened to Becca – that panic, when she called this morning after Shannon Harris? No disrespect to your FLO skills but it was an act. She knew all along that Becca had just done a runner.'

'My god.'

334

'She loves Becca, obviously, but Becca's also the only person connecting her to the outside world. She needs her – she's screwed without her.'

Maggie shook her head. 'What a bloody mess.'

'I know. But I said to Becca, maybe it'll be for the best in the long run. Maybe her mum'll be forced to sort herself out, get some help.'

Maggie took a slow breath, in and out. 'Well, you did it,' she said.

'*We* did – I just got the last bit. We make a good team, you and me.'

'No. Tonight, all this – it was you.'

'Like I said earlier, I wanted to make it up to you. Atone.'

'Atone.' Maggie said the word slowly, as if she were trying the taste. 'God, I don't know – maybe there's no helping you.'

'What?'

'I mean, how many times do you need to be told, Robin? How could you be so high-handed? Doing all this – telling Becca we wouldn't tell Valerie where she was? Who gave you the authority to make that decision?'

Robin had the sudden dizzying realization that she'd got it all wrong.

'It isn't for you to make that call – it's *my* business, *I* hired *you* to work for *me*. I wanted to help you out. Actually, I wanted to help your mother.'

'My mother?'

'You had no right to do this. No right to go and find Tarryn without talking to me, and zero right to make promises to anyone about who we'd tell anything. Valerie's the client here – *my* client – whether she's in the wrong or not, whether you like it or not.' She shook her head again. 'I'm sorry, Robin, I am. You're a good detective, I don't question that, but this isn't going to work.'

* * *

The light was on in the sitting room at Dunnington Road, too, but when she let herself in, no one was up, thank god, they'd just left it on for her. Dennis's snore reached down the stairs, regular and gentle, the sleep of the righteous. She drank a glass of water at the kitchen sink then turned the light off and crept upstairs in the gloom.

'Mum?' Lennie muttered, shifting in the bed, but she was asleep again before Robin replied.

She undressed to her T-shirt then got in and pulled the duvet tight around her shoulders. As ever, the house was subtropical but as she'd left Maggie's, she'd felt cold to her bones and she couldn't get the chill off.

Fired. Again. Fired by *Maggie*.

A family friend. Who, by the sounds of it, only hired her in the first place because she wanted to do her mum a favour.

She remembered Luke's snickering face at the car window. *How the mighty have fallen.* Getting fired by the Met was one thing but to be fired by a one-man band operating out of a shoebox over a hairdresser. Catching scroungers on the sick. No – she stopped herself. She couldn't do that, however much she wanted to make herself feel better. Maggie's business was good – *she* was good. And she'd given Robin a chance; she'd tried to help her.

Freshwater, Gid, Adrian, Samir, now Maggie – the list of people she'd alienated grew longer. All of them – well, no, three out of five – had tried to help her. And there were plenty of others, too, weren't there, said a thin voice of self-knowledge: ex-colleagues, ex-friends, ex-boyfriends. Lennie's dad.

All of them dismissed, written off, expunged from the record. Not all of them, she could admit, with good reason. Or even reasonable justification. Robin Lyons and the Scorched Earth Policy. She was like Stalin, packing her enemies off to Siberia,

336

doctoring the photographs. The only people she'd never pushed away were Corinna and Josh. If she were alive, she'd call Rin now.

Josh is a real killer.

Samir's words ran cold fingers down her spine. Until he'd said it, she'd been sure: Josh would never have hurt Corinna or any woman. He'd killed that man because of what happened to his mother. But last night she'd understood for the first time – really understood – that he'd killed that man because he'd lost control.

What if he'd lost control with Corinna? What if it had been happening for years, all the time she, Robin, had been in London, oblivious to the cuts and the bruises, never around to need lies about where they came from?

Because when the crunch came, Corinna had kept her at arm's length. The loans, the cuts – for all their history, she hadn't told her. Why?

This idea you seem to have that relying on anyone else is a sign of weakness.

But it wasn't a *sign* of weakness, was it? It was *actual* weakness. Rely on other people and you risk them letting you down. And they do. They do.

With a turn in her stomach, she thought about that: her insistence on self-sufficiency, toughness. *I expect it's a good thing to be hard in your line of work.* Had she unwittingly sent a message to Corinna that problems were unacceptable? Surely not – look at the chaos that had been Lennie's arrival, how vulnerable she'd been then. She'd messed up so badly that time, she'd needed Rin to move in with her for a year and a half, for god's sake.

But that was thirteen years ago now. She'd recovered, made a success of herself, at least for a bit. For a decade or so, apparently iron-clad, she'd been charging round, rising through the ranks, doing it all herself. She'd assumed Corinna knew that the armour was borrowed, but maybe, over time – hire purchase – she'd come to own it. Had she made it impossible for Rin to get through to her? Or made her believe she had to put on her own armour? Armour that hadn't been bulletproof.

With an echo of the shame she'd felt at the time, she remembered what her dad had told Thomas and Patel about her constant need to prove herself. Was it true?

She made herself look at it. Becca tonight – had she really done that to atone or had at least part of it been for herself, to make herself feel better after the batterings from Samir and Maggie? Defiance: she *did* have value, she *was* worth something?

Overhead Lennie turned, sighed. *I think you're worth loving.* Robin felt sweat on her top lip and shivered: last night she'd been Valerie, hadn't she, the needy mother looking to a child for reassurance, support in navigating the world. Maybe Luke was right. Maybe Lennie would be Becca in a few years' time, fleeing *her*.

The thought was devastating. Her fear when Lennie had disappeared to London; she'd known beyond doubt that without her, if something happened to her, nothing would ever be right again.

Samir, Gid, Maggie. Corinna.

The drawbridge, chains clanking, leaving her stranded. On her own.

It was her fault. Maybe not Samir but the others. Even Freshwater. *How could you be so high-handed?*

And Corinna. Dead but withdrawing even before that, pulling away.

Was it her fault, Corinna's death? If she'd felt able to talk to Robin, get through to her, would she still be alive? Could she, Robin, have stopped it?

Or was the connection more direct even than that? She lay without moving, without breathing, as she made herself recognize it – own it: she'd been the only other person who knew what Josh had done and she'd let him go. She'd let him go.

Why bother with a judicial system at all, judges and juries, due process?

She'd made the call. She'd let a man's death go unexamined – he was a rapist, he'd attacked them, he'd prejudiced his right to justice, hadn't he? Hadn't he?

And she had allowed Josh never to be held to account. She'd protected him. She'd allowed him to kill that man and walk away.

What she'd also done, she saw, was tell Corinna that it was all right to protect him, too. At seventeen, when she was young and scared, yes – and maybe she could forgive herself for that – but then for years and years afterwards. When she was police, a detective. A homicide detective.

She'd let him go. A real killer.

Chapter Twenty-four

The landline woke her then Christine's voice across the landing as she picked up their bedroom extension. 'Hiya, love.' Luke, Robin thought, rising slowly to the surface, but then her mother said, 'Let her go?'

She lay still as the new reality broke over her again.

'Mum? Are you down there?'

'Morning, lovely.' She tried to sound normal.

'You were back really late – is something going on?'

Robin sat up and swung her legs over the side. When the dizziness passed, she stood and rested her cheek on the bars in front of Lennie's pillow. She stroked the smooth back of her head. My seal, she'd used to call her, back in the days of the bath routine, when Lennie had been small enough to turn in the width of the tub, slosh joyfully from one end to the other.

Last night she'd allowed herself a shred of hope that in the light of day, after some sleep, Maggie would decide she'd been too harsh and give her another chance, however warily. No, judging by her mother's tone – Christine had lowered her voice so much that she couldn't hear the words, a feat in itself – that was not going to happen. She was unemployed again. No salary, no means of supporting Lennie. *She's still investigating, isn't she, in a way?* Not now she wasn't, not even scroungers on the sick. She was screwed. At this point, who would write her a reference for McDonald's, even?

'Sort of,' she said. 'Yes. I'm not going to be working with Maggie any more.'

'What? Why?'

'I did something she didn't agree with. Last night – that's why I was out so late.'

She frowned. 'What did you do?'

'Len, actually, it wasn't just that she didn't agree with it. It was wrong. I shouldn't have done it. I found someone we'd been looking for but then let them go.'

The same thing, again and again.

'What are you going to do?'

'I don't know yet. But don't worry, okay? I'll sort things out.' She stopped before adding, *I promise.*

With a scuff of carpet, the door opened. 'Morning, Lennie, love. Did you sleep well?' Christine crossed the room, the passage between the bunk beds and the little desk so narrow that Robin felt the air move as she went by. She drew the curtains in two crisp moves then turned around again. 'Up and cracking, sweetheart. It's eight already. Grandpa's going to drop you off this morning. Porridge for breakfast, okay?'

'Yes. Thanks, Gran.' Lennie folded back her duvet and Robin moved to let her down the ladder.

Christine waited until Len closed the bathroom door then glared at her. 'We'll talk about this when they've left.'

As Robin was dressing, her mobile rang. *Number withheld.* Here it was then, the call she'd been expecting all yesterday, Samir's considered judgement on how he was going to deal with her.

But there was no way she could have that conversation now, with the others downstairs at the breakfast table. The thought of Christine hearing what Josh had done. What she'd done.

'Can I ring you back, Samir?'

'Is that Robin?' A woman's voice, tentative, young, the accent more Black Country than Birmingham, that shift in the vowels. 'Tarryn gave me your number – I'm her friend.'

It took Robin a moment to put it together – oh. After what Tarryn had said, she'd held out very little real hope. 'Yes, this is Robin. Hi.'

'You're not police, are you? Taz swore. I can't talk to police.'

Robin pushed the door closed and lowered her voice, for what it was worth. 'No, I'm not police.'

You're a pimp.

'She said if I spoke to you, you promised not to tell anyone.'

Robin grimaced. 'Yes. I did.'

'Or to find a way to tell them without them knowing it came from me. Because I really *want* them to know, they have to, but if he knew it was me . . .'

'I understand. As I told Tarryn, I won't do anything that could put you in danger.'

Silence except for her breathing.

'You knew Shannon Harris?' Robin said gently. 'Who died.'

'Yes.'

She waited for the woman to go on but she didn't. She was clearly scared out of her wits. 'Look,' she said, 'why don't I come and meet you somewhere?'

'Meet?' Utter panic.

'You could see me. That might help you know you can trust me.'

Silence again.

'A couple of minutes, that's all. You choose when and where,'

Robin reassured her. 'I'll come to you, wherever you feel safest. I've got a photograph I need to show you – if we meet, I won't have to email or text you. You won't have to give me your number.'

'Okay.' Her voice was barely audible. 'Somewhere busy – Grand Central. There's benches by platform six.'

'I'll find them.'

'At nine?'

Robin glanced at the clock on the desk – just about possible.

'How will I recognize you?' the girl said.

'You've got a smartphone? Google Robin Lyons – Lyons with a y – *Daily Mail*.' The photograph would be spot-on today.

'What? You *can't* have anywhere to be without breakfast *now*,' said Christine when Robin appeared in the kitchen doorway, jacket on. 'Where are you going?'

'Into town.'

'You're not going to the office? It won't make any difference. She won't change her mind, she told me.'

'I'm not going to the office.'

'Seeing a man about a dog, are you?' said Dennis, all about the conflict-avoidance.

'Something like that.' As she passed to kiss Lennie goodbye, she squeezed his shoulder.

She half walked, half ran up Stratford Road to Hall Green station. The train would be quicker than the car at this time of day, the ride itself only ten or so minutes and no parking at the other end. When the train arrived, it was packed with commuters, not a seat to be had if she'd wanted one. She stood in the vestibule, shifting her weight from foot to foot. She was doing it again, the exact same thing, taking matters into her own hands. Playing the teen ninja, ignoring the proper channels, trapped in a cycle of repetition like some character from Greek myth.

This was police work. A woman was dead, her killer – as far as Robin knew – not caught. So what was she doing? Hoping to prove them all wrong by catching him then riding off into the sunset on a beam of pure ego – See, I *do* have value? No, this was different. Both Tarryn and the girl herself had been emphatic: it couldn't be police, she wouldn't talk to them. It had to be someone on the outside.

Through Bordesley, the track ran on a viaduct, up among the rooftops of factories and offices and car showrooms wet with overnight rain, shining in the feeble early sun. Ahead she could see the last of Digbeth's Victorian buildings, then the city centre, the dark spire of St Martin's, the multi-storey car parks, Selfridges. Resilient, she thought, this city. It took what came and dealt with it. It evolved.

The Hall Green line came into Moor Street station but New Street was only minutes' walk away. She swiped through the barriers and jogged towards the pedestrian crossing on the hill outside. It had been late afternoon when she'd met Lucy, the day almost gone, but as she came into Grand Central now, light was streaming through the soaring glass roof, almost too bright to look at. She hadn't been wrong about *that*, she thought: yes, it was a shopping centre over a railway station but it was a cathedral, too, one just right for Birmingham – big, mercantile, non-denominational.

She found platform six and a line of chairs that she took to be the benches. It was three minutes to nine but she didn't see anyone who appeared to be waiting or looking. She touched the photograph in her inside pocket. *Pimp.*

'Is it Robin?'

A small blonde woman materialized in front of her. She looked shell-shocked, absent in the eyes, but her face was pretty, the eyes brown under the peak of a pale baseball cap, ponytail spilling

344

from the notch at the back. She was twenty-three, Tarryn had told her, but in her pink polo neck and denim jacket, no make-up, she looked about fifteen. She was probably popular among the clientele who would have liked them younger, ideally, Robin thought. The idea made her chest hurt.

'Do you want to sit?'

'Can we . . . move around?' Her eyes darted as if she were afraid someone had followed her in.

Robin wandered after her into the gloomier covered area back towards the entrance. The girl kept her eyes lowered, the cap shading the top of her face.

'Taz told you how I got into this?' she said. 'I don't want you to think . . . If someone had told me a year ago that I'd . . .'

'What happened to you is criminal. The man who did it should be in jail.'

They'd come to a lingering stop outside a shop selling bags and aprons and crockery in twee retro floral prints, the 1940s redux. They faced the plate glass as if they were window-shopping, side by side.

'Shannon Harris,' Robin said, keeping her own head bowed.

A mute nod.

'She was his girlfriend?'

Another nod. Robin saw the girl's eyes move in the shop window. She was using it as a mirror, she realized, watching the passage behind them.

'Did he kill her?'

Her body did a sort of hard shiver. She nodded infinitesimally. 'I think so.'

'What happened? Can you tell me?' Robin moved along a bit, closer to the window, as if she were examining a pair of printed blue teacups.

'When I started, she looked after me. He has sex with all the new girls – training,' she swallowed, 'but then they work for him. Shannon was his actual girlfriend. When I met her.'

'Where did you work? Were you on the street?'

'No. He's got a couple of flats, somewhere out. And a house, where we lived.' Another darting look, this one seeming to linger on someone before she lowered her head again. Robin saw her chest fall – relief.

'We left,' she said, mouth barely moving. 'After Christmas. Shannon had to get away – she split up with him but he wasn't having it. She'd been looking for ways to get out and she said she'd heard of a better place and she wanted me to go with her. It *was* better – a lot – but it didn't matter in the end because he found us.'

'What happened?'

'He came there. He forced his way in, like he does. He went . . . crazy. It was . . .' She shook her head. 'Everyone was screaming. He kicked the cloakroom door in, glass everywhere. He hit the woman who ran it in the face. Then he picked up this bit of broken glass.'

She was back there, Robin could tell, seeing it again.

'He said he'd kill them for what they'd done. Taking his girls. Her and Shannon – he'd kill them both. He got hold of Shannon and started dragging her but they had security – Greg, one of the bouncers, managed to get her away. He kicked him out.'

'Why didn't you leave?' Robin said. 'I mean, when you got away from his place – why did you go to another one?'

She'd started crying, her cheeks were wet. 'Because of Shannon – she protected me. She looked after me.' She paused. 'And I need the money.'

'There's other ways to earn money. You were doing something else before, weren't you, before you met him?'

'But I wasn't . . .' She looked at Robin. Without saying a word,

346

she pushed up the sleeve of her jacket, revealing the bruised inside of her elbow.

Jesus. She'd guessed but still. 'What's his name?' she said. 'His real name.'

'What are you going to do?' The panic again, knife-sharp.

'I've got a contact in the police, a friend.' Well, not exactly but she didn't have to know that. 'I'm going to tell him what you've told me but not who you are or anything about you that would help him find you, okay? I don't even know your name.'

'You promise.'

'Yes.'

Another furtive look in the glass then, lips barely moving, she muttered, 'Daniel Staverton. Danny.'

'Do you know where he lives?'

A head-shake. 'The flats are in Handsworth or Sandwell – somewhere there, I don't know the area.'

'Do you know the street? The name?'

'No. We went there in a van. Into a garage.'

She moved suddenly, slipping round the shop corner like a wraith. Robin followed.

'I have to go,' she whispered. 'I can't do this – I feel like I'm going to have a heart attack.'

'Okay. But thank you. For talking to me – doing this. It was very brave.'

'I want them to get him. For Shannon. And the rest of us. I just want to feel safe.'

'When they do,' Robin said, 'and they will, there *are* ways out. This doesn't have to be it. You've got my number – call me whenever you want, any time, I'll do whatever I can to help you. I mean it. Or here.' She patted her pockets and found the little Muji case of cards Maggie had given her. *Robin Lyons, Private Investigator, MH Investigation Services*. 'If you'd prefer, there's this woman, Maggie Hammond. It's her business. She works with women who need help, that's her thing, and she's good. The top one's her office number. She wouldn't charge you.'

'You work for her?' The girl looked at the card.

Robin hesitated. 'Sometimes. And she's a friend. You can trust her.'

'Thank you.' She slipped it into her pocket and turned to move away.

'Wait,' Robin said. 'One more thing. The picture I wanted to show you . . .'

The girl looked stricken but she stopped.

Robin gave her the photograph she'd ripped from Ana's corkboard, Ana, Marta and their housemates in the garden, peering into the afternoon sun. 'This woman,' she said. 'The blonde one. Do you know her?'

She nodded. 'She worked at the new place. The better one – where we went after. She worked on reception, organized who went with who, took the money.'

Heart pounding, Robin took out her phone and scrolled to a picture she'd taken at the end of November. Before she'd been fired from the Met, before any of this had started. Before – she'd actually believed until two days ago – it was thinkable. Josh and Corinna.

She turned the phone around and handed it to the girl. In her head she was praying, Robin realized. *Please.* 'What about him? Do you know him?'

With a sensation like a fist in the stomach, she saw the girl's expression soften.

'No,' she said.

'*No?*' An absurd swell of hope.

'I know her.' She pointed at Corinna. 'Holly.'

'*Her?* She was . . . working?'

'No.'

'Then . . . I don't understand.'

'It was her place. She ran it.'

Robin's hand shook as she took the card from her wallet. She fumbled as she entered the number.

The call was answered after two rings, a crisp 'Thomas.'

'It's Robin Lyons.'

'Hello.' *Interesting*, said the tone, not a moment's hesitation about who she was. They probably had her picture up on their whiteboard; she was probably looking at it right now.

'Is your guv'nor in?' she asked. 'Jafferi.'

'Yeah. Shall I put you through or do you want me to give him a message?'

'I'd like to speak to him, please.'

'Hold on.'

Perhaps ten seconds later, 'Robin?'

'I think I know who killed Shannon Harris.'

Chapter Twenty-five

As she came down the long steps to Station Street, she saw the black VW saloon on the other side. A double-decker barrelled round the corner; she crossed the road in a whirl of exhaust.

He leaned over and opened the door. 'Get in.' She did as she was told. The door clunked shut, locked automatically as he indicated out. 'Put your seatbelt on.'

Through the tunnel under Smallbrook Queensway, traffic thumping overhead. He had his coat on and a dark plaid scarf but the heaters were going and the car was warm. As she got in, she'd been sideswiped by déjà vu. The smell – like his old Golf, like his T-shirts, when she'd lain on lawns and beaches and beds with her head on his shoulder. His skin.

He took the lane signposted for the ring road. 'Where are we going?' she said.

'Don't know yet.' Samir checked the wing mirror. 'Tell me. All of it – from the beginning.'

'You know that I've been working for Maggie Hammond,' she said. 'And that we've been looking for a girl who was missing, Rebecca Woodson?'

'Referral from Alan Nuttall last week. Yes.'

'Last night, I spoke to a friend of hers, Tarryn. She's Australian, they met working at The Spot in town. I'd been trying and trying to get hold of her, and after we heard about Shannon Harris, I was worried. I went to The Spot to see if she was there. When I told Tarryn I'd been worried because of Shannon, she was confused. "*But she was a prostitute*," she said.'

Samir looked over. 'But that hasn't been publicly released.'

'I prodded her and she told me that another friend of hers, a girl who'd been working at The Spot when she started – who'd got *her* the job there, in fact – had rung her in a panic yesterday. *This* girl knew Shannon and she'd heard Daniel Staverton threaten to kill her. Shannon had been going out with him until she dumped him but he'd been her pimp as well.'

'What do you know about him? Staverton.'

'Heard his name for the first time this morning. Tarryn told me a bit yesterday.'

'He's vicious. I saw some interviews he did last year for something else – wasn't him in the end, that one, but he's nasty. His usual thing's protection rackets, though; collection. I hadn't heard he'd diversified.'

Robin took a moment to get it straight in her own mind, to give herself a fighting chance of communicating it. 'I think he killed Corinna, too.'

Samir's head whipped round. 'Daniel Staverton?' He looked back at the road as an articulated lorry curved round them on a bend, sides so high they momentarily lost their view. 'What?'

'Tarryn's friend said he'd threatened them both, Shannon and Corinna.'

He gave her a look of complete bewilderment – had she been drinking? Or had she finally lost her sanity? 'No. Robin, I told you – the post mortem. I mean, come on, how would Staverton even have known her? That's—'

351

'Shannon was working for her.'

'For . . . ? Doing what?'

'Working as a prostitute. At a massage parlour.' Massage parlour, brothel, knocking shop – however she said it, she knew how insane it sounded. It was why she hadn't even hinted at this part on the phone. 'Staverton said he'd kill her for pimping out his woman.'

He dipped his forehead towards the wheel. 'You're doing my head in.'

'Samir,' she said, 'I showed the girl a photograph of them. Josh and Corinna. I thought maybe Josh . . . he'd taken out loans, maybe he'd come into contact with Staverton that way, maybe that was how he'd paid them off . . . but Tarryn's friend identified Corinna. She knew her as Holly but it was definitely her, she was positive.'

'Why did you even *show* this girl a photograph?'

'Because of Ana. The babysitter. When I went to the Serbian church, a bloke there – probably the one who reported me to you – called me a pimp. They knew I was looking for Ana. Why would he call me a pimp unless he thought she was a prostitute?'

'But Ana *isn't* a prostitute.'

'No,' Robin said. 'She was front of house.'

Silence.

'Where?'

'Alum Rock. Just a house. This girl said it was different from Staverton's place, as decent as it could be, clean. There was security – food. She said Corinna looked after them. She said she was kind. Samir, it's been closed for ten days. They've been going there, to work, but it's all shut up.'

* * *

He stopped in a layby and made two calls, one to Lara Morton, the SIO on Shannon's case, the other to DI Webster.

When he hung up, he sat back in his seat. Traffic streamed past the window, feet away but distant. He'd had a haircut since she'd last seen him, or shaved the sides himself; the hair above his ear was short, the greys like iron filings.

'Weren't you supposed to be keeping out of it?' he said.

She looked through the windscreen at the long winter grass on the verge. 'Selling other women's bodies,' she said. 'Girls.' In the pocket of her door, tucked behind a copy of the *Post*, she could see a unicorn sticker book like the ones Lennie used to have. His daughter must be six or seven by now. Leila, she was called.

'How would she ever have got into it?'

Robin thought of Kev, his insistence that history would not repeat itself. *It's not fucking happening to my kids.*

'Remember her dad,' she said. 'Trevor. How much Di struggled when they were growing up, moving all the time because he'd drunk the rent or never earned it in the first place? All the times he went AWOL. Corinna wanted Peter to have stability. She thought that's what she was getting with Josh – it must have looked like a pretty safe bet.'

'That's why, not how. And where does *he* fit into this, Josh? Where is he?'

'I don't know.'

Neither of them spoke. Robin watched the traffic pass the window and had the idea that it was a river flowing, time, the layby a slow pool at the edge, a brief pause before the onward rush.

'Our friends,' she said. She heard him take a deep breath then he sat forward and started the engine. 'Where are we going now?'

'I'm taking you home.'

* * *

353

He parked outside the house and undid his seatbelt. 'I'll walk you to the door.'

'It's fifteen feet, I think I can handle it.'

He ignored her and got out, locking the car behind him as he followed her up the path. She'd gone about three steps when she was overtaken by a wave of nausea so intense she gagged. She managed not to throw up but Samir had heard; he took the keys from her hand and opened the front door. She ran up the stairs, catching a glimpse of Christine's startled face in the archway before she reached the top and slammed the bathroom door shut. There was nothing much to come up but it didn't stop her body trying. Between retches, she heard the low murmur of voices downstairs.

By the time she could safely move, the house was quiet. She opened the bathroom window to look for his car and saw it was gone. The chill was back in her bones, she was actually shivering. She crossed the landing and got into bed.

How could you?

I had to.

That's bullshit!

Easy for you to say.

Really? Because I've got to tell you, Corinna, things aren't that great here but I would never – ever – do that.

For Lennie, you would. Your child.

No. I wouldn't. Because I could never look her in the eye again.

Living off immoral earnings. That was the criminal charge for selling women's bodies, letting them be physically penetrated for money so you could take a cut of it. And it wasn't just their bodies. Corinna must have known that. Robin thought of the girl at Grand Central, the vacancy in her eyes. You couldn't do it, sell yourself, and walk away the same.

'It could still be a mistake,' Samir had said as they'd come up

Stratford Road. 'She could be lying about Corinna for some reason; she could have got it wrong.'

Robin had shaken her head. 'I remembered something else.'

'What?'

'The black eye. Staverton did it when he forced his way in there. The girl said he hit her in the face. The woman who ran it.'

She sensed her mother before she saw her. She was sitting on the edge of the bed, her head cocked bird-like under the edge of the upper bunk. Through the duvet, her hand felt heavy on Robin's ribcage, steadying.

'Samir told me, love,' she said.

'Is there any news? Have they arrested him?'

'Not that I've heard. But no one's called. How are you feeling?'

Literally and metaphorically empty. Like someone had scooped out her insides with a metal spoon. 'How long was I asleep?'

'About three hours. He said to remind you that you could still be wrong.'

'There's nothing I want more. But I'm not.'

When Lennie came home from school, she sat with her on the sofa and told her. It was worse than telling her Corinna had died. At least then the emotion had been simple. Pure. How did you explain what she'd done to someone of thirteen? Corinna, whom she'd loved and looked up to.

But she had to. It was going to come out, it would be all over the *Post* and the *Mail, Midlands Today*. It would probably make the national papers. At least if she told her, she would have some control over the narrative. She could give Lennie a gentler version of the story before she heard the ones that would be far, far worse.

She told her everything, step by step, from Becca to Samir. She was frank, she didn't try to minimize it, but she told Len about Corinna's childhood in the hope that one day, when it settled, she might find a way not to condemn her entirely even if she, Robin, failed. When she went to the kitchen afterwards to get them all a cup of tea, Christine had nodded, *Well done.*

After dinner, she washed up then told her mother she was going to ring Maggie. She saw trepidation flicker across her face.

'Really?' Christine said. 'Why don't you wait?'

'No. I need to tell her I'm sorry.'

It was cool in the conservatory, beyond reach of the central heating. She dialled Maggie's number and it rang and rang. She'd started to think she wasn't going to answer – she was probably standing next to it, waiting for it to stop – when suddenly she did.

'Robin?'

Well?

'Maggie, I'm calling to apologize. I shouldn't have done it – gone off and found Becca like that. Or Tarryn. I'm sorry.' Or emailed Nuttall. Or cut corners on the benefits work to go off-piste. But one step at a time.

'Nuttall called me this afternoon,' Maggie said. 'He told me about the girl you spoke to this morning. What she told you.'

'Tarryn said she wouldn't speak to police. She wasn't even sure she'd speak to *me* so when she rang, I went for it in case—'

'I don't want to talk about the methodology,' Maggie said, dry, 'but well done.'

Robin was taken aback. *Really?* she almost said. 'Have you heard of him?' she said instead. 'Staverton?'

'I had a girl about eighteen months ago who'd been involved with him. He's not without his charms, apparently, in the

356

beginning, but then she wanted out, big time. She wouldn't talk to police, either, but luckily, her parents found me.'

'Have there been any developments? I've been at home all afternoon, I . . .' It dawned on her that of course she'd been at home – where else did she have to go?

'Not that I've heard. If I do hear anything, I'll let you know.'

'Thank you.' She hesitated. 'Maggie, did Nuttall tell you about Corinna?'

'Yes, he did. I'm so sorry, love.'

For a couple of seconds, neither of them said anything. 'Well,' Robin said, awkward, 'I'll leave you in peace. I just wanted you to know I'm sorry. And to thank you for giving me a chance, even if I blew it.'

'Well – thank you.' Maggie sounded embarrassed. 'Look, Robin, I'm not saying we should work together any more, that ship has sailed, but I've been feeling bad about something I said last night. The heat of the moment, you know. I *did* want to help your mother, obviously – she's one of my best friends – but of course it wasn't the only reason I offered you a job.'

From the sitting room came the pulsing music of the evening news, silenced abruptly as Dennis switched channels. Robin sat down in the egg-shaped wicker chair that hung from the conservatory's central beam, his present to Christine a few Christmases ago. It creaked under her weight as she pressed back into the overstuffed cushions.

Every time she thought about it she was amazed again. *How could you, Corinna? How could you do it?*

They were doing it anyway. I helped them, Rob, I got them away from people like him. I looked after them.

You sold them.

I kept them safe – safer. Where will they go now? The streets?

That was how she'd sold it to herself, Robin knew. Corinna the care-taker, Corinna the kind. Corinna who'd salted the steps the day she'd brought Lennie home from hospital, who'd moved across the country from her fiancé so she could support Robin when she needed her. Corinna who sold young women's bodies for profit.

Her phone buzzed in her lap. *Gid.* Had the news reached London already?

'Hi.'

'So guess what?' he said. No preamble, not even an hello. 'Hinton made a *really* bad decision. *Epically* bad.'

Hinton? It was a moment before Robin got her mental orientation.

'He was putting it where he shouldn't – *really* shouldn't. If you were him, who would be the one person whose girlfriend you wouldn't mess with?'

'Who?' she said. 'I can't do games today, Gid.'

'Richie Liddle.'

'*Who?*'

'You know, Richie Liddle?' Gid sounded startled – who was he talking to here? Had she lost the plot? *Have aliens stolen your brain?*

'No, I don't mean . . . I know who he is.' A man intimidating enough to be called Richard Liddle and never have heard a joke about it. The legitimate part of his operation was a collection of bars and clubs where East End faces got bottle service alongside C-list celebrities. 'I mean, why the hell . . . ? Of all the women in the world.'

'Well, she *does* look like Britney Spears. In her heyday.'

'Forget Britney, it'd take bloody Cleopatra, mate. Or Idris Elba, for me. How did you get this?'

'The tape. We went up north to visit the club. Hinton wasn't trying to give himself an alibi, Britney's a Geordie, he was meeting her mum. They thought they were far enough away from London to risk a night out together. We missed the point of the tape first off; it's not about him being in Newcastle, it's about who he's *with* in Newcastle.'

'So where's he now, Hinton? Has he surfaced?'

'Nope. He's either halfway to Australia or Liddle's got him. And we can't find *him*, either. Unsurprisingly, no one has any idea where he might be.'

'So what about Farrell? Where does he fit in to this?'

'It was him who set them up, Hinton and Britney – she'd been to a couple of his raves. She's quite a lot younger than Liddle; I imagine they were more her scene.'

He was quiet for a couple of seconds – respect for the dead – but then Gid laughed his low, bubbling laugh. 'Oh, you should have seen Freshwater this afternoon, Guv. He was *spitting*.'

Chapter Twenty-six

She parked around the corner, as stipulated, and turned off the engine. Silence rushed in, punctured only by the muted hubbub from the playground across the road. A gaggle of kids aged five or six were hanging upside down on the climbing frames like giant, Troll-haired bats, and Robin felt a pang for the days when Lennie was that size, when she still had to lift her up to reach the top bars.

For perhaps the third time in the ten years of Len's school career to date, Robin was early. This was what life was like when you had nothing to do, she remembered it from two weeks ago – the last time she was unemployed. Time billowed. When you were used to every waking hour being occupied, to find yourself with so much of it was frightening, a kind of temporal agoraphobia.

Twenty to four – school finished at quarter to. Rather than spend five minutes thinking, she steeled herself and rang Kath.

'Robin? I was just about to call *you*. I'm outside the hospital, I've just been with Pete.' Her tone said good news even before she did. 'He's starting to respond to the antibiotics – his bloods have started coming back better. Last night and this morning – better each time.'

'Oh – thank god.'

'I spoke to the consultant. He said if it carries on, they'll start to lighten the sedation tomorrow morning, try to bring him up. We're not out of the woods yet, he said, don't count your chickens, all the usual medical caveats, but it's looking better. Though, Robin, when he does come out of the coma – if and when – it's going to be so hard.' She paused. 'Samir rang us. He told us about Corinna. What you found out. That it wasn't Josh.'

'We don't know that for sure yet, Kath. We still have no idea what his involvement was. What he might have done.'

'Well, *we* know he didn't hurt her or Peter,' she said, apparently oblivious. 'And we know you do, too. Whatever happens, you saying what you did last week, it meant everything to us – me and Dad, the boys.'

At three forty-seven, the first wave of uniforms came flooding down the pavement. Hundreds of pairs of scissoring nylon trousers – someone should try and harness the static, she thought, renewable energy.

She scanned the kids as they streamed past, shouting and pushing. Their language was as bad as any she'd heard in the police – at RPG, they'd have been lined up and executed. Surely there was a happy medium to be found somewhere, wasn't there? It occurred to her that it was probably *her* school, the grammar. Could she get Lennie in there in September, have her sit the test? But no, she wouldn't need to. They'd be long gone by then, wouldn't they, back to London – if not to the Met in her case, then somewhere.

Savvy's was huge, over a thousand kids. They kept coming and coming, like a football stadium emptying out. She chose to interpret it as a good sign that Lennie wasn't in the vanguard today, her need to flee the place at least marginally less urgent.

By four, though, the torrent along the pavement had dwindled to a thin stream and she pinged her a text. *I'm outside – where are you?*

Five minutes later, having had no response, she rang Christine. 'Mum, am I being stupid? Did you pick Len up just now?'

'She was here for last period.' Wheeze. 'Definitely. I've just rung the staffroom. She had French. Mr Stratton. He had a full house, no one missing.'

'Thanks for checking, Mrs Travis. I'm so sorry about this. Twice.'

'Oh, call me Pam.' Wheeze. 'Let me know if there's anything I can do, all right, love? I'll be here until half six or so.'

'Thank you.'

'Hard, changing schools mid-term, but don't worry, she'll get there. Teething troubles, that's all.'

Robin hung up and called Lennie again. Voicemail again. She called her mother back. 'The school secretary says she was there until the end of the day this time. That's something.'

'Would she go to Adrian again, do you think?'

'I don't know. Not to try and get us back together but maybe for her own sake, to talk to him? But if she left at the end of school, she can't have got far yet. If she's going to London, she'll be going to Moor Street, won't she? We might even still catch her at Hall Green.'

'On my way.'

'Thanks, Mum. I'll head for Moor Street – I'll call Ade on the way.'

He didn't answer his mobile so in case he was ignoring her, she called his office and left a message with his assistant. Next she rang Carly.

362

'Oh, hi, how are you?' Jolly, no wariness.

'I'm okay. Carly, have you heard from Len at all?'

'You mean today? No.' To one side, more quietly, 'It's Lennie's mum.'

'When you spoke to her last time, did she mention going anywhere at all?'

'How d'you mean?'

'I don't know. Anywhere – anything. Coming to see you, maybe.'

'Hold on.' Another rustle. 'Em, have *you* spoken to her? Did she say anything to you?'

'No,' said an awed voice in the background. 'Is she missing?'

A minute or so later, her mother called. 'She's not at Hall Green. I asked the man in the ticket office, I showed him the picture in my purse, but he hadn't seen her. He says she definitely hasn't bought a ticket.'

It was half past four now and the road into town was barely moving, three cars at the most getting through at each change of the lights. The road was clotted with buses; they seemed to pull out from every stop she passed, one after another.

A phone rang but not through the Bluetooth. It sounded faintly muffled and on the third ring, she realized it was coming from under the passenger seat. The pay-as-you-go – it must have fallen down there last night on the way either to or from Bath. She undid her seatbelt and leaned over, only just getting her finger-tips on it.

Number withheld.

'Hello?'

'Is this Robin?' A man's voice, deep, local. Friendly. She didn't recognize it.

363

'Yes, speaking,' she said. 'Who's this?'

A rustling sound as if the phone were being handed over. 'Say hello, sweetheart,' she heard him say.

'Mum?'

Lennie? What? She was confused – what was going on?

'*Mum!*'

She was crying, sobbing. She was frightened. No, not frightened. Terrified.

Robin's heart stopped. A cold hand took hold of it, squeezed – she couldn't get a breath. She couldn't breathe.

'Give me that back now,' said the voice, warm, paternal, a dad taking his phone from a child who'd sneaked it to watch YouTube videos.

'Right,' he said to Robin. 'You know what all this is about, don't you? You get it?'

Her mind emptied and then, with a roar like an oncoming truck, it filled with a thousand things, swirling, incoherent. Images, voices, bits of information, all scrambled. Becca, Tarryn. Corinna, Ana. A parade of women – girls. And a smiling face leaning across to open the car door.

Did she get it? What *was* it about? It suddenly seemed very important, vital, that she get the right answer. *Think*. She tried to muster her police training, to listen – where were they? Was there anything to give her a clue – but all she could hear was Lennie's desperate sobbing. Muffled now; he – no, someone else: he hadn't had time, she hadn't heard it – had gagged her. 'Lennie!' she shouted.

'Come on,' he said, encouraging.

'Shannon,' she managed.

'That's right.' He sounded pleased: she'd done well. 'Your mate took something of mine so I'm taking something in return: this pretty girl. That's fair, isn't it?'

'What do you want?' Her voice shook.

'Nothing,' he said. 'I just told you: we're square.'

'Lennie!' she shouted. 'Lennie!'

They were gone.

She pulled over, bumping the car up onto the kerb. She opened the door and was sick onto the tarmac. That was how she'd first discovered she was pregnant, the morning sickness that had come out of nowhere. *Lennie.* When her hand reached for her mobile, she saw it as if it belonged to someone else. Useless fingers. *Recent calls.* The number she was looking for.

Again, thank god, she answered almost at once. 'DS Thomas.'

'It's Robin Lyons. Is he there?'

Seconds but it seemed like a long, long time. 'Robin?'

'Samir? Staverton's got Lennie.'

Chapter Twenty-seven

'But she grew up surrounded by police – if there's one person who would never, ever go with a stranger, it's her. And she would have rung to check if anyone she didn't know told her there was a change of plan, that they'd been sent by me or Mum.' Robin looked at Christine across the table. Her eyes were huge, her face white. 'He must have forced her – but how, outside school? Teachers, parents, literally a thousand other kids – there's a freaking *lollipop lady*.'

'*Because* it was so busy? And it was only her second week, right?' DS Thomas frowned. 'So she hasn't got a gang yet, a group of friends who'd look out for her?'

Robin saw Lennie as she had on Friday, head down, crossing the playground alone.

'She didn't know anyone at the school before she started?'

'No. I haven't lived here for a long time. She never has.'

'He's done this because you've been investigating Corinna,' said Samir. 'I think we can assume that much. He knows you're the reason we're looking for him and, almost certainly, he knows that because someone you talked to has talked to him.'

'I did this, in other words. I've made this happen to her.'

'No. Don't do that, Robin,' Dennis put his hand on her arm.

'Just try to concentrate,' said Samir. 'Tell us again who you spoke to. Everyone.'

Who she spoke to – fuck. The powerlessness – sitting here at her parents' dining-room table *talking* when Lennie was out there, god knows where, alone, scared out of her mind. She should be out driving, combing the streets . . . *No, stop. Concentrate.*

'Kath was first,' she said. 'The morning after I saw you at the hospital. When you told me about the factory and you seemed to believe Josh had done it.' She looked at him, looked away. 'Ana the same day – that afternoon – then Kevin Young.'

'Kev?'

'When I thought it was about a dodgy loan – in case he could find anything out on the vine. That's why I thought it was Josh who was involved with Staverton – debts. Then Marta, Ana's housemate, when I went back there to try and find her the second time. The people at the Serbian church – there were seven or eight of them.' And the young couple, too. 'No, ten. And Tarryn.' So many people. It could be any of them. 'And then there was the girl yesterday morning, Shannon Harris's friend.'

'Which of them did you give your card to?' said Thomas.

'What?'

'He called you on the pay-as-you-go Maggie Hammond gave you, didn't he, not your own phone. Did you ever give out that number to anyone other than via the card?'

Robin saw Samir glance at her, *Good work.*

'No,' she said. 'I gave Ana a card – it was on their corkboard when I went back there. And the girl yesterday morning – Shannon's friend. Tarryn's friend. It has to be her, doesn't it? Yes. It couldn't be anyone else – I didn't know that it was Corinna until then, I hadn't made the connection . . .'

'Right, so we need to get someone to The Spot straight away,' said Samir. 'Talk to Tarryn, get hold of her now, get her to help us find this woman.' He nodded to Thomas who got up and walked into the kitchen, scrolling as she went. 'Hi,' they heard her say. 'The Spot, Hurst Street.' The sound of the conservatory door.

'She was terrified,' Robin said. 'Shannon's friend, I mean. Scared senseless. She kept looking around all the time as if someone was watching her. I thought it was paranoia, I didn't see anyone, but there could have been – it was nine o'clock, the place was packed. I gave her the card for when this was over, when Staverton was caught. It has Maggie's office number on it; I thought she could contact her if she didn't want me.'

'Assuming that's right – which seems likely – it tells us how he found out about *you*,' Samir said, standing again, 'but not Lennie. How would he know you had a daughter? Did you tell her, this woman?'

Robin shook her head.

'Who, then, of the people you spoke to?'

'Kath and Kevin Young know anyway,' said Christine.

'Who knew she was at Savvy's?' asked Samir. 'How would Staverton have known to find her there? Or what she looked like.'

'Kev knew that.'

They looked at each other then shook their heads at the same time. 'No. No way.'

'Who else?'

She closed her eyes again, tried to shut out everything else. She groped through the blizzard in her head. *Focus.* She thought of the cool feel of the metal Muji case, the shape of the cards in her hand. The pang for her badge, every time.

You want to ask questions. You're not police? Corinna said you're police in London.

368

Not any more. We live in Birmingham now, we live with my
parents in Hall Green, Lennie's at St Saviour's. I work for a friend
– here, look, this is my card.

'Ana,' she said. The word was a fist. 'And she knows what
Lennie looks like – she was there with Peter when we went to
Corinna's house. She probably has a photo on her phone. Samir
– Lennie knows her.'

'What?' said Dennis, looking between them. 'What does that
mean?'

'If Ana's with Staverton,' Samir said, 'he might have used her
to get Lennie into the car.'

Silence.

'Samir,' Christine said, 'how did he know you were on to him?
The police.'

'He couldn't really not, Mrs Lyons. We've been turning the
city upside down since yesterday lunchtime – we've been to every
address he's ever been associated with, spoken to basically anyone
he's ever met.'

'And you haven't found him.'

'Right.' Samir stood up, took his phone off the table and put it
in his pocket. 'You're good here?' He looked at Thomas, who
nodded. 'Guv.'

'You're leaving?' said Christine, panicked.

'Malia's going to stay with you. I'll keep in touch with her by
phone. If you need to for any reason,' he said, turning to Robin,
'you can call me direct. Here, give me your phone.' She handed
it to him, watched him enter his number.

As she walked him to the door, the landline rang on the hall
table. In the dining room, Christine gave a small cry of alarm.

'There's no caller recognition on it,' Robin said. 'It's too old.'

Dennis appeared in the arch. 'Should I answer it?'

Samir nodded.

His hand hovered above the receiver and then he snatched it up. 'Hello? Oh, hello, son.' He covered the receiver. 'It's Luke,' he said, 'Robin's brother.'

'Dad?' said a tiny voice from the earpiece. 'Have you got someone there?'

As soon as Samir left, Christine hurried into the kitchen to make tea that no one wanted. Keeping busy was one of her mantras even at the best of times, though; to insist that she sit down and deny her any distraction now would be tantamount to cruelty. Robin had watched her anxiety building as the minutes ticked by, her hunched shoulders and unblinking eyes an exact reflection of how she herself was feeling.

Time stretched. Without the restraint of Samir's presence, she wanted to throw herself on Thomas and shake information out of her: Who's leading this? How much experience do they have? How many cases like this have they handled? How many – *if any* – have they resolved successfully? It was taking every shred of self-discipline she had to keep a lid on it.

The boss had made some comment about liking them young.

He has sex with all the new girls.

'We'll organize a trace on the phones just in case,' Samir had said. *Just in case.* In case Staverton changed his mind. Because otherwise, this wasn't a kidnapping, he wasn't asking for anything. *I just told you: we're square.*

Up in the bathroom, Robin washed the sweat off her face, rinsed her mouth with Listerine to try to combat the taste of bile in her throat.

Lennie – her Lennie, her girl. Where was she? Were they still in Birmingham? The more she thought, the less likely it seemed.

370

He knew he was the most wanted man in the city tonight – why would he stay?

But where would he go?

Eight o'clock came, then half past. More than four and a half hours since the bell had rung at St Saviour's and Lennie had walked out to meet the nightmare of a lifetime. Four hours since the phone call and since then, nothing. Zip.

Her mobile rang, causing group alarm, but it was Adrian. He'd been at a site visit with clients, he said – had they found her? He listened in horrified silence as she told him what had happened. 'Keep me posted,' he said, shaken. 'Not now, obviously, but when you can. Let me know.'

Dennis went outside for another cigarette, the tip a bright point in the dark beyond the window. His third so far, all three in plain sight of her mother, who hadn't said a word.

The landline rang again. 'Mum, do you want to get it?'

Christine shook her head. 'No, you. I can't.'

Thomas – she couldn't call her Malia – stood by.

'Robin, is that you? It's me – Maggie. I've just finished having a bite with a friend and picked up a message from Alan Nuttall. What the hell's going on?'

Just before nine Luke and Natalie arrived, Natalie carrying a tin of shortbread biscuits. 'I made them earlier,' she said, 'for Ben in the office. It's his birthday tomorrow, they're his favourite, but I thought they might be needed here more. I can make him another batch.' She put the tin down on the table and gave Christine a tight hug. To Robin's discomfort, she hugged her, too, briefly.

Luke's eyes landed on DS Thomas, on the phone to Samir in the conservatory. 'Is that it – her? Is that all the police are giving us?'

'She's our contact person, keeping us updated here as far as they can,' said Dennis. 'They've got a lot of manpower out looking for Lennie, Luke – a lot – but there's a limit to how much good they could do in our conservatory, don't you think?'

Samir rang. The search teams were working back through Staverton's list of known addresses again, Thomas reported – his friends, his mother's house. What was that like? Robin thought about it in court sometimes, seeing the parents of men being tried for murder, the life sentences coming down. She'd watched their faces. What was it like to know that the child you'd breastfed, held in your arms, brought to maturity was capable of murder?

But Josh was a killer. Her friend, who'd held the child she'd breastfed in *his* arms, carried her in the BabyBjörn, her little feet bumping against his thighs.

'So, nothing,' she said.

'Yet,' Thomas said. 'Nothing yet.'

Another pot of sodding tea. Robin watched hers go cold, a greasy disc of milk separating on the surface.

Mum!

She pushed her chair back.

'Robin?' Christine shrieked. 'Where are you going?'

Out in the garden, she put her hands on her knees and sucked in lungful after lungful of cold air. The dew had settled, it was already starting to freeze. Was Lennie warm enough wherever she was? Where was he keeping her?

She would give anything – literally anything – if her daughter could be unharmed. Her own life, without a moment's hesitation, she wouldn't think about it. Lennie *was* her life – without her, what was the point? If anything happened to her, would she even survive? The scratchy green sofa in their old garden flat in

London, the small hours of the morning. *Together we can do anything.* Without her, Robin thought, if she lost her, she didn't know if she could do anything. If she'd even want to go on.

Natalie was playing spiritual cheerleader, trying to keep them afloat with a constant stream of upbeat chatter about abductees who'd returned safely home, 'even after years and years,' she said. 'There was this girl in Germany, I think – it might have been Switzerland. Or Austria. Anyway, she'd been missing for, like, five years, I read about it, and everyone had given up hope, and then suddenly one day, just like that, she reappeared – she'd escaped. The really weird part was that she could have escaped earlier, she said, it would have been easy, but she didn't want to. There was something really weird going on, like, I think she'd actually fallen in *love* with him, they'd had a *relationship* . . .' She saw DS Thomas's face and stopped. Embarrassed, she took a shortbread – 'Shouldn't, really' – and nibbled an edge before balancing it on her saucer. 'Would you like one, Malia?'

'I'm all right, thanks.'

'So how long have you been in the police, then? Do you like it?'

Just after ten, Thomas's phone rang again. She stood and went to the dining-room window, drawing the curtain a foot or so for a view out into the street. Samir: Robin could see it by her body language, the way she stood even straighter. 'Right,' she said. 'Right. Yes. Okay.' She hung up and came back into the sitting room.

'Jafferi,' she said. 'There's movement.'

'What does that mean?' Luke said. 'Actually?'

'Maggie Hammond called him. About eighteen months ago,

she had a client who'd been involved with Staverton, who she'd helped get away from him.'

Luke pulled a face of cartoonish confusion. 'What do you mean, get away? She does benefit fraud cases, doesn't she?'

'Luke, shut up,' their mother snapped.

'She managed to speak to her about an hour ago. She wasn't answering her phone so Maggie drove over there, to her parents' house. She told her what was going on, asked if she had any clue where he might have taken Lennie, somewhere other than the places we know about.'

'And . . . ?'

'She remembered a place out near Studley that he'd used to keep on the down-low. A farm building he used for storage, paid for cash-in-hand. She didn't know where exactly but she thought she might recognize it – he kept a stolen car there, a sports car; she'd been out with him in it a couple of times. Maggie drove her there – they're there now.'

'Are *they* there?' Robin heard her own voice.

'They think so. There's been a light, Maggie told him – a torch, she thinks, moving around. And voices – male and female.'

'So what now?' Dennis was gripping the arms of his chair.

'There's a team on their way there. Jafferi's following them. Twenty minutes.'

She went to the loo just to get away. She couldn't take it – Natalie's nervous prattle, her mother jumping every time anyone shifted. Luke, in Lennie's chair.

She put her phone on the shelf below the mirror while she washed her hands. In the glass, she looked half-mad, pallid and fervid, wild. Next to her, the empty space. The reflection of the wall.

Love you, you know.

Physical repulsion welled inside her. *Fuck you, Corinna.* She stared at herself. *Fuck you.*

The phone went, the vibration on the glass shelf like a drill, nearly giving her a coronary.

Maggie H.

What? Wasn't she there? But she wouldn't call her, would she, if there was any chance she'd be overheard? She hit the button. 'Maggie?' she whispered.

'Robin.' She was whispering, too.

'Thank you – *thank you*. I—'

'Ssh, Rob, listen. I can only talk a moment. I just wanted to tell you, the police are here – they've arrived. They're nearly ready. They're going to surround the barn.'

'Are they inside? Staverton, I mean – Lennie? Are you sure it's them? It could be someone else, couldn't it? Tramps – travellers?'

She heard heavy footsteps – two men or more, moving, a muttered '*Madam*'.

'Rob, I've got to go,' she whispered.

'Now, madam!' The male voice, low but sharp. 'Get back – back!'

There was a small thud then a series of footsteps, lighter, receding.

'Maggie?'

No reply.

For a second or two there was nothing but then Robin heard a rustling whistle, wind gusting across the receiver. A low mutter, male, and a soft crunch, like a foot on muddy gravel.

Maggie had dropped the phone.

Robin looked at herself in the mirror. Could she? But how could she not?

As quietly as she could, she crept back downstairs and

slipped into her seat. She moved her phone to the centre of the table.

'What—?' Luke started but she shook her head violently.

The wind again, a louder gust. They were somewhere exposed – the top of a hill, maybe. A male grunt, assent, and a sort of Kevlar slither. Wind again then a metallic click. Christine gasped. 'Guns?'

Thomas stood up. She leaned over the table and muted the call, checking the screen to make sure it was actually done. 'Robin, you shouldn't listen to this.'

'I *should*,' she growled. 'I *have* to.'

From the phone came the sound of boots on the move, heavy but quiet, moving away. She pictured it, a farm courtyard in darkness, the group of men moving in the shadows, edging closer, darting moves one at a time, getting into position.

For fifteen or twenty seconds there was nothing but the wind. Christine swiped at her cheeks.

They heard a single low word, male, swallowed.

Robin made eye contact with Thomas, both of them stiff, then, in the distance, a smashing sound, splintering wood, then another.

'*Go – go, go, go.*'

A distant shout, male again and then – they all heard it – a scream. Female – a woman. A girl.

Thomas's eyes stayed locked on hers: *Hold steady.*

Shouting carried on the wind – barked instructions, words inaudible. Another voice. Then another, male but different, higher. Panicked, panicking. 'Don't,' they heard – and then a single shot.

Silence round the table. A whistle of wind that contained every human sorrow.

'Turn it off,' said Dennis. 'Now. *Now*, Robin.'

'No.' She snatched it up, away from him, and as she did, they heard running feet then a low 'Shit!' Maggie's voice. 'Rob? Are you there?'

'Yes. I'm here.'

'What did you . . . ? I dropped the phone, I . . .'

'What's happening?' Her voice echoed. 'What's happening?'

'Love – hold on. They're . . .'

In the distance, a shouted exchange.

'Oh, thank god – thank god.' A long breath. 'They've got her, Rob. She's all right. She's all right.'

Chapter Twenty-eight

Thomas drove them to the hospital, Robin and Christine in the back, Dennis next to her in the passenger seat. 'I've never been in a police car before,' he said, looking at the adapted dashboard.

'Try not to make a habit of it,' Thomas said.

The city at night, Dunnington Road dark except for two upstairs windows, the pub on the corner of Stratford Road closed and locked up, car park empty. Through Sparkhill, the sari shops and travel agents were shuttered, light pooling instead outside late-night curry houses and taxi firms. Blue sanitizing lamps shone behind Gamil's huge plate-glass windows. Robin thought of Valerie, alone in her tiny house.

Her own life lay in pieces around her, everything she'd worked for, and she didn't give a rat's arse. She felt ecstatic, other-worldly. Intensely, joyously alive.

They'd taken Lennie to A&E to be checked over and when they arrived, she was sitting up in bed, waiting. She saw Robin rounding the corner and started to get up, flinging the blankets off. A nurse ordered her back in. Robin squeezed her until her arms ached, all the words she'd wanted to say gone. 'I love you,' she managed eventually, 'so much, and I'm so sorry.'

'It's not your fault.'

'It is. It is.'

'No, it was *my* fault. I should have known that you wouldn't change pick-up plans without telling me.'

'Lennie, come on . . .'

'But when I saw her, Ana, Peter's babysitter . . . She told me that we were going to see him, that you were going to meet us there. Mum, I'm so sorry.'

'Don't – no. None of this is your fault, Lennie, none of it. Please never, never think that.'

Ana, Thomas told them, had been found gagged and bound in Staverton's van on a disused access road to the farm. She'd been mute with fright, unable to say anything for almost an hour. Staverton had followed her home one night from the massage parlour, she said eventually, and found out where she lived. When she'd moved, he'd traced her to the new place. He'd taken her from there. If she didn't help him with Lennie, he'd said, tell her the story about visiting Peter, he'd kill her. She'd been afraid he would anyway. Why would he keep her alive, she'd said, when she knew what he'd done to Shannon and Corinna?

Robin sat on the edge of the bed, clutching Lennie's hand. If it was possible, she'd never let go of it again – she'd go to college with her, surgically attached. She wondered if she'd ever be able to articulate the terror of those minutes that her life, both their lives, had hung in the balance.

In the strip lighting, Lennie looked bleached out, almost green. 'They shot him, Mum.'

'I know.' Now that Lennie was safe – bodily safe – a whole new set of anxieties had sprung into Robin's mind. What would the long-term consequences be? The psychological ones. How terrified must she have been in the dark, the door smashed in, the shouting? She'd been ten feet away from him, he hadn't used her as a shield; there'd been no danger, in fact, that she might be shot by accident, but what had happened tonight would live with her forever.

'Is he dead?'

'No, love.' Staverton had regained consciousness in the ambulance. The bullet had only hit him in the shoulder but as he'd fallen, he'd smacked his head on the barn's poured concrete floor and knocked himself out. Webster had travelled in with him, said Thomas, to talk to him, start piecing some of it together.

'Is he here? This hospital?' Lennie sat up. Her eyes went wide.

'No. This is the children's hospital, just for kids. You're okay – you're safe.'

'Mum, what about Peter's dad?'

Robin glanced at Thomas, who'd slipped into their curtained-off bay and taken the chair at the bottom of the bed until Luke and Natalie had arrived and booted her out of it, apparently unabashed.

Should I? You think she's up to it?

Robin nodded.

'We won't get the whole story until he's interviewed formally,' said Thomas. 'I don't have to tell you that, you're a detective's daughter, aren't you?' She was nervous, Robin realized, scared to tell her. 'He told us that it was him who drove Peter's dad's car to Warwick so that it would look like *he* was the one who'd done it, the fire, then gone into hiding.'

'But that's not what happened?'

'No.'

'So what did?'

Thomas shot Robin a pained look. 'Again, we don't know the details yet but we believe that Staverton killed him, too.'

Lennie leaned back against the pillows. She looked at her hands on the blanket and a tear ran down her cheek.

Robin couldn't bear it. 'But love, what I haven't told you yet – Peter's getting better.'

Lennie made a crooning sound, beyond words, pure grief. 'But he'll be an orphan, won't he?' she said. 'Both of his parents are dead.'

The doctor was held up. There'd been an accident, two seriously injured. They'd heard the paramedics bringing them in, urgent voices. Not for them, Robin thought guiltily, not today.

'Can I have a cup of tea? While we wait? My mouth's really dry.'

'Of course, love. I'll go and get some. Give Gran a cuddle while I'm gone – she needs one, too.'

The café was closed but a porter directed her to a bank of vending machines a couple of minutes away. She walked as if on air: Lennie was safe, back from the edge of the void, safe.

When she rounded the corner on her return, Samir was standing at the department entrance. His head was bent, his hands in his trouser pockets. His cheeks were dark with stubble. On days when he had somewhere to be in the evenings, she remembered suddenly, he'd used to shave twice a day.

As she approached, he looked up and saw her. 'I was just on my way to the station,' he said. 'I wanted to drop in, see if she was okay.'

'She is. Traumatized, of course, but physically . . . Come – come and see her. She's awake. This is for her.' She nodded at the cup that was burning her fingers.

'I just have. I saw her, and your parents. I was on my way out.'

They stood aside for a nurse wheeling a blood-pressure monitor. For a few seconds afterwards, neither of them spoke.

'Well,' he said. 'I'd better get going. Don't stay too long if you can help it. Get home and get some sleep – you need to.'

'Samir.' She looked at him, meeting his eye with the usual charge of recognition. 'Thank you.' She hesitated then stepped forward and hugged him. His chest felt different under her arms, bigger, more solid, but the smell of him was unchanged, clean and warm, with an earthy, sensual note that she'd never been able to describe. After a moment, he put his arms around her.

'She's everything to me,' she said into the grey wool of his lapel.

'I know.'

When she moved away again, he was looking at her, his face serious.

'What are you going to do?' she said.

'What?'

'About what I told you. Josh – back then.'

'He's dead, Rob. There *is* nothing to do.'

'And me?'

He shook his head.

'Thank you.' She felt dizzy all of a sudden, as if she might tip over. There was a line of plastic seats bolted against the wall; she went to them and sat down. After a moment, he came to sit next to her.

'How did we end up here?' she asked him.

'The children's hospital, two a.m.?' His eyebrows flicked up.

She rolled her eyes. 'Josh, Corinna, me. You're doing all right but the rest of us . . . I mean, for fuck's sake.'

She saw him smile. In the olden days, back then, she would have bumped her head against his shoulder, moved closer. He'd have moved his arm out and put it round her, pressed his nose into her hair. Kissed her.

'Samir,' she said, 'why did you break up with me? Not the bullshit reason – the truth.'

He shifted. 'Really? Now?'

'Yeah, I think so.'

He glanced back towards the swing doors. She looked sideways at him, saw the new lines on his forehead draw closer together. *Now?* 'Your brother,' he said.

'What?'

'Luke told me that if we stayed together, you and me, got married, had kids, it'd finish your relationship with your mum and dad. I couldn't do it, Robin. I know you've had your issues with them but I wanted you to have your family. It's important. Also, when the time came, I wanted a family where I would feel welcome. Where my kids would be welcome.'

The world shifted, things she'd believed for nearly twenty years falling away. *Luke.*

She stared at him. 'No,' she said. 'That wasn't true. The only person who wouldn't have welcomed you with open arms – wide open – was him.'

After he'd gone, she sat for a few minutes, trying to absorb it. When she stood and picked it up again, Lennie's tea had gone cold. She left it by the bin and went back to the machine for a new one.

She adjusted her grip as she carried it, her fingers scalding, blood pounding in her temples. She pulled the curtain aside and put the cup on Lennie's table, kissing her head. 'Sorry I took so long.'

'You missed Samir,' said Luke, smirking from his chair on the other side.

She looked at him, made sure he was looking at her. *Not today, not here. Soon, though.* She watched his expression change.

'No,' she said. 'I didn't.'

Epilogue

She hadn't told him she was coming; why give him an opportunity to say no? It was a risk, it might be a wasted journey, but then, what else was she doing? It wasn't like she'd been pushed for time lately.

But no, to her surprise, the bloke at the desk – new, she hadn't seen him before – hung up the phone and told her to take a seat. 'He's coming down.'

And five minutes later, when the door clicked open, there he was, more ferrety even than she remembered, tall Starbucks cup in his pallid, ginger-dusted hand.

She stood. 'Sir.'

'Lyons.' He kicked the door open for her again with a flick of his foot. So cool.

She'd expected the room to go quiet as she walked through behind him, the usual bloodthirsty rubbernecking at the disgraced, but to her surprise there were three waves, two 'Hey, how are you?'s.

Freshwater didn't turn to look at her again until they were in his office, the door closed, the Venetian blinds in the long internal window yanked shut. He sat in his chair, picked up his fountain pen by the ends and started to twist it between his fingers, giving it his best Dr. Evil. 'So.'

So he was as fucking irritating as ever, then. What wouldn't she give to go round the desk, tip him off the chair and kick his furry ginger arse? If she could do it without consequences. Instead she made a face she hoped looked vaguely like a smile. 'Thanks for seeing me, sir.'

'Well . . .' He held out his hands, palms up, as if to say, what did she expect, given his reputation for magnanimity?

Do it before you change your mind. 'I came to apologize,' she said.

His face – as if he'd just heard a dog talk.

'For not following your instructions . . .'

'Orders, Lyons.'

'Orders, sir, that day.' God, she was going to barf.

Another turn of the pen, making her wait for it. 'Well, good,' he said. 'It seems your time away has been good for you, doesn't it? Given you some thinking time?'

'Yes, sir.'

'No doubt you know,' he said, glancing up from underneath his eyebrows, 'that there's been some movement on the Farrell case.'

'Movement? I heard that perhaps there might have been a more complex reason for his disappearance.'

The eyes narrowed: *Don't push it.* 'We received an anonymous package with CCTV tape of Hinton with Richie Liddle's girlfriend in a Newcastle nightclub. As you may have heard.'

'Hm.' She nodded slowly. *Really? Interesting.* She'd texted Boz last week: *Muchas gracias, amigo.* Five minutes later, *De nada.* He and Lauren took Spanish evening classes through the borough council; their dream, he'd told Robin once, was to open a bar in Spain.

'Under the circumstances,' Freshwater said, leaning back in his chair, 'and given what we hear about your *cooperation* with West Midlands,' he looked at her, 'we could be prepared to review your case internally. Perhaps look at reinstating you sooner rather than later. Given our current caseload.'

'That's very kind of you. Sir.'

She took the Tube back out to Hammersmith, where she'd left the car. She'd done it, she'd got her job back, they could move back to London and, all being well, meaning if the bank would advance her some money and RPG agreed, Lennie could go back for the summer term.

She should have been euphoric but as she swung round the roundabout and took the slip road up to the main drag out of town, she felt strangely flat. Tired, she thought, just tired. She needed some kind of break. A holiday – imagine. Maybe she and Lennie could take one now if she got a loan. Yes, it was a good idea. It would be good for both of them, some time away together on their own, after what Len had experienced.

What she'd *had* to experience – what Corinna had *made* her experience. The anger flared. Corinna had brought that violence into their lives, she'd brought Lennie face to face with a killer. But – in the weeks that had passed, she'd made herself own it, *really* own it – so had she.

BIRMINGHAM said the sign on the overhead gantry. She glanced across at the passenger seat – empty today, of course, with Lennie at school. She thought of that drive, her churning stomach. That bloody Burger King. Three things had kept her going that day: Lennie, the job with Maggie, and the thought of Corinna, her friend, waiting for her like a beacon in her orange fern-patterned coat. The human night-light. Today she was driving back to only one of those things and yet, she realized, her stomach wasn't churning. She'd have dinner with her parents tonight and she'd sleep in the bunk beds, her thirteen-year-old daughter overhead, and that would be all right. Except for the temperature. She'd still be sleeping with the windows open. Maybe she'd buy a fan.

As she joined the M40, her phone rang through the Bluetooth. Samir's name on the screen.

'Hi,' he said. 'Have you got a minute?'

'Yeah, of course. I'm driving but I'm hands-free, so . . .'

'It's okay, I'll be quick. I just wanted to say, we're about to advertise a DCI vacancy here. In Homicide.' He paused. 'I wanted you to know.'

Acknowledgements

From the start, this book has benefited from the talents of two excellent women, my agent, Victoria Hobbs, and editor, Helen Garnons-Williams. Your enthusiasm and guidance have been invaluable. Thank you both.

At A.M. Heath, my thanks go to Alexandra McNicoll and Jo Thompson. At 4th Estate, a big thank you to Matt Clacher, Patrick Hargadon and Fran Fabriczki (with special mention for your patience). Thank you to Jack Flag for the great cover design and to Amber Burlinson for your copy-editing skill.

Thank you to Liz Vengen, Cathy Pankhurst and Suzy Vinciguerra Rosen for all your kindness and help over the past six years. This wouldn't have been possible without you.

Danny van Emden at West End Lane Books in London, champion to many of my favorite crime writers – you're appreciated!

Finally, but especially, thank you to Joe – husband, friend and Captain Logistics – and Bridget. Thank you for all the fun.